KING OF MASTERS

THE FOUR FAMILIES | O'SHEA SPIN-OFF

BRYNN FORD

King of Masters
Copyright © 2021 Brynn Ford
Published by Brynn Ford

Cover Design Copyright © 2021 Qamber Designs
Interior Formatting Template by Qamber Designs
Editing by Silvia Curry at Silvia's Reading Corner

More from the Author
www.brynnford.com
brynnfordauthor@gmail.com

For Danielle, Mary, and Maria.

Your enthusiasm gave this story life.

PLAYLIST

Stream the Playlist on Spotify at
bit.ly/kingofmasters

Blood // Water by grandson
Man or a Monster by Sam Tinnesz ft. Zayde Wølf
Come With Me Now by KONGOS
Queen by Loren Gray
Best Friend by Saweetie ft. Doja Cat
Never Be the Same by Camila Cabello
Anywhere by Rita Ora
I'm a Wanted Man by Royal Deluxe
Ruin My Life by Zara Larsson
I Think I'm OKAY by Machine Gun Kelly w/YUNGBLUD, Travis Barker
I Get Off by Halestorm
I Hate Everything About You by Three Days Grace
Toxic by 2WEI
Monsters by Ruelle
Lion by Saint Mesa
Power Over Me by Dermot Kennedy
save me from the monster in my head by Welshly Arms
Shadow Preachers by Zella Day
Pieces by Andrew Belle
Lover. Fighter. by SVRCINA
Call Out My Name by Seraphim
Dynasty by MIAA
Gallows by Katie Garfield
Grace by Lewis Capaldi
Kings & Queens by Ava Max

CONTENT WARNING

This dark romance book involves many triggering elements which may be upsetting for some readers. A complete list of tropes and triggers can be found on the author's website. at brynnford.com/triggers.

SERIES NOTE

This book is a spin-off from the *Four Families* trilogy. It can be read as a standalone, but the author highly recommends reading the trilogy first, starting with *Counts of Eight*. This book contains major spoilers from the *Four Families* trilogy—this is your spoiler warning!

BOOKS BY BRYNN FORD

THE FOUR FAMILIES
Counts of Eight
Dance with Death
Pas de Trois

THE FOUR FAMILIES SPIN-OFF
King of Masters

EMBER GLEN
Spark of Madness
Blaze of Misery
Embers of Mercy

STANDALONES
Sugar Wood
Jagged Line Paradise

LAWLESS
Coming Soon!
The Darkness We Hide

PROLOGUE

Murphy

EIGHT YEARS OLD

THE FLOOR IS hard and gray. It reminds me of the walking stones that line a path from the fountain to the back door of our home. I really want to go home. It took forever on the plane to get here, and I'm tired, hungry, annoyed. But Dad says I'm getting older and he wants to show me the factory.

Mam finishes zipping my younger brother's jacket and turns toward me. The moment her hands fall away, Declan takes off running across the hard floor.

"Declan, careful!" I call after him as I lunge, ready to run and catch him, though Mam grabs hold of my elbow to stop me.

"He'll fall, Mam. He'll hit his head on the floor."

She glances off after him for only a second before returning her attention to me. "He'll be fine, my love. You mustn't worry about him anymore. You have greater responsibilities than worrying about your brothers."

My forehead feels crinkly as I look at her, confused, trying to understand. "I'm the big brother, Mam. I always look after them."

She shakes her head. "No more, Murphy." She grabs my hands and tugs me forward, and I squeeze her palms, holding on tight. She speaks quietly, like she's telling me a secret. "You're special, my love. You're the

1

oldest and someday, you will be the Head of House for our family. Do you know what that means?"

I shake my head. "No."

"It means you're going to be a great leader, the leader of our family. It means you have to walk away from childish things and learn what it means to be an O'Shea man."

"But…I'm just a boy."

"Not just any boy. My special boy." She lifts her head and looks over my shoulder, smiling. I turn my head to see she's looking at my dad, who is talking to some men I don't know. When Mam and I look back at each other, she runs her hands down my arms and I feel warm, loved. "You're going to be like your dad one day. You're going to follow his footsteps and take over the family business."

"I don't know how to run a business!"

"Shh, my love. Not too soon. When you're older. But today, your dad wants to show you what we do."

"What do we do?"

Declan runs into my side, hugging his arms around my leg. He's the youngest—only three and a half—but he's my favorite. My other brother Cormac is five, and I love him, too, but Declan is my best little buddy.

"We work with people," Mam says and pushes to stand tall as Dad and Cormac come over with the two men I don't know.

"Is he ready?" Dad asks Mam.

"Are you sure he's not too young for this?" she asks as her head leans to the side.

"I was his age when I saw the assets for the first time. He needs to learn. He's the youngest future Head of House of all the families."

"I know…I just worry about nightmares."

Nightmares?

I rush to her side and grab her hand. "I don't want to have nightmares."

Dad puts his hands on his knees as he bends over to look me in the eyes. "Nothing you see today will give you nightmares. Not if you learn the first rule of the O'Shea family business and learn it well."

"W-what is it?"

"Business is business."

"Business is business?"

"That's right, my love." Mam wraps her arm around my shoulders and tucks me against her side. "Remember that you are always safe, always protected, always loved. And the assets we sell are nothing."

"I don't understand."

Dad stands and holds out his hand. "Come with me, I'll show you."

I'm nervous, but I take his hand. He leads me across the hard, gray floor and I hear my mother follow, her heels clicking with each step. I turn to look over my shoulder at my brothers. My aunt and uncle, Moira and Colin, and my fourteen-year-old cousin, Cordelia, corral Cormac and Declan to watch them as my mother and father march me toward a door at the far corner of the warehouse.

We stop in front of it and I squeeze Dad's hand tighter. It looks like jail. In front of a regular, wooden door is another door made of metal bars, running from top to bottom. The man I don't know pushes numbered buttons on a square that's built into the barred door. It beeps and clicks, and the man wraps his palm around one of the bars to tug it outward, swinging it open. He then pulls out a key, unlocks one deadbolt, then does it again with another key and another lock.

Why are there so many locks on this door?

Is it a monster?

Is the family business keeping the world safe from a nightmare?

I don't want to have nightmares!

"Mam!" I try to step back, tugging my arm, but my dad grips me tighter, pulling me to stand beside him. "I'm afraid."

"Nothing to be afraid of, my boy." Mam's soft voice croons from behind me and I feel her hand on my shoulder. I glance sideways to see her red-painted nails as her fingers curl, squeezing me and giving me comfort.

The wooden door opens inward to reveal a dark staircase.

Monsters!

I bring my free hand up to grip my dad's wrist, pressing myself against his side. "Dad, what's down there?"

"Assets and inventory," he says calmly. "It's all business, my boy, nothing more. It's time for you to see what it's all about."

He moves us forward, following the man with the keys, who flips on a light switch before stepping down the staircase. Light floods the dark space from overhead, but it's still scary. The steps are enclosed by walls on either side, hiding the basement until we reach the bottom.

We step down onto another gray, concrete floor and a wall of cold, dank air hits me. It doesn't smell very good down here. I feel my nose scrunch as I press my face into Dad's jacket.

"This way," he says as we turn right, and he moves us forward again.

The man I don't know speaks as we walk, while voices and moans hit my ears, gradually growing louder. "We did a cleansing and inspection of the assets yesterday, so you should be seeing them in their best condition."

"Good," my dad replies. "Open your eyes, Murphy."

I didn't realize I'd closed them, but now I know they're pinched tightly shut. I don't want to look. I don't want to see.

A girl's voice whimpers and cries, "Please…please, let us go!"

My eyes snap open because the voice sounds like my cousin Cordelia, though I know it can't be because I just saw her upstairs.

The girl speaks again, "Don't put that child in here with us." *Is she talking about me?* "Oh, God. Please. Don't hurt that child!"

I frantically look for my mother, who moves between me and the girl, blocking my view. She crouches in front of me and my wide eyes snap to meet hers.

"Murphy," she smiles at me, "everything is fine. Don't listen to them. These girls are right where they are meant to be. They only want out because they are afraid."

"I'm afraid, too!"

"But you don't need to be." She strokes the side of my face and it relaxes me a little. "They can't hurt you."

"Why are they here?" I ask as she stands again, her heels clicking across the floor as she walks toward what I think may be a prison room.

I turn my head, taking in my surroundings for the first time. It's a long and dark hallway, the concrete floor running all the way down to the end, and cages line the walls. Little prison boxes—I think that's what they're called. People, lots of people, are behind a wall made of metal bars. My eyes dart up and down the row, but I don't spot any boys, just girls.

"Where are the boys?" I ask.

My dad squeezes my hand and leads me forward down the hall. "Our business doesn't have a demand for boys. Not now, at least."

"I don't get it. What did they do? You have to do something bad to go to prison, don't you? Did they do something bad? Is that why they're here?"

"Don't think of this as a prison; think of it as a factory. Think of these girls as a product. We purchase raw goods, bring them to the factory for processing, and distribute them to buyers who intend to use them…our clients."

I've heard him use those words before, so I kind of understand, though not entirely. "So, they're not bad. They're…products?"

"That's right."

"But who chose them to be products?"

"There are certain traits our clients want to see in the product they purchase. We have a large network of collectors who go out into the world and look for assets with those traits. They collect them and bring them to our factories."

"But they look so upset, Dad. What if they don't want to be here?"

"None of them want to be here, son, but sometimes your fate is chosen for you. They aren't given a choice."

"But…that's not fair."

"Life isn't fair. That's just the way it goes. We all have to play the hand we're dealt. Your hand is running the family business while theirs is to be sold, to serve our clients, to make us money so our family can be fed. You want our family fed, don't you, boy?"

I nod. I don't want to be hungry.

"Then this is what we must do to ensure that all the O'Sheas remain fed, to ensure we keep our power and wealth. This is all so you can have a good life…your brothers and cousins, too. One day you'll take over and be the leader of our business."

"Why me? Why can't Cormac do it?"

"Because it's your birthright as my oldest son."

"I'm not ready, Dad. I can't do this!"

"Don't fret. I'll teach you everything you need to know in time." My father smiles at me, stands, and pats me on the head.

He and my mother stride forward down the hall with the other man, talking about things I don't understand.

"I'm starving…please," one of the girls says after them, but my parents ignore her. "We haven't eaten in two days…please."

I reach into my jacket pocket, my fingers curling around the butterscotch candy Mam gave me earlier. I squeeze the candy in my palm, the wrapper crinkling.

If the business is going to be mine one day, then surely I can decide how to run it, can't I?

I cautiously step forward, moving toward the bars that separate me from the girls on the other side. The one who said she was hungry grips two of the bars with both her hands. She has dirt on her knuckles, and she's dressed only in a plain white shirt that stops just above her knees.

"Aren't you cold?" I whisper.

Her head tilts slowly to the side as a sad look washes over her face. "Yes," she replies softly. "I'm cold and I'm hungry. We all are."

"Oh…" I look down at my shoes. "Um, I have this." Gripping the candy, I slowly pull my hand out of my pocket and take another careful step forward. I hold out my fist toward her, looking down the hall to make sure Mam and Dad aren't watching, and I open my palm, revealing the candy. "Here. Go on. You can have it. I just had lunch."

Her eyes widen and the corners of her lips twist upward into a small smile. It makes me smile, too. I like making people happy.

"I can't take that from you, but thank you," she says.

"Why not? I don't want it."

She glances down the hallway after my parents. "I could get into trouble. They could find the wrapper."

"Oh." I pluck the candy from my palm, unwrap it, and shove the wrapper back into my pocket. I pinch the candy between my finger and thumb and hold it out to her again. "Now you can take it. Just suck on it for a while and it will all disappear into your belly. No one will know."

Her throat bobs as she swallows and she looks nervous, but she can't take her eyes off the candy. I know she wants it. I don't understand why she won't just take it. I step closer and reach my hand through the bars. It scares her and she takes a step back.

"It's okay, it's yours." I smile, trying to make her feel better.

She glances up at my face, then down at my hand. Finally, she snatches the candy, quickly shoving it into her mouth. Her eyes flutter shut and she sighs, rolling the candy around in her mouth.

"Do you like it?"

She nods, opening her eyes and smiling at me.

That makes me happy. "Butterscotch is my favorite. Mam always has them in her purse because she knows it's my favorite."

She tilts her head in their direction. "Is that your mother?"

I nod. "Yeah, that's her."

"Is she kind to you?"

I'm confused by the question. "Of course, she is. She loves me."

"Good. And what about your…Is that your dad?"

"He's kind to me, too, though sometimes he's mean to other people."

She steps forward again, wrapping her hands around the bars. "He's being mean to us," she says, and it makes me flinch. "We don't want to be here. He's keeping us here against our will. Can you tell someone? Can you help us?"

My eyes narrow and I feel my face scrunch up. "I'm just a boy. I can't do anything."

"You're not just a boy. You can do anything you want. You can… you can call the police. Tell them where we are."

I shake my head. "The Gardaí? No. I'm not allowed to call the guards when we're traveling. There's only five guards that our family knows and they're back home in Ireland. I'm not allowed to talk to anyone else. I can only talk to Aidan Walsh, Brendan Byrne—"

"Murphy!" My dad comes rushing back and steps in between me and the girl. "Don't you fucking talk to my son." I slap my hands over my ears. I don't like hearing Dad angry and cussing. "Stupid fucking whores, the lot of you!"

He spins to face me, crouching and coming level with my eyes. He pulls my hands down from my ears. "What did she say to you? Did she harm you?"

I shake my head. "No, Dad. She was nice."

"They aren't *nice*, Murphy. They will say and do anything to get you to let them out. Do you know what we call a woman who is willing to do anything with a man to save her own skin? We call her a whore. These women are whores. They're going to do whatever they have to do to try to get free."

"But we can't just let them go?"

"No. Our clients demand them, and they will get them."

I'm still trying to understand all of this.

Dad sighs and looks at me softly. "You said you were afraid of monsters before…of nightmares?"

"Yes. I'm terrified of monsters!"

He leans in close, his eyes burning mine as he looks at me. "Think of our clients as monsters. Monsters who need to be fed to be kept under control. We feed the monsters, Murphy. We feed them these girls, these assets."

"Like…like a sacrifice?"

"What do you know about sacrifices?"

"I heard that word in a movie. They were talking about taking a princess to a cave and leaving her there as a sacrifice for the dragon. They said it would keep him away from the village for another year and keep everyone safe."

"Right. It's like that. Our clients are like dragons, monsters, and we have to sacrifice a few princesses to keep them away from our villages. To keep our family safe. To keep our women safe. Your mother, your aunts, your cousins. We sacrifice others to save ourselves. We feed the monsters to provide for our family."

I think I'm starting to get it now. "I don't want anything to happen to my family."

"That's right."

I look over at the girl I gave my candy to and smile as I wave. "Thank you for saving us from the dragons, princess."

Her face falls and she starts to cry, but I don't know why. They must be happy tears. Mam told me sometimes she cries happy tears when I find her sobbing alone. She appears beside me, reaching out with her hand and her red-painted fingernails, and I look up at her to find her smiling at me.

I smile back at her, take her hand, and skip along beside her as we walk back toward the staircase.

CHAPTER 1

Murphy

FIONA HAS FINALLY stopped crying, thank fuck. The whining and whimpering has ebbed to silence, and I take in a deep breath, letting my head fall back against the headrest. I turn my eyes to peer out through the window from the back of the sedan, glad she's finally calmed herself down.

She's not calm.

I can feel her anxiety pulsing beside me and I clench my fists, steeling myself against the waves of nausea that roll through my stomach. I lift my head and look over at her. She sits up straight and rigid, her spine arched away from the back of the seat, her thin arms pinned behind her with a cable tie securing her wrists.

Her chest lifts and lowers with rapid, shallow breaths, and her face is hard, impassive. Her head is turned toward me, but her eyes aren't on me. They're glaring past me, out beyond the window, focused on the dense fog surrounding our path.

My lips twitch with the urge to form a small, comforting smile against the ominous mood that the untimely weather sets for her arrival at the O'Shea castle. I'd always had that urge to comfort them—the slaves, the women we sell for profit. It's an old habit I thought I'd effectively ended as I rose to become the O'Shea Head of House. But now that I'm bringing my talent slave home for the final transition of power, I'm feeling that old punch-in-the-gut feeling of unease.

It's just the bit of humanity left in me…humanity I can't afford if I wish to keep my family safe, healthy, and prosperous.

Business is business as Boyd would always say.

I haven't called him dad in years. He's been Boyd O'Shea, the cutthroat king of our territory, since the day I picked Fiona to become my talent slave almost ten years ago. At his insistence, I was no longer able to see him as a parent after that day. He was my boss, my mentor… and I was his apprentice.

Now that he's retired, I'm in charge and I'm responsible for everything. The entire O'Shea territory is mine—to control, to find prosperity with, to fuck it all up and ruin if I make a mistake.

So long as my humanity doesn't creep its way back in with its morality and ethically righteous bullshit, I won't fuck it all up. My family can't afford the repercussions of human decency, so I force indecency with Fiona to prove a point.

I reach over and wrap my palm around Fiona's elbow, yanking her toward me across the leather bench seat. She whimpers, her eyes darting down to where I touch her arm as I drag her closer. I lift away from the back of my seat, sitting up straight to level myself with her eyes, and she shrinks back as I hold her stare.

"Who do you belong to now, Fiona?"

She shakes her head, a tear slipping out from the corner of her eye. She refuses to respond to me, and I won't have that. My hand slips up her arm, over her shoulder, creeping around behind her neck, and grabbing hold of her.

I give her another chance. "Who do you belong to?"

"No…" she whispers. "Please."

I grit my teeth as I shift her in my grip, forcing her to bend, pushing her down over my lap until her face lands on my thigh. She turns her cheek as I harshly press her into tense muscle. Her eyes pinch shut as I slide her head toward me, until the tip of her dainty nose touches my leather belt.

"Tell me who you belong to, or I'll show you."

Her eyes pop wide when she catches my meaning with her chin brushing against my cock, and she flounders in panic. Her lithe body wriggles, struggling against me, though I hardly have to press to keep her face against my thick thigh.

She's small and weak, and it almost makes me regret choosing her years ago. My dick isn't even hard for her. Yet I've spent a great deal of time and money funding her talent as a secret benefactor over the years, so it is what it is.

I angle her face toward my cock, reaching down with my free hand to work the buckle of my belt.

"No!" she yells. "No. I…I belong to you. I belong to you, master."

My hand goes still, almost thankful she spoke up and said something because I'm not in the mood for this. I loosen my grip on the back of her neck and stroke my palm over her strawberry-blonde hair, petting her for being a good girl, like she's a fucking pet.

But that's exactly what she is.

A pet, and my responsibility.

A fucking burden.

She remains in my lap for the final ten minutes of our journey, huffing in shallow breaths and whimpering. She can cry all she wants, though it changes nothing. Still, I stroke her hair, unable to quell the instinct to comfort.

The fog dissipates as we round the curved drive. We come to a stop beside the front steps leading up to our grand estate. I peer out the window as Fiona trembles, realizing our journey has come to an end and unable to control her fear for what's to come.

Boyd and my mother Bridget stand side-by-side on the landing at the top step of the stone staircase. Their talent slave, Esmerelda, kneels beside them. Impressive, they can still command her to kneel given her bad knee, though it's really rather cruel. One would think my father, at his advanced age of seventy-five, might have more compassion for his aging slave.

Esmerelda is fifty-six, two years younger than my mother, but in far worse shape. I can't really say whether that's from my father's use and abuse over the years or it's just poor luck on Esmerelda's part.

I watch them a moment longer while my family gathers behind them. My brothers, my cousins, my aunt and uncle. The entire thing is a spectacle, a procession of degradation to welcome our new talent. I shake my head, pulling my attention away from them and their expectant stares.

"Give us a minute," I say to my driver. He nods and cuts the engine, stepping out of the vehicle. I continue to stroke Fiona's hair as tremors quake through her. "Look at me."

She blinks through tears, but tilts her head slightly so she can meet my eyes.

"This is your new home. I am your master. You will be at my beck and call, and you will do as I say when I say it. If you behave and do as I say, then we won't have any problems. If you decide to test me, you will be met with punishment. You're my pet, but others will want to play with you. And you'll happily oblige them if I tell you to…won't you?"

Her throat bobs and her lips part slowly, her tears soaking through my slacks. "Y-yes."

I curl my fingers into her hair, digging into her scalp, mashing the metal of the two rings on my left hand against her skull. "Yes, *what?*"

She closes her eyes in defeat. "Yes, master."

Good.

"I'm going to remove the binding from your wrists. If you want to avoid humiliation and pain on your first night here, I suggest you keep your tiny hands at your sides unless you're asked to put them to good use. Understood?"

"U-understood," she stutters.

I fist her hair and tug, lifting her upright from my lap. I tilt my hip off the seat to pull my knife from my back pocket and quickly slice the cable tie. Fiona whips her arms around in front of her, rubbing her wrists in turn. I reach out to smooth her hair and swipe tears from her cheeks in an attempt to make her look minimally presentable.

She's my talent slave—her appearance, her actions, her behavior are all a reflection of me, and I won't be made a fool of.

"We're going to greet my family on the way to your new room. You'll be put in your place. You will not react to them. You will not cry, you will not scream, you will not speak. You will follow me quietly. You will watch and wait for us to finish our final transition of power, and you will *not* interrupt. If you do that, you'll be given time to rest and recover alone."

She looks at me like a child with wide, wondering, fearful eyes. It makes me think of the first time I saw our human assets in one of our factories in Oslo, back when I was a child with the same wide, wondering, fearful eyes. A ripple of unease flows through me and I blow out a heavy breath to force it away as her head bobs in something resembling a nod.

That's good enough acknowledgment for me.

I grab the handle and pop open the door, stepping out and smoothing down my waistcoat before holding out my palm to her. A few seconds pass before her hand lands in mine and I help her out of the car. She tugs at the hem of her jumper to adjust it over her jeans.

I shut the door behind her, letting go of her hand as Bailey, my black and white Border Collie, circles my legs. I bend to scruff behind her ears, then ask my driver to take her around the back to play on the hills.

"You walk behind me," I tell Fiona. "Never beside me."

I turn and head up the steps. I glance over my shoulder, fully expecting to see her still standing there like a fawn caught in headlights, afraid to move. She looks frightened, but I'm happily surprised to see her follow me immediately.

I reach the landing as the family parts to allow me to pass, naturally forming two queues that line either side of the entryway. The dreary fog surrounding the stone castle walls creates an eerie mood for the scene ahead, though I don't think sunshine would've done much to alter the general sense of dread with what's to come.

I stop when I reach my parents and hold out my palm to Esmerelda. She looks dreadful kneeling beside my father with her head bowed. I almost feel bad for her considering what's to happen next—that awful tick of humanity fisting my heart for a moment longer than it should have.

I look to see Fiona still behind me, waiting though she shakes. Esmerelda takes my hand and I help her to her feet before guiding her forward. She walks beside me for this…her final walk.

Boyd and Bridget join the queue lining the entrance to our home. Esmeralda and I pass them first, and as Fiona crosses their path, I hear my father.

"Whore," he says behind us to Fiona. "Slut."

"Worthless tramp." That comes from my brother, Cormac.

Then his fiancée, Tallulah. "Slag."

"Scum," my mother hisses.

"Cheap tramp," Saoirse taunts.

Then my cousin, Cordelia mutters, "Nasty twat."

The degradation of my new talent slave continues down the line as we enter the large, circular foyer. The family moves around us, lining the circular space as we come to a stop beneath the large, crystalline chandelier that hangs overhead, shining a spotlight above us.

"Kneel," I instruct Esmerelda, feeling as cruel as my father for making her bend on her bum knee. Yet, she does so without hesitation, effectively broken after decades of slavery and abuse at the hands of Boyd and Bridget O'Shea.

But it doesn't matter anyway.

It's the last time she'll ever have to kneel.

Esmerelda quietly cries, lifting her palms to cover her face as I glance up to see my parents move in front of me. Bridget looks heartbroken, and it tugs at my tattered heartstrings. But then I remember why she's heartbroken and my sympathy wanes. She's a part of this, too—we all are. None of us have the right to be upset about it.

I step back beside Fiona, who quivers beyond control, tears streaming down her porcelain cheeks as her arms protectively crisscross over her chest.

I take in a deep breath then speak loudly and clearly, ready to get this mess the fuck over with.

"Esmerelda, we thank you for your service to the O'Shea family. You will not be forgotten. Your grave has been dug and you will be laid to rest among the talent slaves of generations past. You will be visited and remembered dearly by your masters."

Bridget blows Esmerelda a sad kiss and my father gives her a curt, passive nod. "Thank you for your service," they each say in turn.

I look around the circle, meeting each person's eyes before I sigh and tilt my chin down. "A moment of silence for Esmerelda."

Everyone bows their heads, and the room goes quiet…except for the echoing sob that slips from Esmerelda's stuttering chest. She leans forward, placing her palms on her thighs and chants in a hushed whisper, "Please, please, please."

It's the only time in my memory that I've heard her speak out of turn, but it's no matter. Time for rewards and punishments has passed.

This is the end for her.

After a brief silence, I lift my head and speak somberly. "Family, please thank Esmerelda for her service."

Boyd and Bridget step back as everyone else steps forward, each brandishing a blade. My cousin Cordelia is the first to reach Esmerelda, and I'm not surprised at how eager she is for bloodshed.

"Thank you for your service, Esmerelda," Cordelia draws her arm back and thrusts her blade forward, slicing into Esmerelda's side, forcing blood to spatter.

Esmerelda screams as Cordelia pulls the knife out and steps back, as the remainder of my family each takes a turn stabbing her, stealing her blood, spilling the life force of her servitude all over the tan tile.

Fiona is shocked into silence behind me. I wonder if she makes the connection that she'll share the same fate one day, decades in the future.

Esmerelda topples sideways, her white gown soaked red from the multiple wounds inflicted by my immediate family. Blood pools, flowing out from her prone form, and all eyes turn to me.

This twisted tradition has been carried out by the O'Sheas since the four families first began their partnership generations ago. The Mikhailovs, the Vittoris, the Campbells…they all have their own ways of welcoming their new talent. They don't all end the life of their previous talent slave like we do. This is an O'Shea family tradition, uniquely our own, a rite that we perform for each new Head of House when the newest talent slave is brought to the estate.

It's a ritual that puts a stamp on our family's brutality. We are as we always have been—ruthless masters, quiet and unassuming until the time comes to do our work. And when that time comes, our family spills blood together. No one's hands remain clean.

Boyd and Bridget step forward, and though it's clear Esmerelda has already drawn her last breath, they brandish their blade together. Boyd wraps his palm around the handle and Bridget's fingers curl around his wrist. They bend together and drive a final thrust of their blade into the soft flesh of Esmerelda's stomach. Bridget lets out a sob as Boyd gradually loosens his grip and removes his palm from the handle, leaving the blade stuck inside her.

The eyes of my family cast a glare that burns, heating me with intensity as they recognize my ultimate, unquestionable authority. I lift my chin, my lips twisting into a smirk as I feel the power wash over me.

Power and responsibility.

Apprehension.

Ultimate command.

No one's hands remain clean.

I stride forward, stepping in Esmerelda's blood as I move in close. I bend, grip the handle of the single blade still stuck in her flesh, and rip it out with force. Blood sprays from the wound, spattering my clothes.

I regard the dagger with care, marveling at the fact that it's now mine. It's the dagger my father owned before me, a precious item in this family. It's kept only by the Head of House, and I regard it with care— it's a signifier of power amongst the O'Sheas.

I run my finger over the totem pole of skulls that make the grip, the cross-guard that's formed by two crossbones at its base.

This object is sacred, and it now belongs to me.

"Is that it?" I hear Tallulah whisper, and my neck seizes with tension at the sound of her grating voice interrupting this moment.

My head whips toward her to say something, but thankfully, my brother has a handle on his soon-to-be bride. He grabs her, forcing her behind him, and he snarls, "Shut the fuck up."

I return my attention to the dagger and my reverie reminds me that this is it. The transition is complete. I'm the O'Shea family Head of House.

I'm the leader of this brutal horde of bastards, these masters of our realm.

And I am their ruthless king.

I am the king of masters.

CHAPTER 2

MURPHY

I OPEN THE door and push Fiona inside her new bedroom—the room adjoined to mine. This is a traditional living arrangement for the O'Shea Heads of House and their talent slaves. Our rooms are connected so I'll have access to her at all times, though I'm not entirely certain yet that it's warranted. I understand the purpose of her, and I'm well acquainted with the various manners in which the other Heads of House use their slaves, but I have no particular urge to indulge with her.

I direct Bailey back down the hall after a quick scruff behind her ears, then step inside the room and close the door behind me. Fiona practically runs across the room to get away from me, pressing her back into the far corner, her palms hitting the walls on either side of her hips as she trembles, regarding me with fear in her eyes.

I casually saunter to the armchair angled toward her bed and plop down on the seat, crossing my ankle over my knee. I glance around the room, looking at the recently redecorated space. I had it redone in her favorite color—light green—with shades of cream and ivory.

Boyd and Bridget had decorated the room darkly when they brought Esmerelda home. I recall it changing once when I was a teenager from shades of gray and black to a dark navy, but it always felt like a void to me—not that I spent much time in their talent slave's living space.

The green is nice, a soft shade of mint that feels crisp, clean, and bright. It's quite a luxurious space for a slave. She should be grateful to have an attentive master who thinks of her comfort. She could've ended up belonging to a monster, like any of the clients to which we sell. Women everywhere are at risk—and frankly, Fiona's lucky I chose her to be my talent.

I catch sight of the blood on my slacks and follow the line of it, seeing how it soaks through my waistcoat. It's gruesome and it's probably upsetting to Fiona. I unbutton the waistcoat and take it off, dropping it onto the floor before leaning back in my seat again.

At least my button-up beneath was protected from the splatter, though it's no real matter to me. My clothes, the chair, the carpet, it can all be covered in gore and it doesn't matter. We can replace all of it. We have hired help to clean it. There's no problem that can't be solved if you throw enough money at it. And because I now control the family fortune, I can throw our money wherever the fuck I want to, though I'm not a frivolous man—I intend to run our business shrewdly and with good sense.

"You did well, Fiona. Exactly as you were told. As promised, you'll be given some time to rest."

"You're…you're all monsters."

"*We're* not monsters. There are monsters in this world, yes, but you won't find them here."

Her face twists and contorts in confusion. She doesn't understand. These girls, these slaves…they never fucking understand.

I push to my feet and stalk across the room, watching the way she leans into the corner, as if she could melt through the wall.

"The real monsters…? They're out there. Living where you were before I brought you here. They were in your goddamn living room, Fiona. Your father, your brother…They hurt you, I know they did. And you would've crossed paths with more monsters out there in the real world. But you have talent." I grip her cheeks with both hands to hold her eyes to mine. "You have a beautiful voice, and we want to hear it. So,

I chose you. I chose you to have a better life as our talent slave. You were born to be a sacrificial lamb, to be thrown to the wolves, but I saved you from that fate. I brought you here to give you purpose. You'll sing for us, perform for the four families, and we'll revere your talent. You'll be safe here, protected as one of our own."

"You…you *killed* her."

"Yes, we killed her, but she loyally served the family with her talent for decades. She grew to love her masters and in time, you will, too."

She shakes her head against my palms. "No."

I lean forward and plant my lips on hers, kissing her softly, kindly, but I feel nothing from it.

I feel nothing.

I'm meant to own her, use her, make her mine. I thought she was beautiful when I chose her all those years ago, and she *is* beautiful— creamy fair skin, long strawberry-blonde hair, slender, but not without curves. Beautiful, but she's weak. Her body slumps down the wall at the slightest brush of my lips over hers and a whimper escapes her. I pull back immediately.

Her lips part with a gasp, looking up at me as if she wants something more. I could give her something more…I *should* give her something more. I should strip her, fuck her, leave her raw and wanting so she knows her place. It's what I was instructed to do. Now that I'm here with her, alone in what will be her bedroom for years to come, I feel a black hole pulse inside my bleeding heart that was never there before.

It's a hollow spot, a twinge of emptiness.

Push through it and fuck her.

Maybe I'll grow to like her once I have a taste.

I step back. "Take off your clothes."

She gasps again, surprise marring her features. I expect a fight—I *want* a fight—but that's not what I get. With quaking fingers, she begins to remove her clothing. I suppose the ritual murder in the foyer was enough to break her and somehow, I'm annoyed by that. I should be the one to break her, and it shouldn't be this easy.

Is this how it's going to be? Have I adopted a puppy when I really wanted a wildcat?

I want her to feel like I do—annoyed, frustrated, agitated. She should fill any emptiness I feel, but I think I already know that she won't.

It takes time.

I'll grow to like her.

I grab her hands and toss them away from the button on her jeans, taking control and doing it for her. She stands still as I pull down the zipper and yank her jeans and underwear down her legs. I don't even bother to look at her as I push them down to her ankles and nudge her shin, telling her without words to step out.

She complies, and I hate it.

I hate the way she gives in so easily.

She should be fighting me, yelling at me, trying to make me stop. She should give me something, anything resembling passion or hate.

Just fuck her.

Show her where she stands and maybe it'll piss her off enough to give you something more next time.

I reach around to grab a fistful of her hair and spin her, shoving her toward the four-post bed. I force her to bend, slamming her down face-first with her ass exposed to me.

She finally shows some emotion as I unbuckle my belt with one hand, holding her down with the other.

"Don't," she cries quietly. "Please…don't do this…"

My heart punches an extra beat as I watch the tears roll down her cheek. My belt buckle is undone, my zipper is down, and her ass is bared to me. I'm the fucking king here, and I can do whatever the fuck I want.

So why isn't my cock hard?

Not a single fucking twitch.

I slip my hands inside my boxer briefs and wrap my fist around my cock, trying to work it into something resembling a hard-on, but I still fail to get it up. I reach my hand between her clenched thighs and run my finger across her slit. She jolts, but she doesn't move.

Dry as a bone.

This isn't working.

I pull my hand out of my pants and buckle up, then I take a step back. "Get some rest, Fiona. I want to hear you sing tomorrow. I'll have someone bring you dinner. Don't try anything stupid."

I march across the room to the adjoining door that connects our rooms and check the handle to ensure the lock is engaged from the other side. Then I head for the door leading into the hallway and rush out of the room without giving her another glance.

I lock her door and head back to my room. I peel off my bloody clothes and toss them into the hamper before stepping inside my walk-in shower. I flip the faucet handle and step beneath the cold spray. It slowly warms, and I finally huff out an agitated breath.

"Fuck it all."

I'm put off by how easy it was to strip her and bend her over. I expected a fight. I was *prepared* for a fight. I needed a strong talent slave, someone who would challenge me.

I understand a challenge.

I can connect with a challenge.

I wanted a connection because I think I might lose myself to loneliness in the responsibility of this role. I lost myself for a while in my twenties when the reality of what I was destined to become hit me for the first time. I forgot who I was. I forgot where my loyalties lie. I became lazy. I drank too much. I turned into a right fucking wanker and created problems just to have something to solve, just to have something to *do*.

But Fiona poses no challenge, thus no connection, and I'm pissed.

This isn't what I expected and it's not what I wanted. I wanted a fucking fighter, but all I got was a weak little girl. Christ, she may as well be one of Vigo Vittori's broken dolls. The Vittori Head of House likes his playthings submissive and broken inside. I wanted a fighter, like what Nikolai Mikhailov has with his talent slave, Anya. She fought him for years before breaking, but he keeps things interesting by bringing in partners for her to dance with. Maybe I should reach out to him for advice…

I finish scrubbing the blood from my forearms.

A partner.

Perhaps if I had a partner of my own, it would make Fiona more interesting. Boyd and Bridget loved Esmerelda, and she served them both well—not that I want to think about my parents and their plaything. But my parents have always been affectionate and have loyally loved each other for decades—they've always seemed happy with their lot in life. Bridget was always there to soothe Boyd's troubled mind while he ruled the business. Yet, here I am, running the business alone.

I could turn Fiona into a companion—it's what I'm meant to do for another five years until I turn forty and will be required to take a wife and start a family.

How can I find companionship with someone so feeble, so weak, so submissive?

I can't see that with her. I don't think she'll ever be anything more than a slave to me.

And I want so much more than that.

Bridget finds me first as I enter the living room hours later. Her brown eyes land on mine as she rises from the sofa where she sat beside Boyd. The chatter stops as she crosses the room to me and tugs me into an unwanted embrace—unwanted, but appreciated.

She envelopes me in warmth and love and it seeps inside my cold bones. After a moment's hesitation, I return the hug, giving her a quick squeeze before nudging her away.

She looks up at me. "Is she settling in? Behaving?"

"Of course. I know my way around a slave."

I glance around the room, a party interrupted by my presence. I'm sure I'll adjust to the attention my authority brings in time. I wish I could tell them all to behave as they normally would in my presence, but I don't dare. I don't dare set a precedent for comfort in my presence or else my power diminishes in their eyes.

I know how my father ran the show for his decades as the Head of House, and I intend to follow his lead. He's yet to lead me astray, and I want to command the same tone of authority that came before us.

Cordelia lifts her glass of wine, setting it on the mantle above the fireplace, and takes a step forward. "Did you chain her to the bed as I suggested?"

Delia is the oldest O'Shea of my generation—six years my senior—though she could never become the leader of the O'Shea family because she's a woman. We don't allow women to lead.

"No, Cordelia, I didn't." I cock my head to the side. "Didn't I ask you to keep your opinions to yourself unless they're requested?"

"You did," her eyebrows lift and the corners of her lips curl into a smile, "though I was hoping you'd taken my advice, anyway. The room will be destroyed by morning if you left her with her arms and legs untied and free to roam."

I step past my mother, down into the sunken living room. I stride past the couch where Tally sits on Cormac's lap beside my younger brother, Declan. "She won't destroy the room." I move to the bar cart beside the fireplace and pour myself a glass. "I doubt she'll do much of anything. She's already broken."

"Well, that's no fun," Cormac says. I watch as he wiggles his fingers into his fiancée's side, making Tally squeal with laughter. She smacks his shoulder and they smile at each other.

A twinge of jealousy pricks in my chest.

My eyes narrow on him. "She's not here for fun. She's here to be our talent slave. She doesn't have to be anything more than that."

"She's here for you." Boyd tilts his glass, taking a sip of his whiskey on the rocks. "She's here to serve you while you work. I've told you before that being the Head of House is stressful business. She's here for you to work out your frustrations and tension on."

Bridget slowly returns to him, lowering to sit on the arm of the cushioned chair where he's perched with one ankle crossed over his knee. I don't think I've ever seen him look so relaxed. The weight of the world has been lifted from his shoulders and has instead, settled over mine.

"I'll use her as necessary."

"If she gets out of line, feel free to send her to me. I'll be happy to straighten her out," Cordelia reminds me.

She would be happy to play with slaves all day if we let her. She wears a beautiful mask, but her core is as ugly as any one of us—even more so, truthfully. She has a quiet bloodlust rushing through her veins.

O'Shea blood, through and through.

"I'll send her to you as a last resort," I tell her. "I'm afraid you'd rip out her vocal cords just to spite her, and then I'd be left with no talent."

"Too right," Declan snorts.

I smile at my youngest brother over my glass before I take a sip.

"When will she sing for us?" Bridget asks.

"When I'm ready for her to sing. Has Esmerelda been taken care of?"

Her throat bobs as she swallows. "Yes. Buried in the family cemetery." Boyd reaches over and rubs his hand over the small of her back. She looks down at him from her spot on the arm of the chair. "I do wish we could have kept her..."

"I know, my love," Boyd comforts. "But family tradition prevents it."

Family tradition.

He smiles at her lovingly, with the same tenderness he's always had for her. He's loved my mother differently than he's loved anyone else— loved her better, more fiercely…even more so than his own children.

Heads of House aren't allowed to marry until they turn forty. They're required to sink themselves and their identities into the business and are only allowed to marry with the approval of the board. Bridget was one of three women selected by the board when he was forty—the women were presented to my father as file folders, and Bridget was the woman he chose. I suppose she read the best on paper, and in time, they grew to love each other deeply.

I want what they have.

I almost want to gift them Fiona. They would find much greater joy in having a puppy than I will. I'm already frustrated by the responsibility of her, and she's been here less than a day.

I sigh. I've made my appearance, reassured the family that our new talent slave is tucked away, settled, and locked in. But I'm tired and annoyed, and I don't wish to spend another moment entertaining their questions and feeling their watching eyes.

I set my half-drunk glass on the bar cart and head in the direction I came. "I'm knackered. No one disturb me unless a fucking factory is on fire."

"Murphy." Bridget grabs my arm as I stalk past her and I halt.

There are only two people in this room who can control me so effectively with the mere pulse of their shifting emotions, and she's one of them…the other is Declan.

"I'm proud of you," she whispers, leaning her head against the side of my arm.

I reach over with my other hand, placing it on the back of her head to give her a quick squeeze. When I release her, I look down and grant her the small token of appreciation she deserves. "Thank you, Mam."

She smiles, and that makes me glad—at least I've made her proud.

"Cormac was thinking of taking Tally to New York in a couple of weeks." Her voice is soft as chatter picks up around us. "She's always wanted to see the Christmas tree at Rockefeller and do a little holiday shopping. You should go with them. Take a few days and spend some time with your brothers. Christmas will be busy with sales and preparing for the quarterly meeting at the Mikhailovs' in January. Your dad and I will make sure Fiona gets fed."

I sigh. "I really don't have time—"

"You make time for what's important, my love. Always remember that. Your life won't be your own anymore. Your relationship with Cormac and Declan will change. Go. Be brothers on holiday one last time. Do it for me?"

I won't agree to such a thing now. This transition has been smooth chaos, but chaos nonetheless, and I don't think a holiday is such a good idea.

"We'll see."

"Please, Murphy."

I hate when she looks at me like that. I'm soft for her just as Boyd is, just as my brothers are. She's the only unconditional love I've ever known.

"I'll consider it," I promise.

She grins at me, and I squeeze her hand before walking away.

Someday I hope to have a wife that my children revere as much as we revere my mother. Because I'll be cold and hard and my affection will be fickle with them, just like my father was with us. Because the family business will run me just as much as I run it.

Fuck it all.

Maybe a last holiday wouldn't be such a bad thing.

That settles it.

I'm going to New York with my brothers before I lose myself completely.

CHAPTER 3

Stella

"WHAT TIME DO you get off?"

I lift the tip of my tattoo machine from my client's arm and turn it off, raising my eyes to glare up at him. "Are you serious?"

"Yeah, baby girl. I wanna take you out after you finish me off." He arches an overgrown eyebrow. "Then maybe I can finish you off…"

I sit up straight and push back, rolling along with my stool as I back away from his chair. "Did you ever consider asking if I was interested first?"

The moron must have a death wish teasing my last nerve like that, especially when I'm controlling the needles stabbing ink into his flesh.

"You're down for a good time, aren't you, honey?" He smiles crookedly, shifting in his seat to lean toward me.

I look him dead in the eye. "No."

"No? Bet I can turn that no into a yes."

I stand, my rolling stool whipping out behind me and crashing against the wall. "Oh, fuck no. Get out."

"What?"

"Get out."

"Are you serious, baby?"

"Call me baby one more time. One. More. Time. I fucking *dare* you."

His amused expression slips to shock and his eyes widen. "Hey, calm down. I didn't mean anything by it." He gestures at his outstretched arm. "You haven't even finished my tattoo yet."

"And I'm not going to. Get the fuck out."

Shock switches to anger. "I paid in full. You're gonna fucking finish it."

I shake my head. "No, I'm not."

I'm so sick of these fuck-boys thinking they can mess around with me in my own damn tattoo shop.

Anger becomes outright rage as he leaps out of his chair, rushing into my space. "Fucking finish or give me my money back."

He's trying to threaten me, trying to force my back to the wall, but I widen my stance and hold firm, unwilling to back down. I didn't make it this far in life backing down to shit stains like him.

"It's half done. I'll send a partial refund to your credit card after you kindly leave the premises. You have my full blessing to let some other unfortunate artist finish my work."

It's a damn shame. It would've been a masterpiece, but I'm not putting up with that bullshit. I've learned that if you give guys like this an inch, you ought to be prepared for them to take a mile.

"Where's the shop owner? I wanna talk to him about your fucking attitude, bitch."

I slowly tilt my head and lift the corner of my lips. "Go ahead. Talk to the shop owner."

"Where the fuck is he?" He turns his head to glance around the open shop, and I let my eyes track where his go.

I note Cora stifling a laugh and dipping her head lower as she continues to ink her client a few feet away. It almost makes me want to smile, but I won't give this asshat the satisfaction. My eyes meet his again as his gaze returns to me.

"Hello, sir. I'm the owner. I understand you've had an experience you interpret to be less than desirable in my shop today. We're happy to resolve this non-issue with a partial refund to your card the moment your feet hit the pavement outside. I'm afraid we don't tolerate misogynist losers who think our female artists owe them something." I point toward the register. "As you can see, we have a sign."

He glances back to see the *WE DON'T SERVE ASSHOLES* sign that I actually made myself and posted behind the desk. I'm proud to employ more female artists than males at my shop. It's not that I have anything against men specifically—though most of the ones I've met are as obnoxious as this one. We've dealt with enough pushy customers who think they can take advantage of us, and I've had enough of it.

I have a zero-tolerance policy for bullshit.

Moving quickly, I grab hold of his arm, wipe it down, and carefully but furiously slap a bandage over it. "Judging by the rest of your shitty artwork, I trust you know how to take care of this one while it heals." I let go just as he jerks his arm away with a scowl on his face.

I flick my fingers, shooing him toward the door. "Go on now. Don't make me gather the girls. I promise you don't want to be seen getting shoved out the door by a bunch of wicked females. That would be a blow to your ego that I just don't think you can handle."

He stares me down, unable to speak, surely shocked that one, I didn't want to go out with a gem like him, and two, that I'm kicking him out with a half-done skull tattoo.

I give him five more seconds before I charge for the front, pushing the metal bar on the glass door to swing it open. I hold it wide with my back against it as I sweep my arm out toward the busy sidewalk.

It's a Saturday night and it's noisy outside—not a surprise since my shop is nestled between a nightclub and a bar. While we don't give tattoos to drunk people, we do get a lot of drunk traffic on the weekends—people we will gladly take non-refundable deposits from for future sober appointments.

Business is good and I fucking love it.

Now if I can just get this asshole to leave.

Eventually, once he realizes there's literally nothing else he can do, he rages toward the exit. He rambles off a final, "Fuck you!" before disappearing into the crowd outside.

I let the door swing shut behind me as I come back in.

Cora doesn't even look up. "I'm too fucking tired to give you a standing ovation for that, Stell. Would you settle for an *atta girl?*"

Her perfectly pleasant client chuckles.

"I don't do it for the fame and fortune, but I do enjoy the praise."

Her eyes flicker up at me from behind her clear-framed glasses to give me a quick, approving look. "You're my hero."

I flash her an appreciative smile as I move back to my station. "Well, I guess that's it for me tonight." I start to put away my supplies. "Just threw out my last client."

"You know you can head out if you want. I can close up shop," Cora offers, tossing her head to the side to knock away an obstructive strand of mermaid blue hair from her face.

"I don't know why you even bother offering. You know I don't leave any of my artists alone to close. Despite the sign," I nod back toward the *WE DON'T SERVE ASSHOLES* sign at the desk, "assholes and creeps do wander in here from time to time."

We both laugh.

After cleaning up my station, I head behind the desk to issue a partial refund to the creep I kicked out, and then I prep for closing while Cora finishes up. Once finished, I head back to my client's chair and make myself comfortable. I breathe deeply and let my eyes drift shut, taking a moment of meditation to clear my head and calm my nerves.

Truthfully, it's hard to be a tough woman in this world. I don't have a problem speaking my mind and standing up against men who think they're owed something—entitled pricks—but I'd be lying to say it didn't bother me at all when I have to.

I don't care which bad bitch you ask, we can look as confident as the next motherfucker on the outside, but standing ground against a big, tall, and furiously unpredictable man can be unnerving.

After another thirty minutes, Cora's done with her client and she heads to the register to take his payment. When I hear the door open and shut again, I open my eyes and sit up slowly. "We should get a drink."

"Yeah? I'm down," Cora replies.

I swing my legs over the side of the chair, letting them dangle. "You wanna go to Serendipity or The Jaded Wingman?

"Well, that depends. Do you wanna get hit on by dancing drunks or fighting drunks?"

We both look toward the door as the bell overhead rings and it opens with a sharp tug from the outside.

"Where are you going?" a man's voice says from the sidewalk as another man stumbles inside.

I raise my eyebrows at Cora. "I guess we don't even have to leave the premises. The drunks are on their way to us."

She laughs, leaning forward with her elbows on the counter. "Can we help you?" she asks the tall, lean guy stumbling toward the desk.

He topples sideways, and Cora and I both reach out a hand on reflex, as if we could catch him from as far away as we both are. Luckily, another slightly shorter man with dark hair rushes in to catch him…and thank God, because clearly mine and Cora's psychic catching abilities have suddenly gone on hiatus.

"You'll have to excuse my brother," the dark-haired man says, clearly much more sober than his brother. "We're on holiday and he's had a few too many."

"I'm getting married!" the drunk man enthusiastically states, punching a fist into the air.

Cora and I both laugh as the two men saunter toward the counter. The bells on the door chime as it's opened once again, and my attention is diverted. A third man walks in, more serious and somber. He's tall and stylish with his black overcoat, tailored gray slacks, and sleek dress shoes. He's far too fancy to have found his way in here on his own. His ashen blond hair has a ginger tint and is too perfectly styled, his beard too well-groomed and manicured.

Damn, there's just something about a man with a good beard.

My eyes lock onto him, and I feel a little something extra pulse inside me when he enters the shop. He's got a strong aura. Something within him demands to take up a lot of space, and when I somehow forget to breathe, I think it has to be because he's sucked all the air from the room.

"I want a tattoo," the drunk man at the counter says.

The man at the door catches me staring and with a sharp turn of his head, our eyes meet.

"Sorry, we can't ink you when you're drunk." I hear Cora explain, but her voice sounds far away. "Shop policy."

"I told you that," the sober guy holding him up says.

My eyes are still on the man at the door.

"But I want my bride's name tattooed right over my heart."

"Aw, that's sweet," Cora says. "What's her name?"

"Tallulah. My perfect, beautiful Tally."

"Tally-ho!" both men shout after him in unison.

The timbre of the man at the door's voice strikes me. I can feel it vibrate in my chest from across the room as our eyes remain locked. His lips quirk up at one side and fuck, if mine don't twist up the same way.

These boys have an accent and damn, it's sexy.

Irish? Scottish? Cockney? Shit, is it offensive that I don't know the difference?

I stand and saunter toward the counter, moving behind the desk to stand beside Cora. "Where are you boys from?"

"Ireland," the sober, dark-haired man says. "We came in for a little holiday with his fiancée, but she didn't want to come out with us, so it's just us boys tonight."

The gorgeous piece of man at the door moves closer and somehow, he still has my attention. His light, bewitching eyes scan my face, and I feel the scrutiny under my skin. His coarse beard frames his plump lips, so obviously kissable that looking at them has me biting mine.

I need to calm myself down and stop eye-fucking him. But his hair is thick—the kind you want to comb your fingers through—and his open collar hints at artwork on his chest, hiding beneath. I'm dying to see his chest…For the artwork, of course, not because I want to know how strong his pecs are.

I'm a woman with standards for God's sake.

"Sorry to bother you ladies," the sober guy says after glancing around the empty shop. "Looks like you're shutting down."

"It's no bother," I tell him politely, finally dragging my eyes away from his beautiful friend. "But we can't do anything with your drunk brother tonight. If you guys are gonna be in town, we'd be happy to take a deposit and you can schedule an appointment to come back."

"We're only here for another night."

"You should check out Serendipity next door. Get a drink, do some dancing," Cora suggests. I feel her amused smile and see her head turn to look at me from the corner of my eye. "We were actually just talking about grabbing a drink."

I dare to look over at the man who's stolen my attention, and he offers me a grin. His crow's feet crinkle at the corners of his eyes, effectively triggering all my daddy issues.

Fuckity fuck fuck.

He takes a step toward the counter, moving straight toward me, and though there's an entire desk separating us, the sheer demand of his presence makes my spine straighten, and I lean back.

He speaks directly to me. "Serendipity sounds like fun. If you lasses happened to wind up there in the next hour, we just might see you there?"

I feel Cora's eyes on me as I open my mouth to impulsively reject, but she saves me.

"Yes," she says. "Yep. You'll see us there."

I snap my head to look at her. "They will?" She looks at me sternly—so sternly it nearly scares me enough to take a step back. I hold up a palm to her as a white flag. "Okay, yeah, you will."

"I'm Declan," the dark-haired man says. "This one is Cormac."

Then the man who's caught my attention tells me, "I'm Murphy."

I've already forgotten the names of the other two.

"Cora," she pipes up beside me to introduce herself, then gestures toward me. "And this gorgeous thing is Stella. She owns the shop, you know."

"You don't say?" Murphy cocks an eyebrow, though his expression remains somewhat impassive.

He's tough, this one—a hard shell to crack. It's written so clearly in the way he presents himself. He seems like a challenge, and that's something I haven't had for a while. To speak minimally, he's piqued my interest…and it doesn't hurt that he's drop dead gorgeous, too.

"I'm quite impressive, I realize that," I say with a mock-cocky tone.

"Aye," he replies with a scan of his eyes down the front of my body. *Oh, my fucking, God.*

I hear Cora chuckle beside me, probably expecting me to read him the riot act for so overtly implying that my looks are what's impressive to him, and by all means, I should.

But for some reason, I don't…because I guess I find his looks impressive, too.

"All right, mates," Declan says, "let's head on out, then. Ladies, we look forward to seeing you." He gives a small appreciative nod and drunken Cormac awkwardly salutes as they hobble toward the door.

Murphy remains standing in front of me and I can't help the curl of my lip. "See you soon," I tell him.

"I look forward to it."

He leaves and I make no effort to pretend I'm not watching him walk away. I rush to lock the door behind them after he exits and spin around quickly to face Cora, pressing my back to the door with my arms behind me. I blow out a breath and she grins at me.

"You're crushing hard, babe."

I can feel my cheeks warm. "Not crushing."

"Totally crushing."

"That's not a crush. That's just plain fucking lust."

She chuckles at me. "Well, I hope you wore your good panties today."

My face falls. "Well, shit."

"What? Are you wearing granny panties?"

I knock my head against the door and shut my eyes. "I am. I actually fucking am."

"Go take them off," she says with all the seriousness in the world. "Go commando."

I cock a brow at her. "Seriously?"

"Seriously. Do it."

"Jesus, I'll get a wet spot on my jeans." I laugh.

"So what? He'll probably think that's hot."

"I don't know. He doesn't seem like a typical guy."

"No shit. That's why you have a lady boner for him. Stella Scott doesn't like typical guys. You've always been about that strong, silent type, babe."

I sigh. "Yeah, totally. But he's only in town for a night."

"So? That's perfect! You don't want a relationship. Have a one-night stand."

I tilt my head. "Can I do that?"

"Yes, girl! Why not? Own your feminine sexual prowess or whatever."

"Right." I nod. "Yeah, you're right. I can do whatever I want to." I rake my fingers through my hair. "That's if he even wants to…"

"Shut the fuck up right now. He totally wants to. Did you see the way he eye-fucked you?"

I let out a long, slow breath. "Yeah. He eye-fucks really good, too."

I haven't wanted anyone in a long damn time, and this random guy just walks in and makes my stomach feel like it's literally filled with butterflies. He gives me that gnawing ache deep down in my gut that sets an anticipatory blaze in my veins.

I can't remember the last time I felt such urgency to get out of my shop, but damn, I feel it now.

Excitement.

A mad rush.

An odd—and unexpected—need to spend some time with a random, sexy Irishman who stumbled into my shop. His drunken brother did the stumbling, but that stumbling brought him here, nonetheless.

I rush off to the bathroom in the back so I can take off my stupid granny panties.

CHAPTER 4

Murphy

STELLA.

Latin for star.

She certainly shines brighter than most girls I've met. There's a little something extra to her that I can't quite put my finger on, but I certainly hope to put my finger on it tonight. She caught my attention before I even heard her speak, which is quite unusual for me. Few people in my life have managed to catch my attention.

Fiona caught my attention a decade ago, but I was wrong about who she would grow to be.

Perhaps my judgment is off…

Or perhaps my judgment is better now than it was before.

Something in my gut twists at the thought of Stella and it's a little unsettling. It makes me feel uneasy in a way, but hopeful at the same time. Hopeful is a feeling I haven't had since I was a child.

I feel childlike now in the way she grabbed hold of me so easily, wrung me out until I was dripping with curiosity. She's beautiful, but what really caught me was the fire blazing behind her eyes—the intensity was bright through an interaction as simple as a polite introduction.

She has some fight in her.

I could sense it immediately.

Declan tosses Cormac down on the black leather seat of a booth he talked someone out of near the back of the club. It will never cease to amaze me the way that Declan can charm just about everyone he comes into contact with. He's a people pleaser, a coping mechanism he developed to deal with the worst parts of our family business. I think on some level he thinks he can make up for our crimes against humanity by being polite and charming to everyone we don't seek to exploit.

He's very naïve, but I don't want him to change. If he changed, he wouldn't be Declan, and Declan provides a necessary balance to our cruel reality.

I slide into the curved booth, big enough to seat five or six people, and tug my phone from my pocket. I do an internet search for the tattoo shop next door.

"You think those girls are gonna join us?" Declan grins at me across the table.

"I don't know."

"You liked that girl with the dark hair. Stella, was it?"

I lift my eyes from the screen and glare at him. "She was interesting."

"You hardly spoke to each other. How do you know she's interesting?"

"It's a feeling."

"Aye, a feeling. Are you going in for the shift when she comes by?"

"What's it to you?"

"You need a good ride, mate. Blow off some steam. I'm worried about you."

"What are you worried about, then?"

Cormac leans back, stretching his long arms across the back of the booth. "Your mind is always on the job." His speech is slow and slurred, but he's fully cognizant. "Have a little fun, will you? I'm getting married soon. It's the last time the three of us will be single all at the same time."

I snort. "Declan will be single forever unless he wants to pretend he's straight and play house with a woman."

Declan's cheeks drop out of his constant smile, and I feel a pang in my chest for saying it. "You know what? Fuck you. I was fixing to be your wingman tonight. You're on your own now."

Declan's sexual preference is a bit of a sore spot. I assume Boyd and Bridget know—the rest of us do—but their expectations of us have always been quite clear. The O'Shea sons will marry women and have children to carry on the O'Shea name, whether they want to or not.

I sigh. When Declan gets upset, it bothers me on a molecular level. He has always been my baby brother and there's not an ounce of me that can think of him any other way. It's one thing for him to be pissed off about something, but if he's pissed off because of something *I* said, it's on me to fix it. I scoot out of the seat and tuck my phone into my back pocket mid-search.

"You need a drink. I'll head to the bar. What are you having?"

"Round of shots!" Cormac shouts, his voice overly enthusiastic in comparison to the unenthusiastic way his body slumps against the back of the seat. He's going to have some regrets in the morning.

I shake my head and walk toward the front of the club, heading for the bar. Halfway there, some lass puts her hand on my arm and squeezes, halting me mid-stride. My heart beats double as my eyes fall on her hand and follow her arm up, hoping to see a certain face with bronze skin and dark brown eyes. But I'm disappointed to find that the face belongs to some trashy girl with dark roots and bleached blond hair trying to take something from me that I have no interest in giving.

Instantly, I find myself appraising her value as an asset, but I don't think she'd be worth enough to bother with. She's rail thin, hardly any curves to speak of, and she looks like she'd be a screamer. There's a market for that, of course, but it's small. Our buyers want weak, submissive, quiet women, not girls who'll blast their eardrums every time they play.

I snatch the girl's bony wrist in my hand and spin to face her, tugging her in close. She gasps, her lips parting in surprise as I lean in to speak directly against her ear. "Girls like you should be careful. You have no worth to men like me. I'd sell you in a heartbeat for a nicer car, you worthless piece of trash."

I pull back to smile and toss her hand away just as her eyes pop wide. She stumbles backward a step before turning sharply on her heel and pushing her way through the dancing crowd. I've forgotten about her by the time I make my way to the bar and order drinks for the table.

I pull out my phone, leaning my elbows on the bar top, and resume my search of Stella's shop next door. It's impressive that it belongs to her. The women in my life generally don't work, let alone run a business of their own, so it's easy to recognize that she's not like any of the women who surround me on a daily basis. I reason that must be why I find her interesting.

I find the *Artists* section on her website and scroll through the page until I find a picture of her. It's not a professional picture, which should put me off.

It's actually kind of trashy, but I actually kind of love it.

Her eyes are closed, her mouth is open, and her tongue is out as she holds up her hand with her middle and ring finger down, flashing the universal "rock and roll" hand sign.

I want to spit on her fucking tongue.

"Are you Googling me?"

I turn my head over my shoulder and find her standing behind me, looking at me with a smirk that triggers my own.

She puts her hands on her hips. "Oh, my God. You *stalker.* You were totally Googling me." She laughs and I like how it sounds. It's not a forced, flirtatious giggle; no, it's a real laugh from a real woman.

Unashamed, I click off the screen and put my phone back in my pocket as I turn toward her. She slides up to the bar beside me, leaning on one elbow.

"Hi," she says with a tilt of her head.

"Hello, Stella."

She swallows visibly and licks her lips.

It's the accent.

"You remembered my name."

"Of course, I did."

"I'm impressed."

I raise a brow. "Is that all it takes to impress you?"

"Honestly, it'll take a hell of a lot more than that, but my history with terrible men has set my standards pretty low."

"Why have you spent so much time with terrible men?"

She shrugs a shoulder, and the movement draws my eyes to her slender neck and her smooth, warm-beige skin. "There are more terrible men than good men, so the odds are against me."

If only she knew…

"I can't argue that point."

"Cora," she points behind us, "found your brothers. But, uh, I found you, here, so…" she trails off.

A smile spreads across my face. "I'm glad you found me, Stella."

Her cheeks flush red with a hint of heat.

The bartender slides over a tray of shots and I lift it. "Ladies first," I tell her and wait for her to move.

She strolls away toward the dance floor, heading across in the direction of our booth at the back, and I watch the way her hips sway. It's not intentional. She's not trying overtly to pull my attention straight for her arse, but it's happening all the same.

Stella is a natural beauty, a woman who doesn't have to try, and she's all the more appealing to me that she doesn't. She has curves that could kill, flesh to grab hold of, to grip tightly and dig my fingers into.

I set the tray on the table and wait for Stella to slide in next to Cora before sitting beside her, trapping her in the booth.

"That's what I told Stell," Cora nudges her with an elbow as she speaks to Declan—Cormac is between them, reaching for another drink, "but she has a way of scaring men off. And she doesn't believe she's fuckable."

Stella looks at her, stunned. "What the fuck?" But Cora just shrugs with a smile and my brother laughs.

Declan looks at me, leaning on his elbows against the tabletop. "We were just discussing how overworked and pent-up you are. Apparently, Stella has the same issue. It's the general consensus of the table that you two," he indicates me and Stella sitting side by side with his finger, "should spend some time *alone*." He grins mischievously at me before throwing back a shot.

If anyone else said that to me—even Cormac—they'd be nursing a black eye. Declan gets a free pass. I don't know when that free pass expires, if it ever does, but I think he's determined to find out.

"Wow." Stella's eyes widen and she reaches for a glass from the tray. "I guess I'd better loosen up a little since the table has decided my fate for me. Fuck." She tosses back the shot like a champ.

She doesn't know that every man at this table has a say in her fate, whether she likes it or not. She has no idea what power we wield and how deep our commitment to the family and the business runs.

If I wanted to take her tonight and send her to one of our factories to be processed as a human asset, I could. If I wanted to force her back to my hotel room, use her, and then leave her behind, I could. If I wanted to slit her throat and dump her body in the dark alley behind the club, I could. No judge in the world would convict me because our family is above the goddamn law.

I don't feel an urge to do any of those things, and for that, she's lucky. Her blue-haired friend is, too. I'm more interested in the challenge Stella poses. It's all telling in her eyes. Her spirit is filled with passion, determination, hard-headedness, and bravery. That much was easy to figure out, but the motivations behind those traits are a mystery to me. The mystery has me drawn to her in a way that makes my pulse quicken.

I look at her and wait until her captivating dark-brown eyes meet mine. "If anyone chooses your fate tonight, lass, it'll be me, not them." I look at her plump lips, at the deep dimple in the center of her upper lip that defines their perfect shape.

She doesn't try to hide her flirtatious smile. "So then tell me…"

She leans in close. "What's my fate tonight?"

The corner of my lips quirk up as I stare her down, wondering if the intensity and assuredness of my gaze will outlast hers, wondering if she'll back down and look away before I do.

Several beats pass.

"I need another drink." While I hear Cora, I hold Stella's eyes to keep her attention on me. "You guys buying?"

"Aye," Declan says. "Come on, Cormac, let's go buy the lady a drink."

"Spot on. I need another one, too," Cormac slurs.

I search Stella's expression for a tell as they all scoot out of the booth, but I can't find one in her scrutinizing gaze. All I find is absolution—the stare of a woman who knows exactly what she wants.

"I'm still waiting for your answer," she says.

"My answer?"

She turns her body toward mine, puts her elbow up on the table, and tilts her cheek against her fist as she grins at me. "What's my fate tonight? Actually, I should be asking what you *wish* my fate were tonight, because God knows I don't let any man choose for me."

"Oh, lass, you have no idea who you're dealing with here."

"Enlighten me."

"Enlighten you?" I reach out, slipping two fingers into her black hair and brushing them down the small section peeking out from behind her ear that's dyed a bright, unnatural red.

She lifts her head from her hand. "Didn't your mother ever teach you not to touch a woman without her permission?"

I push her hair back over her shoulder and lean in close to whisper against her ear. "I'd rather ask for forgiveness than permission."

I move back again so I can look at her and her jaw twitches as she forces her lips to curl down. She's displeased, but she's still fighting a smile.

I lean back casually and lift my eyebrows at her as I smirk. "Are you offended?"

Her brown eyes flash down to my chest, then back to my eyes. "I haven't made up my mind about you yet."

"Let me help you sort it out, then. Tell me what you're thinking."

"I'm thinking you might be a bit of a narcissist."

"Spot on." I grin. "What else?"

Her thick eyebrows furrow toward her nose. "Well, there goes that theory. A narcissist would never admit to being a narcissist."

"How would you know?"

"Trust. I've wasted enough time with them to know."

"Bad ex-boyfriends?"

"Quite a few of them."

"Hmm. So I hear you're not used to being taken care of."

"I guess you could say that."

"And what if I wanted to take care of you for the night?" I rub my hand over my beard as I watch her chest sharply rise and fall heavily.

"I guess it depends on what you mean by *take care of*..."

I turn and come in close enough for my beard to scratch her cheek, my lips brushing the shell of her ear. Her spine straightens, but she doesn't pull away. "What do you want it to mean, lass? Tell me."

The woman radiates heat, like fire burns beneath her skin. Maybe that blaze is what pulls me in, like a moth to a flame. Except there is no way for her to burn me.

She turns her cheek toward mine, as if she wants to feel me there, and shrugs her shoulder a little as I lean into her. "That *almost* sounds like asking for permission."

I reach around behind her and press my palm to her back, then drag her in a little closer. "If I were, what would you let me do to you?"

This conversation wouldn't be necessary if she were my slave... not to say it's exactly necessary now. I can take what I want when I want it, though I suppose that's exactly what repels me from Fiona. I'm supposed to use her, abuse her, take what I want without asking, without regret. But the lack of challenge bores me.

It bores me and it bothers me on a fundamental level when my fucking humanity slithers its way back into my heart. I have to snatch the slimy creature, yank it free, and toss it away…or else it sinks its teeth into me and injects poisonous guilt into my veins.

There's no room for guilt in the heart of an O'Shea.

But this, with Stella…this little back and forth with her…this is fun. It's like playing a game.

What can I convince her to let me do to her?

How satisfying will it be to get her to give up control?

What will her face look like when I make her come?

"Just one night," she whispers next to my ear and my stomach clenches. "I'm not looking for a relationship. And you're only here for the night. I probably won't see you again." My shoulders tense. "So I won't have anything to be ashamed of when you leave, right?"

Her hand lands on my thigh and my muscles twitch at the overt confidence. I'm not sure whether I like it. I need to take back control and make her think she gave it to me.

I grab her wrist and toss her hand back onto her lap. She gasps and pulls back to look at me. I slip my hand up to grasp the back of her neck and forcefully slam my lips against hers. There's a moment where she pauses in surprise, but then there she goes again, trying to lead us.

No, lass, no.

I splay my hand over the back of her head and hold her firmly in place as I open my mouth, slip my tongue between her lips, and devour her. She tugs backward once, twice, and then she stills. She sighs, whimpering into my mouth as she gives in and lets me taste her.

She tastes like a woman, a goddamn warrior. Kissing her makes me feel something and it's fucking good. I want to possess her, though not as a slave.

But then, as what?

Her hands slide up my chest, spreading her blaze over my body with the trail of her touch. My breath quivers as I inhale, the touch of her igniting something feral inside me.

What is this feeling?

I stay close when I break our lips apart. "We're leaving. You're coming with me to my hotel. You can walk beside me or behind me or I can carry you out of here kicking and screaming over my shoulder, but one way or another, I'm gonna find out what your pretty little cunt tastes like."

She pulls back with a snap, her lips parting with shock and her eyebrows slanting inward in horror. I wonder which part of what I said horrified her. I flash her a true smile because the look on her face shoots straight through me and makes my cock twitch.

She shoves against my chest to push me back and it only makes me want her more. I hold true to the back of her head and pull her in for another kiss. She tries to shove me, but she abruptly stops when I deepen the kiss, sweeping my tongue so deep inside her that she doesn't know how to respond. Her fingers curl over the fabric of my shirt, trying to find something to hold on to.

I drag myself away with a snap and slide out of the booth unceremoniously. I grab my lapels and straighten them with a quick lift before smoothing down my blazer, then I grab my overcoat from the seat. I look at her and cock an eyebrow, enjoying the flush of red around her kiss-swollen lips.

What will she do?

How will this end?

She licks her lips, then slides out and stands in front of me. Without any shame, she steps in close, slaps her hand over my cock and looks up at me with sin in her deep, dark eyes.

"Don't say *cunt*. I find it offensive."

"Oh, I'll have *you* saying cunt before the end of the night. I'll make you beg me to taste your sweet, swollen cunt before we're through."

Her half-smile returns, twitching at her cheek. "I'd like to see you try."

I take a step forward, pushing her a step back. "Am I dragging you out of here or what?"

Her eyes flicker, sizing me up. "I have two feet and I'll walk my own damn self wherever the fuck I wanna go. And I'm not walking beside you or behind you. I'm walking in front of you. Because I'm the one making the rules here."

"Whatever you need to tell yourself, princess."

She rolls her eyes and laughs. "I'm no fucking princess. You have no idea what you've gotten yourself into with this bitch." She points to herself.

I look at her sideways. "Does this bitch need a shorter leash, perhaps?"

"Wow. *Wow.*" She chuckles and spins away, walking a few steps before spinning around to face me again. "This bitch fucking *leads.*" She claps her hands at me like a dog. "Come on, boy, come fetch your bitch." She widens her stance, crosses her arms over her chest, and scowls at me.

Fuck, I have to hide my smile.

She waits.

She hasn't left yet.

She's enjoying this as much as I am.

I hold up a finger and twirl it. "Start walking then, bitch. Lead the way."

I smirk and her expression instantly mirrors mine, filled with hate and humor all at once. She gives me a quick once over and humor wins, playing at her cheeks. She turns and starts walking.

I like her...I like her a hell of a lot more than I expected.

She has heat. I can imagine it's too hot for most men she meets, but she's never met anyone quite like me. I like the way her fire burns, the way it fuels me with flames that lick hot across my skin.

She needs a man who doesn't back down when faced with her

heat. She needs a man who can put her in her place. She needs a man who can effectively reward her submission when she finally breaks.

She needs *me*.

CHAPTER 5

Stella

"CORA. CORA!" I snap at her as I approach her at the bar. I grab her by the elbow and pull her away from Murphy's brothers. "I'm about to do something really fucking stupid."

"Great! I always knew you had it in you."

"I'm serious. This guy is all kinds of intense and he's a total jerk. But I'm kind of totally into it?"

"Okay, so?"

"So…I shouldn't be leaving with him right now, right?"

She laughs. "Are you asking me for permission? Or are you trying to get me to talk you out of it or what?"

"I don't know. He's just…he's everything that I hate but everything that makes me horny all wrapped in one asshole package."

"Do you want to fuck him?"

I sink a little at the thought of it and nod.

"Go fuck him, Stella. Fuck him and dump him. He's only here for another night. Give him a night to remember and send him on his merry way."

"Yeah. Okay. Yeah, you're right. Why am I so in my head about this?"

"Because you haven't been railed in like, six months."

"Jesus, don't remind me."

"Stella," Murphy suddenly barks from right behind me, grabbing my wrist and pulling me back. I jump when he startles me and my pulse hums beneath his touch. "Are you coming or not?"

"She'd better be coming tonight," Cora says to him with an expression that is far too serious.

I tilt my head and lift my eyebrows at her. "Bye, Cora."

"Send me and Josh a text with the address when you get there." Josh is her on-again-off-again boyfriend-slash-roommate.

"I will. You be careful, babe. Call Josh to walk you home later, will you?"

She nods. "Yep, don't worry about me. Worry about yourself. Stay safe."

Is any of this safe?

I yank my wrist from Murphy's grip so I can blow her a quick kiss, which she returns, before I stride right on past him to the door. I told him I was walking in front of him, and I meant it. This little power play with him is unlike anything I've experienced with a guy before, and I've messed with my fair share of assholes. It's not so much that he's an asshole...he *is*, but I just get this feeling there's more to him than that.

And for some reason, I kind of like the power he exudes. It's sexy when it shouldn't be. It makes me want to keep up this fight for control between us because I want to see how far I can push him before he snaps, before he takes the lead for good and dominates me.

Shit, I can't remember the last time I was this stupidly horny.

I reach the exit and stop, starting to turn so I can wait for Murphy to catch up, but he's right there beside me. He hooks his arm around my waist, his fingers digging into my side, and pulls me against him. He drags me out the door and onto the sidewalk. His strides are long and quick, and I struggle to keep up.

"Slow down," I tell him.

His fingers dig deep into the side of my waist, bruising me. "Keep up."

"I hope this rushing isn't a preview of how the night's gonna go.

You're not a three-pumps-and-done kind of guy, are you?"

He stops us abruptly beside the curb and moves to stand in front of me, his arm sliding along my back as he shifts to grip my hips with both hands. He stands close and his energy pulses through me from his palms. "Do I give you that impression? Does anything about me make you think I don't know what I'm doing?"

"I mean, how should I know? I just met you."

"That's right. You have no idea."

His arms move around my waist to tug me close. Then his lips land on mine. He kisses me, but it's not hard like the first time he kissed me inside Serendipity. It's soft, warm, deceptively so. This kiss is a tease because I know this softness will be absent once we're alone. His strong aura radiates rough, hard, and wild. I really need that tonight. I need him to wrestle the fight out of me and take me.

Does that make me a bad feminist?

Well, fuck me if it does, because I'm doing this tonight, anyway.

He hails a cab and his hands are all over me the entire ride. I don't even know where we are when we tumble out because he's already got me so worked up. I'm sex-drunk from nothing more than simple, mostly innocent touching—he was stroking my thigh, running his fingers down my arm, brushing his nose along my jawline.

It's not until we hit the luxurious hotel lobby that I realize this guy is way out of my league.

"What do you do for a living?" I ask as he leads me along to the elevator bank with his hand on the small of my back.

The sound of water splashing from the fountain as we pass it draws my attention, and I turn my head toward it to take in my surroundings. Marble floors, elegant fountain, terrible soothing piano music echoing from the corridor.

"I run our family business. We do well."

"I'll say."

We get on the elevator, and he has to use his keycard to access a top-level floor. My heart flurries with excitement, not just for getting laid for the first time in half a century, but for getting laid by a hot older man with a sexy accent in a fancy hotel.

Living the dream.

"How old are you?" I ask as he backs me into the corner of the elevator.

"Thirty-five. How old are you?"

"Twenty-six."

"Hmm," he hums, slamming his body against mine and bending to kiss the side of my neck.

I let my head fall back into the corner as he licks a line along the curve of my neck, but then I jolt when he sinks his teeth in—not playfully but fucking hard.

"Hey, easy!" I put my hands on his chest and push. He does it again. I yelp and shove until he takes a step back. He looms above me, looking down at me with narrowed eyes as he licks his bottom lip.

"You wanna leave?" he challenges me.

The elevator stops and the doors slide open. He walks backward off it, cocking an eyebrow and waiting for me to choose—stay on the elevator and go home, or get off the elevator and get it on with him.

I get off the damn elevator.

"Twenty-three fifty-two. Lead the way, I wanna watch you walk," he commands.

The breath I take in is shaky at best. Part of me wants to rebel, stand my ground, let him drag me to his room kicking and screaming like he had promised. But I decide to give him this one and stride forward.

Room twenty-three fifty-two is the last room at the end of the hallway. I stop when I reach it to pull my phone from my bag.

"Hang on," I tell him.

I snap a quick picture of the door number, then take a quick candid shot of his face without warning and bring up a text. "I'm sending the hotel name, room number, and your face to Cora and Josh. If you were thinking about murdering me and cutting me up into little pieces… well, you could probably still do it, but I'd think twice if I were you. They'll know exactly who did it and they'll send you to prison. I'm willing to bet some guy would make you his bitch within the first week."

I tap send and shove my phone into my bag, looking up at him with a cheeky grin. His expression nearly matches mine, his energy nearly matches mine…his vibe, his aura, the electric hum of his beating heart.

I feel him under my skin and the intensity of it is pure, clean, sparking lust.

I step aside and let Murphy unlock and push open the door for me. I barely step over the threshold before I'm attacked. The door clicks shut, and he grabs me from behind, wrapping his arms around me, and molding to my backside.

One of his hands slips down as the other roams up, reaching between my legs while he squeezes my breast. I gasp, folding forward, my insides coiling around his touch. He bends over me, folding with me as he cups his hand between my legs, and my excitement swells.

"God, I need this," I whimper.

He jerks me back, lifting me upright as his hand slips from my breast to my throat. His hand is large, big enough to snap my neck like a twig if he really wanted to, and a pulse of fear shoots through my veins—but right behind the fear is desire. The rings on his fingers dig into my flesh. I want to feel the metal drawing lines across my skin as his hands touch me everywhere.

He marches me forward across the enormous suite, turning us left and forcing me to a half-shut door. His hand leaves my body for as long as it takes to shove the door wide, and he pushes me inside roughly, but not rudely.

I spin around to face him, dropping my bag onto the floor, shrugging off my coat, peeling my shirt up and over my head, and tossing it away. He saunters toward me. His eyes, which seem to change color with the lighting, are a misty gray-green as they zero in on my mouth, and they look…transcendent.

He reaches out, grips me by the side of my neck, and drags me against him. My body collides with his and he kisses me with aggression. It's like the kiss in the booth from before—rough, consuming, almost painful.

I don't think I've ever been kissed this way, not even by a man who once claimed he was in love with me. I don't know if I can handle this much testosterone, but fuck, I want to find out.

This kiss is dangerous in the way it takes hold of me. It demands control that I'm not entirely sure I want to give up. It's so insistent, it could convince me that I want to give it up and that's what scares me.

Give up control to a stranger?

The little twinge of fear is intoxicating, even if it does make me stupid, and the tension of it tugs at something deep, waking me up inside.

Murphy backs me up, rushing us toward the bed as he kisses me, breaking away just as the backs of my knees hit the mattress. He shoves me and I fall back onto the bed.

He steps back and smiles at me, removes his overcoat and blazer, and works at the cufflinks on his wrists. "Take off your clothes."

"A *please* wouldn't hurt," I reply, though I instantly reach for the button on my jeans and start to pull down the zipper.

His cheek twitches as his head falls to the side. "Do you want me to be polite or do you want me to make you come?"

I laugh, pushing myself off the bed to stand. I reach behind me and unhook my black bra. "I have to choose?"

"With me, you do."

"That's such bullshit." I remove my bra and toss it dramatically, then shimmy my jeans down my legs, step out of them, and kick them aside, grateful I took Cora's advice and removed my granny panties earlier.

I have no shame, and I proudly stand naked in front of this stranger. Though I have to say, the extra pulse from my heart shoots a brief ripple of nervousness through me.

I want him to approve of me.

Why do I care if he approves of me?

I only want to fuck him for one night.

He sets his cufflinks on a dresser and turns to face me, his fingers working the buttons of his shirt. When he sees me, we both freeze, still as statues. Our eyes lock and there's a tick of connection there before he scans my body. My eyes fall to his broad chest as his fingers move again to open his shirt. He'd have to physically force me to look away right now because I've been itching to see the ink on his chest since he walked into my shop.

He slinks toward me as he works his buttons and I feel hotter the closer he gets. When he's finally in front of me, my eyes are wide on his artwork. A skull sits on the center of his broad and muscular chest, detailed to perfection with dark, sunken eye sockets and drawn with a technique that almost makes it look three-dimensional. Two skeleton hands, one coming down across each pec, hold the skull from either side, as if presenting it to the viewer. An ornate crown sits atop the skull.

The image itself is black ink only, and I'm glad he didn't put color there—it would only hide the beauty of the detail work. But surrounding the image are drips and splashes of purple. The color is added brilliantly, framing the shape of the image without overpowering it.

"Finish undressing me, Stella," he demands.

"That tattoo is incredible." My hands move to push the open shirt from his shoulders, and he lets it slip from his arms to fall on the floor. He has tattoos everywhere, over his shoulders, down both arms all the way to his wrists—mostly black ink, but there's color where it counts.

I want to know who did this work.

I want to look at every image, trace my fingers over every line.

I can feel him looking at me as I draw my fingers across his skin.

"I was beginning to wonder where yours were."

"Huh?" I lift my chin to look up at him, but his eyes scan my body.

His fingertips gently graze my hip, finding the end of the cluster of black-drawn flowers that are splashed with shades of blue and purple watercolor. "I wondered where I would find your artwork hidden beneath your clothes. Your long sleeves and jeans made it hard to guess."

I draw my finger across my collarbone. "You didn't see this one?"

"Aye, I saw it. The cursive is difficult to read. What does it say?"

"Lost soul." I put my hand on his chest again, pressing my palm to the skull. "What does this mean?"

"It's personal."

"So is mine."

It's personal, yet we're both obsessing over each other's ink, touching each other, tracing lines, and exploring with our eyes. He draws over my artwork, his fingers gliding sideways across my stomach, angling upward over the floral and lace design that wraps across my mid-section, curving around my side and ending just beside my breast. I shiver as his knuckles graze the mound, fingers brushing over my nipple.

I breathe out, and suddenly, I'm frantic. My fingers find his belt buckle and work quickly to unlatch it. I push his pants down to his ankles and drop to my knees with them, letting myself come face to face with his cock hidden behind gray boxer briefs. He steps out of his pants and kicks them aside. His hand lands heavily on the top of my head and his fingers curl, digging into my scalp as he grips my hair and jerks me straight up. I clamber quickly to my feet, my hands shooting up to reach for his wrist.

When I'm on my feet again, face to face with him, he pulls my head sideways. "You're not ready for that yet," he practically growls.

And I fucking believe him.

But I also don't because I'm literally dripping, and we've hardly begun.

His eyelids droop as his gaze intensifies. For a moment we just stand and stare, and I feel like I can't breathe. My lips part with my ragged breaths and his free hand falls gently on my cheek. His thumb brushes over my chin and moves upward, touching my bottom lip, running across it, and tugging it down.

He pushes inside and drags the pad of his thumb down my tongue. The way he presses down and swirls his thumb in a slow circle over my tongue makes me tremble with hope that he'll repeat the motion over my clit.

He pulls his thumb out gradually, scraping over my bottom teeth, hooking inside my mouth, and tugging my lip down. When his thumb falls away, my lips remain parted, and I'm panting.

He drops his forehead to mine, staring into my eyes. "You might be the most beautiful woman I've ever laid eyes on."

My heart hammers. I don't need a man to affirm my beauty, and my appearance doesn't define my worth. But the knowledge that he thinks I'm beautiful sends warmth rolling through my belly. I want him inside me like this, pressed against me, faces close, and eyes on mine. He penetrates my soul with a single look, and I've never felt more vulnerable or bare in my life.

Who the hell is this guy?

I press my eyes shut and lick my lips, moving my hands to his waist. When a heated breath and a groan rushes out from him at my touch, it relaxes me. I sigh as I dare to slip my arms around his hard body and hug myself to him. I raise my chin and our lips meet for a kiss that isn't urgent, but sensual. Our tongues taste and push and swirl, and we melt together.

He releases his grip on my hair and brings both hands to my face, holding my cheeks as he arches me backward, bending over me to deepen our sensual kiss. It lasts for minutes this way, tongues softly tasting, skin brushing skin, our bodies sinking and molding together as something electric builds between our writhing flesh.

I didn't expect this bold sensuality from him.

I expected instant fucking, roughness, and a mixture of pleasure and pain.

I suppose there is some pain in this with the way my body hums, my skin burning and prickling with the need to be touched, to fuse with him, and to do nothing but feel.

My knees sink and he dips with me to hold onto our kiss as one of his hands trails down my throat and over my chest. His palm rubs across the mound of my breast. His thumb follows, quickly swirling around my nipple, making me jolt. My lips part with a gasp and it breaks the kiss against my will.

"Open your eyes, look at me," he groans.

I blink them open, though they want to flutter shut. His thumb continues to move around the hardened peak.

"Murphy," I breathe his name.

He growls, a primal noise that rumbles from his chest, and the next thing I know, I'm on my back. I wiggle myself up the bed as he pauses to remove his socks—thank God, because no girl wants to be fucked by a naked man with only his socks on—and he casually slips off his underwear like it's no big deal.

It's a big deal.

It's a *big* deal.

"Oh, my God." I press up onto my elbows as he climbs over me. "Where do you think you're gonna put that?"

"Shut your smart mouth or I'll shove it down your throat." I can tell he's serious, but the twitch of a good-humored smirk pulls at the corner of his lips.

"Promises, stranger."

He settles over me, thick thighs touching the insides of mine as he nudges my legs apart. "You want a promise? Just know, I don't make empty ones."

He lays down on top of me, trapping me between his hard body and the soft mattress. I feel every inch of him touching every inch of me, his heat merging with mine, his inferno meeting my blaze and igniting a flash fire over my skin.

His hand finds its way between my legs, his fingers skating across my opening. "Are you this wet for all the lads you let take you home? "

"I'm never this fucking wet—"

I'm cut off by my own gasp as he drives his hips forward and slams inside me, his monster cock nearly splitting me in two as he fills me completely. My mouth drops open and my eyes snap wide at the thoroughly unexpected intrusion. My hands shoot up against his chest and press, the instinct to fight him off me sends waves of adrenaline coursing through my veins.

"Shit. Do you have a condom?" My good sense finally returns to me. My dry spell has apparently turned me in to a moron who didn't even think of this until he was inside me.

He sits back on his knees as he rears up, dragging his cock out and slamming it back inside. "Do we actually need one? Aren't you on birth control or something?"

"I am, but…" I trail off as my belly clenches against the way he shifts inside me.

Shit, this feels so good.

"Then it's fine, Stella. I'm clean." He pulls out, thrusts inside me again, and my spine tingles.

I struggle to wrap my mind around what the hell is happening.

Do I want this?

Am I okay?

There was no foreplay, no lead up, no warning.

He groans from deep in his gut as his hand lands on my knee, bending my leg, and pushing it back. His other hand falls to my stomach, splaying across my tender flesh. His thumb scoops downward. It only takes him seconds to find my clit and…

Oh, my fucking, God!

"Yes!" I gasp, arching my back.

I'm bewildered, mystified, stunned beyond belief. He was inside me before I had any time to mentally prepare for it, but he moves with precision and touches me with perfect, swirling strokes. Everything within me coils around my center.

And shit, the way he looks down at me—his hazy, gray-green eyes scanning every inch of me—makes me feel wanted.

I want him to want me.

I comb my fingers into my hair from my forehead and grip the strands, needing something to hold onto as he fucks me.

"You feel so fucking good," he says through gritted teeth. "So fucking good."

I feel like I can't breathe. He's on top of me, inside me, *everywhere*. Every sense is filled from the heat of his touch to the gruff sound of his voice and the peppermint candy scent of his beard. And the way he looks at me, with narrowed eyes in scrutiny, watching me as if he's discovering something brand-new with me here right now.

The only sense unfilled is taste.

"Kiss me. Let me taste you."

I'm almost shocked when he bends and immediately opens his mouth against mine, giving me exactly what I asked for. I move my hands to his hair and grip his ashen, strawberry-blond locks between my fingers.

Everything between us feels warm, wet, filthy, and perfect. Then he thrusts into me with an almost painful stroke and pauses, buried to the hilt inside me.

He lifts his head and looks at me as one of his hands sneaks up to wrap around my throat. The curve of his hand mashes against the underside of my chin and his fingertips push in on my cheeks with bruising force as he tilts my chin skyward.

He smirks. "Tell me you want me to fuck your pretty little cunt."

Shit, I hate that word.

I told him I hated that word before we left the club…and he told me he'd have me saying it before the end of the night.

I'm not gonna give him the satisfaction so easily. I try to shake my head against his grip, but it's no use because he keeps me still. He dips, runs the flat expanse of his tongue across my closed lips, and it makes me shiver. My hips buck and rock beneath him, trying to make him move, trying to get him to fuck me, but he holds firm to his position, pinning my hips with his weight settling over my midsection.

"Tell me. To fuck. Your pretty. Little. Cunt."

His fingers on my cheeks loosen enough for me to form the shape of words with my mouth. "Fuck my pussy. Fuck it hard. Destroy me," I dare.

He groans, punching inside me a little deeper, but still unwilling to stroke. His face drops beside mine and he runs his nose along the back of my jaw, toward my ear. "I didn't say *pussy*. Tell me what I wanna hear. I'm not moving until you do."

"Fuck you. I'm not saying shit I don't want to say. Fuck me or don't."

He pulls out gradually, every thick inch of him scraping along my insides before he violently shoves back inside. I gasp and whimper, my body convulsing around a lightning strike in my core.

"Say it," he says. His free hand wanders between us and I sigh as his fingertips brush over my nipple, but then he takes the hardened peak between his thumb and forefinger and tugs, twisting painfully.

"Fuck!" I hiss, hating and loving the pain at the same time.

His face is right in front of mine, the tips of our noses touch and his eyes slice into me, deeper than I imagined they could. "Fucking say it, Stella."

That gruff quality to his voice twists inside me. It makes me want to bend over for him and let him do whatever he wants.

"Fuck me," I manage to say. "Fuck my pretty little cunt."

He releases my nipple, rears back, and slaps the side of my breast with a *thwack,* the metal of his rings biting into my flesh. Then he pounds me. His fingers rub my clit quickly, aggressively, in a way that almost hurts while it also drives me up that mountain side faster than anything in my life. I know my poor lady bits are going to be raw and sore after this, and I don't even care.

This is how I like it. It's how I need it. It's how I touch myself to get off—rough and hard and fast. He knows what he's doing. He does it almost too well, almost well enough to have me fooled that maybe, somehow, he sees me, gets me…knows me.

I swear to God, it's only seconds later when I feel it pulsing, when I feel that heavy rush between my legs that crashes against the dam wall until it shatters. I split right down the middle, a tsunami bursting from inside me and splashing pulsing waves throughout my body.

My back arches, hips rising off the bed, and my body is shocked into stiffness as the climax takes hold and doesn't let go, wave after wave after wave.

"What the *fuck…*" I mutter as it finally recedes and my ass hits the bed again.

I dig my fingers into my hair as I pant through the drop-off. It takes me a few seconds to realize he's holding still inside me, watching me with a sickeningly sexy half-smile on his face. When I calm enough to blow out a heavy breath, he pulls out of me and I whimper.

Empty.

Hollow.

A missing piece.

I suddenly don't feel right without him inside me.

Talk about an orgasm high, I've lost my damn mind.

He moves his legs to straddle my waist and shimmies higher, coming up until his knees are beside my breasts. I reach my arms around his thick, muscular thighs and slide my palms up to cup his firm, perfect, absolutely splendid ass cheeks.

"Open your mouth and stick out your tongue." His massive hand slips up my throat, moving to cradle my cheek as his thumb presses up against the bottom of my chin.

He tilts my head back as I give him what he wants, opening my mouth wide and letting my tongue drop out. I curl my fingers, digging my nails into his flesh, and he sighs as he grips his cock with his free hand, stroking himself rhythmically.

That's it.

I'm in love with his cock.

It's never really been that big of a deal to me before, but his monster dick is sexy, masculine, and challenging—just like him.

"Give it to me," I tell him. "Come on, let me taste it, come on my tongue." I open wider for him, stick my tongue out farther.

His chest rises and falls, faster and faster, and his nostrils flare as his expression turns dark, clouding with intensity that shoots right through me, making me wish I could reach around him far enough to rub my clit again. He groans, low and long and deep. His lips part, his eyes shut for a moment, and then instantly snap open again. His entire body shudders as he comes hard, his ass and thigh muscles twitching beneath my touch. He angles his cock down, spilling all over my tongue.

He tugs his cock until every last drop is spilled and then he scoots back, his knees moving down to straddle my hips again. He leans over me, bringing his face down to mine as he presses his palm lightly to my throat.

"Swallow it."

As soon as I gulp down the sticky fluid, his lips are on mine, kissing me deeply, tasting himself on my tongue. It makes me moan. It makes me want more of him. I squirm beneath him, aching to be filled again, though I know he won't recover for a while. I whimper.

"You want to come again?" His thumb softly strokes along my jaw and over my chin, brushing my bottom lip.

"Yeah," I manage, swallowing again.

"Good. Because I wanna taste your cunt."

I don't even care anymore what he calls it, I just want him to put his tongue on it.

CHAPTER 6

MURPHY

A ONE-NIGHT STAND.

That was all it was meant to be.

That's all it was.

But then why can't I stop thinking about her?

Stella Scott.

I type her name into the search engine for the millionth time over the last month, and easily find her public social media profile. I click on her profile picture—it's the same one she used on the website for her tattoo shop, Soul Story. I scroll to see if she's posted anything new, and she has, though her posts tell me nothing about her. It's always just pictures of the tattoos she's done. I enjoy seeing her new posts, and her work is fucking spectacular.

Stella is a wickedly talented artist.

I sit back in my chair, linking my fingers behind my head as I stretch. I vaguely wish she could've been my talent slave, though I don't think the four families would have been too keen on tattoo artistry.

Who would she perform her talent on? Other slaves?

It doesn't matter. She isn't the beneficiary I chose when I was younger. Fiona is my talent slave and that's the end of it. Though, I suppose if something unfortunate were to happen to Fiona…then I could select another.

No.

I wouldn't want Stella as a talent slave. I'd have to share her with others. Everyone in the household benefits from Fiona's various services and talents, and the thought of sharing Stella with anyone makes my nostrils flare and my jaw tense. It would be a way to make her mine, yes, but it's not an option because my chest hurts to think of it.

I shouldn't be thinking of it, anyway. It was a one-night stand. A fun night to blow off some steam and nothing more than that. She didn't give me her number and I didn't ask for it—though that wouldn't stop me if I really wanted to get in touch with her.

I really want to get in touch with her.

I lean forward, staring at her profile photo, the one with her eyes shut, her mouth open wide, and her tongue out. I shudder, remembering how I came on that very tongue, and how she swallowed it with pride.

I don't have time for this kind of…obsession. That's what it will become if I don't get her out of my mind, yet my hands are on my cell phone, fingers dancing across the screen, typing the number to her tattoo shop that I've memorized and typed too many times before. Only this time, I press the green button to dial through. It's around midnight here in Ireland, so I know her shop will still be open in New York—I've already memorized the fucking hours.

"Soul Story Tattoos, this is Cora."

"Cora, hi. My name is Murphy O'Shea, I'm—"

"Sexy Irishman?" she cuts me off before I can finish my sentence.

"Excuse me?"

"Hey, yeah, I remember you," she drops her voice to a whisper, "Stella won't shut up about you."

My cheeks twitch and an unashamed smile lifts my lips. "I shouldn't be surprised."

"Don't be smug. It's not a good look for a white man these days."

"Cora, listen, I'd like to get in touch with Stella. Would you mind giving me her cell phone number so I can text her?"

I could find her cell phone number on my own, but I feel the need to legitimize the way in which I came into possession of it. I shouldn't feel the need to legitimize anything, but my feelings about her have been strange since the moment I laid eyes on her.

Obsession.

"I don't know…" Cora says with skepticism in her tone. "I'm not sure I'm allowed to do that. You're practically a stranger."

A stranger who made her come on his face.

"Then will you give her my number and ask her to text me?"

"Sure," she agrees. "I'll send it to her right now. I can't guarantee she'll reach out though."

"Why wouldn't she reach out to someone she can't shut up about?"

"Girls are weird, dude. Don't you know that by your age? Just give me your number."

I recite to her and we end our short conversation just as Cormac bursts into my office, unannounced and without the courtesy of a knock. I guess I need to start locking the damn door. Bailey hops up from the floor and lets out a single bark as he shoves the door open wide.

I push to my feet as he enters, patting my thigh to call Bailey back over. "Go back out and try that again. *Knock* and wait for me to—"

"There was an escape attempt in Oslo," he says, stopping dead in his tracks. He lifts his palms in weak surrender as fury washes over my face, and I grip my palms into fists at my sides. "Excuse me. I thought you'd want to know straight away."

"I would like to know straight away, but you can inform me with respect, Cormac. I'm not your brother when it comes to business."

He swallows his injured pride and takes a step back. "Aye. Understood."

"What's it all about then?"

"Three of the assets attempted to incite a riot, which of course, was just noise with them all behind bars. But I guess that was their intent? The noise distracted the guards and the three of them made a run for it while they were on the floor for inspection."

"Did they get away?"

"No. Two of them were killed in the shuffle. The third has been sufficiently subdued."

Fuck.

Now I'll have to find two more human assets to replace the ones we lost. Each one is profitable when they're sold, though finding the right owner and processing each sale takes time. Acquisition costs are high for a single human asset—we have to pay for capture, holding, travel, and we pay our hired help well.

Money is the only way to keep people quiet.

My phone pings, and I reach to lift it from my desk, turning it over, expecting to see a notification from my father asking me if I'm awake and handling business—as if he's still Head of fucking House and has to manage his apprentice son.

I swipe open the new text message, ready to tell him to fuck off, but the message I see is from an unknown number.

UNKNOWN: *Hey, stranger.*

I pause.

My lips twist into a half-smile.

Stella sure didn't waste any time reaching out once she had my number. Her eager return has my pulse quickening. I add her number as a contact right away while three dots tell me she's typing something else. I wait, watching my screen, until the new message pops up.

STELLA: *Cora told me you called the shop. I was surprised to hear from you.*

I start to type a response, but Cormac speaks, jerking me from thoughts that drift to my night with Stella, bringing me back to reality.

"Do we need to do an inspection? You know Declan and I can do it for you. I could take Tally. She hasn't seen one of our factories yet. It'd do her good to see one before I lock her down."

His fiancée, Tallulah, was well vetted through our families connections. She knows everything about our business, as does her family. The McCarthy's trade similarly as we do—in a criminal fashion—though their stock is in weaponry.

"I don't care if you come and bring her along, but I need to handle the inspections myself. We'll leave in the morning."

"You can't do it all alone. Learn to delegate."

"Cormac, I swear, I'll knock you on your fucking arse if you don't mind your place with me. I'm your *boss*, not your brother."

His eyes narrow. "Fucking right you are. And you're gonna be fucking lonely with that attitude."

"I have my companion."

"Right," he scoffs. "Because you really enjoy Fiona's company. She's boring, mate."

"I'm well aware, but that's none of your business."

He sighs. "Yeah, well, when you realize how lonely it is at the top, you can stop pretending to be like Boyd and come have a drink with your brothers. At least with Declan. He feels fucking abandoned."

I feel that hit me like a punch to the gut.

"Bridget's trying to set him up with one of Tally's sisters," he says.

"She's not."

"She is. So, if you insist on being the king, I suggest you straighten her out, for Declan's sake."

"I don't insist on being the king, I *am* the fucking king." I sigh. "I'll talk to her."

"All hail the fucking king." He bows dramatically like the moron brother he is, and I have to force away the grin that threatens at his pure idiocy.

"Get the fuck out, Cormac."

"Yes, your highness."

He ducks out of the room, and I lower to sit, pulling up email on my laptop. I type out a quick message to Nikolai, Vigo, and the new American Head of House Leo, letting them know about the situation at our factory in Oslo. As soon as I press send, I feel something tug at my spirit…a pull toward my phone sitting on my right.

Stella.

Once her image is in my mind, I forget about all else, and that's dangerous. I shouldn't respond. I should leave well enough alone. But I pick up my phone and type out a response to her message, and she replies almost immediately.

MURPHY: *I tried to get your number, but Cora wouldn't give it to me. Good friend.*

STELLA: *Well, now you have it.*

MURPHY: *Now I do.*

STELLA: *So, what did you want?*

What did I want?
I'm not entirely certain I have a good answer for that.

MURPHY: *You've been popping into my head.*

STELLA: *Oh???*

The three question marks seem excessive, but leading. She sends another text before I reply.

STELLA: *Maybe you've popped into my head once or twice.*

MURPHY: *Oh???*

I repeat her punctuation overkill.

STELLA: *I had fun with you. Kind of a bummer that you don't live in NYC.*

MURPHY: *Maybe I'll find my way back there soon on holiday.*

Why did I say that?

I have no plans to return to the States anytime soon. We ended up there on a whim for holiday. I can't really do business there since the Leblancs—the new American family—have claim to that territory.

STELLA: *Maybe if you did, you might swing by my shop.*

MURPHY: *Maybe I would.*

STELLA: *Maybe you should, stranger.*

MURPHY: *Would you be happy to see me?*

STELLA: *I should probably play it cool, but my answer is an overly eager yes.*

My smile twists and pulls at my cheeks and my facial muscles aren't used to the feeling of it.

MURPHY: *My answer would be the same…if you're wondering.*

STELLA: *God, you really know how to get a girl's heart beating, you know?*

MURPHY: *I don't know. Tell me.*

STELLA: *What do you want me to tell you? That I like you? Does it really matter?*

MURPHY: *It matters to me.*

STELLA: *I hardly know you.*

MURPHY: *You know enough.*

STELLA: *Wow. Okay, then. Well, I guess that's that.*

I narrow my eyes at the screen. I don't know what she means, but I read sarcasm in the tone of her message. Fuck this texting bullshit. I tap on her number to call her. Her phone rings and rings and the longer I wait, the more my frustration ticks. Tension pulls tight across my shoulders and my jaw sets, wondering if she's going to send me to voicemail.

I'm going to lose my shit if she sends me to voicemail.

She picks up at the last possible second.

"Hi," she says, her tone sweet, but perhaps a little sad. I can't say for sure.

"What did you mean, *I guess that's that*?"

She sighs. "Why did you call?"

"I asked you a question first."

"And I reserve the right to refuse to answer. Woman's prerogative."

My teeth grind. "Too bad I'm not there to make you talk."

"*Make* me talk? Are you kidding me?" she scoffs, then pauses. I open my mouth to speak, but she starts again before I can. "How exactly would you *make* me talk, Murphy? Hold me down? Grip my chin and force my mouth open with your thumb?" Her breath catches, rolling into a hiccup. "Shit. Full disclosure…I've been drinking. Which means I probably shouldn't be talking to you right now."

I sit back in my chair, kicking up my foot to rest my ankle over my knee. "Actually, I think you should be talking more." This ought to be interesting. "I rather enjoy hearing you talk about my thumb in your mouth."

She sighs, her voice going distant for a moment as she mumbles a quick, "Jesus Christ," before returning to full volume. "Why did you call, Murphy? Why did you reach out to me?"

"Are you upset that I did?"

"No. I just don't understand."

"What don't you understand?"

"You're in Ireland, right? That's where you live? There's an ocean between us. What we had was a one-night stand. That's it. That's all it was ever supposed to be. We had a good time and parted ways, so I don't understand why you wanna talk."

"I wanted to hear your voice again." I'm surprised when I say it. It's true, but I don't understand why any more than she does.

"You did?"

"Aye. I enjoyed spending time with you, Stella. It's unfortunate that we're so far apart."

She's quiet for a moment. "Let's just say that you and I were closer. Say you were here…Do you think we would've had a repeat by now?"

"A repeat?"

"A second night together."

I don't hesitate. "Yes."

She lets out an audible breath, a deep exhale, as if it relieves her to know that. "I think so, too. I…we were pretty good together."

I rub my hand over my beard, tilting my chair back as I look up at the ceiling. "You were fucking fun. The most fun I've had in a very long time."

"I'll bet you say that to all the girls."

"I really don't."

"I think I kind of like you," she says, and my chest tightens.

Fuck, I want her.

Hearing her voice has triggered something inside me that aches to claim her again—something that aches to claim her fully.

But I have to recognize that this foolishness is a dangerous distraction. These feelings she stirs make me soft when I need to remain rigid, a wall of rock that can't be moved or swayed against my will. Because no woman will ever cloud my judgment when it comes to the business…except, my mind already feels muddled after five minutes on the phone with her.

The O'Shea name is what's at stake, and I can't let a good piece of arse make me forget that. I hang up the phone on her without saying another word and leave well enough alone.

My phone pings, startling me awake from a dreamless sleep. I blink, coming into awareness that I've fallen asleep on the brown leather armchair in my office, my laptop somehow still teetering where it's balanced on my thigh, having slipped between my leg and the armrest.

I groan, moving my laptop to the side table and stretching my arms over my head. My phone pings again and I reach for it, blinking as I pull up the two new text messages. I brace myself for a barrage of texts from the four families wanting news about the attempted escape in Oslo, though there's nothing new to report.

I'm shocked Vigo Vittori hasn't called me personally by now to hash out all the details. Though, I suppose Cordelia has already been on the phone with him about it all. I don't understand their connection with each other, and it pisses me off how often she undermines my authority with him.

I look at my screen, and I'm surprised to find that the texts aren't from Vigo or any of the other families.

They're from Stella.

I glance at the time—four hours since I hung up on her. If she was drunk four hours ago, she's either sobered up or is completely wankered by now. I open the messages.

STELLA: *Rude.*
STELLA: *RUDE.*

And then, another text slips through.

STELLA: *RUUUDDDDEEE.*

Completely wankered, then.

I should delete the messages, ignore them, and go and get a few hours of sleep. Yet my fingers move to type a reply without any good sense at all.

MURPHY: *Care to elaborate?*

STELLA: *YOU HUNG UP ON ME.*

MURPHY: *Dial it down a notch, sweetheart. You should only be screaming at me when I'm between your legs.*

STELLA: *HOW DARE YOU.*

MURPHY: *Just how drunk are you?*

My mind wanders. I wonder where she is, whether she's drinking alone at home or out at a bar…maybe at the club we went to when I was on holiday.

I imagine a dance floor, Stella in the middle, surrounded by filthy monster men, all trying to paw at her and take her home with them. My chest aches as fury slips through, prickling awareness beneath my skin and heating me from the inside out.

I shift in my seat, leaning forward with my elbows on my knees, the phone in my hands as I type faster.

MURPHY: *Where the fuck are you?*

STELLA: *Excuse me?*

MURPHY: *Where are you?*

I asked her the question, and I don't know why I bothered. I can have surveillance on her in thirty minutes or less if I wanted it.

And fuck, do I want it.

Nikolai Mikhailov has contractors in New York who do surveillance on close contacts to his talent slaves who used to live there. Before Stella responds, I've shot off a text to him with her name and the address of her tattoo shop. His associates will gather the rest of the information on her from there.

Five minutes go by with no response from Stella and a strange sensation washes over me. It's an aching, tingling feeling of anxiety that tightens my muscles, pumps blood faster through my veins, and puts me on high alert. I've felt it before, I just don't know why I'm feeling it now.

Anxiety.

I've got fucking anxiety over Stella Scott and her relative safety.

STELLA: *I'm at Serendipity. What do you care?*

I've never shot to my feet so fast in my life.

MURPHY: *Stella, go home.*

STELLA: *I'll do what I want, thank you very much. Not like you care. You hung up on me.*

MURPHY: *I care. Go home.*

STELLA: *Why are you like this?*

I scoff. I'm like this because of who I am…who I was born to be. And apparently, she was born to be a headstrong pain in my arse. I could go round in circles with her demanding that she go home, but I gather she's the type of woman who digs her heels in when told what to do.

She's not O'Shea wife material at all.

She's such a goddamn challenge…and I love it.

I try a different approach.

MURPHY: *Please. For me. I can't stand the thought of you drinking and dancing with another man.*

It's intended to be a carefully placed lie to persuade her into leaving, but it's not a lie at all. I truthfully can't stand the thought of it.

STELLA: *What do you mean???*

MURPHY: *Just go home, sweetheart. Sleep it off and call me tomorrow.*

STELLA: *I will NOT call you tomorrow.*

MURPHY: *Then I'll call you.*

STELLA: *Fine. Whatever. Do what you want.*

MURPHY: *Are you leaving?*

STELLA: *YES, I'M FUCKING LEAVING.*

Her next text comes a full ten seconds later.

STELLA: *But not because of you.*

I don't care why she leaves, just as long as she leaves. I let out an unintentionally held breath of relief.

I don't hear from Stella again all night, but I don't need to. Nikolai received my text and had surveillance on her forty-three minutes after she sent her last text to me. His men watched her make her way safely back home, her address texted back to me within the hour.

It's a relief to know she's safe, tucked away in her modest apartment in New York City with eyes on her every movement. She'll be safe from the predatory monsters who swarm the vulnerable, drunk women in every city in every country of this godforsaken planet.

I'll keep her safe from those monsters.

But I can't guarantee she'll be safe from me.

CHAPTER 7

Stella

CORA PUTS A mug of coffee in my hand as soon as I round the counter at the shop. I bend, leaning down on my elbows as I grip the ceramic cup with both hands and tip it to my lips. I'm still wearing my oversized sunglasses, but not because it's sunny outside in mid-January. No, my head is pounding from one too many drinks last night and I'm being a little dramatic about it.

"Good morning, sunshine," she sings with a small laugh.

I set my mug down on the counter and straighten, turning to face her at my side, placing a hand on my hip.

"Don't give me that chipper bullshit today. I am *not* in the mood."

"Okay, sassy pants. What happened to you last night?"

"You know what happened. You sent me the Irish guy's phone number after two glasses of wine. Obviously, I drunk-texted him."

She chuckles. "Oh, shit. What did you say?"

"I don't know," I groan. "But then he called."

Her eyes pop wide, feigning horror. "You texted him and he *called* you? The nerve of this guy."

"I know, right?" I push my sunglasses up on top of my head and take another sip of coffee. "He said I was the most fun he's had in a long time. I told him I liked him," I lean forward for emphasis, "and then he hung up on me."

"Rude."

"That's what *I* said…when I texted him several hours later."

"You didn't."

"I did. Shit, Cora, I was wasted."

"What did you say?"

"Well, I told him how rude he was, and he told me to leave Serendipity and go home." I pause. "He called me *sweetheart*."

She laughs. "Seriously?"

I tilt my head. "I didn't hate that, actually."

She stares at me, an odd beat passing between us. "Stella. You hate when guys give you nicknames."

I squint as I think about it. "Yeah, I know. Usually, I do. I don't know…" I wave it off. "Maybe it just sounded okay through text."

Cora's head turns slightly to the side, and she looks at me out of the corner of her eye. "You okay, Stell?"

"Yeah. I just…he said he'd call me today and I think I kind of want him to." I rest my hip against the edge of the counter, leaning against it as I cross my arms. "I don't know why I want him to."

She shakes her head with a look of concern. "Maybe I shouldn't have given you his number…maybe I should have pretended that he didn't call."

"No, then I would've been pissed at you for not giving me the message."

"You wouldn't have known about the message if I hadn't given it."

"Do you think I shouldn't be talking to him or something?"

"I just don't want you to go down this road again with an unavailable man. You're gonna end up hurt in the end. It was supposed to be a night of fun, Stell…a night to get you back on your feet after your break-up with Nathan."

"I know." I lift one arm, absently chewing on the side of my thumb. "I *know,* but—"

"But nothing. Stella, come on. There's an entire ocean between you. It's not like he's ever coming back. Don't go getting all emotionally invested like you do."

"But it's kind of my signature style of toxic, self-defeating behavior." I smile.

"Funny." She grins but tilts her head disapprovingly. "Seriously, this makes me nervous for you. I just don't want to see you get hurt again."

My lips part to speak, but the ping of my phone draws my attention away. I dig through my purse and pull out my cell phone. My heart skips a beat when I see his name flash across the screen.

Shit, Cora's right.

Talking to a guy right now feels new and exciting, but there's literally no potential here. We can't date. We can't touch. We can't kiss. We can't fuck…

Damnit, the sex with him was amazing.

I open his message.

MURPHY: *Are you free? Let's video chat.*

My heart drops into my gut and the heavy fall makes me feel weak in my knees. I turn my screen to show Cora.

"He wants to video chat with me. What do I do?"

She shrugs. "I don't know. Talk to him or don't. But you know you're walking a thin line if you talk to him."

I stare at the screen, thinking it through. I know I should ignore him, delete his messages, and block his number. I should because I hardly know him, and he was kind of a prick. I fucked him once a month ago and that was that.

He left and I moved on.

But I didn't.

I didn't really move on because I still think about it. I don't know. Maybe that's normal to keep replaying the best sex of your life over and over in your head until you find a real relationship with a real person who isn't a walking, talking sex-god with the world's most arousing accent.

The way he made me feel was just so…

"I'm gonna talk to him," I tell Cora. "Maybe he won't look as hot as he did that night, and then I can put him out of my head for good."

She bobs her head, eyeing me skeptically. "Okay."

"Be right back," I tell her, then head for the private bathroom at the back of the shop.

I shut the door and lock it, taking a moment to comb my fingers through my wavy hair and pinch my cheeks to brighten them up a bit. I respond to his text, telling him to call me on video, and take deep breaths until his call comes through.

"Fuck, fuck, fuck," I mutter to myself, then plaster a smile to my face and tap to answer.

The black screen blinks and suddenly, his face appears.

Oh, my fucking wet panties.

He's every bit as hot as I remember. And when he sees me and smiles—he fucking smiles with those damn sexy crow's feet wrinkling the corners of his eyes—I know I'm done for.

This was a bad idea.

A bad, bad idea, and Cora should've tried harder to warn me.

"Hey," I say, taking a step backward to lean against the far wall.

"Stella," he says, his eyes scanning the screen from bottom to top. "Well, it looks like you're standing upright on your own two feet. Slept it off, did you?"

"Yep. Wicked hangover, but nothing I can't manage."

"You shouldn't be out drinking alone."

I flinch. "I can do whatever I want."

"Sure you can, but you know better, don't you? You know what could happen to a beautiful woman like you, out by herself, drunk and vulnerable."

My eyes narrow. "Yeah, I'm well aware, asshat. I know all the things I'm supposed to do to protect myself from men. Walk with my keys between my fingers, don't wear a long ponytail someone can grab, never walk alone at night." I roll my eyes. "Men know they're the reason women are unsafe, right? Not because I chose to go out and drink. *You're* the problem."

Christ, he really flipped my feminist switch and it's not even ten o'clock.

"*I'm* the problem? Was I out watching you dance around drunk last night, trying to get under your skirt?"

"Okay, first of all, I wasn't dancing around drunk. Second, no one was watching me. Third, it's commanding, alpha assholes like *you* who make it unsafe for women like *me* to go on living their lives. Christ," I huff. "This was a mistake, I'm hanging up."

"Wait," he says.

My finger hovers over the "end call" button, but the way he runs his tongue across his bottom lip gives me pause.

"Tell me more about how much you hate men like me. It's really doing something for me." He smiles and it shoots lightning straight through the screen, striking my stupid pussy and making her throb.

What the hell is wrong with me?

I smile, goddammit. "Shut up."

"The size of your attitude is massive, did you know that, sweetheart?"

"Don't call me sweetheart. I have a name."

"Oh, I know your name, sweetheart."

I hold up my middle finger and put it right in front of the camera, making sure he can't miss it.

He sighs heavily. "If you were here, I'd bite your fucking finger and make you put it to better use between your legs."

Oh, my god.

My stomach tingles, drawing tension low and making me shiver. I have never reacted like that to anyone before—least of all to someone I'm watching through a screen.

Someone who lives on the other side of the world.

Someone who doesn't even have their hands on me.

It feels exciting and new and so, so good. But rationally, I know that physical feeling is fleeting. It will only last as long as we're on opposite sides of the screen, as long as it's all talk and no reality.

Reality is a fickle bitch and I hate her.

I blink, leaning my head back against the wall, just to steady myself. "I can't believe you. Is this just a sex call?"

"A sex call? You think I just called to toy with you?" He cocks his head to the side, licks his lips, and smirks.

I glance at the small square on my screen that shows me how I look on camera. I realize I look hot and bothered leaning against the wall this way. I *am* hot and bothered, but he doesn't need to know that.

I kind of want him to know that.

"I'm at work, okay? I have a client coming in ten minutes. So, what did you call for?"

"Ten minutes? Too bad I'm not there with you. I could make you come twice in ten minutes."

"Jesus fucking Christ," the words slip out a little breathier than I intended, "you can't…I'm…Listen, you and me? This isn't a thing, okay? We're too far away from each other for this to be a thing. One-night stand. Over. Done."

"Do you want me to stop calling you, then?"

My lips part as I suck in a shaky breath.

Why isn't the word yes *slipping easily and clearly from my mouth?*

"I don't…I have a problem with jumping into things I shouldn't, you know? I invest too much of myself and get caught up in my feels, and it always ends badly for me. I'm not interested in getting hurt like that again."

He watches me carefully as I speak, his cheeky expression shifting into something softer, more serious. "It's actually not my intention to hurt you, Stella." He sounds as surprised by his own words as I am, and

I know I should read into that—I know it should worry me that he's surprised he doesn't want to hurt me.

"There is no way for you and me to communicate without it leading to hurt, for one or both of us. That night with you was so good...*so* good. I don't think I can just have a friendship with you, and that's all this could ever be with us being so far apart."

"And if distance weren't an issue?"

"If distance weren't an issue?" I sigh. "I don't know. You're kind of an asshole. I feel like you're the kind of guy who could rip my heart out. I'm not really interested in going through that again."

He nods and I'm thankful, thinking he understands. "I understand what you're saying, but I'm not interested in stepping back. I think it's best if you come to terms with the fact that you and I have crossed paths, and there is no uncrossing me." He smiles a charming, devilish smile that twists my insides. "I also think it's best if you shove your mouthy middle finger inside your perfect cunt and make yourself come before your first client. I wouldn't want someone giving me a tattoo with that much pent-up tension, would you? You need to relax, sweetheart."

My mouth gapes open in shock and he ends the call.

I exhale, slumping back against the wall. "Shit."

I bring my phone to my chest, holding it over my pounding heart.

He's a cocky, arrogant, entitled prick if I ever met one. But damn, he's pricked me like a needle and injected me with infatuation. I have to wonder what he wants with me, why he's contacted me now after a full month has passed.

Has he thought about me so much that he just had to reach out?

Tiny, stupid wings flutter around my heart and I have no rational explanation for it. He's probably the most attractive man I've ever seen in real life, so there's that, but aside from his looks, I can't see there being more.

He puts me on edge. He makes me grind my teeth. He sets a fire inside me that makes me want to yell and fight against every misogynistic comment he makes. I shouldn't want a man who makes me feel that way.

He makes me feel…passionate.

Passionate with rage and passionate with need.

I know from my past that passion leads to heartache and overwhelming hurt when it all comes crashing down. I know I should be smart and block his number, vow to never speak to him again. Yet some of the fluttering wings around my heart escape, floating down through my stomach, triggering a wave of good feelings that make me ache to be desired by him—feelings that make me ache with desire *for* him.

I already know that if he calls or texts again, I'll be running to my phone to answer.

CHAPTER 8

Stella

I'VE BEEN RUNNING to my phone every day for the last month. Surprisingly, my daily talks with Murphy have become the highlight of my day. I get on the phone with him each day after work and we chat until I get home safely.

Sometimes, when the mood is right, we stay on a bit longer, switch over to webcams on our laptops, and indulge ourselves in some rather obscene adult time.

Murphy's obscenity is mystical.

His filth is transcendental.

And that's all just through a computer screen.

But today has been something else entirely. We've been shooting filthy texts back and forth all day, and I don't think I've ever been this recklessly horny. I just finished with a client, and I've only got one more before we close. I have ten minutes before my appointment though, and Murphy insisted he needed to see my face, only if just for a minute.

I tell Cora I'm going to the bathroom and proceed to the back of the shop. I lock myself in the private space, then start a video call, popping in my wireless ear buds so no one can hear him.

He comes up on the screen and my smile stretches across my cheeks. His face is close to the screen, and it looks like he's outside walking somewhere.

"Hey, I've got a few minutes. Where are you?"

"Nowhere," he says, letting a half-smile curl his lips. "I just wanted to see if you were blushing after the last few texts."

"Blushing?" I lower my voice. "Honey, if you could only see between my legs."

"Show me."

"What?"

"You heard me."

"I've only got one more client, then I'm heading straight home. I'll show you everything then. Promise."

"I want you to show me now, Stella."

"Are there people around you?" It's noisy, wherever he is. "They'll see."

"I have a tinted privacy screen on my phone. No one will see except for me. Show me, Stella."

"Murphy—"

"Stella, put your phone between your legs and show me how wet your panties are. I need to know." His grin is cheeky. "I need to know *right now.*"

"What if I told you I'm wearing jeans?"

"Then I'd tell you to pull them down. Are you wearing jeans?"

"No, I'm wearing a perfectly adorable polka dot dress."

"Perfect. Show me."

I bite my lip, debating whether I should. I want to. I *really* want to. He's clearly out in public somewhere, so it's not exactly a private call, but knowing that edges my excitement to peak heights.

"Okay," I say quickly, shimmying up my skirt with one hand.

It's not like he hasn't seen the goodies on screen before, I've just never done it with my phone and while I'm at work…and without being able to finish myself off, no less. If I'm gonna do it, I'm gonna make a fucking show out of it.

He brings the wildness out of me.

I lean my back against the wall and jut my hips forward, slowly moving my phone between my legs, turning it until I get the angle right. I can see the wet spot soaked through my white cotton panties on the screen. I only show him for a few seconds before I bring my phone back up to my face. His eyes are narrowed on the screen and it tugs a sinful smile from my lips.

"Satisfied?"

"Hardly, but it'll have to do. I'm heading in for an appointment now, so I guess we'll both have to wait a bit to finish off."

"Send me another dirty text if you can later…Keep me warmed up for you, you know?"

"I know, sweetheart. Don't worry. I have no doubt you'll be plenty warm the next time you see my face."

"No doubt," I agree, warmth spreading through my belly. I hear the bells clang against our front door and know my next client is on their way in. "I've gotta go. I'll call when I'm leaving, okay?"

"Go tend to your client. And Stella…I expect you to do your best work ever."

I chuckle. "While I'm all hot and bothered like this?"

He smiles and my whole world brightens. "Be a good girl," he tells me and I literally swoon.

I might've fainted dramatically on the floor if I weren't a goddamn professional with a business to run. He ends the call abruptly, as he often does. When the conversation is over with him, it's over.

I take a minute to straighten myself out, brushing down my skirt before exiting the bathroom. It's just me and Cora in the shop, and she's already done with her last appointment. So, when I step out, I know the man standing near the door with his back to me is my next client. I approach, but Cora catches my eye from where she stands behind the counter. She looks positively gobsmacked, her eyes wide and staring at the waiting man.

"What?" I ask her.

I fully stop when I turn my gaze to him again, when I look at him—really look at him—and a punch of adrenaline shoots through my veins. I take a step back. I draw in a deep breath as I assess the truth in front of me. The man is wearing a familiar sleek black peacoat, perfectly pressed gray slacks, and black dress shoes.

"Oh, my fucking God."

He turns to face me as I nearly stumble backward from shock.

It's Murphy.

Murphy O'Shea is here.

He's grinning at me.

And I'm standing here with my mouth gaping open in shock, realizing I'm an absolute moron—the name of my next client is John Smith. *John Smith.* The fakest of fake names I've ever heard.

"Are you John fucking Smith?"

"Of course not, but I did schedule an appointment under that name so I could surprise you." He smiles and I lose my shit.

I run for him, throwing myself into his open arms. He lifts me easily from the floor, squeezing me tight. I melt into his hold, an odd relief washing over me, a feeling like finding my way home after being lost for so long.

He nudges his nose against my hair and whispers into my ear, "Do you greet all your clients like this?"

"Only the sexy ones."

Begrudgingly, I let go of him and take a step back, but he takes my face in his hands, tilting it up as his smile brightens. "Hello there, sweetheart."

I disintegrate into ash. A gentle breeze could blow me away right now. The metal of the rings on his hands digs into my skin as he dips to plant a bruising kiss to my lips.

We groan in unison. The ache of lust that's been building between us shatters like a dam wall, flooding me with swelling excitement for finally feeling his touch, his kiss.

"What are you doing here?" I ask when the kiss ends.

"I needed a tattoo. Figured I'd come to the best." He brushes his thumb over my bottom lip.

Oh, my God.

Oh, my God.

Oh, my God.

I whimper. My chest hurts and my stomach swirls, tingles rippling beneath my skin as need pulses through me. I'm shaking—literally shaking—for this man, and I've never, ever felt this way before.

I snake my arms around his waist and hug him close, forcing him to drop his hands from my cheeks. "I missed you. I fucking missed you so much, Murphy."

He slowly exhales and I can feel tension leave him as his chest sinks. "I missed you." He kisses my hair and it puts me straight into swoon-mode.

I'm feeling way too much for this man.

"How long are you here for?"

"A day, maybe two if I can swing it."

I pull back and lift my chin to look up at him. "I'll bet you can swing it."

"We'll see…" His eyes narrow a little as he looks at me. "You're every bit as perfect as I remember."

I sigh happily. "So are you."

Cora makes a noise from behind me and suddenly, I remember where I am. I wipe my hand across my mouth—as if that will clear away the flush of my warming skin—and spin around to face her. "Cora, you remember Murphy." I mouth the words *"Oh, my God,"* to her.

She gives a polite smile and nods a little. "Yeah, I remember. Good to see you." Her voice is kind, though her expression is strained.

"Likewise," he replies kindly from behind me.

He takes a step closer and I feel his hand land secretly on my ass. I press my lips together to stifle a whimper.

"So, you don't have to stay," I tell Cora. "I'm fine to do him…um…

do his *tattoo*. And then I'll close up." I nod toward the door, giving her the hint. "You can head on out."

She tilts her head appraisingly. "And what about your very strict rule that no female artist closes shop alone?"

"Well, I won't be alone, will I?"

She shakes her head. "Nah. I'll stick around until you're done."

"Cora."

"Stella."

Murphy squeezes my ass and I nearly yelp. I twirl to face him. "Go have a seat over at my station," I point behind me, "and I'll be right over."

He gives me a once over with his brilliant eyes, the corner of his lips curving into a half-smile. He nods and moves past me to my station at the back.

I rush around the counter to Cora, moving in close and bringing my voice down to a whisper. "I swear, I'll be fine. You can go home."

"I don't feel comfortable with this. Did he just fly across the ocean and show up unannounced?"

I raise a brow. "Disturbingly romantic, right?"

"Disturbing, maybe. I mean, he's kind of got you on the hook now, right? What if you didn't want to see him? I'm reading toxic behavior all over this, babe."

"You're reading too much into it. You don't understand the connection we have."

"I understand you're a bit obsessed with each other."

I sigh, my shoulders drooping. "Cora, I'm *happy*. I'm fucking ecstatic that he's here."

She tilts her head with a look of disapproval. "I'm sorry. I'm really not trying to rain on your parade, but damn, Stella. I'm just shocked at your reaction to this."

"Then that should be telling you that I'm seriously into him. And I promise, I'm absolutely safe with him. So will you please let me have this unexpected time alone with him?" I beg her with my eyes.

She stares at me for a minute before softening, letting out a slow breath. "Fine. I'll go. But I'm on the record about feeling uncomfortable with this."

"Duly noted."

"I want you to call me in one hour. If you don't, I'm gonna hunt you down to make sure you're okay. Fair?"

"Fair, babe."

She gives me a hug. "I'm happy you're happy, just guard your heart with this one, okay?" She pulls back and gives me a smile. "Love you."

I nod. "I will. Love you, too."

"Don't forget to use a condom this time," she says loud enough for him to hear.

"Cora!" I swat at her arm.

I turn to head back to my station and she swats me on the ass. "Don't forget to put your back into it, ho."

I flip my hair over my shoulder to look back at her with a grin. "Always."

I hear Cora's purse hit the counter and her keys jingle behind me as she preps to leave. I steel myself as I head over to my station at the back. Murphy has taken off his coat and sits in the chair with his feet up. The sleeves of his button-down shirt are rolled up to his elbows, showing off his arm tattoos.

I'm already feeling flustered by the time I arrive at his side, plopping down onto my rolling stool beside him.

I tilt my head to the side as our eyes meet. My heart flutters and my stomach rolls into nervous but pleasant knots.

"Bye, babe!" Cora yells as she exits, and I give her a quick wave.

"So, you wanted new ink?"

"Aye."

"Tell me what you want."

"Come here," he commands, sitting up, turning so his legs dangle off the side of the chair. "Stand up."

Lust and excitement rush through my veins with every pulse, my skin humming with desire. I push to my feet and move to stand in front of him. He spreads his legs apart, grabs my waist, and tugs me between them. My lips part to let out a heavy sigh.

One hand slips down my side, slowly running over my hip. I don't breathe as our eyes lock with passionate intensity. His fingers graze my thigh as they grasp the hem of my skirt, slowly pushing it up, exposing my hip. I gasp as he dips his head to press a kiss there.

"I want this," he says, his warm breath heating my skin.

"Yeah," I hum with a moan.

He pulls his head back to look up at me while he traces his finger around a spot on my hip. "This purple rose you have on your hip...I want you to put one on me, too."

I'm breathless and lost to lust, my body swaying toward his. "Oh, I can put it on you."

"Sweetheart," he croons, the crow's feet wrinkling around the corners of his smoky eyes as he smiles brighter, "I want you to put the *tattoo* on me."

"Oh." I shake my head to snap out of my trance. "Right. The purple rose."

He lets go of the hem of my dress, letting it slip down, but his hand sneaks between my legs. I feel two fingers press and drag over my panties, straight across the wet spot he gave me with all his dirty texting earlier.

I put my hands on his shoulders and hang on for dear life, because my body sways and my knees dip at his touch.

"Though perhaps I should do something for you first," he says, holding my gaze with passion. "You seem to be a little...flustered. You're trembling."

"That's your fault."

"I know," he says with pride. "Should I resolve that for you?"

I nod. "Yeah, I think you should."

"Slip off your panties."

Oh, my God.

"Seriously?"

His expression morphs into something insistent. "Seriously."

My chest rises and falls as I reach beneath my dress, grab hold of my underwear, and quickly slip it down my legs. My clit already throbs with an ache to be touched, and my stomach clenches as he helps me tug the fabric off my high-heeled, knee-high black boots. He takes them away from me, folds them up, and shoves them into his pants pocket.

"Those are mine now," he says.

"Fuck," I breathe, "that's so hot."

He chuckles, watching my face carefully as his hand returns beneath the skirt, his fingers quickly finding my wet, aching center. He rubs two fingers along my slit and my knees buckle, causing me to drift toward him. I wrap my arms around his neck and hang on. His free hand reaches around and grips me behind the knee. He pulls my leg up, and I place my knee on the chair beside his hip.

"Come fast for me." He dips his fingers inside me, pushing in deep, gathering my wetness and dragging it out and over my clit. "Give me a sweet little orgasm to satisfy your nerves, and later, I'll destroy your cunt to satisfy your soul."

"Shit." My hips rock forward into his touch, his fingers pumping in and out for a minute before he draws them back and rubs my clit in hot, little circles.

"Fuck. You're already right there on the edge, aren't you, you filthy girl?"

"Yes." I absolutely fucking am because he's been edging me with dirty texts all day. I'm ready to fucking explode.

He circles faster, pressing in, driving me up a steep mountain of pleasure with his impressive skill. I guess that's one benefit of fucking a man who's nearly ten years older. He's not messing around here. He knows exactly what he's doing and how to get me there.

I'm fucking his hand as I get closer, my arms clenched around him, holding him against my body. His lips brush across my chest, over bare skin exposed by the V of my dress. He kisses and licks at my flesh, overwhelming me with touch that I've been longing for.

God, he's here.

He's really here.

The excitement of that sends a rush of pleasure straight through my clenching belly, and with the next twist of his perfect fingers, I come undone.

"Murphy!" I call out as my hips rock frantically, as my fingers curl around the back of his neck and dig into his hair.

My body trembles as I come. I let out the most satisfied sigh, rocking through my release, until I gradually come back down from the high.

I loosen my grip on him just enough so I can look down at him. He's grinning up at me like he's just won the award for giving the best orgasm of the year. I'd say he has; except I know how incredible it feels to come on his tongue.

Fighting to catch my breath, I pant, "I'm definitely gonna sit on your face later."

"I'd be disappointed if you didn't." His hand raises between us, and he brings his fingers, glistening with the evidence of my climax, to his lips. He sucks them into his mouth, licking them clean.

My lips part and I gasp, his eyes locked on mine as he tastes me. When he drags his fingers out, I grab his cheeks and kiss him hard, my tongue diving inside his mouth and swirling to pick up the flavor of the orgasm he just gave me.

It tastes like sin in heaven.

When the kiss breaks, I press my forehead to his and work to catch my breath while I watch his flickering gray-green eyes.

"Now," he says, "how about that tattoo?"

CHAPTER 9

Stella

MURPHY'S SOFT LIPS and bristly beard sweep across my collarbone. "Tell me what this means."

"My tattoo?"

He draws his fingers across the black ink just beneath my collarbone, painting my skin with the scent of my arousal. "Aye. *Lost soul*," he reads.

"I've always felt like a lost soul."

He watches me, softly stroking across my skin.

"It was my first tattoo," I tell him, "which, believe it or not, I didn't get until I was twenty-one."

"Why did you get it?"

"It's a whole story…"

"I want to hear it." He tucks my hair behind my ear, and it gives me goosebumps. "Tell me while you give me a matching purple rose."

I lower my leg from the chair and take a small step back, smoothing down my skirt. "Okay. Let me get things prepped." Murphy gives me a wink and my heart beats frantically. "And stop being so charming."

"Never," he says with a smile. Turning on the chair, he leans back and casually lifts his legs onto the footrest.

I fan myself with my hand, sweaty and flustered, before I finally drag myself away to prep my materials. "Where do you want me to put it?"

"Are you talking about your arse or the tattoo?"

I flash him a grin. "The tattoo."

He starts unbuttoning his shirt and I hold my breath to see the masterpiece that is this man's chest—not just the tattoo he has there, but the sculpted, delicious muscle. He's so beautiful that I have no problem momentarily defying my staunch feminism to reverse objectify the fuck out of him.

"Right here." He points to a spot on his left pec. "Partially behind the skull and crown."

"You mean right there…over your heart?"

"That's the spot."

Should I read into that?

My fluttering heart says yes.

I try to play it cool. "You know it doesn't mean anything special. The rose, I mean."

"It's special to me."

"It is?"

"You always turn to your left when you take off your panties on camera for me." His eyes drink me in. "That purple rose on your perfectly curved hip is the first thing I see when you strip yourself bare for me. It's an image I want to keep close at heart."

I think I must be blushing because my cheeks are warm. I don't know the last time I felt so flattered by a man.

"And purple is my favorite color," he adds with a cheeky grin.

I let out a satisfied sigh. "Murphy O'Shea, you might just be the most fascinating man I've ever met."

An oddly comfortable silence falls between us as I sketch out a similar version of the rose on my hip. I print it out, place the template on his chest, let him verify it's where he wants it, and pick up my tattoo machine to get right to work.

"You'd probably have an easier time if you straddled my lap, sweetheart."

Fuck me.

"Well, I was waiting for the invitation." I set down my machine and climb onto his lap, straddling his hips and sitting back on his thighs. I reach over and drag my rolling tray closer to have access to my supplies. When I grab my machine and settle comfortably to begin, I feel the electricity of our connection spark between us, and I actually flinch at the shock of it.

We share a look and a mutual sigh, relief at our proximity after all this time apart. I can feel how he wants me—his cock half-hard between my legs. I'm aware that I might leave a wet spot on his pants, but I rather like the idea of claiming him that way. I give a little wiggle of my hips before sinking into stillness.

I wouldn't dare do this with any other client. I'm probably pushing it to do it with him, but fuck, he makes me forget my ethics—which I know is dangerous, but the way I feel about him draws out something within me so beyond the scope of human awareness that it makes the morally gray feel comfortable.

He puts his hands on my hips and strokes up and down my sides as I settle into a quiet rhythm. The art always lulls me into calmness, the hum of the machine working to soothe my nerves like white noise and meditation. But the stirring in my core from being pressed so closely to him creates a heavenly contrast of serenity and sensation. A few minutes pass beautifully before he speaks again.

"Now tell me about *lost soul.*"

"Oh. Hmm. Well, I was raised by a single mom…didn't know my dad until I was twenty. I actually still haven't met him, and I doubt I ever will. When my mom was in college, she studied abroad in Athens for a semester. She met my father, a local, while she was there, and I guess they just clicked with each other for a while. She always said it was a whirlwind romance that she'd never forget.

"Long story short, he knocked her up. I guess it was kind of a big deal for him that they'd hooked up at all because his family was pretty conservative…didn't go for the whole sex before marriage thing. Anyway, she told him she was pregnant, he spooked, and they never saw each other again. She came back to New York and dropped out of college a year before she would've graduated."

"Why do you say you won't ever meet him? Did she keep him a secret from you?"

"It wasn't a secret; I just never asked. She did the best she could raising me on her own. It was just the two of us until…" I trail off, feeling an ache throb across my forehead from the serious turn this conversation has taken.

"Until what? Tell me. I want to know."

I glance up briefly to meet his eyes, then focus intently on my work. "When I was nineteen, about seven years ago, she was driving out of town to meet this guy she met online. They'd been chatting for about a year and she was really excited to meet him. I didn't know she was going, otherwise, I would've insisted on going with her. You can't be too careful these days, you know. Anyway, she got hit by a drunk driver on the way there…died on impact."

His hands curl around my waist, holding me with heavy palms, authoritatively drawing comfort in the way his touch anchors me.

"When she died, I was the same age that she was when she had me." He sucks in a breath through his teeth when I move across a particularly sensitive part of his flesh. "Sorry. You okay?"

His thumbs circle over my flesh and I look up to catch his nod. "I'm fine. Go on."

I continue working. "Losing her really fucked me up for a while, you know? I was on my own, with no support, without the only person who was ever really there for me. I went through a slew of bad relationships with a bunch of assholes and kind of hit rock bottom for a while. I started digging into ancestry stuff online and I managed to track my dad down, but when I reached out to him, he just wasn't interested in talking to me. He was married and had a whole family. He didn't want anyone finding out about his *youthful indiscretion.*

"By the time I'd finally managed to get in contact with him, I'd completely lost myself. I was trying to make sense of who I was and who I wanted to be. I felt so confused, so lost, so alone. I was trying to find something I could cling to that made me feel grounded in some way. My mom was dead, and I couldn't get her back. My dad didn't want to know me, and I felt rejected. I *was* rejected.

"I'd sort of developed this negative mantra in my head. I told myself over and over that I was a lost soul because really, I was. I was completely lost. And at some point, I decided I needed to own that. I decided I wanted to wear it on my body. I don't know, I guess I thought that maybe one day some other lost soul would see it, recognize me, and we wouldn't be lost anymore."

I pause to shift, wriggling a little over his hips before settling again. "It was my first tattoo, and it did so much more for me emotionally than I ever expected it could. As soon as it was on my body, I felt different. I felt stronger. It was like taking all my heartache and confusion, and then acknowledging and accepting it. I intended it to mark me, to identify me for what I felt I was, but instead, it became something more like a badge of honor. I was a lost soul, but that didn't mean I couldn't find myself again.

"It was so empowering that tattoo artistry became a calling. It dragged me in and didn't let me go. Three months later, I started an apprenticeship with the artist who did this tattoo and it's all I've been doing ever since. I worked crazy hours, became obsessed with it, saved every penny I earned, and was finally able to open this shop a little over a year ago."

I'm suddenly aware of just how much I've been talking. This always happens with him on the phone. He makes me feel open; he makes me feel brave enough to be vulnerable.

I have a fleeting thought that maybe he's the other lost soul I was hoping would find me someday. Except, I know that's not true because he's got his shit together. He has his bad days, but he knows who he is, he knows his purpose, he has his family. And that kind of magical soulmate thinking will only lead me to heartache when this is all over.

I don't want this to end.

I don't ever want him to leave.

I pause and look up at Murphy to see him grinning at me, wrinkles framing the corners of his hypnotizing eyes.

I draw in a breath. "Cora and Josh are the only other people who know all that. I don't usually talk about it. There must be something about you that makes me want to share all my dark secrets." I smile at him.

"You know you're making everything so much harder than it has to be." I see the humor glint in his expression and know he's not speaking literally.

"How so?"

"I like you a little bit more every time you talk."

"Does that mean you're not just in this for the pussy?"

"And then you go and open your beautiful, smart mouth, and say something crass like that—"

"And that makes you like me even more?"

"Impossibly more, sweetheart."

I watch his transcendent eyes for a beat before I turn off the machine and lean against him, placing my free hand on his shoulder to steady myself as I press my lips to his. I let him lead this kiss and he keeps it gentle, soft, slow, and sensual. When it breaks, we just smile and I feel something resembling peace…maybe even hope.

"So, I told you mine. Are you going to tell me yours?" I ask.

"Hmm?"

I place my palm against the center of his chest, over the tattoo of the crowned skull held between skeleton hands, one of which is now partially obscured by the half-drawn rose. "Your tattoo."

"Have you ever heard of a Claddagh ring?"

"No."

"It's a ring worn by some lovers in Ireland. Traditionally, it's a heart at the center held by two hands, and the crown sits on top of the heart. It represents love, loyalty, and friendship."

I pull back a little to look at his chest and trace one finger over the lines. "I see the hands and I see the crown…"

He inhales and exhales deeply, his eyes fluttering shut for a beat at my touch. Seeing the way he reacts to me spreads warmth across my belly.

"The hands represent friendship," he tells me. "The crown is loyalty."

"But this…" I draw my finger around the outlines of the skull in the center of his chest. "Why a skull and not a heart?"

"It's a family symbol."

"Your family's symbol is a skull?"

He grabs my hand, halts my tracing finger, and holds it over his heart. "O'Sheas love passionately. Our devotion is bone deep and remains even in death. That kind of love requires a stronger symbol than a simple heart."

My heart flutters. "That's morbidly romantic."

He grins, his eyes flickering across my features. "It is. The tattoo serves to remind me of what's most important when the daily challenges of our business threaten to make me forget. Love, loyalty, and friendship."

Much like the purple rose I drew over his heart, my affection for him blooms, flowering in my lost soul. I can feel how easy it would be to fall for him.

I breathe out slowly, letting my fingers creep over his chest. "I still can't believe you're here. Why *are* you here?"

He reaches up to touch my cheek, his thumb rubbing over my skin. "I needed to know if this is real."

I swallow a dry lump in my throat, hesitant to ask. "And…what did you find out?"

A cheeky grin slips across his cheeks. "I'll tell you in the morning."

I smack his chest. "Stop it. Tell me now."

"What do you think I found out, Stella?"

"Do you want to know what I found out?"

He slips his hand around to grip the back of my neck, his hold possessive, yet gentle. "Of course, I do."

I press my palm to the center of his chest, looking down at his tattoo, and I feel his breath stutter in his lungs, his fingers curling around the side of my neck. "Murphy, this is all real for me. Frighteningly real."

"Look at me." I lift my eyes and suck in a sharp breath at the way his meet mine. His palm squeezes and he pulls my head down to his until the tips of our noses touch. "You're right, sweetheart. It's frighteningly real."

My eyes fall shut as the warmth of his breath kisses my lips. "I already miss you."

"Eyes on mine." His voice is soft, a commanding whisper that I'm compelled to obey. "I know there's an ocean between us, but I will always answer when you call."

I lay my forehead against his. "Any time?"

"Any time."

"It's not the same over the phone."

"I know it's not." He sighs. "I'm not going to lie to you and tell you things will ever be different than this for us."

"Different than separation, lonely phone calls, and a visit once every couple of months?" I smile sadly.

"I can't even promise you every couple of months, Stella. My work is…unpredictable."

"Just for argument's sake, if I lived closer to where you work, would it be any different?"

"I'd like to think it would be, but there are things about my family that you don't know. Things I can't ever tell you. Things that make this vastly more complicated than I can ever explain to you."

"Try me."

"I can't tell you what I can't tell you."

"Why can't you?"

"Because I can't."

His hand drops from my cheek, trailing over my shoulder, and down my arm. His grip on my waist tightens. I can see the way his shoulders tense at the conversation. He sits up, taking the machine from my hand, and setting it on the tray. He plays it off, trying to distract me by kissing my cheek, trailing down my jawline, nuzzling my neck. I wrap my hands around him and hold him against me because I don't want to let him go…even if it means using our physical chemistry to emotionally distract ourselves from the gravity of his unwillingness to tell me more.

"Can you at least tell me that I'll see you again? Tell me that you won't leave and never come back."

He sits back again to look up at me. "You'll see me again, sweetheart. I can at least promise you that. I'd miss the taste of you too much if I never returned."

He pulls me down, running his tongue across his lips before they fall against mine. I sigh into his kiss, quickly seeking his tongue, and letting him devour me, letting hope and sadness fill me for the uncertainty of a future with another lost soul.

CHAPTER 10

Murphy

"WHERE THE BLOODY hell have you been?" Cordelia stomps down the front steps of the estate as soon as I exit the car on my return home.

"Great to see you, too," I murmur sarcastically.

I finish replying to the email on my phone as I wait for my driver to pull my suitcase from the trunk. Bailey races Cordelia down the stone steps and circles around my calves. I reach down to give her a pet as my cousin lands in front of me on the gravel driveway.

"I've been calling you for two days," she hisses.

I raise my eyes to glance at her over my phone. "I'm aware, Cordelia. It's why my phone has been silenced for the last twelve hours. You've been a real pain in my arse."

I hit send and grab the handle of my black suitcase, lifting it as I pocket my phone and trudge up the steps, Bailey obediently at my side.

"You can't just disappear like that," she says, stomping back up the steps behind me. "You're a Head of House, Murphy. You need to behave as such."

I stop on the landing and whirl around to look at her as she stops a step beneath me—exactly where she belongs. "I *am* the Head of House and leader of this family, Cordelia. I don't answer to you. You have no claim over my time or how I spend it."

Fiona stands on the landing with her head bowed, waiting to welcome me home. She's boring, but she's compliant, easy to master, easy to care for. I put my fingers beneath her chin and lift, dipping to meet her eyes. "Take the night for yourself. I don't require anything from you."

"Boyd asked for me to—"

"I'll remind Boyd that requests for your services go through me."

I stalk off into the house to end both conversations, but Cordelia can't leave well enough alone. She chases after me through the foyer and down the hall to my office, her impractical high heels clicking over the tiled floors.

"I'll remind you that you still answer to the board."

"I'm aware that I answer to the board. I've done nothing that warrants answering for." I scan my fingerprint at my office door, then type in my pin, the two-factor locking mechanism necessary to maintain my privacy. I open the door and step inside, Cordelia pushing through to follow me before I can slam the door on her.

I sigh as I round my desk and plop into the leather executive chair.

"You took off and disappeared for two days and didn't tell anyone where you were going." She gracefully lowers into the armchair angled toward the opposite side of my desk. "What if something had happened while you were gone?"

I lean back in my seat, exhausted from the eight-hour flight. "Declan knew where I was—someone had to look after Fiona. And if there had been an urgent business matter, you would have called my emergency line and I would've handled it."

Her pin-straight strawberry-blonde hair drops over her shoulder as she tilts her head appraisingly. "How could I have had any confidence that you would respond? You've never silenced your phone before."

I sit up and power on my laptop, looking at the screen rather than meet her eyes. "I was taking care of something important."

Stella.

I was taking care of Stella, and she is fucking important.

I know Cordelia is right. I know I shouldn't be so distracted, especially not this early into my tenure as the O'Shea Head of House. It was never my intention to meet a woman on that trip to New York two months ago, but I met *her* and she's had a hold of me ever since.

After hours of business dealings and tough decisions, regardless of how exhausted I've been, I would still find a thrill knowing I'd be on the phone with Stella before long.

We talked every goddamn night.

If it were purely the sexual nature of our texts and occasional filthy video chats, I would write it off and leave it be. I wouldn't have flown across the ocean just to see her because my stupid fucking heart couldn't take it anymore.

I needed to lay eyes on her in person, put my hands on her, see what my soul felt being close to her after all this time. My hope was that I'd feel nothing; that we'd have sex, get it out of our system, and let the lust fade, but that's not what happened.

I fucked her and I wanted more.

Cordelia drags me from my thoughts with a dramatic sigh. "It's the girl, isn't it?"

"Hmm?" I play dumb because I don't want to deal with her bossy attitude right now.

"Bloody hell, Murphy. It's the girl. I knew it. When were you going to tell us about this?"

"Nothing to tell. And what do you know, anyway?"

She glances toward the bookcase on her right, avoiding my eyes. "It may have slipped to Vigo that I wanted to see your phone records, and he may have told me what he saw. Daily phone calls and texts to a girl named Stella Scott in New York."

I slam my palm against the desk, making her jump in her seat. "What the *fuck* is wrong with you? Head of House records are private." I point my index finger at her. "You could've been punished just for asking. What the *fuck* were you thinking, Cordelia?"

Her eyes narrow on me. "I was thinking that my cousin is struggling in his new role and needs someone looking out for him. Besides, it's better I review the records and clear things up with you now, rather than one of the other Heads."

I pinch the bridge of my nose. "Cordelia, you *alerted* Vigo to the fact that there was some reason to look at my phone records. Now everything I do will be *fucking* monitored." I shove away from the desk and walk around it.

"Everything you do is being monitored anyway." She waves her hand flippantly. "It's why you all have access to each other's records in the first place. Checks and balances."

I scoff, "Checks and bloody balances, Cordelia." I lean my arse back on the edge of my desk, crossing my arms over my chest. "Well good on you and your fucked-up relationship with Vigo. Now this is something I'll have to address with the board."

"You'd have to anyway. If you're seeing someone this early into your tenure, they'll need to know. It's required."

"We're not seeing each other. Not exactly."

But aren't we?

I drop my arms, curving my palms around the edge of the desk at either side of my hips.

"Murphy, tell me the truth. What's going on? Did you go see that girl?"

I lift my palm, as if I'm going to emphasize a point, but the words are lost. Instead, I bring my hand to rub across my beard, letting out a heavy breath. "I went to see her. She's the girl I met in New York when I went with Declan and Cormac in December."

She looks surprised. "Do you like her?"

"Very much."

"So much that you're speaking every day?"

I raise an eyebrow at her. "You ought to know if you saw the phone records."

"I thought there must be some explanation."

"The explanation is that I met a woman, and I can't get her out of my head. That's why I left this weekend. I went to see her in New York."

"Oh, Murphy," she sighs, leaning back in the chair and setting her arms up on the rests. She gazes off toward the bookcase, her eyebrows dipping in the middle as if she's thinking of some way out of a sticky situation. "Did you sleep with her?"

"We did a hell of a lot more than sleeping."

"Well, that's good then, isn't it? You fucked her and got her out of your system."

"Not exactly…"

She raises a brow.

I push off the desk and wander toward the books lining the shelves along the wall. "She's special."

I feel the force of Cordelia rising from her chair and crossing the room toward me, coming up on my side. "You can't be serious."

I turn my head to look at her. "Do you think I would joke about something like this?"

She rolls her eyes. "I never really know with you."

"It's not a joke." I turn to face her, leaning sideways with my elbow on the shelf. "I went to see her, hoping I could fuck her out of my system, but it didn't work." My jaw tenses. "I care about her."

Delia lets out a single sharp laugh. "You *care* about her? Some cheap twat you had a one-night stand with?"

My chest puffs out with indignation. "First of all, she's not a twat. I swear I'll break your fucking jaw if you talk about her like that again."

"Talk about her? I don't even *know* her. You haven't told me a bloody thing!"

"And you've proven why I couldn't, tipping off Vigo that he should monitor my phone records. The only cheap twat I know is you when it comes to that man." I push off the shelf and walk around her toward my desk. "Get the fuck out, Cordelia. I'm too tired for your bullshit."

"Nothing can come of this. You know that, Murphy. Why are you torturing yourself? Quit talking to her. Cut her off and be done with it. Get back to work and do what's necessary to put us back on top of the four families. We should be outselling them all by millions, what with Nikolai's family gone and the changeover with the Americans. Yet we aren't. Because *our leader* is off having an affair with a whore in New York."

"It's not an affair. It's so much more than that."

Her shoulders slump, her expression softening before she crosses to me. "It can't be more. The board will help you select your wife when you're forty. You'll be happy then. The women always do amazing work in selecting wives. You'll have someone who can make you happy. Just like Boyd and Bridget have each other. And let's not forget that you have a perfectly lovely talent slave to satisfy you until then. That's what she's here for. I don't know why you don't use her for her intended—"

"Stop. Just stop. I know you're trying to be helpful, but you're failing miserably. Fiona does nothing for me. She's weak. Complacent."

"Exactly as she's meant to be."

"And it does *nothing* for me. Stella…she's strong, smart, capable. She's kind and stunning, and she fucking challenges me."

"And that's the last goddamn thing you need."

"I can't get her out of my head."

She throws her hands up in exasperation. "Well, what do you think is going to come of this? You can't marry her."

"Like fuck I can't." I can feel my eyebrows pinch together in fury at the challenge.

Her eyes widen and she leans forward, speaking slowly and deliberately, as if I'm a child. "Murphy. You can't marry her. The board won't allow it."

"You don't know that. You alone don't speak for the board. What makes you think they'd deny my request?"

She huffs, "You wouldn't dare ask for such a thing. We don't know who she is."

"I know who she is. Why isn't that enough?"

Her lip twitches. "Nothing is ever enough for the four families, you know that. Don't be stupid. Don't try to waste away the best years of your life on a wife. What if she gets pregnant, for god's sake?"

I cock my head to the side, challenging her with a cocky smirk. "Then I'll thank my lucky stars." She opens her mouth to speak, but I snatch her by the elbow, roughly marching her to the door. "Now leave me the fuck alone. I have work to do." I shove her carelessly out into the hallway, and she stumbles before righting herself, whipping around to face me.

"Murphy!"

I lift my eyebrows at her and slam the door shut, engaging the lock so she can't get back in. I hear her huff, then the sound of her high heels as she furiously clicks away.

I move to the armchair and drop to sit, leaning my head back and rubbing my hands over my face. Bailey's nose nudges my knee and I lift my head, pulling my hands away to place them on the sides of her head. I give her a good pet and scruff her ears as I bend close, letting her lick my cheek.

"I'm gonna train you to chase her away every time she comes near me...take a piss on her Prada shoes."

Bailey's head tilts to the side as if she understands me, and I smile at her waggling tail. I thought Bailey would be the only girl who could make me smile like that...until I met Stella Scott. She's crawled inside me like a stray seeking shelter during a winter storm, and all I want to do is keep her warm and cared for.

I've never cared for any woman that way before.

Though I'd hoped seeing her again after all this time would've been the reality check I needed—a time to fuck her out of my system and move on with my life—I'm more desperate for her now than I was before.

I don't care what Cordelia thinks. My position entitles me to have what I want, and I want Stella.

So, I'll fucking take her and make her mine.

CHAPTER 11

MURPHY

IT WAS NEARLY two months ago that I decided Stella would be mine—nearly two months of patience and worry over how the board would react to my decision to petition for a wife five years before I'm meant to have one.

I sit at the table in the Americans' boardroom at the Leblancs' estate in Louisiana. I'm focused on the business at hand, but I'm getting antsy waiting for my agenda item to come up. It would already have been discussed by now except for the unexpected suicide attempt by a talent slave tonight.

I scribble a note about last quarter's earnings in my folio as I listen to the latest drama over Nikolai Mikhailov's talent slaves.

"Anya's been quite the little rebel in recent months, hasn't she?" Renata Vittori states. "First, letting Nikolai's boy into her bed and now this. Perhaps she should be sold outside of the families to a client."

"Selling her would only be offloading the problem to a customer," Cordelia says. "I would never sell a rebellious commodity to one of our loyals—unless they requested it, of course, which in my experience, is rare. It might be best to decommission her and be done with it. Or let her do it herself if she's so desperate for death."

Nikolai's head snaps rather aggressively in Cordelia's direction and I look up to watch the exchange. "No. Her transgression doesn't warrant decommissioning."

Anya—Nikolai's former talent slave, whom he recently sold to Vigo Vittori—is the one who tried to commit suicide earlier this evening.

"Agreed," Vigo adds. "Why should we give her exactly what she wants? Regardless, I'm not done with her yet."

Sick wanker.

"Then what do you propose?" Vigo's sister, Renata asks.

Vigo straightens in his seat, a sick smile spreading across his face. It's telling that he's got some twisted notion about abusing Anya more than he already has—she already looked rather unhealthy when I saw her earlier with Vigo in the Leblancs' ballroom. He opens his mouth to say something, but Nikolai jumps in to cut him off before he can get a word out.

"Give her to me tonight," Nikolai says.

My eyebrows raise in surprise. He'd sold her to Vigo in the first place, so it's curious why he'd want to have her again.

"Are you serious?" Renata chuckles.

"Yes," Nikolai replies. "She needs to be put in her place. Clearly, Vigo has pushed her too far. I can put her right again."

Vigo leans forward, presses his elbows to the table, and rests his chin on his hands. "And what makes you think that?"

Nikolai leans back, letting out a sigh. "Because I know her better than you do, Vigo. And let's not fool ourselves. She never once tried to end her life in my care. You've broken her to pieces, and someone needs to put them back together if you intend to keep her."

"What makes you think—"

"You signed a contract with me," Nikolai snaps, "and I expect you to honor the agreement. You've already breached several clauses you agreed to for her welfare, so I suggest you stop pretending that I'm *asking* for a night with her. Your lack of decorum necessitates it."

I regard Nikolai with narrowed eyes. There's some hint of desperation there—something inside him that begs—and it makes me think he still has some longing for Anya. Pity he didn't see what he had and treated her with care while he could.

Renata's head tilts to the side as she looks at her brother. "Is that true? Have you neglected to abide by your contract?"

Vigo tilts away from the table with a smile. "It depends on how you look at it."

"Bullshit," I chime in, crossing my arms over my chest as I lean back in my chair.

"Aye," Cordelia surprises me with her agreement, given her strange fondness for the monster who is Vigo Vittori. "I'd be happy to review the contract with you if you're having trouble interpreting it, Vigo. I'm sure Nikolai has laid out clear terms for you in his sale." Vigo's smile begins to fade as he listens to the only woman I think he's ever had an ounce of affection for as she calls him out. "What are the consequences set forth for breach of contract, or has that not been laid out? I assure you that the board would lay out an appropriate consequence if Nikolai neglected to write one into the contract."

Delia tosses her hair over her shoulder and Vigo watches her intently. The skill of seduction is one the women of the four families possess in equal measure—it's the only power they have in our world. Cordelia once helped the O'Shea family negotiate a trade deal through Lisbon—a territory previously owned by the Vittoris—and she did it all by seducing Vigo. That's when their twisted little back and forth truly began.

"Fine," Vigo finally says to Nikolai. "Have her for the night. Straighten her out and set her right."

"And?" Cordelia's voice rises in a feminine timbre.

"And I'll sit with you to review the contract," Vigo replies. "Let you straighten me out and set me right."

Cordelia grins. "My pleasure."

"Very well," Renata says. "Nikolai will have Anya tonight and return her to Vigo in the morning. Leo, why don't you move us along to the next agenda item?"

I shift in my seat.

Leo leans forward on his elbows, reaching for the paper agenda laid in front of him. "Yes. Next item is the matter of Murphy's…his bride?"

Leo Leblanc is new to this world. He was brought in to replace the former American family—the Campbells—after it was discovered that they had plotted and successfully murdered Nikolai's family by tampering with their aircraft.

There has always been, and always will be, unspoken rituals of competition between the four families. For one, our talent slaves perform at the beginning of each quarterly meeting—there isn't a Head of House among us who doesn't want their talent slave to be perceived as the best among us. There's competition in our acquisition of assets and their assessed value. There's competition in our sales and unspoken rivalries between certain families. But sometimes said rivalries get out of hand—as was the case with the Campbells. It led to their unprecedented dethroning, leaving way for their cousins, the Leblancs, to take control of the American sector.

And poor Leo was thrust into his role at the young age of twenty-seven, making him the youngest Head of House of our generation. I'd always been the youngest before him—it was why I was exposed to the cruel details of our trade at such a young age.

"Murphy has petitioned for an early bride," Renata explains.

Nikolai's eyebrows lift in surprise. "Really?"

"I'm impatient." I shrug, not wanting to divulge too many details of my plan too soon. "What's the point in waiting until I'm forty to find a suitable wife?"

Cordelia sighs. "I've tried to talk him into waiting until it's his time," she casts me a judgmental gaze, "but he insists he wants a bride now."

"All of the Heads of House must agree for us to move forward with an early petition. What are your votes?" Renata asks the group.

"Agreed," Nikolai replies readily, and I give him a nod of gratitude.

Vigo follows in quick agreement. "Agreed."

The room looks to Leo, who shifts uncomfortably in his seat. "You're petitioning to get married?"

"Aye."

Leo clears his throat, then smartly follows suit. "Agreed."

"Petition granted. Congratulations." Renata's voice is congenial in offering her cheers. That's good for me because I'll need to rub elbows with her to get approval for Stella to be my bride. "I'll prepare you a portfolio of suitable women to join the four families."

"Actually…" I place my elbows on the table and lean forward. "I already have someone in mind. A fiery little thing I had the pleasure of meeting by chance last time I visited the States."

"Murphy." Renata folds her hands. "You know your bride must be approved."

"And she will be." I flash her a grin. "I'll send her details to you for approval, and you can pass it along to the Heads of House for the final vote."

She stares at me, her eyes narrowing as she searches for something in my gaze. "Fine, then," she finally says. "Send me the details and we'll make a decision at the next quarterly meeting. Fair?"

"Fair." My grin broadens and I lean back in my chair.

Petition—done.

Now I just need to get Renata on my side to approve an unusual choice of bride—an innocent bride who knows nothing about the four families.

"Renata," I call after her before she escapes down the hallway.

She halts, turns, and slowly walks in my direction. I move toward her, meeting her in the middle, just in front of the Leblancs' ballroom.

I only speak when we're close enough that I can lower my voice to a whisper. "I wonder what I might do to convince you to push for my selection of bride."

Her head falls slowly to the side as a small smile creeps across her cheeks. "Murphy. You know that's not how it works."

I lift an eyebrow at her. "I have it on good authority that you have the most influential voice when it comes to the women on the board. I need to ensure buy-in before the official decision is made at the next board meeting."

"Ensure buy-in," she repeats slowly. "And how do you expect that will happen?"

I start to speak, but a sudden commotion down the hall forces us both to turn our heads and look. Nikolai has Anya by the wrist and is dragging her along, moving toward us from the end of the hall.

"Why are you taking me?" I hear her say as they approach. "You sold me to Vigo. Why am I going with you?"

"Don't speak." He gives her wrist a tug and she stumbles, but he catches her frail body before she falls, bending, wedging his shoulder into her stomach, and lifting her.

My eyes narrow at her condition—her chest and wrist caked in dried blood. I can't blame the lass for trying to off herself—I'd likely do the same if I belonged to Vigo. The reminder of his sickness punches a sense of urgency through my veins. Monsters like Vigo are the reason why I do what I do—to protect the women in my family by selling strangers to the monsters instead. But until I make Stella mine, she's vulnerable. Anyone could snatch her up, ruin her, hurt her, take control of her. She's not safe until she's mine.

I need to make her mine as soon as possible.

Nikolai and Anya pass and the commotion softens into quiet chatter among the others passing by.

Renata pulls my attention back to her with her fingers trailing down my arm. "You know how things get done with me, Murphy. What are you willing to do to have your bride?"

My shoulders tense as my eyes zero in on her hand. I have to fight the urge to toss off her arm, whip it around behind her back, and slam her against the wall. Instead, I let a smile touch the corners of my lips.

"We both know I'm not your type."

"Oh? Do I have a type?" She feigns innocence, as if she doesn't know that we all know she likes her men young and subservient.

"Let's not play games. You have a price for your influence, and I understand that. I'm willing to pay that price for Stella."

"Stella." She smiles. "Now I know I've heard that name before."

"From your brother, no doubt. He and Cordelia talk far more often than they should."

"Now that's something we both can agree on."

"So. Your price?"

She takes a step forward, moving into my space and I allow it, only for the situation at hand. "Why don't you find your way to my room in an hour, and we can work something out?"

I should've known she'd take it there. I'd slept with her once before—the bitch preyed on me when I was in my twenties. She was an older, experienced woman; I was going through a particularly rebellious stage in my life where I sought out deviancy to quell the anxiety of the overwhelming responsibility of my fate.

Renata did as she always does and effectively seduced me into her bed. She's an attractive woman by standard means so it didn't take much for me back then, but I'm not the same man I was before. I know her family's particular brand of evil, and there's nothing about her that appeals to me that way.

"Murphy," she croons, "you know my influence will be important for your family. If I don't find her worthy of assimilating to become the wife of a Head of House, your family will never accept her. Don't you want their acceptance?"

I *need* their acceptance.

I can't bring her home without their acceptance.

"Of course, I do. But certainly, you understand why I can't just slip into bed with you like it means nothing."

"The only one of us who has to enjoy it is me. In fact, I prefer it if you *don't* enjoy it."

A tight, frustrated grin tugs at my cheeks. "We all know how you get off on having all the power."

She shrugs a shoulder. "If you don't want to do it, fine. I'll just have to find another bride more suitable for you."

She starts to turn, and I grab her by the elbow, tugging her toward me, and she crashes against my chest. She blinks at me with her sinister smirk, molding her body to mine. I feel my upper lip snarl in contempt. "You'll approve Stella."

"We'll see. Satisfy my terms and you'll get your approval."

I release her and step back with a huff.

"I'll see you in an hour, Murphy." She turns, giving me a final appraising glance over her shoulder before sauntering down the hallway.

My fists clench at my sides and I seethe because I know what I have to do. It's not that I can't just marry Stella on my own and force everyone to accept it, but doing that could get her killed.

If she doesn't have the enthusiastic approval of the board—if Renata doesn't use her influence to convince my family that's she's worthy—it will put her at risk. They could hurt her, kill her, and though they would be met with dire consequences, those consequences wouldn't undo any harm that befell her.

The process has to play out properly.

The formalities must be tended to.

But I can't do what Renata wants to win her favor.

I won't sully my honor for Stella by jumping into bed with Renata just for her approval and influence.

I jog down the hall to catch up with her, wrap my fingers around her elbow and tug until she stops. She spins to face me, and I shove her back to the wall.

"In a hurry to get started?"

I dig the heel of my hand into her shoulder, keeping her firmly against the wall as I step in closer, aiming my index finger at her chin. "You listen here. I've had about enough of you and your family's bullshit. You'll approve Stella to be my bride, and you'll do it as a goddamn favor to me. Or may I remind you that my dear cousin Cordelia is reviewing a contract with Vigo at this very moment…Do you recall how easily she convinced him to hand over that trade deal through Lisbon? Perhaps I'll call her now and ask her to talk him into handing over Barcelona, too. You and I both know he'd give her anything she asked for. What would happen to your sales then?"

Her grin fades into a sneer, her eyes flickering across my face, reading my expression. When she takes too long to respond, I step back, pull out my cell phone, and dial Cordelia.

She answers and I put it on speakerphone.

"Are you with Vigo?"

"I'm on my way to his room. What do you need?"

I cock my head to the side. "Renata, what do I need?"

Renata shakes her head slowly, narrows her eyes, and then a slight smile curves the corners of her lips. "Fine, Murphy. You win."

"Never mind, Delia. Enjoy your night." I hang up and pocket my phone.

She sighs. "I appreciate your tactics. You're growing into your role, Murphy. I'll approve your bride as a favor to you so long as Cordelia doesn't convince my brother to give up more of our territory. He's a cunt-blind moron when it comes to her."

"Another thing we can agree on. I'll ensure your territory remains firmly in your family's possession."

She holds out her hand. "Then we have a deal."

I feel relief wash over me as my palm touches hers.

The board has approved for me to marry early.

Renata will ensure Stella Scott is the woman selected.

Soon, that stunning wildcat will be safely in my possession.

CHAPTER 12

Stella

"JUST SPEAKING MY truth here, but I think it's safe to say that you've taken this obsession to an unhealthy level."

"Cora." I tilt my head, giving her an admonishing look. "I don't want to go there right now." I lift my glass to take another sip of my margarita.

I turn my body so my back is nestled in the corner of the booth at the back of The Jaded Wingman, the bar next door to my shop. I put my legs up on the seat, pulling back my knees. Cora and Josh share a look of frustration with each other and anger prickles through my spine. I know my face does nothing to hide that. I'm sick of this conversation.

"You never want to go there." Cora rolls her eyes at me. "I'm just trying to help you see what I see." She gives Josh a nudge with her elbow. "What *we* see."

"Oh, she's got you convinced now, too?" I glare at Josh. "Are you going to tell me I should block his number and forget about him?"

Josh raises his palms. "I'm not gonna tell you to do anything. And this isn't just coming from Cora." He lowers his hands. "I'm worried about it, too."

My shoulders shrug with tension as I wrap my arms around my legs, hugging them to my chest. "Why? What are you worried about?"

"You're falling hard, Stella. Which is…great." I roll my eyes at the way she says *great*. "But you've only seen this guy in person twice since you met him. And that was what, four months ago when you first met?"

"What's your point?"

"You don't know anything about him."

I push my legs to the floor and sit up with a snap, leaning forward with my arms on the tabletop and my hands folded in front of me. "I talk to him every day, Cora. Literally, every damn day. I *know* him."

"Yeah, but he could say anything over the phone, right? He can paint whatever picture of himself he wants you to see because you never actually spend time together in person. You don't even know what he does for a living."

"He runs his family business."

Cora snaps, raising her voice, "*What* business? *What* is the family business, Stella?" She huffs out a frustrated breath, leaning back in her seat. "It's so obvious he's lying to you."

"It's not obvious to me."

"That's what I'm worried about. You don't see it!"

"Because there's nothing to see!"

Cora crosses her arms, looking over at Josh with a shrug, though she still speaks to me. "I don't know what else to say about it. You're not listening to me. That's the problem. You're so obsessed with him that you can't even see what's wrong with the situation."

"Because there's nothing wrong with it." I sit back and cross my arms, mirroring her.

She tosses up her hands, rolls her eyes, and shakes her head.

I'm so over this.

From where it's placed next to my drink, I see my cell phone screen light up just before it starts ringing.

"Is it him?" Cora asks.

I glare at her. "Yeah, it's him."

She starts moving, scooting toward Josh until he gets the hint and slides out of the booth. "I'm tired anyway, and I don't want to fight with you anymore. Do what you want. Let it drag out another six months."

She gets to her feet. "I'll be here for you when you get your heart broken, but I can't keep watching you fall in love with this liar."

My eyes are hot, tears threatening to slip out from the corners. Cora and Josh leave the bar together, leaving me alone after making me feel so shitty. I don't understand why they can't see what I see, why they have to be such assholes about it all. I just want their support, and I don't understand why they can't give it.

I sniff back my tears as I reach for my phone and answer Murphy's call. "Hey, stranger."

I hear him sigh. "There she is."

God, I really am falling for him.

"Where are you?" he asks. "It's noisy."

"I'm at the bar next to my shop. Cora and Josh wanted to take me out for a drink." I sigh. "It didn't go so well."

"They're with you now?"

"No. Cora got upset with me and they just left."

"So, you're alone at a bar?" I hear the agitation in his voice kick-up.

"Technically, I'm surrounded by people."

"Stella, go home."

"I need to finish my drink."

"Fine, finish your drink but stay on the phone with me until you get home."

I lift my glass to take another sip. "Well, my day sucked. How was yours?"

He goes quiet for a few breaths and the passing silence makes me nervous. "I've been traveling for work. Long day."

"What's wrong?"

"I can't tell you about it. I wish I could tell you about it."

I take another sip and set my glass down, leaning back in my seat. "Talk to me. You can tell me anything."

"You know I can't."

I feel my forehead crease. "I know that you always say that.

What's the worst that could happen if you told me about your job, your family business?" I chuckle. "Are you a hit man? An arms dealer? An international spy?"

"I just needed to hear your voice, Stella." His voice cracks—something I've never heard before—and my heart starts pounding.

"Murphy, are you okay?"

"No. I'm not okay. I fucking miss you."

I take a final swig of my drink as I start moving, sweeping my purse strap up onto my shoulder and pushing my way through the crowd. "Talk to me. I'm on my way home now. We can get on a video call."

"No," he says sharply and without hesitation. "Sweetheart, I can't do that right now. I told you I've been traveling."

I push through the door and step out onto the sidewalk. "So what? I want to see your face."

"I can't do that here. Our work is private."

"I'm not interested in your work, Murphy. I just want to see your face."

My feet move quickly beneath me, as if walking back to my apartment could carry me straight to him. There's a sinking feeling in my stomach as I remember that I'm not walking home to him. I'm walking back to my apartment, alone, with hopes I can comfort him through a screen.

"I'm not going to be able to see you for a while."

I stop dead in my tracks. "What do you mean by that?"

"Don't make assumptions. There's nothing to read into. I'm just stating a fact."

"It's a stupid fact. One you didn't need to remind me of."

"Then let me follow up with a better fact."

I move forward again, walking at a more reasonable pace than before. "What?"

"I'm making plans for us."

I can't stop my eyes from rolling. "I've heard that before."

"It was never untrue. I want you to remember that my decisions are always made with us in mind. Every choice I make is for us and for our future. I need you to remember that, even if you're angry with me."

What the fuck is he talking about?

I stop and someone who was walking behind me bumps into me before circling around. "Watch where you're going, bitch!"

My face scrunches in irritation and I hold up my middle finger to her back as she and her friends continue down the sidewalk.

"What the fuck was that?" Murphy demands.

"Forget about it. What do you mean *if I'm angry with you?* Why would I be angry with you?"

"Forget about it," he repeats me.

"No. What the hell are you talking about?"

"Stella. All I want you to know is that things are coming together, okay? I'm doing everything I can for us."

"Us?" My shoulders shrug in confusion. "I don't understand."

"Certain things have to be settled for you and me to be together. And it will be a while before I can come visit you again, but when I finally do, it will count."

"Are you telling me there's," I pause to swallow a dry lump in my throat, "maybe a chance we can be together…as in, more than this?"

"You want that, don't you, sweetheart?"

"I do. I do want that, Murphy, I just don't know how—"

"Don't worry about how. I just need to know you're not going to be impatient."

I chuckle. "Me? Impatient? *Never.*"

He laughs a little and I feel relief to hear it—his voice was rife with stress when he called, and it was killing me. "I know, it's like asking the Pope not to pray."

"Exactly."

"Just promise me you're not fucking around with other men."

"Murphy, you're the only guy I'm fucking around with. I haven't wanted to fuck around with anyone but you since I met you.”

He lets out a long breath. “Good girl.”

“Babe, don’t say that to me in public.” I start moving. “Wait until I get home.”

“I can’t do that with you tonight.”

“Why not?”

“Stella, I told you, I’m away on business. I can’t do that with you right now,” he says with a note of finality.

Frustration wraps around me, but there’s nothing I can do about it. “Okay. Fine. I understand.”

He sighs. “I hate denying you what you want.”

“It’s fine…We’ll just do it another time. Okay?”

“I *will* make time for you later this week. I promise.”

He’ll make time for me.

It’s such a minimal promise for normal relationships, but something I’ve never been given without having to put up a fight for it. I’ve never had to fight for time with Murphy because we talk every day. He’s never missed a phone call. Cora and Josh can call that obsessive all they want, but I don’t see it that way. I see it as commitment.

“You always make time for me,” I praise him.

With sincerity that pricks me like a needle, he promises, “And I always will.”

CHAPTER 13

MURPHY

"DID YOU GET a report on the two new assets in Amsterdam? When will they be ready for sale?"

Declan sighs. "The training team requested that we transfer one of them to Oslo or Copenhagen."

"Why?" I look up at him, peering over my laptop. He sits in one of the armchairs on the opposite side of my desk, Fiona in the other beside him, quietly reading a book.

He looks down at his laptop, reading from the screen. "It says, *'They were captured together—sisters. They find too much strength in each other and need to be separated to be broken.'*" He pinches the bridge of his nose.

I know the details are often wearing on him, but more often than not, having him help with the day-to-day operation of our factories is the only time we get to spend together.

"Let's transfer one of the sisters and two other assets to Copenhagen, then. Numbers are low there right now, so it'll even things out."

"How should they select the other two assets?"

I wave my hand dismissively. "Doesn't matter. Allow the trainers to select—they can usually find the right balance of personalities."

His fingers move across the keyboard. "Noted."

"Inform the trainers in Amsterdam that we need the girls ready in eight weeks. I have twelve new buyers lined up this quarter, and I want them to have a varied selection to choose from."

"Got it." He continues to type.

It's quiet for a minute or two as I finish checking through a facility report.

Then Declan quietly notifies me, "It's seven o'clock."

I glance down at my gold Rolex to confirm, then quickly send off the report and shut my laptop lid.

"You don't look as excited as you should be for a man who's about to bring home his bride."

"I'll be ecstatic when this discussion with the family is through."

"Nothing to worry about. You got full board approval."

"Minus Vigo and Nikolai's Head of House votes."

"Well, it's not your fault they were so terrible they went and got themselves murdered on the same night."

Three months ago, I'd successfully petitioned the board to take on a bride early, and I'd secured Renata's influence to ensure Stella was the bride selected. But earlier this week, the quarterly meeting hosted at the Vittori mansion was fucking chaos. The Russian Head of House, Nikolai, used one slave to help steal back another slave he'd recently sold to the Italian Head of House, Vigo. Vigo was killed before they fled, and Nikolai got caught with a stray bullet and died later that night. It was a goddamn mess.

But since business is business, and it always comes first, the quarterly board meeting went on as scheduled. I was still met with final approval to marry Stella Scott, minus Nikolai's and Vigo's verbal votes.

It was helpful that I had written correspondence with each of them prior to that meeting where they sent their premature congratulatory remarks after receiving the agenda. That, and Renata's glowing recommendation was what I needed to cement Stella's safety with my family—some of whom don't approve my decision to marry early.

Cordelia is the only member of the board who questioned the selection of Stella beyond the reasonable line of questioning that always comes with these decisions. But even she was ultimately swayed by Renata's influence.

The decision was made, board approval was given, and I won't put up with any further bullshit from those in my family who feel less than thrilled about it. That's the reason I've asked my family to gather tonight in the living room. I'll be bringing Stella home this weekend, and I need to ensure they'll be on their most welcoming behavior.

I let out an agitated breath and push to my feet. "Let's get this over with. Fiona," I alert her, and she closes her book.

She quietly places it on the side table before rising to her feet and following behind me and Declan as we exit my office. I lock the door behind us before heading down the hallway, Bailey and Declan beside me, Fiona behind me.

Fiona's proving to be a good pet—obedient, calm, and eager to please. She ought to be gracious given the living situation I pulled her from. She's settled in nicely. She's blended easily into my care, earning rank with Bailey in no time, who trots along beside me. Fiona and Bailey each have freedom to roam around the grounds as they please, but they heel when I call them to.

I hear the pleasantries of chatter as we approach from the hallway, but it fades to silence as I enter the living room.

"Get me a drink," I tell Fiona, and she darts off toward the bar cart to get my usual.

The family is gathered in the sunken living room, their expectant eyes on me, waiting for me to speak. I step down and lower to sit on my chair near the fireplace. It faces outward toward the family so I can see everyone from where I'm perched.

Fiona hands me my drink and kneels beside my chair. On reflex, I reach out to stroke her hair in recognition, just as I would with Bailey.

"I've asked you all here tonight to discuss your expectations for Stella's arrival this weekend. As you already know, she's not bred from the world of criminal activity, and she knows nothing of our business and what we do. When I bring her home, she will only just have learned, and I expect it will be a shock to her. I expect she'll be angry. I'll expect her to fight, perhaps even attempt to escape. The security team has been briefed and extra precautions will be put in place for a number of months."

"We wouldn't need security measures if you'd allowed your bride to be selected the traditional way," Cordelia says.

"And that's the kind of bullshit I'm not going to tolerate." I take a slow sip, lean back, and cross an ankle over my knee. "You had your time to speak, and your vote was counted. I received board approval and that's the end of the argument. Stella Scott will be my wife, and there's no need for your attitude about it. If you're too displeased to play nice, Delia, then you're welcome to leave my good graces. You're welcome to choose to live on your own without benefitting from the family wealth."

I cock an eyebrow at her and her jaw tenses, but she doesn't open her mouth to speak again.

"As I was saying, this is going to be a shock for her and I can tell you, she's not going to concede to our way of life easily. She's a fighter, and I expect a fight from her."

"Tell us what you expect from us, my love," Bridget says softly. "How can we help with her transition?"

I grant my mother a small smile in appreciation of her grace and acceptance.

"I think the best that everyone can do is go about business as usual. Welcome her with kindness, recognize her place above you, and for the love of God, don't talk about our trade. It will only upset her and lead to an argument—one I'm certain none of you will win. If she has questions about the business, *I* will answer them."

"Walk on eggshells is what I'm hearing," Cordelia snips.

I snap my head in her direction. "I see you're overdue for a lesson in hierarchy. Do you understand her place will be above yours, dear cousin?"

She glowers at me, but thankfully, shuts her mouth. "When she arrives on Saturday, I expect you all to be waiting to greet her in the foyer. We'll do quick introductions and that will be all for the day. She'll require an adjustment period." I look to my brother, standing off to the side. "Declan, I'll need you to look after Fiona while I'm absent retrieving Stella."

"We can look after her," Cormac offers, and I sense Fiona shrinking back on her heels.

"Absolutely fucking not. Last time you and Tally had her, she was returned with bruises on her arse so tender she couldn't sit on it for a week."

"So?" Tally asks, looking genuinely confused, the fucking dimwit.

"The answer is no. Declan will be responsible for Fiona and no one else will bother her. Understood?"

I'm met with nods and murmurs of agreement.

"So we're all settled, then. Everyone's understood?" Thankfully, the room remains silent—no dumb questions. "Great." I push to my feet, toss back my drink to empty the glass, then hand it to Fiona. "I'm off then. I need to prepare my bedroom to welcome home my bride-to-be."

"Murphy, wait," Bridget says, standing and moving in front of me. She places her hands on my shoulders to hold me steady, looking up into my eyes with happiness reflecting in hers. "I'm not thrilled that you're doing this so early in your tenure, my love. But I am thrilled that you've found someone to share it all with. She'll be welcomed as family."

Her gentleness makes my cheeks twitch and my lips curl into a smile. I lean in to press a quick kiss to her forehead. "Thank you."

I pat my leg for Bailey to follow, and Fiona comes right along, too. It makes that twinge of humanity tense in my muscles for a moment to think that she's trained to behave like my pet. But who am I to fight the fact that she feels comfortable to belong, to know her expectations, and obey them?

That's where Stella will give me trouble. She's not comfortable with the status quo. She doesn't know what it means to belong to someone. She doesn't follow expectations, and she certainly doesn't blindly obey. My heart races to think of the challenge she poses. I crave it. I crave her fight. I crave her anger. I crave the contempt she'll have for everything we stand for.

My soul begs for hers, just as hers begs for a home.

And I'm finally bringing her home.

I raise my fist and knock on Stella's door. I know she's home because the surveillance team had eyes on her, but she doesn't know I'm here. I wanted to surprise her. Both because I think it will be fun to see the look on her face when she sees me and because I need to take her off-guard, get her adrenaline pumping. I want her to make the decision to come with me enthusiastically and impulsively, rather than have my capture team come in and do it by force.

I knock again, anticipation sparking heat that burns beneath my skin. My heart pounds against my ribs as I knock a third time and get no answer. I know she's in there. I pull my cell phone from my back pocket and call her.

"Hey, baby," she answers, and I can hear the echo of her voice on the other side of the door.

"Answer the damn door, Stella."

"Answer the…*what?*"

"Did you hear me knock?"

"Murphy, are you…You're not!"

I hear something clang against her hardwood floor, quickly followed by her footsteps padding across it. I end the call and pocket my phone when I hear her disengage the locks from the inside.

The door swings open, and I find her wide-eyed and hopeful as her beautiful brown eyes take me in. She's wearing gray sweatpants and a white tank top that clings to her curves. Her dark hair is piled on top of her head and she's wearing her glasses, which means she hasn't put in her contacts yet today.

She's fucking stunning.

She's fucking *mine*.

I struggle to keep my cool when she squeals and launches herself into me. She throws her arms around my neck and goes straight in for a kiss, pressing her lips to mine with indecent intent.

There's something about having her in my arms that settles me, something I can't explain. I pull her tightly into my embrace, lifting her feet from the ground and walking her backward into her apartment. I set her down, untangle one of my arms from around her waist, and reach behind me and shut the door.

"You're here," she pants as her eyes flicker across my face.

"I told you I'd see you soon."

"I didn't realize it would be *this* soon." Her brown eyes zero in on my lips as mine lock on hers, both of us aching from the lust that's been building for months. When she speaks again, her voice is soft and sultry. "Can you fuck me now and talk to me later?"

I chuckle, sliding my hands to her hips as I step in closer. "A tempting offer, but I have a proposal for you first."

"A proposal that's better than fucking?" She shifts, wiggling her hips.

"Not exactly better than fucking. But something that will give us far more time to fuck in much more spectacular places."

"Okay, you've piqued my interest. What's your proposal?"

"I want you to come on a trip with me."

"A trip?"

"I want to take you home with me. To Ireland. I want you to meet my family." Not exactly a lie, she *will* be meeting my family…she just doesn't know the circumstances yet.

Her lips part as she gapes at me, her head tilting to the side. "You want me to meet your family?"

I stroke my palm down the side of her head, cupping her cheek. "I want more with you, Stella; more than phone calls and occasional visits. I want to be with you. I want to show you how serious I am about us." All true.

"I'm...I don't know what to say."

"Say you'll come. Let's pack you a bag and get going."

"You mean *now?*"

"I mean now. Right now."

Her eyes dart back and forth across my face. "I can't just leave with no notice. I...I run a business. What about the shop?"

"Ask Cora to take care of things."

She blows out a breath, stepping backward and away from my hold. I drop my arms as she turns, pacing away, and my pulse quickens. "I don't think I could ask her to do that if she knew I was going with you."

"Why? Because she hates me?"

"She doesn't hate you...She just doesn't know you. She's concerned about me." She turns to face me, crossing her arms over her chest.

"That's a little unfair of her."

"How so?"

"She pushed for you and me to hook up the night we met. Now she's back-tracking and trying to talk you out of having a relationship with me."

"It's not like that. She just wants me to be safe and happy."

I cross the space between us, rubbing my palms up and down her arms. "If she really wants that for you, then she'll be happy that you and I have this opportunity to take things to the next level."

She sighs. "I don't know. I don't know that she'll be happy about this. I don't know if I can ask her to run the shop while I'm away. How long would we be gone?"

I don't want to lie to her, but I can't tell her the truth, either. Once she leaves with me, she's never coming back. "Why don't you just call her? See what she says."

She blinks up at me with her expressive eyes, reflecting depth and darkness in which I could dwell, a place where I could lose myself. I'm tempted to throw her in her bedroom, strip her, and fuck her before anything else happens, but I know I can't. I can't allow her that physical release yet. I need our mutual hunger to ensure she has at least one good reason to leave with me—to satiate her sexual craving. I know she'll give in and leave with me anyway, but sex is my fail-safe. Otherwise, I'll have to drug her and call in my capture team to get her on my private jet, and I'd prefer to avoid doing that.

"Sweetheart, please." I bend, taking her face in my hands, laying my forehead to rest on hers. "I need to take you home with me."

Fuck.

I can feel the vibration of her heartbeat cutting through the space between our bodies. The way she already loves me is like an electrical field that reaches out from her heart, grips mine, and pulls me closer.

I feel her body slump and sway toward me, her muscles relaxing. She unfolds her arms and lifts her hands to grip my wrists, her thumbs brushing over my skin.

I've got her right where I want her.

It makes my stomach twist in knots that resemble guilt.

"Okay. I'll come with you," she says softly with a smile. "I want to come with you, of course I do. Just…only for a few days, okay?"

I refuse to agree to that because she's never coming back here, so I choose to show her gratitude for her concession instead. "Thank you, Stella."

"You really flew all the way over here just to pick me up and fly me all the way back?"

"I'd travel around the world for you." That's not a lie.

She nudges forward, arching her back and curving her body into mine. She plants her lips on mine, and I gradually deepen our kiss. My body sinks at the things she makes me feel, knowing that once I have her home, I'll get to feel this way with her every day.

When our kiss fades, she sighs, a happy smile lighting her cheeks. "Okay," she whispers. "Okay, let's do it. Let's go. Just let me call Cora and rip off that band-aid. She's not going to be happy with me."

She's going to be less happy when she realizes Stella isn't returning. But there are plans for handling all of that once I have Stella securely in my home and unable to leave.

I take a step back and shove my hands into my pockets, turning to lean my arse against the back of her couch. "So let her be unhappy for a bit. She'll come around."

Stella twists her lips, then slowly nods before stepping away. She bends to pick up her cell phone from the floor—it looks like she must have dropped it there when she realized it was me at her door. When she stands, she pauses, looks at me, and smiles.

"I can't believe this is happening."

"Believe it. I'm finally taking you home."

CHAPTER 14

Stella

MY FINGERS CURL around the armrests and my lips curve into a smile as I revel in the luxury of Murphy's private aircraft. I knew he and his family had money, but I couldn't have imagined this kind of money. He could buy happiness. He could buy anything he wants.

And he picked me to spend his time with.

I let my head fall back against the headrest, shutting my eyes and breathing deeply as I let myself enjoy the fluttering flaps of butterfly wings in my stomach. As the plane levels out and I start to feel a little more settled, I open my eyes and lift my head to find him watching me.

He sits across from me, his ivory leather seat facing mine. He looks relaxed, resting his chin on his hand and his elbow down on the armrest. When our gaze meets, he grins, those damn wrinkles around his eyes nearly killing me as he sits up straight, scrubbing his hand across his beard.

"You're stunning," he says, his tongue sneaking out to lick his lips. "I'm lucky I found you."

My stomach flips. I'm aching to touch him, hold him, kiss him. It's been a complete whirlwind since he arrived at my apartment this morning—a tense phone conversation with Cora, quick packing, and straight off to the private landing strip that Murphy's family owns.

The whole thing feels like a goddamn fairytale. Though I know I shouldn't be getting off on this whole rom-com scenario—the sexy, wealthy Irishman sweeping his random New York City meet-cute girl off her feet—but I'm totally horny for it.

"Come on over here, sit on my lap."

My seatbelt is unbuckled before he finishes his sentence. I leap across the small space between us and eagerly climb onto his lap. There's plenty of room for me to straddle him in the comfortably wide seat, and I lower my ass to sit on his thighs. I grab his cheeks and kiss him hard and fast as his large hands splay across my back. His rings are hard, digging into my flesh as he pulls me in close. He sinks his tongue inside my mouth, kissing me so deeply, I can hardly even reciprocate.

He wants this kiss and he's taking it.

He can have it.

He can take whatever he fucking wants from me.

I feel like a teenager with the way we want each other. His hands don't stop moving and his tongue doesn't stop tasting me until our heavy breaths are as loud as the aircraft engines rumbling all around us. He doesn't stop until I'm rocking my hips, grinding my weight down heavier on his lap, intoxicated by the feel of him against me.

He breaks from our kiss and trails his lips along my jaw, his breath warm and his lips soft as he moves them down my neck. "Good for both of us you wore this hot little skirt."

He grabs the bottom hem of my black-and-white striped miniskirt and flips it up over my hips, giving me a little more wiggle room to spread my legs wider and sink heavier on his lap.

I smile as I lick my lips and my eyes flutter shut. "You're never gonna see me in pants again, stranger. Easy access from here on out."

He groans as his mouth moves over the hollow of my throat—I can feel the vibration of it buzzing over my skin. "I like your way of thinking."

My hands roam down his chest as he nips at my collarbone. I drop my voice to a whisper. "Can I fuck you here? Is someone going to walk in on us?"

He lifts his head, draining the last bits of concern and rational thought from my mind with the way his eyebrows dip to frame his heated stare. My fingers are already between us, working his belt buckle before he speaks. "If you don't fuck me, then I'll fuck you."

I cock an eyebrow at him. "Is that a threat?"

"It's a fucking promise."

There's a beat that passes between us before we both devolve into frantic creatures, both of our hands between us, fighting to get his pants undone and free his thickening cock. I rise onto my knees and he reaches between my legs, his fingers brushing across my sex, slipping beneath the fabric of my underwear, and tugging it to the side.

I shift forward, prepared to impale myself on him before I'm even fully ready because I need him so desperately. But he stops me with his touch. His fingers swirl, teasing me as he watches with hungry eyes.

"Get wet for me."

He licks me with a single stroke of his thick tongue from the hollow spot of my throat all the way up to my chin, and it makes me shudder. His fingers still move, caressing the sensitive flesh between my legs. I gasp when he gently presses them inside me.

I let my head fall back and enjoy the way he touches me with experienced hands. I'm briefly reminded of how much older he is than me…older and more experienced sexually, but also more powerfully knowledgeable as a white man in a privileged world.

Guard your heart with this one.

Cora's words echo inside my head, but it's too late for that. I'm in too deep and this feels too damn good.

As Murphy draws slickness from my core, I meet his eyes, giving back the intensity he feeds me. His breath hitches as he hooks two fingers inside me and my lips part to puff out a breath.

He grins as reason melts away and drips down my insides, washing away my sanity and rushing liquid straight to my core. "That's my good girl," he says as I soak his fingers.

I shift my position, not only ready, but entirely needy for him. I lower my body and take his cock inside me, slowly and deeply. We breathe together through every inch until he's sunk in completely.

"God, that feels so good…"

His hands rub over my back as I start to gently rock forward and back. His touch is so soft that it makes my chest tighten with a swell of emotion. Our eyes are still locked, our bodies are molded together as one, and all I feel is him.

Fuck yes. I'm ignoring my rationality with him—I have been since the moment I met him. But I'm obsessed with him, intoxicated by him, consumed by him, body and soul. He's taken hold of me in such a significant way that I know I'll never recover from him.

I'll never recover from this.

"I'm falling for you," I say softly.

I didn't mean to say it, but I know the words are true. I've been falling for this privileged prick since the day I met him.

"I know," he replies and the ache of those two words—of simple acknowledgment and nothing more—sinks inside my gut. But then he kisses me, mouths closed, with absolute sincerity. He lets our lips linger before he breaks away and says, "I've already fallen for you, Stella."

His words strike like a lightning burst from my heart, lighting me on fire from the inside out. It takes my breath away, but air isn't what I need. I need his touch. I need to feel him move within me, faster, harder, deeper. As if he knows what I need, he rises abruptly from the seat, lifting me with him and taking me down to the floor, laying me sideways between our seats.

As I settle onto my back, he pulls out, tears my twisted panties down my legs, tosses them away, and slams back inside me. I wrap my legs around him, and he comes down on top of me, smothering me in heat and kissing me breathless as his hips work to pump his thick cock.

I moan against his lips as he roughly thrusts. In moments, we're both so breathless that our panting breaks the kiss. He stays close, his cheek pressed to mine as he moves inside me, through me, all around me.

"Come for me, Stella. I want to feel it. Give it to me. Promise you'll never give it to anyone else."

His words tug deep inside me, dragging pleasure to my center.

Never?

Is that a promise I want to make him?

There's no room for logic with the way he fills me so completely.

"Never," I whisper.

"Say it," he grunts, angling his hips so his cock presses upward, rubbing against that perfect spot inside me. "Promise me."

"I promise."

"Promise me your pussy is mine."

The way he growls and grunts his words is so primal, so erotic, that it makes me say it. My pussy is *mine*, but this dumb, lust-driven version of me is so wrecked that she makes promises she doesn't mean just because it feels so fucking hot to belong to him.

"I promise…my pussy is yours."

That sets him off. He rears back, sitting up on his knees, gripping my hip with one hand as the other lands on my stomach. His fingers spread and his thumb slides down over my dark curls to swirl over my clit.

My hips buck up off the floor as he pounds into me. He fucks me so hard I think I might break…but *fuck*, it feels so good to let him break me. I lift my hands above my head to push them against the wall behind me, just in time to catch myself before hitting my head.

"Murphy…"

"You're fucking mine," he hisses, his jaw tense, his eyes narrowed and focused on me as he thrusts and swirls his thumb.

I can feel how this orgasm is going to wreck me. It keeps building and building, like a bubble expanding through my core, getting bigger and threatening to burst, though it only expands more. "Harder," I tell him. "Move your thumb faster."

Our eyes remain locked as he gives me exactly what I ask for, as he inflates that bubble larger than ever before. "Come for me," he says, his lips parting, his chest expanding as his breaths quicken with his pace. "Come for me, Stella."

It's his look that does me in; the way he starts to lose control as I get closer, as *he* gets closer, as he tenses and fights to hold back his orgasm until I come first. And if that isn't the sexiest thing I've ever seen. The bubble bursts, forcing my entire body rigid as my climax tears through me.

"Yes, fuck, that's a good girl," his growling words blend into a groan. "That's a good fucking girl." He thrusts fast and comes inside me, liquid heating me and claiming me from the inside.

I reach for him as my explosive climax drops from the peak, tumbling down the edge. He bends over me, snaking his arms around me to hug me as he rolls us onto our sides, his cock still sunk all the way inside me. I wiggle my hands up between us to hold his cheeks as I kiss him deeply, slowly, tasting him with my tongue and thanking him without words for making me feel this way—for making me feel so satisfied, so cared for, so wanted.

We hold each other for minutes after the kiss breaks, breathing and coming down from the high together as our hands roam each other. The way he touches me is gentle—such a stark contrast from the way he fucked me.

"I can't give you my heart if you're not going to be careful with it," I say, my voice soft.

He pulls back from our embrace just enough to meet my eyes.

"I told you I was falling, but I can't hit the ground with you unless I know you're going to protect my heart. I've been hurt so much in the past. I don't want to fall for you only to be hurt again."

Something unsettling flickers across his gray-green eyes as he strokes a hand down my hair. "I will take care of you. I'll appreciate you.

I'll give you everything you need, and I'll protect your heart from being hurt by any other man." He sighs and pulls out of me slowly, and the absence of him is profound.

I roll onto my back, gaping at him as he gets to his feet and adjusts his clothes too quickly, buckling back up before holding out his hand to help me from the floor. I let him pull me to my feet.

"The bathroom's back there." He jerks his chin toward the back of the cabin. "Go clean yourself up. I think it's time I told you the truth."

My heart beats double time and I feel a whoosh of adrenaline flood my veins. "What are you talking about? The truth about what?"

"Go clean up. When you come back, we'll talk."

"No. I don't want to clean up." I narrow my eyes at him. "I don't care. Talk now."

"I'm not going to ask you again."

His cum is seeping from inside me, threatening to run down my leg, but I couldn't care less about cleaning up. I need him to talk. *Now.* The air around us is suddenly stale and stagnant, and goosebumps run up my arms. "You're right, you're not going to ask again because I already said *no.* Tell me. Tell me now." His hand clamps around my bicep, squeezing just above my elbow. He tugs, trying to pull me after him toward the bathroom, but I plant my feet, refusing to move. "Murphy, I said *no!*"

"Stella—"

"I. Said. *No!*" I shake my arm from his grip and stare him down, panting from the anger that's burning inside my chest.

What's happening?

Why is he acting like this?

Before I can get answers, his hands come up to grip my shoulders and he pushes me, forcing me to walk backward toward the back of the cabin. He reaches out with one hand to wrench open a small door before shoving me inside the tiny bathroom and following after me. He pulls the door shut behind him and stands in front of it, blocking my exit. I feel breathless as anxiety and adrenaline mix and flood my veins.

"What are you doing?"

He reaches around me to grab toilet paper, then reaches between my legs. My eyebrows shoot up to my forehead in shock at the way he's so blatantly ignoring me. I take a step back and hit the wall beside the toilet, smacking his hands away.

"Stop it!"

But it's like he doesn't hear me at all. He presses against me, stealing my breath as he crowds me against the wall. I feel the pressure of tears behind my eyes. He reaches between my legs again, but I fight him as I smack his hands and shove at his forearms. It's useless, though. He's bigger and stronger than me, and I can't fight him off.

He forces his hand between my legs and I clamp my thighs together, but only manage to trap his hand there. He brings the toilet paper up to my pussy and wipes his cum away. The paper is rough against my sensitive flesh and his hand is forceful.

I hiccup, trying to suck in a sharp breath, but then I start to cry. I shove at his chest, though he doesn't budge. "Stop it! I said *stop!*"

He gives me a stern look and yanks his hand free, dropping the paper into the toilet. "I asked you to do something. You didn't do it, so I did it for you."

That's enough to send me into a raging fury of tears that flow freely as I reach out and slap him across the cheek. "How fucking *dare* you?"

His head turns to the side and he slowly brings his fingers to touch his cheek where I hit him, but I'm not done yet. I backhand him, hitting his other cheek with my knuckles. Then I put my hands on his chest and shove. I can't move him, but I keep shoving. I hit him, punch him, push him.

When he's had enough, he snatches my wrists in both of his hands, lifts them above my head, and slams them to the wall behind me as he comes in close, pinning me in place with his weight against my body.

"What are you doing?" I cry. "We were just making love…" A sob breaks from my chest and I've never heard my own voice sound this sad, this broken.

"Do you really want to talk here? Like this? Or can we go back to our seats and have a civil discussion?"

I spit on his fucking face. I've never been so livid, so disgusted in my entire life.

A scowl shifts his features and I hate how he looks. He reaches up with his hand to wipe my spit from his cheek. "I'm gonna let that slide because I know I've upset you. But please make no mistake…if you do that again, there will be consequences."

I gasp because the look on his face tells me he's painfully serious.

When he's satisfied with my stillness, he speaks again. "I'm sorry. I didn't mean to deal with you so roughly. But that's why it's time for me to tell you the truth about your future. You need to understand what's really happening here."

My eyes widen and air rushes quickly through my nostrils, my chest heaving up and down with my quickening breaths. "What's really happening?"

He sighs. "Are you done fighting me now?"

I take a beat, staring at him intently, trying to figure out what I should do. My instinct is to fight, but I see where that got me—pinned to the goddamn wall, fearful of a man I thought I was falling for only moments ago. I'm trapped with him—not just in this bathroom, but on this plane at thirty-thousand feet, flying over open ocean. It only occurs to me now that I don't really know where we're going. He said he was taking me to Ireland.

But what if that was a lie?

Has it all been lies?

I have no choice but to play it cool and find a way to keep calm so he doesn't hurt me.

I never would've dreamed he could hurt me like this.

Slowly, I nod.

And just as slowly, he loosens his grip on me. When he's satisfied that I'm calm enough, he releases my hands and takes a step back. I drop my arms from the wall, bringing them down to my sides.

"Good girl," he says.

"*Fuck* you. I'm not your fucking dog."

His lips quirk up at the corner. "Right, you aren't. My dog obeys without a fight."

I almost think he means it as a joke, but God, if that isn't the must condescending, disgusting thing I've ever heard a man say to me.

Stay calm.

He gives me a once over, then turns and opens the door. "Come on, let's go have a seat and I'll tell you everything."

He leaves me alone in the bathroom and I start searching, scanning the space for something, *anything* I can take out with me as a weapon because suddenly, I'm afraid of the man I've been falling for. But there's nothing. It's empty aside from a soap dispenser, paper towels, and toilet paper. I push out a heavy breath through my rounded lips, tug down my skirt, and cautiously step out from the bathroom.

I'm hypervigilant as I scan the cabin, my eyes falling on him, and I'm surprised to find him back in his seat, sitting casually and watching me, as if nothing at all had just happened in the bathroom. I swallow my rising fear and move toward my seat. When I reach it, I lower slowly, never taking my eyes off him.

"I'm sorry, sweetheart." He could almost have me fooled that he's being sincere. "I truly didn't mean to get so rough with you. And I won't have to be that way again once we understand each other a little better."

I choose my words carefully, though a flurry of hateful words try to claw their way up my throat. "What do I need to understand?"

"I haven't been entirely honest with you."

My heart beats double time. "What do you mean?"

"I haven't exactly been dishonest with you, either. I haven't told you any lies, but I've omitted some rather important information. But it was necessary in order to get you here."

Oh, my God.

"What information?"

"What my family does…Who we are…Who I want you to be."

I grip the armrests, my fingers feeling like claws as they curl around the leather. "Who do you want me to be?"

"I want you to be you…but *mine.*"

The way he wants me still makes my belly flutter senselessly, though now the flutters are followed quickly by nausea. I press my eyes shut. "I *was* yours. I was."

"You still are. You will always be. Your choice in that is no longer yours to make."

A tear slips down my cheek. "I don't understand. What are you saying?"

"You made the choice to leave with me. I asked you to come away with me and you said yes. You packed your bags and you got on this plane with me. All of your own free will. Isn't that right?"

I nod, opening my eyes.

"You made the choice to be with me, but you no longer have the choice to leave."

A stab of pain shoots through my chest. "What do you mean? What do you mean, Murphy? What do you *mean* I don't have the choice to leave?"

He shifts to sit up straighter and looks at me squarely, seriously, grimly. "It's time for me to tell you about the four families."

CHAPTER 15

Murphy

"YOU'RE DISGUSTING," SHE spits.

My heart thuds against my ribs. I hate this. I hate the way she hates me right now, but I knew this would happen. I'd mentally prepared for it. I'd run through this conversation over and over again in my head to get myself ready for this and it still fucking hurts. I stay silent, watching as she scans me from head to toe, judging me, reevaluating her opinion of me.

"I'm so fucking disgusted by you." Her voice is quieter this time and somehow, that's worse than her yelling.

I sigh, lifting my head from where it rests on my hand, my elbow on the armrest. "Go on," I encourage.

The sooner she gets this out of her system, the sooner we can work on building a better relationship from these ashes. As she sees it, I've burned down our future. But she'll understand soon enough that I've made a future for us where there wasn't one.

It had to be this way.

"Go on?" Her head tilts as her eyes narrow, her upper lip scrunched in a snarl of disgust. "*Go on?* I'll fucking go on, you sick piece of shit." She leans forward, and I know she would have launched herself at me on the attack by now if it weren't for the fact that the plane is in its final descent. Having her buckled in her seat does make this easier for me. "You are the worst kind of creature, preying on women, trafficking them to monsters…monsters like *you*."

My jaw ticks. "Let's be clear on one thing. I'm not a monster. I only feed them."

"Oh, *fuck* you! You're delusional on top of everything else! How can you say you're not a monster? You sell women…you make them *slaves!*"

"It's the family business."

"It's fucking disgusting."

"Depends on your perspective."

I don't know why that's the line that makes her snap, but she snaps spectacularly. As soon as I see her hands move toward her hip to unlatch her belt buckle, I have mine undone, ready to grab her. She has no trouble reaching me since she's facing the front of the descending aircraft and I have my back to it. Still, she takes me off-guard as she throws a side hook toward my cheek and I barely duck in time to miss the impact.

I grab her swinging fist and twist her arm behind her back, spinning her away from me before her arse falls onto my lap. I grab her other arm and put it in the same position, yanking her backward, holding her against my body as she kicks and squirms.

"Let go of me!"

I bring my face over her shoulder, speaking into her ear through her tangled hair. "Keep it up if you want to be on lockdown when we get home. Keep testing my patience and I'll cage you in a windowless room where you won't see sunlight for *days*."

She jerks her head toward me and the expression on her face is a kind of fury I've never seen on her before. Her rage has twisted her into someone entirely unrecognizable, but she still exists in that anger. It's this kind of fiery magnetism that drew me to her in the first place and the way she fights makes my heart beat faster. It makes my muscles tense and twitch. It pumps adrenaline through my veins, and it makes me want to dominate her in every possible way.

She fuels me.

I know without a shadow of a doubt that making her mine was the best decision I've ever made.

She doesn't speak and her squirming stills at my threat, but none of the fight is gone. I see it in the way her chest rises and falls with heavy breaths that make her nostrils flare. I shift my grip to hold both her wrists in one of my hands, bringing the other around to stroke down the side of her hair.

"That's a good girl. There's no reason we can't be civilized about this. I want a partnership with you, Stella. If I'd wanted to make you a slave, I would've made you a slave months ago."

Her eyes flicker and widen as she jerks in my hold, the realization of the power I've held over her since the night we met finally sparking in her mind. "Make me a *slave*? Christ, you're sick. You're so goddamn sick!"

I chuckle. "Trust me, sweetheart. I'm not sick. You and I just come from different worlds. I'll show you what sickness looks like, and it doesn't look a goddamn thing like me."

"Why are you doing this to me?"

"I'm doing this for *us*. There was no other way."

We don't speak as the landing gear touches down onto the pavement, bouncing the cabin before settling as it rolls along the earth. Her body falls heavily against mine as the pilot hits the brakes, the speed quickly decelerating and holding us together before it slows to a stop.

I glance out the window beside us and let out a breath, then turn my face toward hers. I nudge her hair away from her neck with my nose and deeply inhale her sweet vanilla scent.

She hates me right now, yes, but I feel overwhelming relief to have her here with me, back home in Ireland where I can protect her from the monsters in the world and keep her safe with me.

She jerks at the touch of my nose along her neck, and I let go of her wrists, allowing her to jump from my lap. She spins around to face me and backs away. I stand as our flight attendant, Shannon, appears in the cabin while the engines whir with the letdown.

"Just a moment, sir, and we'll have the airstair lowered for you to exit the plane." She grants me a kind smile as she moves past us, ignoring Stella and her outburst, as she should.

"Thank you, Shannon."

I smooth my waistcoat and step toward Stella. My movement startles her, and she takes a step back, but there's nowhere for her to go. She has to pass me to get off the plane. I motion her toward me with my hand. "Come here."

She shakes her head. "No. *No.* I'm not getting off this plane. I'm going back to New York."

"You're not going back to New York. You're coming home with me. I'd like to do this the easy way, but if you force my hand, I will drag you out of here kicking and screaming. And I promise you, no one will bat an eye. Not the flight attendant, not the pilot, not my driver, or any of my other employees. There is no choice for you to stay on board. I suggest you come willingly."

She scoffs, "Like fuck I'm coming willingly."

I watch as her eyes flicker sideways, registering the bathroom door just behind her a few steps away. It's the only place she can run to, and she could lock herself inside, but it doesn't matter if she does. I could easily break down the door to get her out. However, I'd prefer to avoid the expense and hassle of having a new door installed.

I lift my eyebrows and shake my head slowly, giving her the chance to make a better choice for herself. But of course, she chooses incorrectly. I reach for her as soon as her feet turn and she runs for the bathroom. She makes it inside just as my hand clamps around her elbow. She spins, fighting me more frantically than I had ever imagined she could, and frankly, I'm impressed by it.

I'm turned-on by it.

She shoves at my hand as I pull her toward me. She smacks my cheek once, twice, but I catch her wrist before the third time. I slide my grip from her elbow to her wrist and cross her arms in front of her, dragging her so she lands against my chest with a thump that forces the air to leave her lungs all at once.

"Valiant effort, lass, but it's time to go home now."

"Murphy…" She looks up at me, meeting my eyes with raw vulnerability. "Don't do this to me. I thought you cared about me," her voice cracks. "I thought we were falling…" A tear creeps out from the corner of her eye and trails down her flushed cheek.

That fucking hurts me.

"Don't cry, sweetheart. I'm not trying to hurt you. I just can't risk you running away from me before we get home. I can only keep you safe at home."

She shakes her head. "It's not my home. It's not my home. Not with you."

I let go of her wrists and wrap my arms around her, holding her close to me, hugging her. "I'm sorry it has to be like this. I never wanted to hurt you. I never wanted to scare you."

"I'm so fucking scared of you…"

"And that hurts me. It hurts me to know you're afraid of me. You don't need to be. I promise I'll make you happy."

"I won't be happy."

"You will be. I promise."

"Stop it!" she screams against my chest. "Don't make me promises!"

I sigh, stepping backward to pull us both out of the bathroom. I spin to block her from getting back inside again before I let go of her. She steps back and looks at me, scanning me from top to bottom. She takes another small step back. Then, she turns her head to see the cabin door that Shannon's opened behind her.

"Go on," I tell her.

She runs and I huff out a breath.

She's going to try to flee.

Unfortunate for her, there's nowhere for her to run. Our airstrip is private, and security is well-maintained.

I stride after her as she disappears through the cabin door. I arrive at the exit just in time to see her hop off the bottom step onto the tarmac, her bright yellow blouse screaming for attention as she looks both ways to assess her surroundings. I start down the steps as she decides to turn right and runs toward the hangar, away from my driver, who lunges for her.

I jog down the steps. "I've got her," I tell him calmly. "Just bring the car around after us."

"Yes, sir."

The sun is setting as I walk across the concrete after her. She's quick, but there's really nowhere for her to go. She reaches the hangar and stops at a door, though I already know it's locked before she tugs on it. She pulls and pushes, trying to get it open, then runs past the garage to the next door. Again, she pushes and pulls to no avail.

What is she planning to do if she gets inside, anyway?

My lips quirk in amusement at the thought. I love watching her thoughts in action.

"Stella," I yell after her. "It's a private airstrip. There's no one here to help you."

She looks behind her and raises her middle finger at me as I close in on her. She makes a run for the far end of the hangar and darts around the corner. She can run all the way around the hangar if she wants, but she'll only be met with emptiness that's surrounded by a tall fence, topped with barbed wire. She comes to a stop on the other side of the building as she realizes this.

I watch as she realizes her escape attempt is futile, as my driver pulls up in front of her on the opposite side of the hangar. She stops dead in her tracks, her shoulders slump, and she mutters, "Shit."

I'm careful as I approach her, stopping a few feet away. "Get in the car, Stella."

She whips around to face me. "Where are you planning to take me?"

"I told you, I'm taking you home."

"*Your* home."

"*Our* home. I'll make sure you're very comfortable there."

This time, she lifts both hands with raised middle fingers as she scowls at me.

I walk toward her and she stands her ground, her hands raised between us as I come in close. "I suggest you don't do that when you meet my cousin, Cordelia. She might chop off your fingers." I turn and walk past her toward the car, sliding into the backseat where my driver holds the door open for me.

It takes a few moments, but eventually, she gives up, gives in, and climbs into the car.

CHAPTER 16

Stella

NEVER LET THEM *take you to a second location.*

Never, ever *let them take you to a second location.*

I let him take me to a second location on-board his private aircraft, and a third when I got into the car with him.

I feel so stupid.

The car curves around the gravel driveaway, rumbling over pebbles as it slows to a stop at the bottom of a set of beige steps. They lead up to the main entrance of a stone castle—a massive, sprawling *castle.*

I've been cataloguing my surroundings carefully, though there were too many twists and turns through the Ireland countryside for me to easily track my way back to the airstrip. Even if I could track it, it took more than an hour to drive from there to here—too far to make my way back on foot if I could escape.

I could still easily follow the nearly mile-long driveway back to the secured gate we drove in through. The gate and surrounding fence looked sturdy, but I think I could climb it.

Murphy turns sideways to look at me. He sits beside me on the bench seat in the back of the car, blocking my view of the staircase. He has the *audacity* to grin at me. "Welcome home."

I want to spit in his face. "This isn't my home."

"It really doesn't have to be this way."

"You've made it this way," I hiss.

"Would you rather I'd told you sooner?"

I burn a hole through him with my eyes. "I wish I'd never met you."

A lump rises in my throat at the words that feel so wrong to say to the man I've been falling for over the last seven months. I forcefully swallow it down.

He takes in a sharp breath through his nose and clenches his hand into a fist as he lifts his arm to rest it along the back of the seat. "You're angry with me…I understand that. But let me warn you, my patience for your temper only extends so far."

I turn to face him, mimicking his position by propping my elbow on the back of the seat and leaning my head against my hand. "Gosh, I'm so sorry you don't have a greater tolerance for my temper. If you can't take it, perhaps you should send me the fuck home."

He smiles and I curse my wicked hormones for training my body to feel that the twist of his kissable lips should turn me on. I fucking hate him….and I still feel what I felt for him before. There's a raging war of incomprehensible emotion within me.

"I wouldn't dream of it," he says. "We're home, and you're not leaving. Not without me and not until I can trust you."

"Oh, sweetie, you'll never trust me. I'll make sure of it."

"You're sexy when you're angry, did you know that?" He squints at me with a scrutinizing gaze. "The way you furrow your eyebrows…" He opens his fist and reaches out to snatch my wrist. I lift my head away from that hand with a snap just before he tugs, dragging me across the seat. "You do that and bite your lip just before you come."

My thumping heart stills me as he pulls me close, hip to hip, wrapping his arm around my shoulders. I can't take my eyes off him as I wrangle my emotions into a corral of control. I was in love with him hours ago…I was falling hard. My brain is fighting to comprehend everything he's told me that has shattered the illusion so effectively. He's a criminal, a liar, a vile monster who hurts women.

So why does my stomach still flutter?

I just want it to stop…I want to stop falling.

My only defense mechanism is my words.

"You know what you do just before you come?" I pause a beat to gain his intrigue and he looks at me warily. "I don't have a fucking clue. I don't care enough about you to pay attention."

He grins, but I saw the flinch right before his lips curved. "Oh, you beautiful thing. Keep it up. You're just asking me to put you in your place." I try to pull away from him, but his arm tightens around my shoulders and he shifts his ass closer, pressing his thigh against mine. "When I was thirteen, my father's talent slave, Esmerelda, spoke out of turn at a family event. Do you know what he did to her?"

I turn my head away, but he reaches around me with his free hand and grabs my chin, pinching me, forcing my head toward him. "He cut off her little toe. It wasn't a clean cut. He sawed it off with a serrated kitchen knife. Almost took the next toe, too."

I feel my eyes pop wide and I breathe heavily through my nose, trying to maintain some semblance of calm composure. I don't want him to know my fear. "Why are you telling me this? Would you cut off my toe? Am I meant to be your slave? I thought you wanted to give me a comfortable life."

He presses his forehead to mine, making it impossible to look anywhere but at him. "I wouldn't so much as cut a single strand of your hair. I give more than a shit about you. If I'd wanted to treat you like a slave, you'd have been my slave months ago. I'm telling you about my family so you'll understand how little your snarky tone will be tolerated. You have no idea what I've had to do to make this happen, to make you my soon-to-be wife. They're not all happy you're here."

"Then we'll have that in common."

His hand slides from my chin to grip me by the throat. "Not forever. You'll see in time how good I can make your life. You'll see how much I want to make you happy." He lifts his forehead from mine but holds me with his gaze, his eyes softening as he watches me for long seconds. His throat bobs as he swallows, then he leans forward and softly presses his lips to mine.

He's so gentle that it stuns me, and I freeze in his hold.

God, he's everything.

No, he's nothing.

Why did I ever let myself start to fall for him?

This is torture!

He pulls away all at once, releasing me, opening his door, and stepping out of the car. He holds out his hand for me to take. "Come. We'll meet my family and then I'll show you to our room."

I scoff and turn away, opening the door on my side of the car and getting out without his deceptive chivalry. I stomp around the back of the car and smack his hand away as he tries to grab mine. I march up the steps toward the front door with my arms tight across my chest. I stop and wait for him at the landing, turning to watch him walk up the steps after me.

I don't understand how my heart can still see him the way I did only hours before…how it can still beat with hope for a future that's impossible now.

It should be a fairytale—the Irish stranger I met whisked me away to his castle home in Ireland—but he's turned it into a nightmare.

His tattooed forearms flex as he clenches his fists. My eyes are drawn to the rings he wears on both hands. It makes me think of how the metal felt on my cheeks when he held my face in his hands and kissed me. His sleeves rolled up to his elbows make him look so effortlessly stylish. His sway through his perfectly tailored waistcoat and slacks still makes my stomach clench.

How could I fall for his lies, his deception?

Cora was right…

He was always a monster, and I couldn't see it. I *failed* to see it because I let my guard down. I let him in. I let him do this to me. I let him seduce me, make me fall for him. I let him take me and there's nothing I can do about it now.

All I can do is learn and wait for an opportunity.

I drop my hands to my sides as he approaches and I pull my shoulders back, lifting my chin. I'm not letting him win this. I'm not giving him anymore of my anger—he likes it too damn much. He gets off on it.

He smiles as he stops in front of me. "Ready?"

I don't speak. I don't nod. I simply turn my eyes from him to the door and wait for him to open it. He steps forward and swings it wide to reveal a grand foyer, but I can't take in the beauty of the structure. All I can focus on is the throng of people gathered there, standing, watching…waiting.

As a reflex, I look at Murphy—a natural instinct to look for direction in an unfamiliar situation—but I force myself to look away from him just as quickly. He reaches behind me, splaying his hand across the small of my back, and leads me inside. My skin prickles at his possessive touch.

"Everyone, this is Stella. Stella, meet your new family."

Jesus Christ.

My heart drops into my stomach, sending a tsunami of nausea and unease right through me. Silence greets us all, stretching across several uncomfortable beats.

Then, a familiar face attached to a man with a tall frame lifts his arms in the air and shouts, "Sis! Welcome home!" The joviality in his tone is jarring against the eerie feeling inside my soul. "Remember me?" He points to himself.

I recognize him as one of Murphy's brothers, Cormac.

A petite blonde woman standing beside him smacks him in the chest. "How much did you drink? Are you wankered already?"

A woman with long, straight, light-orange hair crosses the tile floor, her high heels clicking as she moves toward us. She stops right in front of me, and I'm tempted to take a step back, but I know better than to show that kind of weakness to anyone. And the way Murphy pushes forward against my back makes me feel like he's intentionally preventing me from backing away from this woman.

I quickly guess that this must be his cousin, Cordelia. He's told me quite a bit about her.

She inclines her head as she regards me. "Stella, welcome. I'm—"

"Delia," I cut her off intentionally. "I know who you are."

I'm not stupid. I know how to play this power game. I sense Murphy's eyes on me, and I glance from the corner of mine, detecting a smirk playing across his lips. I want to smack him to wipe the smugness from his face. I'm not playing this game to entertain him—he forced me into this, and I have no choice but to play.

Cordelia takes in a breath as she blinks, straightening her posture. "We've been looking forward to your arrival."

"Oh?" I tilt my head. "So, you're all in on the kidnapping, then?"

No one bats an eye.

Right…they traffic women for a living. What do they care?

Another woman, much older, with shoulder-length black hair and brown eyes glides forward, a man at her side who looks like a much older version of Murphy. As they step forward, Cordelia steps back and I feel relief. She sets off warning bells that give me goosebumps.

The woman with black hair immediately steps into my space and I want to step back, but again, Murphy doesn't allow it. She wraps her arms around me and squeezes me in a hug that feels deceptively friendly. She pulls back to look at me, but her hands stay on my shoulders. "Stella, I'm so glad to finally meet you. I'm Murphy's mother, Bridget." She shakes her head, then looks at the man beside her. "My love, she reminds me of Esmerelda. Doesn't she look like Esmerelda?"

Murphy's hand slips around my side, his fingers curling and tightening to grip my waist, tugging me harshly against his side. His mother lets go of me and steps back, moving beside her husband.

"She does," the older gentleman murmurs, presumably Murphy's father. "Boyd." He doesn't offer me his hand, just gives me a curt nod, his eyes wandering my form.

The look is unsettling, and I find myself welcoming Murphy's possessive grip. I actually step closer to him and I hate myself for it.

"Quick introductions," Murphy begins. "Boyd and Bridget, my parents. You've met Cordelia there. Cormac you know, and that's his wife, Tally." The petite blonde smiles and waves at me—far too friendly for this scene. "Colin and Moira are Cordelia's parents, and her sister Saoirse. Egan and his wife, Nessa—they don't live here; they were just eager to meet you." I can't keep up with these names, all these strangers. "And there's Declan, you remember."

I remember his brother Declan. I thought he seemed like a nice guy, but apparently, I was wrong about everything.

Fucking monsters, all of them.

"Where's Fiona?" Murphy asks and I turn my head to look at him.

"Locked in her room with Bailey," Declan says. "I didn't think we needed to overwhelm Stella any more than necessary for one day."

"Who is Fiona?"

I know Bailey is Murphy's dog, but I thought he only had one. He's never said anything about a dog named Fiona.

"That's not your decision to make, brother. I asked for everyone to be present to greet Stella."

Declan shrugs. "You left me in charge of her while you were gone, so it was entirely my decision to make at the time. Would you rather leave her with Cormac next time? Cordelia, perhaps?"

Cordelia opens her mouth, but Murphy snaps at her, his fingers incidentally digging too hard into my side. "Shut it. You must be out of your mind if you think I'd ever let you have her."

"My love," Bridget speaks softly to Murphy, "let's leave this for now and receive Stella properly in the dining room. I'm sure she's hungry."

"I'm not."

"No," Murphy replies, equally soft with his mother. I take note of that and lock it away for future reference. "She's quite upset with the circumstances and will need some time to adjust before joining the family. We'll receive dinner in my room tonight."

"Come now." Boyd claps his son on the shoulder and is met with a scowl from Murphy. "She'll be fine. She can sit next to your mother… let the ladies get to know each other."

"No." When Murphy speaks to his father, he's sharp and abrupt— another note to lock away. "If you'll excuse us."

He walks and moves me with him, his family parting for us to pass beneath a grand, crystalline chandelier as he turns us toward a massive hallway. He maintains his grip on my side as he moves us forward, but his fingers loosen after we've passed two doors. They slide along my lower back and lift away just long enough for him to snatch my hand in his instead.

My fingers squeeze around his palm, my brain still crisscrossing synapses that learned to love him while I come to grips with how much I need to hate him right now. In any case, meeting his odd family made me feel uneasy, and I feel a swell of instinct that he's a safer bet than the rest of them. The instinct drives me to hold fast to his hand.

At the end of the hallway, he pulls open a door and leads me through it, but it's not a room. The door swings shut behind us, locking us inside a narrow space with nothing more than a single spiral staircase going up.

He tugs on my hand, pushing me toward the staircase. "Up."

"Where does this go?"

"Upstairs."

My lips pucker in annoyance as my head tilts to the side. "No shit. But what's *upstairs*? Where are you taking me?"

"To our bedroom."

I cross my arms and stare at him, unwilling to move.

"Would you rather go back and spend time with my family?"

I consider, but my choice is quick. I drop my arms with a huff and start up the narrow steps. He follows, locking me in, leaving me no way to go but up. After two flights, at the top of the staircase is another door, so I open it, but he's quickly behind me.

We step out into a hallway that looks much the same as the hallway on the first floor, except this level is carpeted rather than tiled. I pause, not sure where to go from here, but then he grabs my hand and tugs me along, bringing us to one of the doors across from the secret stairwell.

He types in a passcode and scans his thumbprint to unlock it. I gape at him for the over-the-top security measures.

Is it because he means to keep me trapped in here?

My heart is pounding.

He pops open the door and I step back, yanking my hand from his grip. I nearly stumble for the force with which I have to pull, but he doesn't come after me. He stops, turns, and waits.

"This is our bedroom," he says calmly. "This is a safe space for you."

I take another step back. "How the fuck is it a safe space for me with you in it?"

"It's secure, for one. No one else in the home will have access to you here. In any case, I hardly spend any time here except for sleeping. So, if you want time to yourself during the day, you'll have it here." He glances inside. "I like the purple, but we can have it redecorated any way you like."

I shake my head at him, crossing my arms protectively across my body.

He sighs, leaning against the doorframe and mirroring me with crossed arms. "Would you rather have time to explore the grounds? See all the ways in which you can't escape? I promise you, Stella, any escape attempt you could dream up, I've already planned for. There are extra security measures in place in the estate and on the grounds. The sooner you accept your fate, the sooner we work on building mutual trust."

"Mutual trust? *Mutual* fucking trust? Are you kidding me? Do you think I could ever trust you again?"

"You will trust me again. I know it will take time, but how long is up to you. I have faith that you'll come around."

"Come around to what? To being complicit in your heinous crimes against humanity? To *participate* in it?"

"Eventually. You'll be a member of the board and will have a say on some matters. You'll have plenty of time to adjust before then. Until that time, all I expect of you is to be there for me when I need you."

I toss up my hands with a laugh and let them slap against my sides as they fall. I turn, taking a few paces away before marching toward him with determination. "How about when I need you? Will you be there for me?"

"Of course, I will," he says as if it's an obvious statement.

I step closer, pressing into his personal space. He drops his arms, pushing off the doorframe to straighten to his full height. He towers above me, looking down at me.

"I'm telling you now that I *need* you to take me back home. Take me home and fucking forget about me. I want to forget about you."

"You would never be able to forget about me." He takes advantage of my proximity, snatching me by both shoulders and spinning me into the room. He releases me, whips back around, slams the door, and locks it.

"Is the unearned self-confidence a direct consequence of your trade or are you just generally an asshole?"

He gives me a small smile as he turns to face me again. "You knew I was generally an asshole before we started talking on the phone."

"Ah, okay. So, it's just *you,* then. You're just a piece of shit, with or without the family business."

His jaw ticks. "I can handle you being angry at me. But I'm not going to tolerate you insulting me again."

I lean forward and slow my words to emphasize every one of them. "You're a piece of *shit*, Murphy. A rotten, lying, worthless sack of shit, and I feel *sick* that I ever wanted—"

He rushes me, his hand clamping around my throat. I reach for his wrist, but he holds firm as he pushes me back. My knees hit the mattress of the four-post bed and I fall back onto it. He bends over me, settling his weight to pin me down as his fingers clamp and squeeze the sides of my throat.

My lips part as I try to take in a decent breath, but I can't because he's pinching my airway.

Oh, God.

He's going to kill me!

"You're being ungrateful and frankly, your behavior is edging toward trashy. The O'Sheas are not trashy, sweetheart." His fingers release, though his hand hovers over my neck as I gasp in a deep breath. "I expect better from you. It's easier for both of us if you learn your place, straighten up, and act right, but if I need to force your hand, if I need to break you like a goddamn slave, make no mistake, Stella, *I will.*"

I lift my knee as hard as I can and jam it into his fucking ballsack.

Prick.

He grunts, "*Fuck,*" then rolls slightly to the side.

I slap him, then grab his shoulders and shove him off me. I jump to my feet and spin, scanning the ridiculously oversized purple and gold room. I spot an open door in the far corner.

A bathroom.

I run for it. The moment I'm inside, I slam the door shut and slap my palm against the wood to hold it in place. When I glance down at the knob, I'm shocked to see it has a lock on it. It's just a simple lock for the knob—nothing strong enough to hold if he really wanted to break the door down—but it's an extra barrier, nonetheless. I turn it and let my hand drop from the door, taking a step back and letting out a heavy breath.

I start pulling open the drawers of the double-sink vanity, hoping to find something to defend myself with, but the first drawer is empty…

and the second…and the third.

All the drawers are empty.

I spin, finding a small cabinet behind me beside the large, glass-enclosed walk-in shower. I pull open the top and bottom doors, but again, they're empty.

The only thing in this room that isn't attached to the damn wall is toilet paper. There aren't even shampoo or soap bottles in the shower.

"What the fuck?"

Then his voice comes muffled through the door. "Did you think I'd leave anything in there for you to hurt me with? As if I'd let you have so much as a goddamn curling iron right now. You'll have to earn privileges."

"There isn't even any soap," I shout louder than I have to for him to hear me, feeling indignant and bold and biting with sarcasm. "How will I keep myself clean for you to use, *master?*"

He chuckles and it rumbles through me as a dark promise. "Keeping you clean will be my responsibility until you've proven you're trustworthy."

"Go fuck yourself."

"You, too," he says, his tone as malice-filled as mine.

There's a single thump against the door that makes me jump…just one loud thump that makes me think he punched the door.

But then I'm met with silence, and I wait.

I wait until I hear a door slam shut.

Then I wait more…until I'm certain he must be gone.

Now that he's not here for me to unleash my fury upon, my anger breaks. Like a melting glacier breaking free from its shelf, there's an icy rush inside me that washes away the anger and replaces it with sadness and fear.

I start to cry, really truly understanding for the first time that I'm not going home…that a man I was falling for has betrayed me more brutally than I ever could have imagined.

Life as I know it is over, and I've never been more afraid in my life.

CHAPTER 17

Murphy

I LET STELLA have the room last night. I was angry enough to cause her actual harm and thankfully, I had the good mind to remove myself from the situation before I tried. I'd left the lock on the bathroom door to allow her some semblance of privacy, but it's a weak lock and I have a key for it, anyway.

I slowly enter our bedroom after spending the night in one of our many guest bedrooms and lock the door behind me. I glance across the room at the bed, and I'm surprised to see she's not in it. I thought at some point she'd cave and allow herself the comfort of a warm bed to sleep in—it gets cold in this room at night, even in the summer. A glance toward the bathroom shows me the door is still shut, and probably still locked from the inside.

I huff out a breath, wondering what to make of that.

My soon-to-be wife would rather sleep on a drafty bathroom floor for the sake of demonstrating her rebellion than admit defeat and sleep in our bed.

This transition may end up being more challenging than I had anticipated, but that fact doesn't bother me. It fuels me. It will be all that much more rewarding when I finally win her over.

I cross the room and unlock the bathroom door, pocketing the key before opening it. The door swings in and hits something which halts it. I peek my head inside to see that it's her feet. She's sleeping, stretched out across the floor, half on her stomach, half on her side. I wedge the door a little farther, letting it push her feet, and she jolts awake, bolting upright.

She spots me and turns to sit flat on her arse, pushing back and scrambling until her back hits the far wall. I push the door open the rest of the way and enter, then shut it behind me, leaning my back against the door to keep my distance.

"I take it you slept well?" I ask with a tilt of my head as I cross my arms over my chest.

"Fuck off."

"I gave you the room last night. You could've slept in the bed. I didn't stay here."

"I don't want to sleep in your bed."

"*Our* bed," I correct her.

She gives me her middle finger.

"If you play nice, I'm inclined to let you contact Cora today."

She jumps to her feet. "Where's my phone? I want to talk to her."

That got her attention.

"I'll let you talk to her if you cooperate."

"What do you want from me? She'll be worried sick by now. I told her I'd let her know when we landed, and it's been—"

"Too long, I know. It will benefit us both for you to connect."

"Like fuck it will benefit you. I'm telling her everything."

I push off the door and move toward her. "No, you're not going to tell her a damn thing other than how happy you are."

"You can't control what comes out of my mouth."

I edge closer, pressing into her body, holding her to the wall. Her lips part as her eyes flicker up to meet mine. "You're due to think on that one again. You can't tell her the truth. If you do, she'll be dead within an hour."

"*What?*"

"Take off your clothes."

"*No.*"

"Do I need to take them off for you? Cooperate or you won't get to talk to her at all and that probably wouldn't bode well for her. If she starts getting suspicious and hunting for information, she'll have to die. I don't think you want that responsibility weighing on your shoulders."

She visibly swallows and shakes her head. "You're sick. You're *delusional.* How can you think I'd ever care about you when you threaten my best friend's life?"

"You already care about me. Those feelings don't just disappear. They'll return in time when you learn to trust me."

She puts her hands on my chest and shoves, but I don't budge. "I *hate* you."

I give her a smile. "At least you have some passion for me, then. I'd be more concerned if you felt nothing at all." I take a step back to give her some space, then I begin to undress. "Take off your clothes so we can get on with our day."

She's fuming, panting with angry breaths, and her eyes threaten to burn a hole right through me. Yet she remains still, her back to the wall, her palms pressed to it on either side of her hips.

"Stella," I warn, "I won't ask you again. If you want a fight with me, you'll get it. I will strip you myself if I have to, and I don't think you'll feel very good about that right now."

I pull my shirt off and work my belt buckle, keeping my eyes on hers. I watch the way they flicker across my features and dip down to take in my bare chest.

I understand the conflict she feels. Just yesterday, she thought she was falling for me—a version of me that I'd sold her, a version of me that has since shattered in her mind. It aches a little to acknowledge that because the version I'd sold her was a true one—it *would* be true if I lived in her world.

But that version simply can't exist in the world of monsters which I rule. She gets the version of me that was created by the four families—

the real me.

Is that the real me, though?

Regardless, I know she can't just let go of what she felt, and I have to use those feelings carefully, to make her fall for a ruthless king and master.

Slowly, she shakes her head, her throat bobbing as she swallows the anxiety of her continued defiance. Perhaps it's not anxiety at all. Perhaps it's a primal need within her to fight me because she gets off on it as much as I do. She lifts her chin and her head leans against the wall behind her as she remains still, refusing to undress.

I finish removing my clothes as my heart kicks up in rhythm, excited for the challenge of her refusal. I push open the glass shower door and step one foot inside to turn on the water. She lunges, taking the opportunity to try to get around me and out the bathroom door. But it was a useless effort on her part because I anticipated the move. I *wanted* her to do that.

Just as she passes me, I reach out, snatch her by the elbow, and yank her toward me. I tug hard, taking her off-guard, making her stumble over her steps. She collides with my chest as I pull to keep her upright.

With one hand firmly gripping her arm, I snake the other around her waist, holding her close as I take a step backward and pull her into the shower with me. I nudge the glass door shut with my foot and spin her to put her directly under the waterfall.

"Let me go!" she shouts, bringing her arms between us to push and shove.

The shower water soaks her, saturating the fabric of her bright yellow blouse, making it cling deliciously to her skin. "Are you going to take off your clothes now?"

"No!"

I spin her around, wrestle her arms behind her back and shove her face-first against the wall, molding my body to hers. I tug her dampened hair back over her shoulder, exposing her neck as I lean in close to whisper in her ear. "I don't mess around, sweetheart. I don't back down and I don't take *no* for an answer."

"You're disgusting."

I bend and press my lips to the curve of her neck—kissing softly to contrast the roughness in which I handle her. She stills, taken off-guard by the way my lips move across her skin with gentle kisses. "I don't take *no* for an answer," I repeat, "but I'm more than willing to be reasonable, even to change my mind given the proper persuasion." I run my tongue from the curve of her neck up to her ear and she shivers. "But this blatant disrespect does nothing to persuade me. It only makes me want to push your buttons."

I'm not surprised that she hasn't moved yet. It's been less than a day since she wanted me whole-heartedly…less than a day since she eagerly touched and fucked me. I can still feel the pulse of her lust for me in the vein in her neck. I can feel it against my chest in the way her breaths quicken and her lungs rise and fall.

Her voice is quiet. "I hate you for this."

She says it with such conviction, yet her head inclines, allowing me easier access to tease. I continue to make her feel what she doesn't want to feel, kissing along the curve of her neck and down her jawline.

"What do you hate me for?"

"Everything. I wish I'd never met you." I can hear the way she struggles to breathe.

I loosen my grip on her, moving my hands to her hips as I lean forward to pin her in place with my body. "That's quite unfortunate. I thank my lucky stars every day that I found you."

"Don't say shit like that to me. You don't have the right." She tries to bring anger back to her tone, but it only comes out as sadness and hurt—hurt that my lies have caused her. I don't like the way that feeling strikes me, but things could never have been any different.

I had to lie to her to make her mine.

I lift the back of her blouse to find the zipper on the back of her black-and-white miniskirt. She lets me pull it down. Her fight isn't gone, she's just tired. I know she wouldn't give in this easily.

I allow her to turn to face me as I pull off her skirt, letting it fall in a heap around her feet. I grab the hem of her shirt and tug upward. She hesitates, but then lifts her arms for me to peel the clinging fabric from her body.

I tell her to remove her underwear and bra with a simple flick of my eyes and she obeys. With shaking hands, she bares herself to me, and fuck, I want her. I want inside her. I want to make her come. But the glassy sheen that forms suddenly over her beautiful brown eyes quells my lust. It causes a sinking feeling in my gut that I don't think I've ever felt before…and I don't know if I can stand it.

What is this feeling?

I step back as she lets go, as she starts to cry.

I want to hold her, to make her tears stop…but I'm the one making her cry.

I pull open the shower door and step out, shutting it again between us. "Get rinsed off. Your luggage is in the bedroom. Get dressed. I'll be back in thirty minutes, and I'll let you talk to Cora."

I've coached Stella through a script before dialing Cora's number from a burner cell phone. Stella's phone is already gone. I've shown her the photographs that our surveillance team in New York has taken of Cora just this morning, proving to Stella that Cora will be dead in no time at all if she doesn't stick to the prescribed conversation and convince her that everything is as it should be.

Stella rips the phone from my hand as it starts to ring on speakerphone. It only rings once before Cora answers with an eager tone. "Hello?"

"Cora," Stella says, letting out a sigh of relief. "It's Stella."

"Oh, my God! Thank, God. I was getting so worried about you. You said you'd let me know when you landed. Are you okay?"

"Yes, I'm…I'm fine. I'm okay." She looks at me warily and I raise an eyebrow. "I'm sorry I didn't call earlier." She paces my office as she talks. "I was just so caught up, you know?"

"You were too caught up to send a quick text? What am I gonna do with you, girl? You leave on this guy's private plane to fly across the ocean and then don't text as soon as you land? I was ready to call the FBI!"

"No, no, you don't…you don't need to do that." She adds a fake laugh for good measure, and I nod my approval. "Everything's fine. We're here and just…having a great time."

"Where is *here*, exactly?"

"Ireland."

"Yes, I know that, but where in Ireland?"

She turns to look at me. "Dublin," she lies, exactly as I told her to. "We're in Dublin."

"Oh. Well, whose phone are you calling from? I didn't recognize the number."

She glares at me, fuming as she tells the next lie. "I'm so stupid. My phone must have fallen out of my purse before we left. We've looked through all our luggage and everything…can't find it anywhere."

"You lost your cell phone? Before traveling overseas with a practical stranger? Stell. I can't…" I hear the shift in Cora's tone, her suspicion rising. "Are you okay? Really? Are you safe?"

Stella opens her mouth to speak, and I slowly shake my head at her before she does, reminding her what's at stake. "Yes." She brings lightness to her tone, doing her best to convince Cora. "Girl, I'm great." She glares at me. "Really happy, actually. Murphy has just been full of surprises."

"Good surprises, I hope."

"Of course. Would I settle for anything less?" Her shoulders slump in defeat.

"You'd better not."

I twirl my finger at her, indicating the need to wrap it up.

"Anyway, I have to go, babe. I just wanted to let you know I was okay."

"Okay. Well, be safe, okay? Can I call you on this number?"

She looks at me and I nod. "Yes," Stella tells her. "Just…leave a message or text if I don't answer."

"Okay, babe. Love you."

"Love you, too." Stella ends the call, looking down at the cell phone for a few seconds.

I watch her anger bubble and rise, shooting through her fingertips as she hurls the phone across the room, hitting me in the chest with it—impressive aim. I catch it before it falls and set it on the desk.

"You did well," I praise.

"Is she safe now?"

"For now, yes."

"For *now*?"

"There will still be surveillance on her until I can trust you, Stella."

"That's not fair. That's not *right!* She didn't choose you. She wasn't dumb enough to fall for you and fly across a goddamn ocean with you! In fact, she warned me about you. She knew! You can't punish her like this."

"I'm not punishing her. She'll remain safe so long as you remain compliant."

"I'm not fucking compliant! I never have been! Why the fuck did you choose me for this? If you wanted an obedient wife, that's what you should've chosen!"

"I already have an obedient slave and it bores me."

She pauses. "You *what?*"

"I wasn't supposed to be married until I turn forty. I petitioned the board to marry early because I met a woman who challenged me, a woman with so much fire that I couldn't ignore the flame. I met *you.*"

"You have an *obedient slave?* What do you mean?"

I sigh, leaning back in my executive chair behind my desk. "I told you I'm the O'Shea Head of House. We each own a talent slave. I recently acquired Fiona, a singer, and she's—"

"Fiona. What the actual fuck?" She spins away, her hands covering her mouth as she paces. She drops them again as she spins to face me. "I thought Fiona was your dog. You're telling me Fiona is a woman? You have a *slave?*"

"Bailey is my only dog. Fiona is a talented young woman. I can assure you that she's well cared for."

"Oh, my God. Oh, my *God.* You're a fucking monster."

I push to my feet and march toward her. "I'm not a monster."

She nods furiously. "You are. You're a goddamn *monster.*"

I seethe. I'm trying to be patient but her inability to grasp that I'm not a monster is quickly taking me down. "Don't call me that."

"It's what you are! A *monster.*"

I suck in a sharp breath. "Sit down and shut up."

"I hate you."

"Sit down and stop fucking talking. Do it before I lose my patience with you."

She stands her ground. "I'm not afraid of you."

I reach around to grab the back of her neck and jerk her against me. "Well, you should be."

Her eyes widen as she watches me, waits for me to show her my true colors. If she really wants to see me as a monster, then that's what she'll fucking get. I squeeze her neck, spin her around, and march her forward to my desk.

I bend her over the edge, her palms coming up to brace against it as I fold her harshly over the desktop. She bucks against me as I step in close, leaning over her backside and pinning her with my weight.

"Let me up!" She squirms, her arse shifting against my cock, making me lustful when I'm trying to be serious.

I continue to squeeze the back of her neck, holding her down as my other hand drifts of its own free will. It lands against the back of her thigh, my palm stroking over her tight jeans before grabbing a fistful of her arse.

"The more you fight me, the more I want you."

"Because you're a sick fuck who gets off on hurting people," she spits, her voice dripping with venom.

Her fire heats me, spreading warmth across my stomach, making my cock twitch and my balls tighten. "I only get off on your passion for me, sweetheart." Folded over her backside, I nip at the shell of her ear.

She gasps and stills, her muscles tense and body rigid beneath me. I let go of her arse only long enough to land my hand again with a smack to her soft flesh, then I squeeze with a firm palm. She whimpers, her breaths growing heavy as I let my palm wander toward her crack and slip between her thighs. I shove my hand between them and cup her cunt, digging my fingers in roughly, making certain that she can feel me through her jeans.

She doesn't fight me, she doesn't even squirm. She's still as I dig and stroke and press. She can try to pretend she doesn't want me as much as I want her, but I know the truth. I know the lust in her eyes that I've watched through our laptop screens for months.

"You can't deny the way our bodies respond to each other," I groan, shifting to grind my cock against her arse cheek as my fingers continue to play. "If I fucked you right now, you'd let me, and you'd fucking come, wouldn't you?"

Her voice is quiet. "You'd get off on that, wouldn't you? If you could trick my body into coming for you, even when I'm telling you no…I'm telling you *no*, Murphy."

She's mine.

She belongs to me—body, mind, and soul.

I can do whatever the fuck I want to do with her, and I want to fuck her just like this, bent over my desk, gasping and crying for me. Yet I can't bring myself to reach around and unbutton her jeans. I want her screaming for me because she wants me, not because she wants me to stop.

I release her neck and take a harsh step back. She pops upright and spins to face me, backing away from the desk until she hits the bookshelves lining the wall. Her cheeks are flushed—the way they always look when she's aroused—and her eyes dart a quick glance toward my crotch.

She wants me, I know she does. And as much as that makes me want to take her, right here, right now, I know I can use her desire as leverage to draw her back in and win her trust again.

"Sit down on that fucking chair," I tell her, pointing to the armchair across from my desk. "I need to finish up a few things, and then I'll take you to tour your new home."

Her forehead creases as her eyes narrow in defiance. "I'll stand, thanks."

I cock an eyebrow at her. "Suit yourself." I circle my desk and adjust my fucking hard-on before lowering into my seat. I glance up at her to find her watching me as I open my laptop. "Don't look at me like that unless you want me to fuck you, because I will, Stella."

Her lips part as if she wants to snap back at me and I whip my head to glare at her. She folds under the intensity in my gaze and slowly moves toward the armchair. I smirk as I look at my laptop screen.

She plops down onto the seat, and as I start to type a reply to an email, I light a new flame within her with a single, condescending remark that makes both her and Bailey snap their heads up to look at me.

"Good girl."

I spent the better part of an hour showing Stella around the estate, giving her a tour of her new home. She's been far more resistant than I'd anticipated, but I fault myself for that. I knew how feisty she was from the day I met her. It's what drew me to her. It's what makes her different.

Yet it's also what keeps her fighting me. I have to find a way to be patient with her through her fighting. I've only just uprooted her from her entire existence, and though I don't think it was such a great existence, it was the life she knew. I understand that. I just wonder how long it will take for her to understand how much better her life will be now.

It's a beautiful summer day, perfect weather to show her the beauty of our castle grounds. The front of the estate is stunning with a lovely patch of green garden surrounding an ornate fountain just on the opposite side of the gravel driveway. As beautiful as it is, it's nothing compared to the back.

Our castle sits atop a grassy green hill that slopes downward into a rolling meadow. Gently sloping land of varying angles form the landscape, grassy hills sprinkled with the pink buds of bog-rosemary flowers and periwinkle spring squill dotting the way to the pond beneath the willow tree in the distance.

The breeze picks up at the top of the largest slope where I stand beside Stella. I watch as the warm air blows her hair back over her shoulder, the brightly dyed streak of red peeking out and skating along the breeze. Her arms are tightly folded over her chest, and the black of her painted fingernails peeks out from beneath her biceps.

"You can come outside whenever you want. Explore the grounds as much as you like."

She doesn't look at me. "And what if I try to escape?"

"You can't."

She slowly turns her head to look at me. The initial shock of her situation seems to have worn off a bit, but judgment is still ripe behind her deep brown eyes. It would be a lie to say it didn't affect me.

"I'll find a way to escape you," she says quietly, but with confident determination. "You won't be able to stop me."

"You underestimate my reach, the security measures I've already put in place here." I point far out beyond the sloping hills, down across the meadow that fades into a dense tree line. "You would get lost in those woods. It's dense and it surrounds the land we own. But do you know what's beyond it?"

"What?"

"Nothing."

She scoffs, "The rest of Ireland is beyond it. You don't own this world, Murphy."

"Not alone, I don't. But me and the four families? We own it all."

She rolls her eyes, turning her head to look out at the grounds, away from me.

"You don't believe me?"

"Of course not."

"I'm surprised by that. As aware as you are of how men control you, how much influence men have over your freedom as a woman. All that fight in you against the patriarchal systems that oppress you and rob you of the privileges you should be afforded as a woman. I understand your feminism. If I were a woman, I'd probably feel the same as you. But I'm not. And regardless, the truth remains that men rule the world."

"Bad men. Men like you."

"There is no bad or good. There's only truth. And the truth is that once you are involved with the four families, you can never escape us. We're everywhere, Stella. If you somehow managed to make it through the woods and climb the fence beyond, it would only take moments for me to find your location. It would take minutes for my security team to recover you." I turn my body to face her squarely and step closer. She glances at me over her shoulder before looking off in the distance. "If by some miracle you made it farther than that, it would be no time at all before we found you."

"Why me?"

I reach up and run my finger through the strand of red hair mingling with the black. "Because I wanted you."

"And if we'd never met…If your drunken brother had never stumbled into my tattoo shop, and we'd never crossed paths…"

"Nothing would have changed for you. You'd still be living your old life in New York."

She looks down. "Then I wish I'd never met you. I wish I hadn't texted you. I wish I hadn't called you. I wish I never spoke to you at all."

I swallow her words like a bitter pill.

"I wish I hadn't opened up to you. I wish I hadn't thought you were my friend. I wish I hadn't…" she trails off, then lifts her head to look out again.

"Wish you hadn't what?"

"I was falling for you." She turns her head, scanning my features with her discerning eyes. "I was falling so hard for you. I would've given up my life if you'd asked me to. But you didn't ask…you took. You lied to me about who you really are." Her eyes narrow on me. "Do you understand what you've done?" Her body turns to face me, and I drop my hand from her hair. "You say you want my love. You say you want me to be your wife. The way I was falling for you…you could've had that. You could've left your family and had it all with me."

"You really don't understand. There is no choice for me to leave my family."

"Would you have? If I'd asked you to, would you have done it for me?"

I take in a steadying breath before I truthfully tell her, "No."

She shrugs, then bobs her head in a shallow nod before an unhappy smile spreads across her cheeks. "And that's why you'll never have my love. You may as well sell me as a slave. I'll be worth more to you that way because I promise you, you'll never get a goddamn ounce of love from me." She turns and takes a step toward the house before turning back to face me. "And *when* I escape, I will turn you in. I will take you down. And I will show you and your godforsaken family no mercy."

CHAPTER 18

Stella

I MARCH BACK toward the castle, though I don't want to go back inside. That labyrinth of halls and rooms is my prison. He calls it my home, but I can't fathom how he could ever think it would be. He's trapped me here. I'm trapped with a criminal I thought I was falling in love with.

My heart pounds against my ribs, stress grabbing hold of me and stealing my breath. I stop dead in my tracks in the middle of the lawn, place my hand over my aching heart, willing it to slow and steady as my head bows.

"All right there, Stella?"

My head snaps up at the sound of the unexpected voice. Declan must have just come out from the ostentatious home. He crosses the stone patio just outside the French doors to meet me on the grass. I don't feel the need to run from him—his presence doesn't ripple with threatening energy like some of the O'Sheas, but I'm still wary of all of them.

"Fine. I'm fine. Just coping with being ripped from my life and being held captive in a foreign country, but I'm fine."

The side of his lips twist into a half-smile. "Yeah, I suppose I wouldn't be feeling all right in your shoes." He looks off behind me and my head turns to follow his gaze.

Murphy trudges toward us, Bailey walking along beside him, and my pulse quickens with each of his steps. He stops for a moment when he reaches us and casts me a glance that shows some hint of pain behind his eyes, but I refuse to feel sorry for him.

"Stay," he tells Bailey, pointing in my direction.

Bailey comes to sit beside my feet and then Murphy turns to leave. He stalks past, tugging my heart along after him like a magnet. But then, when he's far enough across the stone patio, his hold on it breaks, and my heart snaps painfully back into place. I exhale heavily as he disappears through the French doors.

Bailey rubs her nose against my fingertips, looking for affection, as I finally start breathing again. I turn my palm, letting her nuzzle her nose against my hand.

"I think it's important for you to know that Murphy is a good man," Declan says. "He was born into his role. He could never have chosen differently for his life."

"I suppose you want me to believe that he would have if he could."

"No, you can believe whatever you want. You'll never understand him completely."

For some reason, I feel offended by that. "I understand him well enough."

"Well enough for what? To decide that you hate him because he never had a choice for who he would grow to become?"

"Everyone has a choice. He has power and privilege. You can't fool me to believe otherwise."

"You're right about that. He has more power and privilege than any man deserves to have. But you need to understand something, Stella. The man you met, the one you talked to on the phone all this time… he's the same man who chose you and brought you here to be his. In his role, he's meant to be *appointed* a suitable bride when he's forty. He petitioned to have a bride of his own *choice* five years before he was ever meant to have one because he wanted you that much."

"And I'm supposed to feel good about that? That he chose to

kidnap me and force me to marry him?"

"If you understood our lives…the O'Sheas, the four families… you'd understand why he chose you. You'd understand how much he needs you. Even if some members of the family disagree."

"If they don't want me here, then why did he bring me? Why would he make me join a family who doesn't want me?"

He sighs. "When Murphy was a child, he put on a mask so that he would look like they do. The mask never came off…not until he met you. Every time he looks at you, I see the mask slip." His eyes shift from side to side—as if he's watching for someone who shouldn't be listening—and he leans forward. "He needs you to rip it off for good and let him blow up the world."

I lean back at the intensity of his words.

Blow up the world?

I don't understand exactly what he means, but his words are too powerful to ignore.

"I don't understand what you're talking about."

His head bobs and his gaze softens. "You only just arrived. There'll be plenty of time for you to see it all for yourself." He pauses and I watch the switch flip behind his eyes, changing him from serious to jovial. "Anyway, have you eaten yet?"

I shake my head. "No."

"Well, come on. Let's go grab something from the kitchen. You could probably use a break from his brooding anyway, yeah? Fancy eating outside? It's a lovely day."

I am hungry and it is beautiful outside. And Declan's energy is far more palatable than Murphy's intensity. I don't want to be scavenging around for food with the threat of running into anyone else I don't know.

"Yeah, fine."

Declan and I cross the lawn and the stone patio and head back inside. He holds the door open for me like a gentleman, though in my current state, I want to scoff at him. I have to remind myself that none of this is Declan's fault. It's not like he kidnapped me—though I suppose he must have known Murphy's intent and did nothing to stop it.

"Did you always know he was planning to take me?" I ask as we turn and walk down the tiled hallway on the first level.

"Yes."

"Did you ever discourage it?"

He runs his hand through his dark hair. He looks more like his mother than Murphy and Cormac do. "I encouraged him to consider what it would do to you, but I never protested his decision. You have to understand something. He's the O'Shea Head of House. The born leader of our family. His say is final, and it can't be argued with."

"That doesn't mean you shouldn't have tried."

He stops and turns to face me, putting his hand on my elbow to halt me. "Stella, I'm sorry. I know it's right shit for your end of this, but I wouldn't have stopped it. You can't understand how much your presence is needed here yet." His eyes shift again as he speaks, nervously combing his fingers through his hair. "But just pretend I never said that," he adds with a grin.

I'm compelled to return his smile, though I'm wary to connect with anyone here. Still, I feel a natural comfort with Declan. "Yeah, maybe your family does need the presence of a strong woman who doesn't put up with bullshit, but that doesn't negate the fact that he kidnapped me."

Declan's head inclines. "Did he though? Really? I hear he asked you to go on a trip with him to visit his family in Ireland, and you said yes. And here you are…in Ireland, meeting his family."

I expect to feel anger bubbling in my chest, but it doesn't boil and burst. Declan's tone is tinged with sarcasm and the small smile playing at his lips hints at humor.

"The key word here is *visit*," I emphasize. "I agreed to *visit* the family. Not be trapped here and forced to marry against my will. I mean, honestly, do you all really expect me to just stay quiet and go along with this? I'm going to escape."

"What are you gonna do?" He starts walking again and I move with him. "Climb the fence?"

"Maybe."

"It would be a waste of your time."

"Maybe not."

He lets out a breath, then nudges me with his elbow. "I think you're a stubborn one."

"You bet your ass I am."

"Classy as hell, too."

I can't help the tiny chuckle that slips out past my lips. I can't stop myself from nudging him back with my elbow. "Don't try to be my friend. It won't work. I won't feel sorry for you when I go to the police."

"I'll be impressed if you make it that far. If you can talk the guards into doing anything other than bringing you right back here to us, I'll die of shock."

"Then prepare to die, Declan." I pause. "Wait…what? Why would the police bring me back here?"

"We have a lot of money. I think that's explanation enough."

"Jesus, fuck. You don't have *that* much money."

"You'd be surprised."

"I'm not letting that stop me."

He holds up his palms. "I'm not trying to stop you. I'm just trying to tell you that it's a waste of time."

"Then it's a good thing I have plenty of time to waste."

Murphy told me it was impossible.

Declan warned me it was a waste of time.

But I wouldn't have been able to forgive myself if I didn't at least *try.*

Murphy brought me back to the bedroom at nightfall, and then he left me to my own devices. He showed me how to lock myself into the room, informing me that only he would be able to get in if it were locked. I suppose that was meant to make me feel safer, but if he could still get in, it was no safe space at all.

He showed me how to lock and unlock the door from the outside if I wanted to leave and return later, and then he left me alone for the night.

He left me alone.

As if he had no fear of me roaming freely around the grounds, no fear of me escaping. I didn't know if that was because his security truly was that thorough or if he was just that arrogant to think I wouldn't try anything.

And I did try, but fuck, Murphy and Declan were both right.

It was an impossible waste of my time.

I'd crept out of the castle, darted down hallways, and dodged shadows until I found the foyer and the main entrance where we'd come in earlier today. I'd run down the stone steps two at a time and followed the gravel driveway, jogging the mile to the securely gated entrance at the end. Massive black metal gates hung secured to stone columns, which were connected to a slightly shorter stone wall that stretched on far into the night in both directions.

Atop the stone columns were security cameras, which I'd only spotted because of the blinking red lights. I'd turned away from them and skirted alongside the tall metal fence that was affixed to the stone wall. I padded across soft grass until the spotlight that shone at the center of the gate faded, until I was completely shrouded in darkness.

I climbed up onto the four-foot-tall stone wall, gripping the black metal bars cemented into it. I attempted to climb it. I actually reached the top of it once, but I hadn't thought through how I would get over the barbed wire. It didn't matter, though. By the second time I scaled to the top without falling, security had arrived. They flashed a light on me before I heard them approach and it spooked me so much that my grip loosened, and I fell.

I did a spectacular job of it, too.

My knee caught the top of the stone wall on the way down, slamming against it and ripping a hole in my jeans, taking some of my skin and blood with it. I'd hit my arm pretty hard as I tried to catch my fall, too—not that any of that would deter me from trying again later.

The security guards who found me walk on either side of me as they march me forward down the hall. We come to a stop at Murphy's office door, but it's already open wide. I see Murphy leap to his feet from behind his desk, quickly striding forward to greet us. His eyes land on mine and worry lightens the gray before giving way to anger. He steps aside. "Bring her in."

The guard tries to grab my elbow but I shake him off, stepping inside Murphy's office on my own. He points to the armchair across from his desk and I move to sit. My knee does actually hurt so I don't feel the urge to be defiant about taking a load off.

"Leave us alone," he says, and I hear the door click shut behind me after the guards leave. Murphy circles around in front of me and I raise my chin to look up at him. "Are you satisfied now?"

"No, I'm not satisfied. Obviously, I failed tonight, but I will try again."

"Try all you want. You'll get the same result." He moves behind his desk, reaching down to pull something out of a drawer—it's a small white box with a familiar red mark that shows it's a first-aid kit.

He arrives in front of me again, towering where he stands, glowering down at me as I look up at him with fierce determination. Perhaps I shouldn't look in his eyes anymore—I'm trying to convey that I won't back down but seeing his otherworldly gray-green stare still kicks up speckles of desire within my core that swirl like a vicious tornado inside me.

I hold my breath as he kneels at my feet. He sets the kit on the side table beside the chair and pops it open. He pulls out a small bottle of rubbing alcohol and some gauze, then pauses to look me over. My skin hums beneath his gaze, awareness prickling where his eyes track.

He reaches up, his fingers grazing my forehead, the gentleness making me flinch as he grips the stem of a leaf and plucks it from my tangled hair. "One thing I like about you, Stella…you never do things halfway."

A compliment…that was unexpected.

"I heard you scaled the fence twice before they found you."

"I almost made it over before that asshole spooked me with his flashlight."

"Really?" He cocks an eyebrow. "You *almost* made it over the barbed wire? Your clothes are in decent shape…Tell me, were you hovering over it?" He quirks a smile and I hate it—I hate it because it makes me want to smile back at him.

"I scaled a ten-foot fence of vertical bars. Please, tell me how much better you would've done." I roll my eyes.

"I wouldn't have bothered to try, but I'm impressed by your effort."

He pours rubbing alcohol on some white gauze as he inspects my knee. I look down at it, too. There's a gaping hole in my jeans that exposes my entire kneecap, and the skin is raw, scraped, and bloody.

"This might sting," he warns before pressing the gauze to my wound to clean it.

I tense at the way it burns, but more so at the way he cares for me. He kidnapped me. He's forcing me to marry him. He's a criminal, a lying asshole, but his touch is gentle as he tends to my wound.

He does care about me, but it doesn't matter.

He's taken my power from me and that's unforgivable…it has to be unforgivable.

"I don't need you to be gentle about it."

His brow furrows as he glances up at me from beneath his lashes.

"Did you want me to pour it on? Fuck, Stella." He shakes his head but continues to diligently clean my wound. When he's satisfied with my knee, he sits back on his heels and looks at me. "Where else are you injured?"

He looks different there on his knees, gazing up at me, asking me to tell him where to fix me. It's not my physical injuries I need him to fix. It's the emotional wounds he's caused that need to be healed, but that will never be possible. I will never heal from what he's done to me, what he's done to *us*.

"Stella, you can tell me where you're injured or I can strip you, inspect you, and figure it out for myself. Which would you prefer?"

Air catches in my lungs as a flash of wanting burns behind my eyes—a bursting vision of the man I thought I knew stripping me bare, looking at me with lust, grazing every inch of my body with his fingers, searching for injuries. My body still craves him. I have to swallow down my desire and force the idea of wanting him to fade away to the back of my mind.

"My wrist," I tell him. "I hit it on the stone wall on the way down."

He rises on his knees, reaching forward, gently wrapping fingers around my arm, just beneath my elbow. His touch is soft as he turns my arm, brushing his fingers over my skin in scrutiny.

"Looks like it's bruising here." He frowns as his fingers run over the back of my wrist. "We should probably get an x-ray to make sure you didn't fracture a bone. I'll have the family physician come in tomorrow morning and look at it for you."

"Why don't you just take me to the hospital tonight? They can give me an x-ray now."

And I can get someone to help me.

He chuckles. "You must think I'm stupid. We have a family physician and an entire health clinic here in the castle. We get a lot of injuries in our business and can't afford to have medical records."

"Wow." My voice drips with sarcasm. "You've just thought of

everything, haven't you?"

"I assure you we have. Our trade has been successful for generations. I don't know why you think you're so special that you'll be the one to get away."

I lean forward. "Because I *am* special, and I *will* get away."

"You're right about one of those things." His gaze lingers on mine, but then he sighs. "Any other injuries?"

"Nope, I'm fine."

"Are you?"

My head inclines. "Would you be fine if you were me?"

"No, I wouldn't be. And I don't expect you to be, not right away."

"What exactly do you expect of me, then? Do you expect me to just accept this? To accept that you've chosen my fate and there is no other choice for me?"

"There never was a choice for you. Not from the moment we met each other."

"If you really felt something for me, Murphy, if everything between us was real, then why didn't you cut me off? Why didn't you man up, cut off contact with me, and let me have my life? If you really loved me, you would've let me go rather than condemn me to live a life I didn't choose for myself…a life as the vilest kind of criminal." I feel a lump rising in my throat.

He pauses, his eyes intently on mine, never wavering. "Because I couldn't stand the thought of living my life without you…and I have no choice but to be what I am. I was born to be the O'Shea Head of House and that's what I am. I wanted one thing, one goddamn thing that was just for me, something that I chose for myself. I chose you because I need you, Stella. But I'm not gonna waste my time trying to convince you of that when all you do is argue with me." He pushes to his feet and holds out his hand for me. "I'll walk you back to bed."

"I'm not sleeping with you."

"You don't fucking have to!" he snaps. "You can have your goddamn space.”

I flinch at the force of his words. Avoiding his outstretched palm, I rise slowly to my feet, side-stepping to move away from him. My eyebrows lift with disdain. “So generous of you. Really.” I turn my back on him and move for the door. “I’m so glad you have such respect for my needs.”

I reach for the knob as I feel his energy shift behind me. The back of my neck tingles. I feel his approach before his large hands land on my waist, gripping me tight. He whirls me around so fast it makes my head spin. He slams my back against the door and air escapes my lungs in a rush. I try to take in a gasping breath, but then his mouth lands on mine and there is no air to breathe—there’s nothing except the passion he feeds me with his thick, sweeping tongue.

I kiss him back.

I don’t want to, I don’t mean to, but my stupid lips crave the bruising ache of his as we share our anger with one another.

He pushes against me, his body holding mine to the door as his hands come up to cup my jaw. My back arches toward him as his tongue dives, as mine slips past his to make room.

It would be so easy to let him in, to let him kiss me, touch me, make me feel his passion.

It would be so easy…

I turn my head to the side with a snap, breaking our kiss and I instantly regret it. “I can’t. Please…don’t.”

He pants, his breath warm against my ear. His nose draws a trail down the side of my neck, inhaling me deeply. “I want you.”

My insides liquify and melt, a slow flow of molten lava warming my belly and dripping to my core.

“Don’t say that…” I’m breathless. “It’s not fair.”

“Let me have you, Stella.”

You could let him. You could. It would be so easy.

He plants kisses into the crook of my neck, nipping and licking, teasing me until I'm sinking against him. I put my hands on his chest, but I don't shove. "Please…"

He groans, his hips thrusting forward, his hardening cock grinding against me.

"Murphy…stop." My voice lacks conviction and my body betrays me, rocking against him, seeking friction.

"Let me taste you. Let me make you come."

"No," I whisper but my hips keep moving. "No…" I can't do this. I want this, but I can't do this. If I do this, I'll never forgive myself. I suck in a harsh breath and spit out my words as I push against his chest. "Murphy, no!"

He steps back. Thank God, he steps back because I don't have the strength to push him away again. His eyes narrow on me in desperation as his tongue runs along his bottom lip.

Fuck.

I want to let him taste me. I want his head between my legs. I want the power of clamping his face between my thighs as I let him devour me and taste me as I come on his tongue.

But I can't. I can't let him have that part of me after what he's done to me.

I shake my head at him as I forcefully swallow down my lust. I press my eyes shut. "No, Murphy. *No.*"

There's a beat of silence that stretches on, and I refuse to open my eyes. I don't dare look at him.

"Fine," he finally says with a quiet voice that's filled with pain. "Then leave me the fuck alone so I can work."

CHAPTER 19

Stella

I'M ONLY WEARING the dress because I'm forced to, but I can't deny the effect it has on me. I turn sideways to see my profile in the full-length mirror, obsessed with the way the dress clings to my curves and accentuates my best parts. The black satin is soft against my skin, hugging my body with a precise fit.

Our engagement party is tonight. Murphy had my measurements taken a week ago, and in his severe kindness as my captor, he allowed me to choose from a selection of gowns. I saw this black dress and chose it without a second glance, only because I want him to know I'm not celebrating our engagement—I'm mourning it.

My make-up is done with dark eyeliner and smoky shadow sweeps across my lids. My hair is curled in soft waves, pinned back on one side so that it all rests over the front of one shoulder. My red lipstick matches the bright streak in my hair.

I'm actually excited about the way I look, but I know my excitement is only present as my mind's way of compensating for the horror of being held captive and required to celebrate my impending forced marriage.

So, thank God for this dress that makes me feel like a queen, because I need to feel something resembling power or control in my hopeless situation.

The black silk gown is open at the back, bare down to the curve of my ass, except for the thin straps which crisscross over my back and hold it in place. The V in the front dips between my breasts, but everything is held firmly in place by the spaghetti straps over my shoulders.

I feel strong in this dress, and it's a relief to feel that way. I've felt powerless since we landed in Ireland earlier last week. Correction, I *have* been powerless since we landed in Ireland.

There's a knock on the bedroom door and I cross the room, tugging it open a crack, and peeking out to see who's there. My view of him is obscured by the half-shut door, but the view I have makes me momentarily speechless, nonetheless.

Murphy stands there, dressed like a star in a black tuxedo, white button-down, and simple black necktie. My eyes scan him, admiring the way he looks, almost forgetting the fact that he's not the man I thought he was, almost forgetting that he's my captor, not just my soon-to-be-husband.

Fucking hell.

My heart still isn't in sync with my mind as it grows wings that flutter inside my chest.

"Are you ready?" he asks.

"Emotionally or physically?"

A tight smile pulls at his lips. "Physically."

"Yes," I reply, lifting an eyebrow, trying to remain impassive.

"And emotionally?"

"No."

"How can I help with that?"

I jerk my head away from the cracked door, taken aback by the question.

Does he really care about helping me or is it just that he wants to get me to his party quicker?

"I don't think you can."

"Tell me what you need to help you through this, and I'll do it for you."

I grip the side of the door, yanking it open wide. "What I need is for you to let me go back to my life."

His eyes pop wide as they scan me quickly. He rubs a hand over his perfectly trimmed beard. The way his eyes flash with heat makes my stomach flip.

"Stella, you look incredible."

I fight the urge to smile at his compliment. "I know I do. I don't need you to tell me that."

"I'm telling you anyway."

He moves toward me, but I don't back away. I hold my ground as he presses into my personal space, edging across the invisible boundary and coming in close. He moves until he's as close as he can be without hugging me, and I'm finding it hard to breathe.

He smells like peppermint candy and the musk of a man. My eyes want to flutter shut and inhale him deeply, but I don't dare. I don't dare let him know the physical effect he still has on me.

It's still so fucking strong.

Moments pass as we stare at each other this way. Each breath draws us nearer, tugs us closer, like we're being lassoed together by a cord of heat. My lips part in hope that words will escape my mouth and break the tension that coils us together, because his heat is too much for me to bear.

My body wants his, my heart wants his, my mind hates what he's done to me, and my soul screams incoherently.

Just as I sway toward him, just as I lose control of myself, he takes a step back. "Shall we?"

I blink. "I guess I have no choice."

His expression is somber. "You chose me."

"I didn't choose this life. I didn't choose to marry you."

"You would have. If I'd proposed before you knew about my life, you'd have said yes."

He's not wrong.

"That may be true, but—"

"That's all I need to know." He smiles, though his eyes remain serious. "I'm still the same man you would've said yes to." He turns sideways and holds out his arm. "Come on. We don't want to keep our guests waiting."

"What if I refuse to go?"

Why am I asking instead of just refusing?

He shrugs. "Then I go alone to my own engagement party." His throat bobs as he swallows.

I feel a wave of unearned guilt wash over me. He deserves to be alone at his engagement party. I didn't have a choice in our engagement. I have to become his wife to spare Cora's life, and I'll do it for her a million times over. He's a monster for doing this, and it's not fair that I should have a guilty conscience over the fate he was born to have. If he really cared about me then he wouldn't have pulled me into his life. Instead, he's forcing me to live the nightmare alongside him.

Yet, as he stands there, arm held out, waiting patiently for me to take it, I can't deny the pull of his aching heart to mine.

I sigh. "Well, that would be pathetic, Murphy." I brush my hands down my front to smooth my dress one last time and step forward to link my arm with his.

I see his smug smile from the corner of my eye and choose to ignore it.

Fuck me and my bleeding heart.

We step out into the hallway, and I nearly jump out of my skin when I catch movement from beside us. Another woman stands there waiting. My eyes take her in with a quick scanning glance. She looks a little younger than me, and she's wearing a gold dress, her straight, strawberry-blonde hair hanging down her back. Her head is bowed slightly, and she only glances up at me from beneath her eyelashes.

Fiona.

The talent slave.

I know it must be her before Murphy confirms it.

"Stella, this is Fiona."

My hand comes up to cover my mouth as the reality of who she is ripples through my gut in a nauseating wave. I hadn't forgotten that he told me about her, I'd simply been so preoccupied with my own sordid fate that her fate had slipped to the back of my mind. This is the first time I'm meeting her.

"Fiona, this is my fiancée, Stella. She and I are equals in your ownership."

I jerk, pulling my arm from his, and take a step back from him. Murphy doesn't react, he continues to direct Fiona.

"You obey her the same way you obey me. Her authority overrides the rest of the family. The only one you obey before her is me. Do you understand?"

"Yes, sir," she mutters.

I take another step back.

I'm shocked into silence. I feel like something just snapped inside me, like something has broken beyond repair.

I feel…I don't have words for what I feel.

"Stella?" Murphy says, and I look at him.

I have no words.

I have no emotions.

I feel protectively numb.

"Stella," he says again, and my eyes follow movement as he holds out his arm, "our guests are waiting."

I clench my fists at my sides, my body moving slowly toward him against my will. I'm so stunned with reality that I think it's broken me. I know I'm moving. I know I'm taking his arm. I know we're walking together down the hallway. I know that I'm walking beside my soon-to-be husband while our slave trails behind us.

Our slave.

Our *slave.*

Our slave.

I need to save her…I need to save myself.

But how? If I manage to escape, will anyone listen to me? Will anyone help me?

I'm only barely aware as we arrive at the party. I only half-register the sounds of appreciative welcome as guests cheer and clap at our arrival. My stomach feels hollow and empty.

"I need a drink," I mutter softly.

"Then let's get you a drink. It's our night, sweetheart, you can have as much as you want."

I lean away from him, though he still holds my arm, turning my head to look at him squarely. "I hope you meant that," my eyes scan him with hateful longing, "because I don't think I can do this sober."

CHAPTER 20

Stella

"TO MURPHY AND Stella!" Cormac toasts.

"Cheers!"

"Here, here!"

I've already thrown back another shot before the throng takes a sip in our honor. I've planted myself on a stool beside the bar on the far side of the room. It's a large living space, a sunken square forming the center, which is filled with comfortable couches and seating. Murphy wanted us down there, in the center, but I refused.

I don't want the attention for marrying into a family of fucking traffickers. Besides, he said I could drink as much as I wanted, and that's exactly what I'm doing. I told the bartender to keep them coming, and he hasn't disappointed me yet.

My ass is perched precariously on the varnished wooden stool. The smooth fabric of my gown keeps slipping, threatening to toss me off the damn thing.

Three toasts in, three shots in.

As Declan stands and begins to speak, I wave my hand at the bartender, who works to pour me another. Murphy stands beside me, holding his tumbler of ice-cold beer. It looks good, but I need the strength of straight vodka in my system to get through this shit.

"Marriage was never something that was on my mind, personally," Declan says. "But I always knew it would be something that Murphy would want. He's always been the caretaker of the family, the big brother who looked out for all of us. He made sure we had love before we had anything else."

I spin sideways on my stool, turning to look up at Murphy. He watches his younger brother with kind eyes and a calm expression. I recognize the expression from months of video chats. It was an expression he didn't show me at first…it came over time. I recognize it as a look of attachment.

He grew attached to me over time, but that's nothing.

Attachment isn't love.

"Murphy doesn't give love easily," Declan says, "but once you've earned it, you'll have more of it than you'll ever need."

Murphy grins, then looks over at me, meeting my eyes. I didn't mean for him to see me looking at him, so I quickly turn away and forcefully swallow down my feelings. I grab the newly filled shot glass in front of me and throw it back in the middle of Declan's toast. The bartender's already pouring me another.

"Stella," my heads snaps as Declan calls out my attention, "I know you didn't come to him in the traditional way. You came five years early and you're not from our world, but I hope you'll give Murphy the chance he deserves. Let him love you the way he does and…" he pauses, his eyes holding mine intently, "maybe you can help him grow to become more than he was meant to be. You can help him become better than his destiny."

"Declan," Boyd warns.

A silent beat passes as Declan gives me a look, hope glinting in his eyes. Then, he raises his glass. "To Murphy and Stella."

The crowd takes another drink and I finally drag my eyes away from Declan, turning to face the bar fully, and taking a fifth shot from the bartender.

Murphy's hand lands on the small of my back as he slips in beside me. He sets his beer on the bar top and leans in close. "Five shots in, hmm? Should we thank our guests before you're too drunk to stand?"

"Are you keeping count?"

"I'm always watching you, sweetheart." He presses a quick kiss to my cheek that makes me swoon while also making me want to vomit in equal measure.

"You haven't finished your drink," I point out. "Maybe you ought to catch up."

"I don't think you want me drunk tonight." His hand slips lower, the tips of his fingers graze my ass, and his gentle touch makes me shiver. "Your arse is begging for me in this dress, and I might not be able to control myself."

Goosebumps ripple down my forearms. I hate the way he makes me feel so desired. My lust for him is at war with my mind, and the tug and pull of it is intoxicating.

Maybe that's just the liquor.

"Come on." He steps back and holds out his palm. "Let's say thank you before your speech is too slurred to understand."

"I don't want to say thank you. I'm not thankful."

"Don't test me tonight." His eyes narrow, his hand remains outstretched for me to take.

"You really want me to speak to your family?"

He huffs, his shoulders shrugging with tension. "I want to thank my family for their offers of congratulations and support. I want my wife to be polite and do the same. This is your fucking life now. I suggest you start it on the right foot with my family."

I lean away, glaring up at him. My inebriated eyes see the opportunity in this. "Okay, fine."

I dramatically slap my palm onto his and swivel on the stool, hopping off it onto my heels. I clench his hand in mine when I sway, a little unbalanced. He pulls me into his side to steady me.

"I've got you," he says.

My heart pounds an extra beat.

I reach behind to pick up shot glass number six, and Murphy grabs his unfinished beer from the bar top. He releases my hand, instead placing his on the small of my back, his fingers splaying wide, his little finger creeping down toward my crack—intentionally—and I find myself a little breathless at his touch.

Goddamnit.

"Family," Murphy projects to get the crowd's attention. "Stella and I just wanted to say a quick thank you. I know we weren't meant to be doing this for another five years, but we meet your support of our unusual engagement with gratitude. I'm not sure Stella quite appreciates just how unusual our engagement is." I look at him and he looks at me. "When I met her, I knew she was someone different, someone special. I tried to fight it at first," his eye contact is unwavering, and his voice is nearly painful with sincerity, "but it was clear early on that no other woman could ever match her in my eyes."

My pulse hums behind my ears, blood pumping frantically through my veins.

He looks back out at the crowd. "Stella is to become one of us. She will soon be an O'Shea, and my gratitude for those of you who've already welcomed her graciously as such cannot be expressed with words alone." He pauses. "Stella, would you like to say something?" His hand slips around to the side of my waist, squeezing lightly.

I feel a little dizzy, but I've been given an opportunity to speak my mind, to say what I've wanted to say to these monsters since I learned about their business and the four families.

"Um," I pause to clear my throat, "I don't know most of you people, and it doesn't really matter. I don't have to know you personally to know what you're all about."

Murphy's fingers tighten around my waist, but not in warning... they're claiming and possessive.

My eyes flutter shut at the way his touch makes me feel, but I quickly pop them back open. "I didn't choose to be here. I didn't choose to be a part of your family. I was taken advantage of because I fell in love with Murphy. I did. But it doesn't change the fact that you're all criminal scumbags who—"

"Murphy! Get your woman under control!" Boyd shouts, causing a murmur of dissent from the party.

I glare at Murphy's father with heat in my gaze. "No man controls me, you wrinkly old piece of shit!"

"How dare you?" Boyd pushes to his feet, as if he's going to come after me.

I have to slap my hand over my mouth to hide the laugh that bursts from my lips without warning. This old man is going to stumble across the room to put me in my place. Behind my drunken eyes, I see the image of a graying man waving his cane at me violently as he shuffles at a snail's pace, and I can't stop the laughter. I double over, hiccupping as I snicker.

Murphy's hand moves from my waist and it lands on my ass softly. "Stella." When he doesn't immediately get my attention, his hand lowers and I feel his thumb subtly trace along my crack. Then, he presses it in between my cheeks, and it startles me.

I jolt upright and look over at him. Humor and annoyance mingle in his expression. I think he's unsure of whether to be angry with me or to laugh with me.

"I think we've all had enough toasting for one night," Murphy says, then raises his drink. "To us."

He stares me down as he takes a sip of his beer. I stare right back as I toss back my sixth shot. Gradually, the volume of the crowd increases, but we're still standing together and staring.

The longer our eyes are locked, the quicker my anger grows. Anger I've held on to from the first day we touched down in Ireland. Anger that's been building and building. Anger that needs an outlet. Anger that brews in my gut and tingles in my core with sexual repression.

I don't know how the two exist together, but they do…rage and lust.

I feel the way my upper lip twitches into a snarling scowl the longer I look at him. He tips back his drink, finishing his beer, his eyes on mine, gulp after gulp after gulp. When he's finished and he brings his glass down, I reach out and smack it from his grip. It falls to the floor with a clang, a chip from the top breaking free and sliding across the floor.

I don't feel satisfied by that. I wanted it to shatter. I wanted it to shatter the way he shattered my life by bringing me here. I throw my shot glass down after it and let out a breath of relief when it smashes and splinters, breaking with a satisfying clang into tiny pieces. I dare him with my eyes to do something about it.

"That was unnecessary," he grits.

"You're unnecessary."

Jesus Christ. I'm stupid drunk.

He looks past me. "Fiona, clean that up, will you?"

My head cocks to the side with a snap. "Leave it alone, Fiona."

"Say another word, Stella. Smash another glass. Show me your defiance one more time. I dare you."

I step impossibly close to him, our bodies kissing as I give him unflinching eye contact. "What are you gonna do, spank me?"

His eyes smolder and I sink, weak at the knees. His arms whip around me, encircle my waist, and cage me against his hard body. He pours his heat into me, his aura throbbing, hitting me with pulse after pulse of electric warmth. It radiates through my belly, spreading deep within my womb, melting my fury into hateful hunger.

His lips graze my ear as he whispers, "Is that what you want from me, sweetheart? Is that why you want me angry? So I'll bend you over and spank you like you deserve?"

I put my hands on his chest, but I don't push, even though I know I should. "I don't deserve your violence."

"But you want it, don't you?"

I shove his chest. "Fuck you."

In one swift motion, he releases me, but one of his hands slips down my arm. His hand clamps around my wrist, then he turns and walks, hauling me along behind him. I'm nearly jogging in my heels to keep up with the wicked pace he sets as he drags me through the murmuring crowd and out of the room. He moves us into the hallway, his fingertips painfully digging into my bruised wrist, which still aches from my escape attempt and fall earlier this week.

"Let go of me!"

He doesn't say a word and we don't go far. He pushes open an unlocked door to an unfamiliar bedroom. He flips on a light switch, yanks me inside, and slams the door shut behind us. I spin to face him when he lets go of me.

"You're such an ass—"

He rushes me, we collide, and he kisses me.

He kisses me hard and fast, and then he stops, dragging himself away, leaving me breathless. I step forward, wanting to taste him again, but he grabs me by the back of my neck, turns me to face away from him, and shoves me forward toward the wall.

"Put your hands on the fucking wall," he growls.

I slap my palms against it to catch myself, to try to shove away from it, but he comes in close, pressing his lips to my neck and breathing against my ear. His voice trembles with the same angry, aching lust that I feel for him.

"You're gonna be good for me. You're gonna be a good girl for me and give me what I want, aren't you?" The rumble of his voice twists a tight knot in my stomach, wringing out tension that drips inside me, begging to be released.

I ache for him.

I'm wet for him.

I'm stupid drunk, and I fucking need him.

I nod.

He draws a line with his nose along the curve of my neck and I shiver. "Keep your hands on the wall and don't move unless I tell you to."

His hands grapple at the backs of my thighs, fingers clawing as he works my tight dress up my legs. The fabric skims across my backside as he shoves it up over my hips.

"Fucking hell," he hisses, his fingernails digging a sharp trail up the back of my thigh, cutting into my bare ass cheek, which is exposed from the thong I put on to avoid panty-lines. "That's fucking beautiful."

He grips my hips with both hands and harshly tugs me backward. "Hands stay on the wall," he reminds me as my back arches.

His hand whistles through the air and lands with a sharp *thwack* against my ass, rocking me forward. Whimpering, I jerk my hips away from the impact. He grabs my hips again, towing them back.

"Hands on the wall," he says before smacking me again.

My lips part and I let out a puff of breath on impact. His touch is biting, heating my flesh, sending a shockwave of pain down the back of my thigh.

"Murphy…"

He hits me again and my back arches more, seeking the roughness of his touch, because at least it's honest.

"Tell me to stop," he says.

I can't.

I can't tell him to stop because his touch is twisting something within me. It's drawing out my rage, it's boiling, it's filling me to bursting with explosive energy to lash out at him the way I need to.

I want him to hit me.

I want him to make me furious.

I want him to give me a reason to fight so I don't crumble to my knees and beg for his cock.

"Harder," I demand, deepening the curve of my back as I push my ass out for him. "Fucking do it harder, Murphy."

He pulls his hand back and smacks me powerfully, rocking me toward the wall as I scream out from the bruising impact. Before he can hit me again, I spin, slap his cheek, shove his chest, and throw punches. I attack him off-guard, and he stumbles backward, falling flat on his ass on the carpet as I push and shove.

I drop to my knees over his lap, straddling his hips as I reach back and slap him across his cheek again. His hands shoot up and his fingers wrap around both of my wrists, wrenching my arms between our bodies.

He pulls me to lay on top of him. I try to get my feet beneath me so I can yank my arms from his grasp, but he's quick, flipping us both. I land hard on my back, and it knocks the wind out of me as he crushes me, laying heavily on our hands between us.

I fight and struggle to get my hands free, but he surprises me, releasing them both without warning. I thrash, trying to get myself out from under him, but he sits across my stomach, pinning me beneath him in such a way that I can't even kick my feet. His fingers work at his black necktie, loosening the knot and tugging it free from his collar with a sharp yank.

I try to sit up, but he slams down on top of me. His chest lays heavily on mine as he wrangles my arms up above my head. I can feel him grow hard in our struggle, his thick erection pressing against my belly.

He wraps his tie around my wrists, knotting and tugging, tying them tight as I register the look of longing in his eyes—a look that forces me to pause and take in a steadying breath.

It's a look I only recognize because I've seen it so many times before through a screen.

It's desperation.

It's struggle.

It's the ache of wanting something you can't have.

He'd look at me like that when he told me how much he missed me, how much he wished he could touch me, hold me, fuck me.

I don't even realize that my body has stopped fighting until I feel the drag of his fingertips down my arms. His palms rub over my chest, skating over the mounds of my breasts. I gasp at the contrast of sensation, the jarring transition we've made from fighting to gentle caresses.

His hands travel up again. One slips up my throat, grabs me hard, and tilts up my chin. The other glides over one of my arms stretched above my head, which is tied to the other. He grips both of my bound wrists in his large palm, grinding them down into the carpet.

My back arches beneath him, my breasts heavy, aching for him to touch me again, but my anger hasn't quite let go of me yet. We pant as we watch each other with careful, hungry eyes.

I can't tell him that I want it, that I want him inside me.

I can't say those words and admit defeat.

But fuck, I need it…I need him. Though my words remain sheathed behind my gritted teeth, my body encourages his rough touch. I lift my hips, rocking them from the floor, seeking friction against him.

He groans, his palm clutching my bound wrists, his fingers pinching the sides of my throat, making me gasp for him. He knows that I like this, this rough and reckless kind of sexuality. He knows what turns me on, what makes me come. He knows it all because I bared my soul to him. He can use it against me. He may be using it against me now, but hell…it's working.

It's fucking working.

I let my tongue run over my lips, tempting him, begging him with every physical signal my body will allow me to give, because I can't ask him to fuck me.

I see the shift in his eyes from lightness to smoky gray as they dart across my face, lower to watch the heavy rise and fall of my chest, and finally land on my lips.

He dips his head and our mouths collide, his tongue darting inside me and filling me up. Raw, sexual hunger slips from his tongue and it feeds me, fuels me, rips a moan from deep within me.

He lifts his right leg and moves it in between mine, sliding his knee up against my pussy. I whimper in gratitude for something to move against, and my hips wriggle, rubbing my clit against his knee.

He groans and presses harder, his knee unrelentingly driving against me as he deepens our kiss impossibly more. He's heavy on top of me. I'm completely at his mercy, so lost to anger and drunken lust that I feel like I could lose my mind if he doesn't make me come.

There's no sound around us except for our moaning and panting, our smacking lips that kiss and suck and fuel that linking desire between us.

How can I still desire this monster?

He pulls back with a snap that leaves me breathless and sits back on his heels. He grabs my thong and tears it down my legs. He lets me slip my pinned leg out from between his knees so he can remove them, and though I should probably take advantage of that to kick him and run from the room, I don't…

I can't…

I don't want to run from him.

I don't want to run from this.

That's the most painful thing to acknowledge.

I still want him, though he's vile.

Instead of shoving my stiletto into his gut, I spread my legs for him and invite him to take the last bit of dignity I have left. His hands work his buckle as I bring my tied hands down, shove them between my legs, and stroke my clit with my middle finger.

"I fucking hate you," I tell him, trying to convince myself.

"I know you think you do."

"You took this from us. It should've been like this between us… desperate fucking on a goddamn vacation."

He pulls his belt free from the loops, grips it in one hand, and slams his fist on the floor beside my shoulder. He bends over me, his other hand slapping over my mouth, and pushing down hard. "It can still be like this, sweetheart. All you have to do is let yourself enjoy it."

I try to bite his hand, but my teeth can't clamp down—they only graze his skin. I lick his palm instead. His eyes flash with hazy gray heat. He shifts his hand so he can shove two of his fingers past my lips, pressing them in deep. I gasp at the intrusion and my stomach clenches, my fingers moving faster over my clit as wetness pools.

I hate that this is hot as hell.

I fucking hate it.

I hate him.

"Suck," he commands.

I stare at him unwaveringly as I bite his fingers.

He hisses but doesn't pull them out. He pushes them deeper and triggers my gag reflex. My body lurches and I swallow hard as he draws them back an inch. He drops his head, rubbing his nose against my cheek.

"Suck them, sweetheart."

I moan, need throbbing beneath my circling fingers.

I hollow out my cheeks to suck on his goddamn fingers because I want to...

I fucking want to.

He groans, his body shifting and rubbing against my hip and leg as we watch each other. "That's my good girl."

I turn my head forcefully, spitting out his fingers. "I'm not your good girl."

"Yes, you are."

"Fuck you," I pant.

He sits back on his heels again, lifting the belt in his hand and folding it in half. I hope he hits me. I hope he hurts me. I hope he gives me a reason to hold on to this hate.

But this hate is passion, and that passion is what's dangerous between us.

He shoves my hands away from between my legs, then turns his belt and thwacks it hard against my pussy. My body tenses as a sharp pain shoots through my swelling clit, rippling through my core.

"Shit!"

He pulls it back and hits me again.

My insides twist, rolling desire and pain together, wringing out a need to come like I've never felt before.

I can hate him and fuck him.

I can fuck him and it doesn't have to mean that anything has changed.

Memories of touching myself for him during our video chats flood my mind, all the desires and filthy fantasies we shared with each other. I told him dirty things I wanted to do with him that I've never done with anyone…things I've never even told another man I wanted.

My mind wants to wash me in shame that I ever opened up to him that way—it wants to shut me down, but my body won't allow it. When I look into his eyes, I still see him. I still see the man I fell for, the one I talked to every night on the phone for nearly seven months, the one who knows me better than anyone else ever could.

I can let him have this win.

But I won't let him have the next.

"Fuck me," I breathe the words. "Choke me and fuck me like you promised you would."

His lips part as his breath catches in his throat. He scrubs a hand over his beard, a move so signature of the Murphy O'Shea I thought I knew that it makes me whimper.

He drops the belt beside my hip, shoves down his pants and boxer briefs to free his hard cock, and moves between my spread legs. I pull back my knees to rest against his hips as he angles his tip, and I lift my arms above my head, letting them rest on the carpet. I shudder watching his expression drift from pure passion to relief.

He's not even inside me yet and he feels relief.

Because he wants me…he needs me to want him.

"Oh." Air rushes from my lungs as he presses into me, slowly but steadily burying his cock deep inside me. "Fuck."

We both moan and pant as he holds steady, as I adjust to his girth and the depth in which he penetrates my fucking soul. He moves one hand up the side of my waist, drifting upward, rubbing over my breast, and teasing my hard nipple. Then he clamps it around my throat.

Gradually, he pinches the sides of my neck, restricting my air flow. My lips part as I gasp, as the high of breathlessness forces a smile and makes my eyes flutter shut. I feel him move, slowly dragging his cock out before driving it back inside.

He loosens his grip and I pant to catch my breath, my entire body whispering its need across my skin.

His forehead falls to mine, our eyes locking with lust. "Again?"

I nod. "Again. Do it longer."

He squeezes my throat and thrusts, pounding me with a slow, hard, steady rhythm. He squeezes until I can't pant, can't gasp, can't tell him to stop.

I don't want him to stop.

He releases.

I gasp.

He fucks me.

He squeezes.

Over and over, he grips my throat and fucks me until my hips are rising desperately from the ground, my back is arching, and I'm using the only breath I have between chokings to beg him to make me come.

"Make me come," I beg. "Make me come, make me come."

He lets go of me, rears back, grasps my hips in his large hands, and flips me over onto my stomach. He grips my waist and tugs, making me lift my ass from the floor and present it to him. He rubs his erection over my pussy, gathering wetness before he drags it back along my folds, teasing over my sensitive flesh. Then he reaches the puckered hole at the back.

"Oh, my God," I moan as he pulls his cock away, replacing it with his thumb to rub my wetness all around the spot.

All at once, he thrusts his hardness into my pussy and nudges his thumb inside my back hole. It feels so fucking good, that I scream.

"Good girl. That's a good fucking girl." His voice trembles as he fucks me, slipping his thumb deeper inside me. His fingers are splayed over my cheek, nails digging in to hold me.

It hurts and it feels so fucking good.

We were like this in every fantasy I had of being with him—rough, needy, hopelessly and recklessly passionate.

I'm filled so spectacularly that my climax builds quickly, tingling through my sensitive flesh with a persistent throb that demands my tension against it. I press up onto my elbows, arch my back, and push back against Murphy, meeting him thrust for thrust, taking him with me as we chase a release from the tension that's been building between us.

His thumb sinks deeper, and the overwhelming fullness spurs my release. My pussy pulses as I come hard, clenching around his cock, my whole body stiffening with tension as pleasure explodes in my core and ripples over every inch of me. Just when I think my climax is about to drop, I feel him spill inside me and the warmth of his cum drives me higher, sending one last tsunami of pleasure straight up my spine.

I collapse when it lets me go, and he meets me on the ground. Spinning us sideways with his cock still buried deep, he brings us both down to lay on our hips as he curls around me from behind.

I gasp for air, my lungs begging for it, but I can't catch a good breath. Each inhale catches in my throat, the air building pressure within me that drives tears to burn behind my eyes. I break into sobs. He wraps his arms around me tight and I'm sobbing on the floor.

I'm sobbing because of him, and he tries to comfort me.

He tries to comfort me against the pain he caused me.

He caused me this pain.

I jerk away from his hold, roll over to face him, and slam my fists against his chest. "Untie me. Untie me!" I scream at him.

His eyes hold mine with a calm expression, but it doesn't quell my swelling anger. He unties the knots that bind my wrists together and I shove away from him, stumbling to my feet, swaying, and almost toppling over from the post-orgasm light-headedness and my intoxication. I tug at my gown, shimmying the dress back down over my hips. One of the straps across the back is torn and dangling, and it tickles my bare skin as I move.

"How long are you going to hold on to anger over a future we never could have had?"

I whirl around and point my index finger at him. "You *told* me we could have it."

"No, I didn't. In fact, I distinctly remember telling you that there was a chance we could never be more than what we were. And I remember you wanting more, so I gave you more. I made it happen. I made a future for us where there was none."

I chuckle through my tears. "This? This is no future. You're a criminal, and the most disgusting kind. I could never love you."

I swallow as if my body wants to take the words back and bury them deep inside me.

He buckles his pants and bends to grab his belt from the floor. "Love me or don't, Stella. You'll be my wife either way." He shoves past me, heading for the door. I spin to watch him as he pulls it open. "I'm sleeping in my own damn bed tonight. If you don't want to sleep with me, then I suggest you find another unlocked room you feel safe in. I'm done granting you kindness when I get none in return."

I'm still and silent as he steps from the room and marches off down the hallway.

CHAPTER 21

Murphy

I STOMP DOWN the hall, leaving Stella alone to brood and sulk and sob over her circumstances. She'd let me fuck her. Her body practically begged me to make her come, and then she cried and yelled at me, giving me mental whiplash and a screaming headache.

Fuck.

I'm so angry with her I could punch a goddamn hole in the wall. The fact that she'd let me fuck her when she was still so goddamn angry with me was a tease. I thought we were coming to some sort of understanding, letting the growing tension between us release so explosively, but clearly, I was wrong.

She cried.

I took advantage of her.

I rub my temple as I march past the party. I have no desire to return to it alone, and I'm starting to feel like shit from the alcohol and excessive movement. The movement, the touching, the aggressive fucking…

My skin still burns from the heat of her passion.

I don't know if I'll ever understand how one woman can make me so angry and so hard all at once. She and I are fire meeting fire, and the way I come for her would be ill-defined as explosive—there isn't a word strong enough to describe it.

I make my way upstairs to our bedroom—where I've graciously

allowed her to sleep alone as she adjusts—and head inside. I consider taking a quick shower, but this night has me drained. I remove my clothes, strip naked, and turn off the lights before climbing into bed.

I huff out an agitated breath to rid myself of the fire inside my belly, but it's no use. I'm knackered, but I'm wired. I lay on my back and put my hands behind my head, staring up at the dark ceiling and hoping sleep will come soon. The last thing I want is to lie awake all night wondering whether Stella will join me in bed or find another room.

A wave of nausea rolls through my gut, and it's not the alcohol. I'd be insulted if she chose to sleep in any one of our guest bedrooms. She's been locking herself in here at night, so if she chose to sleep in an unlocked, unsecured bedroom, it would be a slap in the face. It would tell me she'd rather sleep without security than sleep with me—and that would fucking gut me.

My nights have been hell since I brought her home because I've had to sleep without her. It's not exactly how I pictured our life together starting, though I knew this would be a process for her. What she doesn't realize is that it's a process for me, too—a process I feel excluded from.

I stare at the ceiling until my eyelids start to feel heavy, until they begin to droop over my eyes. My body begins to release some of the stress it holds in favor of finding a good night's sleep in my own bed. I couldn't say if minutes or hours have passed.

Just as my eyes flutter shut, just as sleep creeps in to take me away, I hear her at the door, and it jolts me back to awareness. I look toward the door as I hear the failure beep on the locking mechanism, indicating she's entered the pin incorrectly on the keypad. Part of me is pissed at her enough to let her keep failing, but some gentler part of me forces my muscles to twitch, aching to run for the door and help her.

Before I can decide, it beeps its acceptance and the door clicks open. I see her outline in the dark room and I don't make a sound as she stumbles inside. My heart flutters that she's here. She came. She made the choice to sleep here, knowing that I'd be here, too.

Maybe we are making some progress, even if she'd be loath to admit it.

I watch her outline as she disappears into the bathroom, flipping on the light. A minute or two later, she lets out an agitated breath. "Where the fuck are my glasses? Fuck it." The light goes out and her shadowed form returns to the bedroom.

I wonder how bad her vision is without her contacts in. It doesn't matter, she'll find her glasses in the morning where I saw them when I came in, sitting on the bedside table. She only ever wears them at night, anyway.

She rounds the bed, and I feel the mattress jostle as she plops down awkwardly. The sliver of moonlight peeking in through the window casts an angled glow across her midsection.

I turn my head and watch as she bends, probably removing her shoes. Then she stands before bending again, and when she straightens, she slips her gown up her body, slowly revealing the shape of her perfect arse in the moon's glow as she pulls it off over her head.

Quickly, she grabs the covers and slips into bed, the mattress shifting with her weight. It sends a rush of desire through my veins to feel her here with me in my bed. I've dreamed about having her here for so goddamn long.

My fingers itch to touch her.

My arms beg to wrap around her.

My legs tense to tangle with hers.

My mind longs for the peace of falling asleep in her embrace.

I roll onto my side to face her, and she snaps at me, "Don't fucking touch me. Stay on your side and leave me alone."

"Please make this clear for me, Stella." I keep my voice low and steady. "I can fuck you like an animal and make you come, but I can't hold you to sleep in our bed?"

"It's not our bed."

I scoot a little closer toward her back, which she has turned to me. "Then who's bed is it? Is it your bed? Or is it mine? It seems to me that we're both in it now."

"It's *your* bed. I just don't want to sleep alone in a room with an unlocked door with your vile family around."

"I suppose that's fair. But then that must mean I'm the person you feel safest with since you're willing to fall asleep beside me."

"Shut your mouth and go to sleep. I don't want to talk."

I reach forward and trail the backs of my fingers down the side of her arm. She jumps at my touch, and I feel goosebumps forming along her cool skin. "You're cold."

"Yeah, it's fucking cold in this room at night."

All at once, I move against her, molding my front to her back, as I throw my arm around her to lock her into my hold. "That's why you want me here."

"I don't want you here." She bucks her arse against me while pushing at my arm, trying to throw me off. "I don't want to sleep with you."

I grip her tighter. "We could always fuck again if you don't want to sleep."

She struggles against me, somehow managing to flip around and face me. She swats me with her hand, hitting my arm, her palms shoving my chest.

"Let go."

"Calm down. I just want to keep you warm."

She fights. "I want to be cold."

"Bullshit." She kicks at my legs, and I'm stunned when her foot touches me, freezing cold skin shocking mine. "Your feet are freezing."

"I like them that way."

"Liar."

She shoves and kicks and fights as I wrestle her arms between us and lock my leg over hers. I could give this up and let her go, but the fight in her just takes hold of me. She's stubborn. She's fucking freezing, and I just want to keep her warm…but she just won't let go.

Maybe she'll let go if I surprise her.

I take her off-guard in her struggle by planting a soft kiss to her forehead, and thankfully, the shock of it makes her stop.

"Don't," she whispers, and pain fills her soft voice, carrying through the darkness of the room. "Don't be sweet."

"I can be much sweeter than you give me credit for."

"You're not sweet; you're not kind. You kidnapped me."

I pull her tighter against me, wrapping my arms fully around her body to hug her close. Miraculously, she lets me, but she's tense in my hold. Her stillness begs my body, like a silent challenge to push her just a little more, to see if I can take just a little more from her.

I always want to take from her, but I want to give back even more… she just won't let me.

My hips slide forward, and she gasps when she feels my cock touch her leg. I'm not even hard after that fucking explosive orgasm with her, I just need to touch her. My body wants every inch of hers.

I kiss her forehead again, softly, gently. I kiss again, then again, my lips naturally finding a gentle rhythm to press kisses to her face, drawing a line down the side of her cheek, all the way to the corner of her lips.

She lets out a long, slow breath. "I'm so fucking tired."

"Go to sleep." I release my vice-like grip on her to pull my arm back and I brush my hand down the side of her head, tucking her hair behind her ear.

"Stop it. I don't want you to take care of me."

"I'm going to take care of you."

"I hate you."

"You keep singing that song." I continue to stroke her hair and she continues to relax in my grip.

"I just want to go home."

"You *are* home."

"You keep singing that song," she repeats me.

I chuckle.

An oddly comfortable silence falls and I'm happy to let it swirl around us. Stella's breathing gradually slows and deepens as I stroke her hair, and before long, she's fallen asleep…in my arms.

I swallow, feeling strangely sentimental and deeply unworthy. Odd thoughts that I don't deserve to hold her in her peaceful slumber scramble through my brain, building a deep sense of shame in my gut.

No.

I deserve her. I deserve to have her here, in my bed. I did the work to make our future possible and she's *mine*.

I draw her closer and match my breaths to hers until the guilt subsides and I drift into a peaceful sleep.

CHAPTER 22

Stella

"CALL ME OLD-FASHIONED," Cordelia says to Tally, as if I'm not standing right in front of her. "But if I were Stella, I would've chosen a wedding dress that wasn't so blindingly white."

My fists clench in preparation to punch her freckled face every time she opens her damn mouth.

It's been nearly six weeks since our engagement party and I'm getting married today.

It's my wedding day.

I'm marrying a criminal trafficker against my will.

Cordelia's smart mouth isn't doing anything to comfort me as I prepare to meet my fate. She puts a cold hand on my shoulder.

"You know, it has nothing to do with your darker shade of skin, Stella. The white looks lovely with your olive complexion. It's just that I've always subscribed to the belief that you should only wear white to your wedding if you're a virgin."

My jaw clenches and I cock an eyebrow as I speak through gritted teeth. "And what makes you think I'm not a virgin?"

She laughs. "Murphy may have bad taste, but at least he picked a girl with humor."

My knuckles ache to collide with her cheek, to make sure she doesn't say another word to me the rest of the day.

Tally giggles along with her as she throws back the rest of her mimosa in a single gulp. "Delia, you're such a bitch. Leave her alone."

"What?" She tosses her straight orange hair over her shoulder, walking away from me. "I said she had humor."

I turn my head to look back at the bitch over my shoulder. "What did you wear on your wedding day, Delia? I'm certain the groom wore black in mourning."

Tally tosses her head back and laughs as I face forward again, regarding myself in the oversized mirror from where I stand on a round, raised platform.

"I've never been married," Cordelia replies.

"I'm not surprised."

I press my eyes shut and try to forget Cordelia's existence. I breathe deeply to center myself as I try to ignore Tally's obnoxious cackling in the background. I try to imagine myself happy, preparing to walk down the aisle to the version of Murphy I'd fallen for before I found out the truth about him.

I can picture it for a moment, and it nearly brings a smile to my face. But then the vision of him standing in a tux at the end of the aisle becomes tainted with the faces of nameless women filling the rows of seats. They watch me travel down the aisle, and though I don't recognize them, I know who they are. They're the women—the *slaves*—he's trafficked and sold.

The vision makes me gasp and I shake my head to come out of it, brushing my hands over my soft skirt. The dress gives me some comfort in a strange way. Murphy asked me about my preferences for colors and cake and food, but I refused to help plan our wedding. The only thing I selected myself was the dress, and I'm glad I did. Wearing it now gives me the false sense that I still have some control, some ability to decide.

My fingers curl around a swatch of the tulle ball gown, holding it for comfort as a child would their blanket. The hems of the various layers are cut at an angle, rippling down in soft, flowing waves.

The top is a separate piece—a crystal-beaded, long-sleeve crop top that meets the top of the ball gown at the smallest part of my waist. The hand beading covers the entire top, across the bodice, over the shoulders, and down the organza sleeves.

It sparkles when it catches the light, making me feel like sunshine in its glow. The back is cut low in a deep V, and the front sweeps across my chest as a boatneck, the combination of white organza and beading allowing skin to show beneath.

Bridget suddenly appears and puts her hand on my shoulder, making me jump. I didn't even notice the reflection of her approach in the mirror, but there she is, beside me, holding out a champagne flute.

"To calm your nerves?"

I glance at the drink and nod, taking it from her and tossing it back.

She lowers her voice to a whisper. "Just try to ignore them. That's what I do," she says with a friendly smile.

"They're awfully loud."

"Volume doesn't equal power, my love."

"Someone should tell them that."

"That would only make them louder. You, love…you'll keep your voice quiet."

"Excuse me?"

"The less you speak, the more power your words have when you finally do. Be careful not to go the way of the other women in the four families. You're not like them, and I'd be very sad to see you change."

I'm taken aback. Her tone seems sincere. The smile and tender touch as she squeezes my palm makes me miss my mom. I wish she were alive so she could be here for me on my wedding day. Equally, I'm glad she's not, because then I'd have to lie to her about Murphy. She'd be so ashamed of me and what I've become.

My eyes burn and I try to sniff back my tears as there's a knock on the door. Fiona—poor, sweet Fiona—goes to answer it.

The less you speak, the more power your words have when you finally do.

I don't know if Bridget's right about that. For me, being quiet means complacency. I've always raised my voice to shout above those of obnoxious men who think their words have more power. But perhaps I'm wrong. Murphy has tried to give me a voice. He wants me involved; he wants me to be his partner. If he's willing to grant me the power of being his wife, then maybe I should accept it and find the best way to wield it.

Accepting this life means being complacent in their horrific trade, but maybe temporary complacency is necessary to grow my power and do some real damage to their so-called business.

I steel myself with the rising tide of strength that straightens my spine. I pull back my shoulders and lift my chin.

"Stella," Declan comes into the room. "You look stunning. You might give Murphy a heart attack."

"Would serve him right."

He crosses to me and holds out his hand. I take it so he can help me step down from the podium. He looks handsome in his black tux. His dark hair—like his mother's—is smoothed and styled with precision.

"You look nice," I tell him.

"I could've looked better, but I didn't want to upstage the bride." He grins, which makes me grin, too. "I have a surprise for you. Actually, I should say Murphy has planned a surprise for you. I made the arrangements, but it was his idea. He wanted to come tell you himself, but I reminded him that it's bad luck for the groom to see the bride before the wedding."

My eyes narrow. "What surprise?"

"Before I show you, I need to be perfectly clear about how this has to go. You're a very lucky, very happy bride marrying her beloved Murphy O'Shea…by choice, not by force. You know nothing of the four families. If anyone asks, the O'Shea family are wealthy barley farmers."

"Barley farmers?"

"It's important that you don't slip up, Stella." He grabs both my hands and leans forward, granting me unflinching eye contact. "Their lives are still very much at stake if you fuck up and tell them you need saving. If either of them think you're in trouble, they won't leave Ireland alive, do you understand?"

My eyes widen as awareness strikes. "Cora and Josh? They're here?"

Declan nods and smiles. "Now tell me you understand so they can come in."

I nod. "Yes, *yes,* I understand." My heart pounds double time with the knowledge that my best friends are here… and for the fact that their lives are in danger if I can't convince them that this is a happy affair for me.

Declan heads back to the door and opens it wide. A familiar flash of cerulean hair makes my heartache fade away for one brilliant moment.

"Cora!"

Her shoulders relax as she spots me and the widest grin I've ever seen spreads across her cheeks as we rush for each other. I throw my arms around her and hug her hard as Josh appears behind her.

"Oh, my God, you look so beautiful!" She half-sobs into my neck. "I'm sorry I'm crying on you. I don't want to ruin your dress."

"Ruin my dress, you're already making my eyeliner run."

I don't know how long I hold her, but I don't want to let go. When I finally do, I run my knuckles under my eyes, hoping my tears didn't make too much of a mess, before giving Josh a hug, too.

"I'm so sorry I left the way I did, Cora, I feel awful—"

"No, don't. Not today. We can talk about it some other time." She lets out a heavy breath. "You're happy, you're alive, you're safe, and that's all I care about."

I work through a stuttering breath, forcing myself to focus on her in front of me so my smile doesn't fade. "I can't believe you're here."

"Me, too. Honestly, I was surprised when Murphy called and asked us to come. I know things were rough between us when you left. And I was *so* rude to you when you called and told me you were engaged and you weren't coming back. I mean, okay, it was pretty rude of you to leave me behind with your shop like that."

We both laugh. "I know. I'm so sorry."

"It's okay. It's good, actually. It's going really well. We had to hire another artist. She's not as good as you are, but who the fuck could be?"

"I've missed you. I really, really missed you."

"I've missed you, too. Stella, I just…Are you happy? I just wanna know that you're happy."

I feel my face twist as I fight back the swell of tears that threaten to spill. I nod, pinch my eyes shut, and open them again with a smile. "I'm happy, Cora. You don't need to worry about me."

My chest aches, but she looks relieved, her shoulders slumping as she releases tension with a long exhale. "Good. That's all I care about."

"One more surprise," Declan says, approaching with a garment bag. "The maid of honor needs her gown."

"You're gonna be my maid of honor?"

"Of course, I am. I've got you, boo."

"I really need you today. This…" I pause, choosing my words carefully. "It's not an easy family to marry into."

I glance at Declan, and he shrugs, recognizing that my statement is true but not telling. "No lie there," he agrees. He nods in the direction of Cordelia and Tally across the room who stare and whisper. "Bunch of bitches over there trying to play bridesmaid to a queen."

Cora grabs the garment bag from him. "No worries, queen. I'll make sure you get down the aisle to your king without anyone stepping on your toes."

I sigh. "I'll need all the help I can get."

Breathe…just breathe.

My hands are shaking.

My stomach is twisted in knots.

I stand just behind the French doors leading out to the gardens at the back of the castle. They're covered with fabric to conceal me from the guests seated outside…from my husband, who is waiting for me at the altar.

One breath at a time.

Cora stands beside me, our arms linked. I asked her to walk me down the aisle because there was no one else I would've wanted by my side.

"I might throw up," I tell her as the last of my appointed bridesmaids makes her way up the aisle on the other side of the doors.

"You've got this. You're amazing, you're fucking gorgeous, and you're about to marry the man of your dreams. Just forget about the rest. The other people out there? They don't matter. Eyes on the prize, babe."

I flash a tight grin. "Eyes on the prize."

The prize…my captor, my husband.

He's going to be my husband.

"Cora, I—"

Two servants pull the doors open wide as the pianist outside plays Pachelbel's Canon in D Major.

I look at Cora and the sudden urge to tell her everything and ask her to help me escape washes over me. And then she smiles at me, reaches over to squeeze my hand, and I remember…I can't. I can't risk her life. I can never tell her the truth.

I smile at her as she tugs on my arm, encouraging me forward. We step down onto the stone tiles that create the patio overlooking the green hill. I can see the pink and purple flowers dotting the green in the distance, giving the illusion that this place is happy, that this place is bright.

But the illusion only draws out my anxiety. My pulse races as I force myself to look at him, and when I do, his eyes are waiting for me to find him.

Murphy smiles at me from the end of the aisle. There's a beat—a single beat—where the music seems to pause, where the world seems to fade, and I just see him. I see Murphy—the one I longed to see for long, lonely months.

The man I fell in love with.

And then it all comes rushing in—the music, the people, the lies, the rotten fucking truth.

I stop halfway down the aisle, unable to move forward, tugging Cora to a stop with me.

"Almost there, babe," she whispers.

But I can't take another step.

I can't catch my breath.

I can't *breathe*.

My chest hurts.

My fingers tingle and an anxious numbness ripples through my limbs. My grip around the bouquet loosens, and it tumbles from my fingers, falling in slow motion to the ground. I watch it land, and it's as though all other sounds have been muted, except for the crushing, imagined thud of my flowers hitting stone. I place my hand over my thudding heart, swallowing the rising bile in my throat.

"You okay?" Cora asks, but her voice sounds faded.

I bend my knees, crouching toward the ground so I don't fall over. A gentle breeze rustles my gown and sweeps the murmurs of the concerned crowd around me, encircling me, caging me in. Cora crouches beside me, one hand on my back as she leans in close.

"Stella, are you okay, babe? What do you need?"

"I need…" I gasp. "I need…"

"Murphy," I hear her say.

I try to protest, "I don't—"

But he's there before I can say more, crouching in front of me as

Cora stands and steps back, letting him take care of me. Two gentle fingers touch beneath my chin.

My whole body trembles as I lift my head slowly. "I can't."

Transcendent gray-green eyes meet mine, and there's a softness in them I haven't seen since the first time Murphy visited me after two months of phone calls…and we made love.

"It's me, sweetheart," he whispers. "It's still me. I'm still here. I never left you."

I stare at him, searching his eyes, knowing that his words are true. He's telling me that the Murphy I knew is still there, that he didn't leave me when the disgusting truth was revealed.

"Eyes on me," he says. "See me, Stella."

I nod slowly, trying to grab hold of something, anything that can steady me. I grab hold of the vision of who I thought he was—who I thought he would be—and I refuse to let go.

"Take my hand and let me lead you."

I look down at his palm as he turns it over for me.

Taking it is the only choice I have.

I place my hand in his and meet his eyes again, forcing myself to see the Murphy I fell in love with, because I can't do this if I let myself see the rest. But I can do this—I can do this for me, and I can do it for Cora and Josh—if I forget about the monster inside him, if only for a little while.

Murphy helps me slowly to my feet and Cora hands me my bouquet with a smile, none the wiser. She must think I was just an overwhelmed bride seeing the man she loves at the altar.

"You okay?"

I nod at her and smile.

With my hand securely in Murphy's grip, I step up to the altar by his side and become the reluctant queen of his violent empire.

CHAPTER 23

Murphy

I WATCH MY beautiful wife drink and laugh with her best friend at our wedding reception.

My wife.

My cheeks ache from smiling because she's finally mine. We said our vows and made our promises without incident. She was convincing enough that I nearly believed she still loved me when she promised to honor me.

I understand logically that for her it all felt like lies, but my soul and hers have been connected from our first meeting, and I could still feel her pulsing hope for everything she thought we were. Despite her arguments, what we were is what we still are.

The truth of it is that she simply wasn't born and bred into this world, and she's struggling to accept the reality of it.

I have faith that she'll come around in time.

It's not as if she has a choice.

Watching her from afar, she could almost have me fooled that she's truly happy on the day of our wedding. Cora's presence alone has given her a reason to pretend her world wasn't shattered when I stole her away, a reason to be joyful on a day she may have otherwise mourned. I just hope she's careful in what she tells Cora. If she reveals too much, Cora won't be leaving Ireland alive.

But I'll only worry about that if we come to it. Stella's smart enough to understand what my family is capable of; she knows the consequences. And for now, she's smiling, dancing, and laughing with her friend, and that's worth all the risk.

I down the last of my beer with two large gulps, stealing some liquid courage because I can no longer put off telling her what happens next. I've been dreading this because I know she'll hate me all the more for it, but family traditions are family traditions and there is no breaking them.

I stride across the ballroom to meet her and she's so engrossed in whatever story Cora's telling that she doesn't see me approach from behind. I slip my arm around her back as I step up beside her. She jumps, surprised at my touch, and turns her head to look at me.

"Can I steal a dance?"

Her expression goes hard for a beat, but then she looks at Cora, realizing she's meant to play the role of the happy bride. She smiles softly at me and nods.

I intentionally lead her to the center of the ballroom, wanting to ensure eyes are on us so she doesn't react unfavorably. I take one of her hands in mine, lacing our fingers together, and drop my other hand to her waist. I tug her close, pressing my cheek to hers as I lead her in a slow sway.

"Did I tell you how stunning you look?" I whisper against her ear.

"Several times." Her voice is steady, without a hint of emotion.

"I need to tell you something that will upset you."

"And you feel the need to share this now?"

"I want you to be prepared for what happens when the reception is over."

She pulls her head away to look at me, plastering a fake smile to her face. She speaks softly so she can't be heard by anyone else. "When the reception is over, dear husband, I'm going to *sleep*. If you have other expectations of me, I'll encourage you to rethink those."

I smile at her and take her by surprise with a soft kiss before dragging her close again, cheek to cheek.

"They're not my expectations. They're the expectations of the family."

"The family you lead?"

"Yes."

"Then lead your family in another direction."

"Believe me, Stella, I've tried. But family traditions are important to maintain. No one has ever had issue with this tradition before. Even Cormac and Tally had to do it after their wedding."

"Issue with *what*, Murphy? What's the tradition?" Her hand squeezes mine and I feel her body tense against me.

"There will be a ritual with the immediate family."

"Murphy…"

"The consummation of marriage."

She snaps back, jerking out of my hold, but I manage to keep hold of her hand.

"Eyes are on you. Cora's watching," I remind her.

I see her struggle as she works to twist her expression from anger and fear to a tight smile. I pull at her hand, encourage her to twirl to cover the way she pulled away so harshly, then I tug her against me again.

She's the one to lean in close this time, her furious voice forced to a hush beside my ear. "I swear you did not just say *consummation of marriage* to me with an expectation that I would participate in such a thing."

"You will participate because it's required of you."

"You can't convince me you're okay with this."

"It's fine. It's ritual, tradition."

"How honorable of you that you would allow your family to watch me get fucked against my will."

"People who are married fuck each other, sweetheart. Sex is a basic human function. We're all aware of it. We all do it."

"Well, when you put it *that* way. Sweep me off my fucking feet with your romance."

I don't have to see her face to know she's rolling her eyes.

"You don't have to agree with it. You don't even have to enjoy it. It just has to be done."

"I'm glad we both recognize that sex with you is a chore." I feel her pulse in her palm, quickening with her lie.

"We both know you don't believe that."

"This is sick, Murphy. It's disgusting."

"It's necessary. It finalizes the marriage."

"The ceremony and the certificate aren't enough?"

"The consummation makes annulment impossible."

"I'm not Catholic."

"Neither am I. It's not religious, it's symbolic."

"Oh, so your family just makes this shit up?"

"Tradition, Stella. It's important."

Her fingers curve around the back of my neck, digging nails into my flesh to pull me closer, and it sends a shiver of desire down my spine. My dick twitches at her rough touch.

Her lips graze my ear as she whispers, "Are you going to rape me if I say no? Is that how you want this sham of a marriage to start?"

"You won't say no." I turn us sideways and turn my head to look at Cora and Josh having a drink across the room. Stella's head turns to follow my gaze. "You'll say yes and do what you have to because their lives depend on your cooperation."

Her head snaps back to me. "What if I just told them? What if I told them everything?"

"Then my father will have them killed."

"Your father?"

"I never wanted it to be this way with us."

"Then why couldn't you just leave me alone?"

"Because I fucking *need* you." My heart hammers and my chest aches, indignation and fear rising with my truth.

Her eyebrows dip toward her nose as she scrutinizes me with her gaze.

"I *need* you. There is nothing I wouldn't have done to make you mine."

Her throat bobs as she swallows, her eyes drawing a quick line across my face.

"I'm sorry for the pain I've caused you," I tell her truthfully. "But I have a lifetime to make up for it now. If you would just let your guard down and let me in, I could make you happy in this life."

"I could never be happy knowing what you do…what your family does. It's vile."

"It's business."

"It's human lives, Murphy. Women like me, like Cora, like your cousins. You're selling women just like us."

"I do it to protect you all. I do it to keep our family's power and wealth; I do it to ensure your safety."

"Our safety from whom? Traffickers? Like you?"

I sigh. "This isn't the time and place for this conversation."

"Then name the time and place because I have words for you. So many fucking words."

I pause, mesmerized by the intensity in her brown eyes. Her passion is what draws me to her, and though I have no intention of doing anything differently for the business, I somehow know I want to hear her words. I want to hear her fight me, stand up to me, tell me what she really thinks.

"Tomorrow morning. We'll have breakfast in our room, and you will have my undivided attention. You can scream at me, chastise me, tell me how much you hate me and what I do, and I'll listen to every goddamn word." I'm aware of the way her body molds to mine so subtly as I speak. "You'll talk and I'll listen."

"Nothing I say will change your mind." Her voice is quiet, but hopeful.

"You're probably right, but still, I'll listen." I squeeze her hand, leaning into her sway as she unconsciously arches and molds to me, her breath quickening. "Have faith in me." I bend and my lips brush hers. "We'll consummate our marriage tonight and cement our future. Then, you'll have the power and privilege of being my wife, my partner. I promise you will have a voice with me."

Her guard slips as she softens to me. I bend and her forehead touches mine as she takes a slow breath. "Then I'll make sure you hear it."

"I know you will."

"I wish it could be like this between us."

"It is like this between us. You just don't know how to stop fighting."

"My heart is broken, Murphy."

I have the misfortune of seeing the silent tear that slips from the corner of her eye and slides sadly down her smooth cheek.

"Then mine is broken, too."

"You're the one who broke us."

"Then I have a lot of fucking mending to do. But I can't fix your heart if you won't let me have it."

"I don't trust you."

"I know."

"I hate you."

"I know that, too."

Her eyes flutter shut. "Sometimes I don't."

I don't know what to say to that, so I don't say anything at all.

"Sometimes I mourn you," she continues. "Sometimes I loathe you. Sometimes it hurts to look at you." She pauses. "Sometimes I love you."

"Stella—"

"I'll do what I have to do tonight, but I want you to know I'm doing it because you've made me fearful for my friends' lives. I'm not doing it because it's tradition or because you want me to." She lifts her head and looks at me squarely. "You've made me afraid of you. I just hope you can live with that."

CHAPTER 24

Stella

ROUNDING THE CORNER, Tally stumbles, laughing manically as her blonde hair falls from her messy updo after a night of drinking. The whole family has been drinking throughout the reception. I threw back a couple of extra shots after Murphy told me what I had to do at the end of the night.

Of all the disgusting, oppressive rituals, I never could have imagined this would be my reality…his family bearing witness to us consummating our marriage.

I'm horrified.

I'm disgusted.

I'm nauseous.

But I have enough liquid courage coursing through me now to make me stubbornly lift my chin, determined to get through this with what little dignity and grace I have left.

Murphy holds my hand as we turn down the long hallway on the second floor, heading for the bedroom…*our* bedroom.

Where we'll consummate our marriage.

The other wedding guests are still partying on the first-floor ballroom, unaware of the horrid, archaic act I'm being required to participate in.

I take in a steeling breath as my eyes fall on the line of them—Murphy's immediate family all lined up with their backs to the outside wall, facing the center of the hallway. Cormac catches a stumbling, giggling Tally, and they join the line at the end as the family shushes them.

I never thought I'd prefer Tally's obnoxious laughter to silence, but in this moment, I'd welcome it. The line of O'Sheas standing, staring, watching us silently from where they line the hall…it's eerie.

I look at Murphy because looking at everyone else is making me feel sick. He smiles softly, showing me some encouragement in his expression, but it does nothing for my nerves—it does nothing to ease the awkward pain of being required to participate in this.

Yet it has to be done.

My best friends' lives are at stake, and I would do anything to save them. I'm more determined now than I've ever been before to destroy this business—to make myself, my friends, the world safe from these monsters. I can only do that with my voice, with the power I'll gain by fully becoming his wife.

I pull back my shoulders and stand tall as Murphy releases my hand. He bends, tugging up the leg of his pants, unsheathing a dagger from a holster around his calf.

I had no idea that was there.

Does he always carry it?

He adjusts his pant leg and straightens, turning to face me, presenting the dagger on his palm. The handle is formed from stacked skulls while crossbones create the hilt. It's beautifully formed and it's frighteningly representative of this family.

How many lives have they ruined? How many girls have died at the hands of their owners? How many skulls would line the hall, fill the home, overflow into the garden?

"This dagger is passed from Head of House to Head of House. It's been in the O'Shea family since the four families' partnership formed generations ago."

I nod, but remain quiet.

"Give me your palm."

"What?"

"Hold out your hand."

I swallow hard, my pulse kicking up a quick rhythm. My hand trembles as I show him my palm, slowly extending my arm toward him, still so intensely aware of the eyes lining the hall that watch my every move.

Murphy takes my hand, holding it gently, as he lifts his dagger.

"Murphy…"

"Just a nick," he warns, then slices the tip of the dagger across my palm in a small line.

I hiss, wincing at the sting that shoots through my hand. Warm blood pools and starts to drip, burning my skin as it spills from the wound. He holds out the handle of the dagger, offering it to me. I look up to meet his eyes.

"Do the same to me."

I look down at the dagger.

He's giving me his dagger…he's handing me a weapon.

I could take it and thrust.

I could stab him to death right now.

And then what would I do?

I couldn't kill the rest of his family before they stopped me. It wouldn't matter, anyway. The thought of shoving the steel blade inside him makes my stomach roll. It doesn't matter what he's done—our painful connection is written in stone, and I think that if his heart stopped, mine would, too. I hate him so much for what he's done to my life, but my feelings for who I wanted him to be are still so present, so raw, so hopeful, though hope has no place here.

Taking my time, I slip my hand beneath his, his palm up and presented to me. I bring down the tip of the blade, breathe slowly, and make a quick slice on his palm.

"Good girl," he whispers.

Fuck me.

I hate that he still says that. I hate that he uses it against me. It was something he always said to me on our video chats when we were playing together. He trained me so my pleasure was linked to his "good girl" praise, and now he takes advantage of it.

It works.

We both know that and that's why he says it.

My breath catches as he lifts my bloody hand, eyes stealing my attention, holding me in his gaze as he bows his head to press his lips to the cut he made. He kisses my hand sensually, a gentle press of his lips that lingers, so sweet, I imagine it could heal the wound. I watch as he lifts his blood-smeared lips from my hand and gives me a nod, indicating I should do the same.

Oh, my God.

My heart is fluttering.

This ritual is bizarre, something that should immediately horrify and disgust me.

So why doesn't it?

Why does the way he looks at me with my blood staining his lips twist my insides so intensely?

I bend, kissing his wound. His blood is thick as my lips capture it. I straighten and look at him, bringing my fingers up, preparing to wipe the blood from my lips. Before I can, Murphy's clean hand wraps around the back of my neck, jerks me toward him, and crushes my lips in a bruising kiss.

The passion that exists behind his chaste, closed-mouth kiss stuns me. Our lips are slippery from the thick crimson that coats them, but he firmly holds me in the kiss for seconds. When he breaks, he drops his forehead to mine and looks deeply into my eyes, so painfully deep that for a moment, I forget where I am.

But then he reminds me.

"We each choose one person from the family to enter the bedroom with us and bear witness."

"So, they won't all see?"

"They won't all see."

I let out a sigh in partial relief. Two witnesses is easier than the entire family.

"You choose a woman; I choose a man. Kiss the cheek of the one you select to share our blood, and then you'll follow me into the bedroom."

"Why the blood? What is this?"

He moves his bloody hand against mine down at our sides, lacing his fingers with mine. "Our blood is the same now. Yours and mine. We share it with the family because we are all one blood. O'Shea blood."

"Murphy, I—"

"You can do this."

He releases my hand and I feel weaker.

He steps away from me and saunters down the hall, passing his parents, his cousins, his aunt and uncle. He slows to a stop in front of Declan, steps toward him, and kisses his brother on the cheek.

Murphy turns to look back at me, giving me a nod, and I know he made that choice for me. Declan has been kind to me, a friend. He's someone who is as disenchanted with the way things are as I am. Murphy chose Declan to be our male witness because he knew that held no threat to me.

I feel grateful.

But why should I feel gratitude toward any part of this?

Regardless of who he chooses, it's disgusting. And now I have to choose.

His mother has been decent, but I don't want her to see this. Perhaps, Tally. She's obnoxious, but she's non-threatening—hell, she'll probably black out half-way through considering the way she sways drunkenly in the line. Then again, she might giggle through the whole thing and that would be unbearable.

I should choose someone I don't care about.

No.

I should choose someone who needs to bear witness to the power I'll gain when my life is officially tied to Murphy's—my mind is already twisting and morphing to think like they do.

I have to be careful.

I can't become like they are…I won't.

With intention, I stride forward, trying to appear confident though my insides are dripping with apprehension. I move down the line and come to a stop in front of Cordelia. I turn to face her, giving her my eyes, letting her know without words why I'm choosing her.

I want her to witness me taking my place, earning authority as Murphy's wife, inextricably above her in the hierarchy of this family.

What's happening to me?

I'm already feeling the shift, the power of this ritual, the authority of mixing my blood with Murphy's. I want Cordelia to know she's not above me, because it doesn't take a fool to know she poses more of a threat to me than any other person standing in this hallway.

I take a step forward, lean in, and kiss her on the cheek. I immediately turn away from her, quickly putting her at my back. I watch as Murphy and Declan enter our bedroom and somehow, I make my feet follow after them, Cordelia trailing behind me.

I'm surprised when I see Fiona already inside, standing beside the open door. She closes it behind us, instantly creating an eerie silence in the large sitting area. Murphy makes his way toward the bed, standing at the foot of it. He waves his fingers to call me over and I move, thankful for some direction.

I stop in front of him, standing two feet apart.

It feels too close and too far all at once.

Murphy stands still as Declan moves behind him, as I feel Cordelia's presence at my back. I swallow hard as I watch Declan grip Murphy's jacket at his shoulders, tugging it down his arms. I flinch at the touch of Cordelia's cold fingertips brushing my spine as she grabs the zipper of my beaded top and pulls it down.

I hold my breath, my nervous glance darting to my shoulder as she pushes down my sleeve, my skin going from covered to bare in an instant. I tug my hands free from the sleeves, blood from my palm staining the pristine fabric. I let her pull the cropped top over my head, and it drops to the floor. She pulls down the zipper on my tulle skirt as Murphy unbuttons his shirt and unbuckles his pants.

I wonder if they can hear my rapid heartbeat.

My skirt falls and Cordelia bends, tugging where it touches my ankles, encouraging me to step out. I carefully balance on my silver stilettos, standing exposed in my white strapless bra and thong.

Murphy takes in an audible breath, dropping his eyes to my chest as Declan pulls his open button-down shirt down his arms. I let my eyes land on the skull tattoo on his chest, tracing over the lines with my gaze, and falling to rest on the purple rose behind it.

There's something stirring about seeing my artwork on his skin. The purple rose I tattooed over his heart—the one that matches the rose on my hip—rises and falls with his chest and I know his heart is pounding behind it. The rose is a part of him, etched into his skin, and it's a part of me, too. The thought of it is overwhelming.

I lift my shaking hand and glance down at the wedding ring that now adorns my finger. It's not traditional—it's not a giant, sparkling diamond that screams O'Shea wealth. It's the same as his tattoo—his twisted take on the Claddagh ring he told me about—a skull in the center instead of a heart, held by two skeleton hands, and a crown on top. The crown is where the diamonds are, studded across the base.

The ring is not what I expected to wear on my hand, but I imagine that if I had chosen to marry Murphy—if he'd turned out to be a good man instead of a monster—I'd adore this ring and treasure it for what it's meant to represent—love, loyalty, and friendship.

I startle from my thoughts as Cordelia's cold fingers brush my ankles, working to unbuckle the straps of my shoes, first the left, then the right. I step out of them, and she takes them away.

Murphy and I have both been stripped down to our underwear, and my eyes can't avoid him.

It's tragic how beautiful he is. I'm hopelessly attracted to him. It was our physical chemistry that brought us together in the first place, but that wasn't what kept us going through more than a half a year of phone calls and sparse visits. It was what was in his heart, what I felt from his soul.

He's a lost soul.

Just like me.

Even now, in this dreadful moment, I'm drawn to him.

I need his comfort and strength to get me through this, but I only need to get through this because of the life he's chosen for me.

Murphy takes a step forward and I know without words that I'm meant to do the same. We're close enough to touch, but we don't. The silence and the beats of waiting let an electrical current of uncomfortable, yet somehow still erotic energy build between us. In moments, I'm matching him breath for heavy breath as I watch his tattoo rise and fall with his chest.

I see Cordelia and Declan move from the corner of my eye, backing away from us as Fiona appears. She holds up a large, white sheet as a barrier between us, blocking us from Declan and Cordelia's view.

"Turn around," Murphy commands, and I'm so fucking nervous that I obey.

His fingers are warm as they brush my skin, running down my spine before landing on the clasp of my bra.

"Murphy." I don't know why I say his name.

He unhooks the clasp, but he holds the strapless bra in place and steps in close, molding to my backside and pressing his lips to the back of my bare shoulder. "It's just you and me, sweetheart."

I hate myself for letting him get to me the way he does, for letting the touch of his lips set me on fire.

It blazes deep and I need it.

I need that heat in my core to get me through this fucked-up ritual.

I close my eyes and try to forget that we're being watched, try to forget I was forced to marry him, try to imagine it's him and me before I knew he was the O'Shea Head of House.

He lets go of the strap and I tense as he nudges my bra off my breasts, letting it fall away to land on the carpet. "Oh, God."

He lowers behind me, leaving a trail of kisses down my spine, probably painting me with the blood on his lips from our kiss in the hallway. He grabs hold of my panties and takes them off me slowly, fingers and lips heating my skin. It makes me shudder when he drags them down my thighs. When my underwear lands at my feet, I step out.

I feel his alpha energy rise with him as he stands. He nudges my waist, encouraging me to turn and face him.

"Take them off me."

I look down at his black boxer briefs, eyeing the growing bulge beneath them. "Just you and me," I repeat for myself.

I grip the elastic.

"Good girl," he tells me.

His cock is half-hard as I lower to remove his underwear. Some sickness within me makes my stomach clench, giving me the desire to use my mouth on him until he's so painfully hard that he has no choice but to take me and make me come. I look up at him, bite my lip, and he shudders as his eyes meet mine.

I force myself to stand and tear my eyes away from him. I glance over the sheet Fiona holds up. I force myself to see Cordelia and Declan sitting in the armchairs, watching us, witnessing this shame.

Except I don't feel shame…at least, not in the way I expected. The way Murphy looks at me almost makes me feel powerful and proud.

"Get in the bed," Murphy tells me. "Under the covers."

I climb onto the plush comforter, lift the neatly folded top, and quickly hide beneath it. He follows, crawling beneath the covers with me, his hip brushing mine and setting off fireworks along my skin.

Then Fiona drops the sheet and walks away to stand in the corner by the door. I'm a little horrified when I find Cordelia staring, fuming, seething. Declan's eyes are politely shifted away.

We're beneath the sheets, so less of my body is exposed now than it was before when I stood naked behind the white sheet. Yet I feel barer now than before. I feel as though I'm on display.

I sink my body down beneath the sheets, pulling the covers over my head entirely. I expect Murphy to tug them away and force me to face this, but instead, he joins me, slipping down beside me and rolling onto his side to face me.

"What do we do now?" I whisper.

He reaches over to cup my cheek in his hand, his metal rings kissing my soft flesh. "We consummate."

"How much time do we have?"

"As much as we need."

"Are they all out there, just standing in the hallway, waiting for us to finish?"

"No." He slides in close, his body running along the side of mine. He shifts, pressing his hardness against my hip as his lips fall softly to mine. "We chose our witnesses. The others are gone."

I blink at him, expectantly waiting for instructions.

But then he asks me, "How do you want to do this? Do you want me to make you come?"

My eyes narrow. "Was it an option for me not to?"

"If you wanted, I could be quick about it and get it over with."

I snap onto my side to face him. "Well, that wouldn't be fucking fair, would it? Forcing me to consummate a marriage I didn't want without giving me an orgasm. Un-fucking-real."

He grins at me and it's only then that I realize how loud I spoke. "They can hear you." He pulls the cover back and peeks over it. "Did you hear that?"

I smack his chest and pull the covers over us again as Declan says, "Every word, mate. And for what it's worth, I agree with Stella."

I bring both my hands up to cover my face though no one can see me beneath the covers.

Murphy's hands are on my wrists, gently pulling them away. "I love it when you raise your voice and yell at me. If you want to come, I'll make you come." His smile and good humor seems to have diffused some of the awkward tension and fuck, I'm so grateful for that.

"It's the principle of the thing. It's unfair that the expectancy is for you to orgasm, regardless of whether I do. I want equality, sir. If you have to come, I have to come. Period."

I hear a slow clap from the sitting area—undoubtedly from Declan—and I think I might die. I have a problem with the volume of my voice when I'm passionate about something. Maybe that's why Murphy thought he might spare me losing control of my volume if he makes me come, because that will happen. The orgasms he gives me are full of passion.

Shit.

His eyes dart around my face, drawing invisible lines that burn and tingle beneath his gaze. "I'll give you fucking equality, Mrs. O'Shea."

Oh, my God.

His lips come down on mine before I can speak another word, coaxing me to part them so he can kiss me deeply, sensually. His kiss takes my breath away and I fall into him, my body sneaking forward, seeking the warmth of him and his protective embrace. That erotic electricity that was growing before expands, wrapping around us and coiling us together. My skin prickles with the spark of it, flames sparking behind his fingers as they draw a line down my arm.

His hand lands on my waist, trailing down over my hip, sneaking between my legs. I gasp as he reaches my clit, unintentionally breaking our kiss. He dips to kiss my throat as he slowly circles his finger.

His beard is rough against my skin as his lips and tongue softly tease across the hollow of my throat. Everything he's doing feels incredible, but I'm struggling to forget that we're being watched. It doesn't matter that we're under the covers, every movement, every sound, every breath is seen and heard.

As quietly as I can, I whisper, "I changed my mind, just fuck me and get it over with." I hate myself for saying it as soon as the words leave my mouth.

Is it that easy to hand over my sexual power?

What does that say about me?

He stops kissing my throat and lifts his head, shifting against me until our eyes are level. He cocks an eyebrow. "I don't think I can do that now."

"What?"

"You were right." He rolls his hips, his hard cock pressing against my stomach. "The expectation is unfair, and I'm not so sure we can call this a consummation if you don't have your own reward from it." He leans in and runs his tongue flat across the seam of my lips. "You wouldn't want to do this again later, would you?"

I pinch my eyes shut, then open them again. "No."

"Eyes on mine," he says, drawing me into his gray-green stare. "Keep them here. Focus on me."

I inhale deeply through my nose and blow it out through rounded lips. I continue to breathe slowly, eyes locked on his as he nudges me onto my back, his body warm along my side. He props up on one elbow, quickly bringing his other hand to my throat, gently squeezing, interrupting my deep breath.

He knows what it does to me when he steals my breath. He knows it destroys calmness to make me frantic instead. He knows it makes adrenaline rush through my veins at the perceived threat. He knows it turns me on. He knows everything about me.

He knows me and I hate it.

He knows me and I love it.

The light and fuzzy feeling of breathlessness wraps around my brain. My pulse quickens and he gradually releases. That tiniest hint of breath play has my heart pounding, and I'm desperate for more of it.

His hand trails down my chest, rubbing over my breast. He squeezes, then runs his thumb back and forth across my quickly stiffening nipple. My body curls, back arching, pressing up against his touch and begging for more. He pinches the hardening peak, rolling it between his fingers, sending a rush of heat through my core that makes my pussy ache for penetration.

He doesn't stop for minutes…maybe it's only seconds. I only know that he makes me feel more desperate for release than any other man ever has. As I look deep into his light eyes, I see all my silly hopes and dreams. I see the relationship I wanted with him. I see the man who cared about me, who made time to talk to me every day, who crawled inside me and finally made my soul feel at peace.

He made me feel like my lost soul had been found by his…our lost souls colliding.

I see it all now in the way he looks at me, holds my stare, touches, and pleases me like no other could.

The world slips away as his fingers trail down my stomach. They slip between my legs and dip down to tease across my slit. I gasp, arching into his touch, encouraging him to touch me deeper, harder…*more.*

"Tell me you want me," I whisper.

His eyes flash with longing that I can feel throbbing inside my chest—it's a throb of instinct that tells me what's real.

He is a lost soul, just like me.

He doesn't belong in this world, and I want him to know it, I want him to prove it to me.

"Show me you love me. Let me pretend tonight. Give me that and let me go back to hating you tomorrow."

His entire body sighs. "I don't have to pretend to love you. You know that I do." His fingers circle my clit, pulling wetness from my core as my body tenses pleasantly against his touch.

"Show me."

Gratitude softens his features. My heart flutters. My stomach twists into a tight knot. My pussy clenches. He pushes two fingers inside me—achingly slow—as he shifts to move above me.

My eyes search his as he looks down at me, watching me as his fingers sink deeper and curl against my upper wall. I let out a soft moan just before his lips come down on mine and he kisses me slowly.

Fuck, I'm in love with him.

I hate him.

His tongue swirls around mine, tasting me, telling me without words that I have his heart. It aches within me to know that's true. It's painful to hate the man who gives me his love so freely, but it's painful to love the man who stole my freedom.

His fingers swirl and sweep in time with his tongue, making me feel wet and swollen. He groans into our kiss as I spread my legs for him. I want him there just as much as he wants to be there. His body moves against mine, writhing, rubbing, seeking, and mine does the same as he draws me toward frantic need. Our kiss breaks as he pulls his fingers out and finds my clit, pressing in, rubbing it back and forth with swift fingers.

"Oh, God," I moan.

He buries his face in my neck, licking and nipping at my skin, his fingers driving me up a steep cliff. He takes me to a point of pure need, making me so desperate to be filled that my hands reach between us, seeking to find his cock so I can stroke him along with me.

He rises, taking my frantic hands and nudging them away. He lifts one to his lips, kissing my blood-streaked palm before running his tongue flat along the underside of my fingers. Then, he places my hand over my dark curls.

"Touch yourself," he commands with a gruff tone as he wraps his hand around his cock and lines up to enter me.

I reach down at the very moment he pushes himself inside me, slow and deep, and we both moan together. He bends over me, holding himself up on his hands.

"This is home," he whispers, his eye contact unwavering. "Hate me everywhere else, but when I'm inside you, you're mine."

I nod my understanding…my acceptance.

That's a deal I'll eagerly make with him.

My fingers move on my clit as my breaths grow shallow and short, mimicking the way he worked me before with quick side-to-side strokes. He pumps inside me with slow, rhythmic thrusts.

He dips to kiss my lips, my cheek, along the line of my jaw, all the way back to my ear. "I'm not lost when I'm with you. When I'm with you, I know I'm right where I need to be."

My insides coil around his words and the truth in his voice. My body sinks, contracting around my center as he thrusts faster, harder, deeper. My inner walls squeeze around his cock and my throbbing clit swells as I stroke it.

"That's my good girl," he whispers, licking the shell of my ear. "Come for me, sweetheart. Come for me. Let me fucking have it. Squeeze my fucking cock and make me come with you."

Holy fucking hell.

The instant contrast from light to dark flips the switch, igniting my orgasm like a flash fire. It explodes a brilliant flame through my clit that spreads like wildfire, straining every muscle in my body. My lips part—I can't hold back the scream of intense pleasure, but Murphy swallows my sound with a desperate kiss as he fucks me through it, harder and faster. His movement draws out my orgasm impossibly longer. He groans into my mouth as I feel him spill deep within me.

My hands snap to his cheeks, holding his face to mine, deepening our kiss as we tumble down the crest together.

I'm not ready to let go yet.

I'm not ready to start hating him again.

We kiss until our bodies release the tension completely, until our breathing slows and our writhing stills.

He pulls back to look at me and he's still there—the Murphy I love is still there. He smiles at me and my lips curve to return it.

"Congratulations." Cordelia's crude voice rips through the bliss and breaks the spell. "Your union is complete. Welcome to the family, Stella O'Shea."

And then I remember where I am.

I remember how I came to be here.

I remember that he's made me a monster, just like him.

Stella O'Shea.

I close my eyes so I don't have to look at him.

CHAPTER 25

Murphy

I'M UNCHARACTERISTICALLY NERVOUS for tonight's talent show, reception, and board meeting. It's my turn to host this quarter, and it will be Stella's first true experience with the four families.

She knows as much as I've told her, which is to say, nearly everything. I've revealed truths in bits and pieces over our first six weeks of marriage, leaving the most dehumanizing aspects of our trade for the past week.

She's angrier with me than she's been for a while, and an entirely new level of her fury has been unleashed. Her attitude is wearing on me and she's brought it with her into our newly refurbished opera house on our castle grounds.

I stand on the plush, purple carpet at the bottom of the house to look out upon my arriving guests. I'm quite pleased with how the renovations have gone. The opera house is luxurious, a place fit for royalty; the purple and gold opulence is similar to our bedroom.

Nearly everything is new, with the exception of the seating. The rows of wood seats are original to the space, which was built generations ago. I had them stained dark and reupholstered in violet velvet, tacked in gold brackets. Boyd thinks my design choices are garish, but I think his were mind-numbingly dull.

My favorite part is the brand-new crystalline chandelier that hangs from the center. The massive fixture costs as much as a car and was worth every dime. There's just something in the way the modern decoration casts a new light on the old, wood-carved balcony boxes—the intricate flourishes carved on the box walls seem more detailed with the contrast of contemporary fixtures.

Stella sits facing me, in the first row of seats near the stage, a surly expression plastered to her beautiful face. Her legs are crossed and one angry foot bounces with her rage-fueled energy.

I can see she's not open to discussion with the way her arms are folded across her body. She's angry with me for who knows which of the details I shared with her in advance of tonight's events—her first night joining me as a member of the board. And angry as she is, she looks fucking stunning. Her crimson dress hugs her body and the deep V cuts down between perfect breasts.

She's a goddamn distraction, to say the least.

She refuses to stand beside me tonight. As my wife, she has the right to make that choice, but she knows there will be consequences for it in private—personally, I look forward to granting her consequences for her bad attitude. Still, she's pressing her luck with me, and tonight will be quite the test on our relationship.

I reach forward and tap beneath her chin, forcing her to lift her head and look at me. "You're being a brat."

"Well, everyone in this room is an asshole, so we're in good company." She jerks her chin from my grip, and I let my hand fall away.

I flash a tight smile. "You know what being a brat gets you."

"I'm sure you'll enlighten me later."

"You can be certain I will, sweetheart."

"Don't call me sweetheart."

"Fine, princess."

"Fuck you."

"Fuck you, too."

I let out a heavy, frustrated breath and adjust my cufflinks. If she wants to be a bitch tonight, she can be a bitch. I need to make sure my guests are tended to and that everything runs smoothly.

I spot Anya Mikhailov moving toward me from down the aisle. She's looking much healthier these days since she's been in Renata Vittori's care—not that I'd ever credit Renata for caring for anyone other than herself. Renata simply understands what's at stake. Her orders were to ensure Anya's health through her pregnancy until we find out who the child's father is and whether it's a boy or a girl. All of which, we'll find out tonight at the board meeting.

Anya nervously rubs her hands over her skirt on her way to greet me, drawing my eye to her rounded belly that's covered in layers of light pink chiffon. It reminds me that I need to have a discussion with Stella about the expectations for her to produce an heir.

Though, it's not just about producing an heir for me.

I ache to see her belly full like that with my child. She would be an incredible mother—fiercely protective and stubbornly attached to them. She needs to provide a boy to someday take over my position as the O'Shea Head of House, but when I picture my future family with her, I see a baby girl…a strong, powerful daughter who talks back and stands up for herself as much as her mother does.

The vision of it brushes goosebumps down my forearms. Stella has no idea the kind of power she holds over me.

I'm weak for her.

I've allowed her to sit there like a brat, refusing to stand by my side, and it's only because she demands the right to choose. She doesn't even know all the things she could demand from me that I would give her.

But tonight, I need her fucking support.

Anya puts on a smile I easily recognize as forced as she approaches. I greet her kindly, taking her hand and gripping her elbow softly as we lean in to kiss each other on the cheek. "You look well," I tell her. "How are things with the lady Vittori?"

"If you're asking me whether she's doing as she was told to do, then things are going as expected. My care has been managed."

I nod. "Good. I look forward to hearing from your joint family board at the meeting tonight. For your sake, I do hope profits are climbing."

Her eyes flicker with regret. "Yes. Unfortunately for the lives that were stolen, our profits are up."

Stella snickers. "I like her."

My jaw ticks. "Anya, this is my new bride, Stella. She doesn't quite understand her place yet as an O'Shea wife. Perhaps I should develop a training program." I raise my eyebrows at Stella expectantly as she unfolds her arms and straightens in her seat.

"Maybe I'll develop a training program for *you* on the health risks associated with trying to mansplain your way through marriage," my wife snaps. She even has the balls to finger quote the word *marriage*.

My weight shifts as I prepare to round on her, but Kostya Federov appears in front of me, stepping between us.

He turns and extends his hand to Stella, speaking in his thick Russian accent. "Good to finally meet you."

She takes his hand kindly but watches him with a sneer that indicates her wariness. "Charmed, I'm sure."

"Kostya Federov. I'm with the Mikhailov family."

"The Mikhailovs?" Stella turns sideways in her seat, looking around behind her to spot Anya as she retreats. "Anya, that's the one you told me about?" She turns back to look at me. "The slave turned Mikhailov by a forced, secret marriage?" She huffs, slumping in her seat again. "I should go sit with her. We could start a club."

I pinch the bridge of my nose. "You were never a slave, Stella."

"Wasn't I? You had me sunk in so deep, I was a slave to my phone for seven months before you took me."

"Would you like to go speak with Anya and compare experiences? I assure you, sweetheart, you've been treated with nothing but kindness and respect in comparison."

"In comparison to a *slave*. Did you seriously just say that?"

"We'll talk more at the reception, Kostya. Will you excuse us for a moment?"

He walks away and I swiftly move to take the seat beside my wife, quickly putting my arm around her shoulders and harshly tugging her against my side. I let my fingers dig into her shoulder as I hold her against me.

I lean in and put my lips to her ear, whispering softly, "I'm asking for one night…one goddamn night where I don't have to worry about your attitude impacting my business."

She pulls away from me sideways, snapping her head to look at me squarely with a bratty smile on her beautiful fucking face. "If you didn't want a woman with an attitude impacting your business then you shouldn't have fallen for a woman with an attitude."

Bloody fucking hell.

I lean forward and kiss her hard, taking her off-guard. She lets me kiss her because she wants it—she always wants it. Sometimes I think she fights me so hard just because she likes to light a fire under my arse to be rough with her. I pull away to witness her gobsmacked expression and perfect pout.

"I'm gonna tie you to the bed and whip your ass raw with my belt tonight. So please, keep it up, sweetheart; piss me off enough to make you cry."

She narrows her eyes at me, but I don't miss the flush of her cheeks or the sharp rise and fall of her chest. "I fucking dare you to try."

I smirk at her. "Never dare me. You know better than that by now."

I give her a quick kiss on the cheek, then pull my arm away and push to stand. I wink at her once before heading toward the stage to greet our audience and introduce Fiona for her first performance as the O'Shea talent slave.

"Welcome." I stand behind my seat at the head of the table in our boardroom. "I think it's best that we avoid the pomp and circumstance and get right down to handling business, shall we? The changes we've seen in the organizational structure of the four families over the past year have been unprecedented and dramatic. We have some major decisions to make tonight and we're going to dive right in. The finalized agenda is in your folder."

Stella sits in the chair beside me, taking in a noisy breath of annoyance. I'm equally annoyed that she sits with her arms crossed when she should be opening the black leather folio placed in front of her.

"Any changes, additions, or objections?"

"I object to all of this," Stella says loudly and intently.

I snap, leaning across the corner of the table and wrapping my fingers around her throat, knowing it'll turn her on enough to shut her up. "Be quiet, lass, or I'll make certain you won't speak again."

Her eyes flash with hunger for the promises I've made—promises to tie her to the bed and rough her up before I fuck her smart mouth.

I cock an eyebrow at her as I unwrap my fingers one at a time from her delicate throat. She visibly swallows and adjusts in her seat, a little wiggle of her hips that no one else in the room would notice except for me.

I straighten my spine and smooth my waistcoat. "Changes, additions, or objections?" I repeat, looking directly at my stubborn, sexy wife.

Her eyes meet mine with a flash of heat, igniting a spark deep inside my stomach that makes me ache to have her bound, naked, and at my mercy. Perhaps this is the reason they didn't give Heads of House a bride until they were forty. The goddamn distraction of my bride threatens to unravel me entirely, though I know in truth it wouldn't matter what age I was…Stella will slowly unravel me until the day I die.

Begrudgingly, I drag my eyes from hers. "First item of business is the matter of Anya Mikhailov, the gender of her unborn child, and the DNA result which determines family placement."

"You know the gender and the father?" Anya asks nervously.

I open my folio and pull out the white sealed envelope which contains the gender result. I'd had it specially couriered from Anya's physician directly to me to ensure it didn't end up in the wrong hands. I've kept it carefully concealed until tonight. I haven't opened it, so I have no idea what it says. I felt it only fair that Anya should be the first to see it, though I needed her in my presence in case the result is… unfavorable.

I find myself somewhat anxious to know whether her baby is a boy or a girl. If it's a boy, the decision making for tonight will be easy; Anya will be the mother of a future Head of House regardless of the DNA paternity result. Whether the child belongs to Vigo or Nikolai, both now deceased, her boy will be raised as their heir.

But if her baby is a girl, some upsetting decisions will have to be made. My lingering humanity grows stronger each day and sometimes, I fear I won't have the strength to ignore it forever, not when I have the spark of Stella to light it on fire.

I place the envelope on the table and slide it across the tabletop toward Anya. Kostya grabs it and pushes it over to her. Her hands twitch holding the envelope and she looks up at me as if waiting for direction.

"Open it," I tell her.

She tears it open quickly, tugs the paper from the envelope, and unfolds the page…but she doesn't look at it. She places it on the table and pushes it to Kostya. "What does it say?"

I feel Anya's tension from across the room—the concern she has for her own well-being, but also for the well-being of her unborn child. My gut twists with the anxiety she feeds me from across the room.

"Boy," Kostya says.

I struggle to hide my relief with a stoic expression as he slides the paper back across the table to me. I give it a cursory glance, confirming the result Kostya stated. "Alright. Well done, lass. You've created the next Head of House." I tug out the second white envelope from my folio. "Now to find out if he's a Vittori or a Mikhailov."

I slide this envelope to Renata Vittori to read. She's cared for Anya well during her pregnancy and the child might belong to her deceased brother. But truthfully, I hope it reads Mikhailov and that she'll be the first to see that she doesn't have a new nephew to grant her some peace from her brother's death.

Renata tears into the envelope and pulls out the paper inside, her eyes scanning it quickly to find the relevant information. Her face falls with disappointment and I have to fight my smile.

She's already pushing the paper back across the table to me before she says, "He's not a Vittori."

I glance at the page to confirm, but I'm confused. "Hmm. Apparently, the DNA result from Nikolai was inconclusive."

Why would it be inconclusive?

We collected clean DNA samples from Vigo and Nikolai both.

"So, what does this mean for me?" Anya asks.

I rake my hand across my beard, my eyes narrowed on the page in consideration. "Leo?"

"So, we assume the child is a Mikhailov since we know it isn't a Vittori," Leo Leblanc states. "I say, let her remain in the care of the Vittoris. She seems to be doing well there now and it makes sense for her to stay given that the Mikhailovs and Vittoris are making joint business decisions. Let her stay for a year and if she proves herself trustworthy, then she and Kostya can move back to Mikhailov Manor to run the business."

"What about the next quarterly meeting?" Anya asks. "It's the Mikhailovs—it's *our* turn to host. I'd like to host it in my home."

"No," I insist. "It's too close to your due date in January."

"But I'm due a week before the meeting—"

"And will be in no condition to travel to Russia with a newborn. You'll host from the Vittoris' home. That's final."

Cordelia leans forward and I brace myself for frustration. "Why do we need to give her any time with the baby at all?" she asks. "I would gladly take over care of the child after Anya gives birth. We won't need her after that. She can be decommissioned like the slave whore she's proven to be."

Did she really just suggest decommissioning the wife of a Head of House?

I would never stand for such a dishonor to someone in my position, dead or alive. "She's a Mikhailov *wife*. We've been through this, Cordelia. We can't just off her."

"Can't we?" Renata feels the need to chime in.

Fury wraps around my heart and squeezes at the mere thought of it. I slam my fist down on the table to release the tension of this building rage. "No. We *can't*. That's final. You can't just kill a wife because her husband is dead. If *I* died and you pulled this shit with Stella—"

I turn my head to glance at my wife as she slowly uncrosses her arms, her hardened expression softening. She catches my gaze and holds it with her fiercely kind brown eyes, telling me with a single look that she appreciates my defense of her position…of Anya's position. Her unspoken gratitude soothes the rising anger within me as I take a deep breath.

"The matter is *settled*," I affirm. "Renata will continue to coordinate Anya's care for another year. We'll reevaluate at the next O'Shea-hosted meeting."

Renata scoffs and it sets Anya off. "Don't be such a bitch about it. Honestly, Renata, the way you behave is so childish. Sometimes I think you need a keeper. Really, Murphy. That woman is emotionally unstable. She's lucky she has Lorenzo to help make her decisions because otherwise, she wouldn't know what side of the bed to get out of in the morning."

Well done, Anya.

I look at Stella to find her pressing her smiling lips tightly together to hold back her cheer. And I find myself doing the same.

"Darling girl, your lover still belongs to me," Renata says.

I hold up my palm to Stella, sensing her internal preparation to start screaming in Anya's defense. I'm nearly inclined to let her loose on the bitch, but I don't want Stella falling in bad favor with the women of the board—she may someday require their assistance. Still, I feel her electricity spark beside me and I can't wait to strike the match that sets her on fire.

CHAPTER 26

Murphy

"YOU DEFENDED HER," Stella says softly after the boardroom has cleared.

I close my folio and look over at her.

"You defended Anya because of me."

"Did I?"

She nods, her expression questioning. "You told them they couldn't kill the wife of a Head of House. You said that because you fear they'd do the same to me."

"You have nothing to be afraid of. I did my due diligence to ensure your acceptance by the four families." I pause. "I would never let anyone hurt you."

"I'm not afraid of them. They bark loud, but they have no bite."

"Then why do you bring it up?" I push my chair back to stand, waiting for her to follow before moving toward the door. I hold it open for her as we pass through into the hallway, heading for our bedroom upstairs.

"I think you might just be capable of empathy, Murphy O'Shea."

"I never claimed that I wasn't."

"Declan's right about you," she says more to herself than to me. "You wear a mask."

"I don't know what you're talking about. I am who I am. I've never pretended to be someone I'm not."

"Well, obviously, that's bullshit. You lied to me for the first seven months of our relationship."

"I omitted the specifics."

"Don't start. I'm trying to thank you."

I chuckle. "Are you? Because I'm not getting that at all."

We walk beside each other a few paces in silence, and I let it linger. We're always exchanging words, always arguing and fighting each other for power. A few strides in silence is peacefully different for us—and not at all what I expected after her first board meeting. I expected an explosion, but what I'm getting is merely a spark.

Still, heat is heat, and it burns between us all the same.

Rather unexpectedly, she reaches for my hand, her fingers warily grazing mine. I don't give her time to change her mind. I snap my palm around her hand and hold tight.

A fucking firework explodes between our hands, sending flames licking over my body, suddenly fueling me to grab her, touch her, feel her with rough and passionate hands.

I hear the breath she draws in with a gasp as I squeeze her hand tighter. She looks at me, and with my gaze, I wordlessly tell her how I intend to smother her and douse our sparking flame properly once we're alone in our bedroom.

I open the door that leads to the hidden spiral staircase and let go of her hand as she passes, making her way up the steps. I'm quick to follow, laying eyes on her spectacular arse as she climbs. I'd love to drag her down to her knees on these steps and shove my fingers into her from behind, but I let the anticipation build.

A heated, heavy silence lingers as we step onto the landing and move down the hallway. When we reach our bedroom, she stops just outside the door, turning to look at me.

Her forehead creases as her dark eyebrows dip toward her nose. "Do you love me?"

"What kind of question is that? We're married."

"Marriage and love aren't the same. And I don't think you've ever actually said the words to me. *I love you.* But then tonight, it was so clear that the thought of something happening to me if you weren't alive to protect me made you angry."

"Of course, it made me angry."

"Because you love me?"

I search her eyes because I don't understand her question.

Does she not know that I do?

I reach around her to quickly unlock and push the door open, then step forward, forcing her to walk backward until she's inside and I can close it behind us.

"Can you answer the question?" She looks up at me with a serious expression, a confused expression.

I grab her cheeks and step in close. Her fingers land on my wrists delicately as I press my forehead to hers. "I'm angry at myself because you have to ask me that."

"Do you love me?"

I walk her toward the bed. "I have loved you since the moment I met you."

Her eyes quickly flicker as they scan mine for truth. Her gaze is filled with confusion and maybe something that looks like fear. "I wish you didn't."

My eyes narrow and I tug my head back, though my hands stay firmly clamped to her cheeks. "What the fuck is that supposed to mean?"

"I'm grateful for what you said tonight…that you defended Anya, that you defended me."

"But what?"

"But I can never accept who you are with them, with the four families. I can never accept the man you pretend to be with them. I can never love the man who leads depravity instead of fighting it. I can never…" her voice catches, and she pauses. "I can never let myself love you fully. I'm against you, Murphy. I'm against you and what you stand for, and nothing will ever change my mind."

My chest tightens. I drop my hands from her face and spin, pacing away.

"I'm sorry," she says.

I whip around to face her. "You're a terrible liar, sweetheart."

"I'm…what?"

"You're lying to yourself to pretend you don't love every despicable part of me."

She shakes her head. "I know what it feels like to love you because I loved you before you took me from my life. There was even a moment after our wedding that I thought maybe I could love you still, maybe I could teach you, help you understand that what you're doing is wrong—"

"Who the fuck are you to determine what's right and wrong?"

"I'm the woman you claim to love!"

"You say that as if you don't believe me."

"How could I?"

I march toward her, reaching out to snatch her by the throat, her eyes popping wide. "Because you were never meant to be mine, Stella, and I *made* you mine. I loved you so fucking much that I re-wrote our destinies because I had to have you." I grip her tighter, wrangling her around and shoving her back against the wall. "I stole you to keep you safe. I stole you so I could love you and care for you better than any other man ever could."

"This is better, then?" she scoffs. "Grabbing your wife by the throat and shoving her against the wall for speaking her truth?"

"You fucking love it when I do this, so don't pretend you don't." I feel her throat bob against my hand as she swallows, and it spurs me on. "You love when I wrap my fingers around your throat and squeeze." I do what I say, pinching the sides of her neck with care. "You love it when I throw you against the wall, when I bend you over and spank you, when I bruise you, cut you, make you bleed."

She slaps me and I turn my head to the side. She reaches out to do it again but I wrap my palm around her wrist. She grits her teeth, her eyes narrowing with fury as she tries to free herself from my grip, her body writhing against mine as she pushes.

"Say it, Stella. Tell me the truth. Tell me how much you love the way I hurt you."

"Why, so you can justify hurting me again?"

"Then tell me to let go. Tell me to walk away. Tell me and I will."

I stare her down, meeting her intense gaze with my own. We both pant, our furious breaths the only sound between us for heated seconds.

I lean in close enough that our noses touch. "Tell me."

In a mad rush, she tilts her chin and kisses me. She puts her lips on mine, and the madness shifts from rage to pure lust that's so consuming, I can't ignore it. I kiss her back with fury, shoving my tongue into her mouth and lashing hers with mine. I let go of her throat, grab both of her wrists firmly, and slam them to the wall on either side of her head.

She lets out a puff of breath as I break away from her lips to mark a trail down the side of her neck. I grab the strap of her dress with my teeth and drag it down her shoulder. It falls easily, the soft fabric that creates the deep V between her breasts slipping to expose her bare flesh beneath.

I groan as her dark nipple peeks out from the falling fabric, moving quickly to catch it with my teeth and nip at it. Her hips buck against mine as she gasps her approval. I suck and lick frantically, scrubbing my coarse beard over her flesh.

I let go of her wrists and she drops them to grip my shoulders. I move against her, kissing across her chest, working my way up her cleavage to her throat as I rub my hands down the curve of her arse, gripping and cupping, pulling her against me.

What were we even arguing about?

Her breathless panting is fuel to the fire that burns within my gut. Her arms wrap around me, her fingers combing into my hair from the back of my neck and clawing, tugging, holding my face against her sensitive flesh at the hollow of her throat.

I curl my fingers, digging into her arse, lifting her from the floor. She wraps a leg around my hip as I spin her and take her quickly to the bed. I drop her onto the side of it, bending with her, finding her lips, and feeding her my rough intentions—and she feeds it right back.

Her hands land on my chest and she shoves me back as she slips down, falling from the edge of the bed, slumping until she sits on the floor at my feet. Her hands scramble, reaching up to unbuckle my belt, lift the button, and tug the zipper.

I huff with strained breaths as I shove her hands aside, reaching inside my boxer briefs, fisting my cock, and tugging it out for her. She leans her head back to rest on the edge of the bed, licking her lips and opening her mouth for me as her hands come up to knead her swollen breasts.

I spread my legs to stand on either side of her hips. I come in so close that she strains her neck backward to watch me with her intoxicating, deep brown eyes.

"Fucking choke me with it," she begs as one of her hands slips down her dress, reaching beneath to play with her pussy.

I reach down to grab her chin, towering over her. "Show me you want it. Show me your tongue."

Her eyes flash with lust, the corners of her lips quirking into the sinful smile she reserves for these moments where we hate and love each other so much that we forget who the fuck we are. We sink into depravity and use each other to remember our passion and to forget the goddamn world around us.

She drops her mouth open wide and sticks out her beautiful, thick tongue. Holding her chin firm in my grip, I sink my fingers into her hair, combing them back on the side of her head and gripping tight so I can hold her in place. She's at my mercy with the way I control her head.

Lifting her head and shifting my hips forward, I give her the tip. She sucks it into her mouth, making a ripple of electricity shoot up my spine. But it's not the feeling of her perfect lips wrapped around my cock that does it for me. It's the look in her eyes, the way she watches me, searching for my reaction because my pleasure pleases her.

We have the same filthy passion for each other—the kind of passion I'd ruin my own life for. But I ruined her life so I wouldn't have to ruin mine, and I need to remind her who's in charge here.

My fingers curl tighter into her hair. I let go of her chin to slip my hand around the back of her neck. I jerk her forward, thrust my hips, and shove my cock deep enough to gag her. She sputters around my thickness, and I pull back out.

"Can you take it, sweetheart?"

She licks her lips and looks up at me with blinking, needy eyes. She doesn't say a word; instead, she grabs my hips, opens her filthy, beautiful mouth, and leans forward to suck me in deep.

"Fuck," I hiss as she moves, her tongue rubbing wet and warm along the underside of my cock, her lips soft and tight as she moves.

It feels incredible, but I don't want her to move. I want her to fucking choke. I push in deep, pulsing against the back of her throat, watching the way her eyes widen as tears pool and slip from the corners. Her throat bobs as she gags and swallows, as her head instinctively tugs back.

I hold her head steady and thrust quick and sharp until saliva seeps from the corners of her mouth. I pull out all the way and her lips leave my cock with a satisfying smack. I drop to my knees as I slide my hands to her cheeks, lifting her head to look at me as she gasps for a decent breath. Tears and saliva spill, making her look like the most gorgeous fucking mess I've ever seen.

"Are you wet for me?"

She nods in my grip.

"You want to fuck me and come hard on my lap?" I lick the dribble from her lips and feed it back to her with a consuming kiss. I pull back and give her unwavering eye contact. "You want it?"

She nods again, so lost in her lust that I imagine she'd say yes to just about anything.

"You're so lucky you have me, aren't you? Lucky you have me to take care of you. Other men would take advantage of you and your pretty face like this." I let my hands slip along her jaw, brushing my thumb across her bottom lip and giving it a little tug.

"Don't…" she swallows, "don't ruin this with your entitlement."

I grin. "But I am entitled to you, aren't I?"

"When I allow it."

I lean forward, licking just behind the shell of her ear, making her shiver. "Then you're going to allow yourself to ride me until you come."

I reach down to grip her waist as I switch our positions, turning to sit with my back against the side of the bed and tugging her with me. She scrambles to get her feet beneath her and moves quickly, turning to straddle me on her knees and shuffling in close.

"We could do it together," she says cryptically as she lifts her skirt higher over her hips and reaches between us to move her panties to the side. She rubs her cunt over the length of my erection, and I twitch against the pure pleasure of her tempting wetness and heat. "We could work together."

I don't know what she's talking about, but I don't care as she twists her body, grips my cock, and angles the tip to wedge between her wet folds. She sinks down with an agonizingly slow pace, taking me inch by inch, and enjoying every aching second of it.

She sinks me in completely, settling her weight on my lap. "You and I could change everything." She grinds her hips, rocking back and forth in slow, long thrusts. I lift my hands to cup her face, tugging her head forward until her forehead drops to rest against mine. "You don't have to be this man…this criminal…"

I hear her words, but processing is a challenge with the way she grinds and circles her hips, her pussy already pulsing and squeezing around my cock.

Her pace gradually quickens, her gentle grinding transforms into harsh pulsing as her lips drop open and she pants for her release. She's already so close, I can feel it. I can feel the way her walls squeeze around me, begging me, demanding me to lose control and come with her.

"Say it," she breathes. "Say the words. Tell me you love me. Tell me you want me to be yours forever."

"Fuck," I groan, her brown eyes holding me, begging me. "You're mine forever, Stella."

"Tell me you love me. Say it."

I tighten my grip, combing my fingers into her hair, tilting my chin to kiss her. I whisper against her lips, "I love you."

She tenses, her entire body fighting against the orgasm I can feel pulsing around me. Her jaw ticks and she fights to steady her breath so she can speak. "Would you do anything for me?"

Shit.

I know what she's trying to do. She's trying to bait me into making promises I can't keep.

"Come for me," I command. "Fucking come for me."

Her muscles twitch against the tension she holds, tension that begs to be released. I'm rather impressed with her ability to edge herself and stave off her climax with the way she grinds and moves.

"Would you—" she stutters through a gasping moan, her face twisting with need, "would you do anything for me?"

I drop one hand to her chest, slip it down over the mound of her breast, and rub the pad of my thumb across her nipple. She gasps, her back arching against the ache of resistance she causes herself. I roll her nipple between my fingers, a gentle twist that I know throbs right through her clit.

"Murphy…" she breathes my name as she slaps a hand on my shoulder, reaching around the back of my neck, holding onto me tight as her back arches to press her breast against my rolling fingers.

"Come. *Now.*"

She can't help the way her body responds to my insistence. She trembles as she fights it, but it's magic when she explodes. Her face opens from its twisted tension into surprised pleasure, her head falls back, her body stiffens as she thrusts through it, her fingernails slice into the skin at the back of my neck, and she shouts her release. Her writhing, pulsing pussy takes me with her, each wave of her pleasure tugging my own, pulling through my hard cock, making me spill inside.

She collapses forward against me when she's spent, her face dropping to my shoulder. I rub a circle over her lower back with one hand until her breathing slows and gradually steadies.

When she's come down from the high, I grab a fistful of her long, dark hair, and sharply yank to lift her head. She gasps as she meets my eyes, her chin raised as I pull back hard.

"You're becoming one of us, Stella…trying to use sex as a weapon to get what you want from me. If you could've edged that orgasm a little longer, you might have had a shot." I scoff, "Renata and Cordelia would be very proud. Did they give you tips?"

"How dare you compare me to them?"

"Don't attempt it again. If you want to behave like a whore, then I'll treat you as such. I'll deny your pleasure, come in your arsehole, and make sure you're fucking bleeding before I'm through."

Her eyes widen with a flash of fury. "Now who's using sex as a weapon? Against the woman he says he loves, no less."

I feel my face twist in shame as the understanding of what I've just threatened sits heavily on my shoulders. I threatened to hurt her with my cock, fuck her until she bleeds, and deny her enjoyment.

I would never do that to her. I couldn't because I could never handle being the man who hurt her. I open my mouth to apologize for threatening to be like the monsters we sell women to and treat her like a slave, but a flurry of sound outside my door draws my attention.

I hear voices and then someone frantically knocks on the door.

She seethes, breathing heavily through her flaring nostrils as her eyes send me rage. I release her and nudge her to move. She's so disgusted with me that she jumps to her feet as soon as I let go. I know I've just taken a thousand steps back in her mind, and I feel the pressure of that stretching tight across my chest.

"She'll kill her! Please, come quick!" the voice on the other side of the door says. "She has a gun!"

"What?" Stella says in surprise as she quickly pushes her dress down and straightens herself out.

"Get back," I tell her, pulling up my pants and buckling my belt. "I want you in the bathroom until I know what's going on. Lock the door."

Her head bobs a little in agreement as she backs away, though her fucking curiosity makes her retreat slowly.

A second fist pounds with the first one. "Murphy, open the door and get out here! That rotten slave slut has a gun!" It's Cordelia's voice this time.

I rush for the door and tug it open. "What are you talking about?"

I see Renata's little boytoy, Luca, standing there beside Cordelia. "Anya has hold of Lorenzo's gun, and she's holding Renata at gunpoint!" Cordelia says breathlessly. "She won't put it down until she sees you."

"Please, hurry!" Luca says frantically.

"Fucking Vittoris," I mutter. I turn to see Stella inching closer. "Stay here, lock the door behind me. I mean it, Stella."

I rush forward into the hallway, slam the door shut behind me, and head off to find out which of the millions of possible reasons Anya has chosen as the appropriate one to threaten Renata Vittori's life.

CHAPTER 27

Murphy

"THERE'D BETTER BE a damn good reason this slave boy disturbed me and my wife," I bellow down the hall as I come upon the chaotic scene.

"Anya demands to speak with you, Murphy," Renata says without looking at me as I approach.

"Are you fucking—" I groan. "What the fuck is going on here?"

Anya Mikhailov is on her knees in the middle of the hallway, still wearing her soft pink lace and tulle gown from this evening. Her kneeling there is strange enough, but it's the gun in her hands aimed steadily at Renata that really rounds out the crazy.

I pause and take a moment to enjoy the look of terror in Renata's expression, though she fights to hide it—but no one can hide fear from their eyes. She has every reason to be terrified that Anya might actually shoot her. After all, Anya did demonstrate her swift determination when she murdered Renata's brother, Vigo, three months ago.

If that weren't enough, Renata holds Anya's lover, Ezra, hostage as a slave—that boy also oddly placed in my hallway. Clad only in his underwear, he kneels behind Anya with bound hands.

Anya looks fierce there on her knees, a forcefield of protective energy radiating around her and Ezra like an invisible shield. I would never underestimate the willingness of a desperate woman when it comes to protecting those she loves.

Of course…

Fuck.

Anya is in love with Ezra.

Understanding of the inconclusive DNA result clicks inside my mind, and I feel idiotically oblivious that I hadn't immediately made the connection. The result of whether Nikolai Mikhailov was the father of Anya's child was inconclusive because he's not the father.

The child belongs to Ezra.

How could I be so stupid as to not realize that before?

I've been so distracted, so preoccupied with taming Stella that my mind hasn't been focused on my work. My harsh business instincts have faded as humanity and empathy sneakily crept back into my heart because of her…because of Stella.

She's more powerful than she'll ever realize.

But in this moment, none of that matters. I need to deescalate and avoid bloodshed—we had enough of that at the last quarterly meeting.

Anya speaks, though she doesn't look at me as her eyes remain solidly focused on Renata. "Renata has attempted to kill the Mikhailov talent slave. She claimed he attacked and raped her, and I know she's lying. I will *not* have it, Murphy. There is no replacement for his talent, and we will *not* break the tradition of the four families just before my turn to host the quarterly meeting because of her false accusation. This is my chance to prove myself worthy of my name, and I will not have her taking the life of our talent slave over a lie. It's unacceptable."

"You're quite the princess, aren't you?" I say beside her, huffing out a heavy breath.

"He raped me, Murphy," Renata accuses. "He attacked me and Luca and then he raped me! I want him *dead*."

My annoyance ticks at the sound of her voice. "Oh, fuck off. We both know that's not fucking true. This isn't the first time you've cried wolf to get a slave killed."

"I never—"

"Shut your mouth, Renata. Our family has been putting security cameras in Vittori family guest rooms for over a decade of meetings that we've hosted. Your family is always causing problems. Keep talking if you want me to go look at the footage from your room. Always fucking causing trouble, fucking Vittoris."

I rub my hand over my beard, pausing to think. I'm gonna have a bloody mess to clean up if I let Anya return to Italy in Renata's care. One of them will kill the other and we can't afford to lose either of them.

"Let us stay here…" Anya says, "under the care of the O'Sheas. I no longer feel safe with the Vittoris. If she puts Ezra's life at risk, the stress it causes me could be detrimental to the health of my baby. The four families can't afford to lose my child. Give me and Ezra shelter here and send the Vittoris home tonight. The safety of the Mikhailov heir has been threatened."

"I've made no such threat to your child's safety!" Renata marches toward Anya. "You're the one pointing a gun!"

"A gun you meant to have Ezra killed with! A gun Lorenzo nearly shot me in the stomach with because of your lies!"

"Ladies," I sigh, pinching the bridge of my nose, "I'm not in the mood for this bullshit."

"*Please*, Murphy." Anya's voice softens and there's something in her intonation that resonates as familiar. "I've been through enough. You wouldn't put Stella through what I've been through. Don't put me through more."

If I look at Anya indirectly, I could almost say she resembles Stella. Her skin is fairer, and her long hair is brown rather than black. But the whispering, nagging part of me that begs to cement a family with Stella—the part that's eager to see her stomach round with our child— calls my heart to find some gentleness and care for the situation Anya's been put in.

"If I say yes, will you put the gun down?"

"If you say yes and arrange for Renata and Lorenzo to leave tonight, then I will put the gun down."

"Christ. Call your pilot to be ready for departure within the hour," I tell Lorenzo. "I'll bring your gun when I have them settled. You Vittoris cause so much fucking drama."

Anya slowly lowers her gun, but it's clear by the way she grips it that she's not giving it up until she feels safe. I call for Renata's slave, Luca, to retrieve the key that will unlock the dreadful collar that's padlocked around Ezra's neck.

As he works on the lock, my eyes catch on Anya's face. The way she looks at Ezra is…inspiring. She looks at him as if her heart aches for him, as if she loves him so much that she feels his pain along with him. I feel that way for Stella, and I wonder if she sees it when I look at her.

No.

I know she doesn't, but fuck, I wish she'd look at me the way Anya looks at Ezra.

How do I make her love me that way?

When Ezra's collar finally lands on the floor, I order the Vittoris to start packing and lead Anya and Ezra to the room she was given as our guest. She was assigned this guest room strategically. It's close to mine and Stella's because I knew I'd need to keep a careful watch on the rebellious girl. I let them enter the room in front of me and I shut the door behind us.

I hold out my palm for the gun. "Hand it over, lass."

"Where will he be staying?" Her head tilts toward Ezra.

"Am I going to regret it if he stays in your room?" I'm stupid to offer it, but I don't want the responsibility of looking after another slave. I'm giving Anya the grace of trust, but it will be painfully ripped away if she breaks it.

"You would let him stay with me?"

"It's probably against my better judgment, but since my home is a fortress and there are extra security measures in place while my wife…

adjusts to her new lot in life, I'll allow you to keep your talent slave for now. Do you have any plans to point a gun at my head?"

"No." She places the gun in my outstretched palm.

"Fuck, I've gone soft. Listen," I point my finger at her intently, "I'm only doing this for you because Renata is on my last fucking nerve. If you test me, you *will* regret it. If you behave yourselves, then we won't have a fucking problem. Understood? There is no escaping my home, so don't even think about trying."

She nods. "Understood."

I turn away and reach for the doorknob, but then I pause, turning back to look at Ezra. "Do you understand what's at stake here, slave boy? You step out of line and try to cross me, and I will hurt you in ways you never imagined."

"Yeah, I get it," Ezra says.

I look him up and down, his energy humming with an urge for rebellion. "I really hope you do." I look at Anya. "Watch him. You're responsible for his behavior. He fucks up, *you've* fucked up. And you know I'll make you pay for it." I pull open the door. "Lock this," I remind them before I step out.

Once the door is shut behind me, I stop, pause, take a moment to close my eyes and breathe deeply. When I feel steady, I open my eyes and turn to head back to my room. I find Stella standing down the hall, just outside our door.

She watches me with anxiety and worry as I make my way back to her, but the simple acknowledgment of concern in her gaze wraps around me like a lasso. She tugs on that invisible rope and drags me nearer—the mere promise of her attention makes me forget the world and all its challenges. I feel relief that she's there, that she's waiting for me. Whether she's angry with me or not, she's my wife, and she's here, and there's peace in her presence.

"Is she okay?" Stella asks when I'm only a few steps away.

"Renata?"

"I don't give a shit about Renata. Is Anya okay?"

I stop in front of her, reaching to cup her cheek in my palm and brush my thumb across her soft skin. "She's fine. She is now. I invited her to stay with us."

"You did?" Her brow furrows in sincere surprise.

I'm surprised by it myself.

"I did. She held Renata at gunpoint. It was only a matter of time before one of them killed the other. I thought it would be better to avoid the bloodshed."

Her head tilts to the side, falling heavier into my palm. "So, you offered to let them stay?"

I nod.

Her eyes flicker across my face. I don't know what she's hoping to see, but it doesn't matter. I get lost in the beauty of her searching eyes and that's all I care about.

She steps closer, forcing me to drop my hand. She snakes her arms around my waist and hugs me. She offers me affection where she never has before, and my heart hammers against my ribs. My pulse rushes adrenaline through my veins, adrenaline that makes me fall from a cliff, dropping hard and fast with my undying love for her.

I wrap my arms around her, cradling the back of her head in my palm, holding her against me impossibly close…and she lets me.

"Thank you…" she whispers, "for letting her stay."

I don't know how to tell Stella that she's softened me. I don't want her to know that she's already taken away some of the power she wants from me, that she holds it firmly in her grasp and only has to hug me like this, whisper softly like this, to get anything she wants from me. I'd give her anything to feel this affection from her again.

I swallow the harsh fear of losing everything I know for this woman. I press a kiss to the top of her head and inhale her sweet, fragrant scent. My breath trembles when I exhale because a terrifying realization has just hit me fucking hard.

If she ever learns that this is all she has to do to strip my power from me entirely, she'll do it, and our world will burn.

And I fear I'd let myself burn with it just to see her rise from the ashes.

CHAPTER 28

Stella

"I WANT TO have the baby back home, at Mikhailov Manor," Anya says.

Ezra drops his fork on his plate and it clangs loudly in the unusually quiet dining room. He looks at Anya with a surprised expression.

I glance at Murphy, sitting at the opposite end of the long dining table, and find him glaring at Ezra's plate. "Be *careful*. Those were my grandmother's."

"Murphy—"

"I heard you the first time, lass."

I watch Anya and the way she steels herself, preparing to boldly ask my husband again. I want to give her encouragement to push him on this, but I don't think she needs it.

"Then I'd like to hear your response," she says.

Murphy puts down his utensils and pushes his plate forward, folding his hands in front of him, and leaning on his elbows. It's just the four of us dining together tonight—me, Murphy, Anya, and Ezra. It's a much quieter affair than usual at our twice weekly O'Shea family dinners.

Cormac and Declan are off inspecting an O'Shea factory, and Kostya is doing the same with a Mikhailov facility. Much of the rest of the family is off on vacation, and Fiona has gone with them under Boyd and Bridget's care. I tried to convince Murphy to let her stay with us. Bridget may be kind to her, but Boyd can be cruel. Even though he's aging severely, he still holds a great deal of power as the former patriarch of the family—and he abuses it when given the chance.

My husband, ever the opportunist, decided he wanted to take advantage of the empty nest so we could play house. Thus, Fiona is away with them, and I worry for her well-being.

But just as much, I'm annoyed for myself. He wants me to spend time with Anya, though I'm not allowed to speak with her unsupervised. He thinks that seeing her pregnant will convince me to want to have a baby with him.

He wants me to have his baby, for crying out loud.

He's been talking about it more since Anya's been staying here for the past couple of months, and it's a bit of an understatement to say it's a sore spot. I'm not interested in having children at this point in my life, and least of all to raise them in the four families' world.

He's a fucking moron if he thinks I'm going to allow that to happen.

No.

I have more important goals. I'm looking for opportunities to chisel away at the power the four families hold over him. I'm trying to make him see how much better off he'd be if he understood what I knew…This is not a life, it's a death sentence—the only question is how long it will be before he's killed or arrested doing what he calls "work."

I wish I didn't care.

I wish I didn't give a fuck what happens to him.

I'm a captive who's had no willing involvement in his business. My marriage was forced. I like to think I'd be spared any criminal convictions if he were ever found out and arrested. I like to think all I would care about is myself if that ever happened—that I would testify against him and help them prosecute him and his despicable family to the fullest extent of the law.

But something terrible happened the night he decided to let Anya and Ezra stay with us. I accidentally let my guard down and my heart softened. And when that happened, my heart played a dangerous trick on me. My heart saw him only as the man I initially fell in love with, and it's been beating with that image ever since.

I can't shake it.

These days I see the good in him more often than the bad, and the way I'm falling for him now significantly rivals the way I fell for him in the beginning.

I fall a little more for him each day that passes, with each bare-minimum act of kindness he shows me. He gives me a million moments of hardness, but one moment of softness keeps me on the hook for more.

I'm starting to look more for those rare moments, and I know it's foolish. It minimizes his toxicity in my mind and leaves me feeling like a dumb, lost little girl who'll take any attention she can get.

My regular phone conversations with Cora further prove how dumb and lost I am. Since our engagement, I've had to lie to her and convince her how happy I am. Yet more and more, the lies have become truths. They've become my overdramatic retellings of the things he actually has done that make me happy, that make me feel loved. I have her as fooled as I am, and she's happy for me because she thinks it's all worked out.

But she only hears the good moments.

I worry I'm starting to blind myself, only allowing myself to see the good. But I am only human, a captive in our forced marriage, and I crave those moments.

I watch him with the glow of firelight behind him, flames crackling in the fireplace. He's a strong, beautiful man that I could bend for—a man I have bent for—and I need to be careful. I straighten my spine and harden my expression as I look at him, trying to remember who he really is.

His eyes catch mine, almost as if he senses my shields going up, and he lunges after the switch to stop it. "Stella. Tell me your thoughts on this…as…a woman."

I could take him asking for my opinion as a kindness. But I've already given up too much power to him today—I was teasing and playful with him earlier and I regret giving him too much of the real me.

I have to balance it; I have to remind him that I'm still against what he stands for. I think now would be the appropriate time to be a proper pain in the ass. It's only fair since he's been a proper pain in mine about wanting me to get pregnant.

I mimic his position, leaning forward on my elbows and folding my hands just as he does. "You mean you'd like to hear my opinion as the only other child-bearing person in this room? Since that's all I'm good for?"

His jaw sets. "That horse is dead, *wife*. Put your damn stick down."

"Then it's a fucking zombie horse, Murphy, because it keeps getting up to rear its ugly fucking head."

"Watch your fucking foul-mouth. I'll wash it out with soap."

"Promise?" I cock my head to the side, agitation filling me with the same kind of rush I get when I'm horny.

Fucking fuck.

Murphy slams his fist on the table, but I don't flinch. He does that plenty—trying to scare me into bending to his will—but he doesn't scare me. Any violence that comes out of him always turns into sex… spectacular sex. Maybe I sometimes egg him on intentionally knowing that.

I scowl at him, waiting for him to say something, but then he just laughs. "Would you just speak your mind, woman?"

Woman?

Oh, no, sir.

I slam my hands on the table and push my chair back with a screech. My heart pounds because what I'm about to say is going to set him off, and the adrenaline I feel in anticipation of him unleashing is anticipatory bliss.

What the fuck is wrong with me?

I flip him the finger. "Go fuck yourself, you fucking, misogynist pig." I turn and head for the door in a flash.

I see him leap to his feet from the corner of my eye and it forces me to quicken my steps. I get through the swinging door of the private dining room just as he comes up behind me.

The moment we're both through the door, he grabs hold of my hips and tugs me backward against him so I can't run away. He turns and pushes me until I crash forward against the wall. I put out my palms to catch myself and turn my cheek, pressing it against the cold, stone wall.

My heart is beating so fast, fluttering like crazy. I'm instantly turned-on and that pisses me off...and being pissed off at him turns me on even more. It's a vicious circle of lust and anger that maybe I've become a little obsessed with.

He leans against me, his body molding to my backside. He rubs his hands over my hips and waist, and he comes in close, bringing his face next to mine.

"Go fuck yourself? Really, sweetheart?"

I try to disguise the desire in my tone by masking it with sarcasm. "Really, Murphy." I pause. "You really want my opinion?"

He kisses my cheek, shifting his hips forward, and I can feel his cock against my butt. My muscles tense as I try hard not to wiggle my ass against it.

"If I didn't want your opinion, I wouldn't ask for it. You know that."

I push back into him, nudging him to leave just enough space between us so I can turn to face him. He's quick to keep me there, hurriedly coming in close to fill the space between us as he leans into my curves and bends to nip at my neck.

Charming motherfucker.

"If you had to push a human being out of your asshole, would you want to do it in someone else's home? Or would you prefer to be in your own damn home where you're comfortable?"

"I'd rather be in hospital."

I groan with frustration of both the intellectual and physical persuasion. "You've already made it very clear that's not an option for her since you fear she'll out you. Which she should. She should out the entire operation of the four families."

He huffs out a breath and pulls his head back, dragging his lips away from my neck. He looks at me with admonishing eyes. "That's not what we're discussing."

I sigh, trying to ignore my growing fury and lust because I care about Anya. And knowing what little I do of her history, I'd say she's fully deserving of some comfort in her life.

"Let her have the baby wherever she wants. She's been through enough; grant her that small comfort of being in her home."

"I can't just send them off to Russia alone. I don't trust them."

"Then we'll go with them."

His forehead creases as he considers. "That's not a terrible idea."

I narrow my eyes at him. "Um, thanks?"

He tilts his head. "It's a *good* idea. You and I could use some more time away from the family. And you're right, she should have some comfort in the midst of childbirth. Okay," he says with finality, then takes a sudden step back.

My body immediately misses the warmth of his.

"Okay?"

"I heard you, and you were right. I'll make it happen."

I swallow the thick lump of gratitude rising in my throat. "Thank you."

He gives me a once over with his flickering gaze, a small smile creeping up the corners of his lips. "Now go to bed, Stella, and wait for me to join you."

"It's only seven o'clock."

"I didn't say anything about sleeping." He disappears through the swinging door.

I hold my breath until it swings shut, then let it out in a heavy rush, along with all my willpower.

CHAPTER 29

Stella

I'VE JUST WITNESSED a tragically beautiful performance by a talented dancer named Ezra Bell. The routine was moving and his talent was impressive, but my heart aches for his forced service as a talent slave as much as it aches for Fiona.

I was watching Anya during Ezra's performance as much as I was watching him. It's just something I do now—observing the love she has for Ezra has become almost an obsession for me. They are truly star-crossed lovers, their fates not their own to decide. Yet their devotion to each other is palpable…and utterly addictive.

I longed for Murphy that way once. If I'm being honest with myself, I'm starting to long for him that way again. But my blasphemous love for the villain is something I just haven't been able to accept. I haven't allowed myself to accept it fully, and that hurts me more than anything. Yet I can watch Anya and Ezra and find peace in their innocent, acceptable love—though the four families won't accept them forever.

I hear there are already murmurings of dissent from the Vittoris—they want Anya dead after she has the baby, who they want to raise as their own. They think the Russian line should end with Anya. They'd rather see three powerful families than have one where Anya has such great influence over the child who will become its Head of House one day.

Part of me wants Anya to rise, to fight the families along with me as we both grow in power. But if the rumors are true, then Anya's life is in danger the moment she gives birth…and there may be nothing I can do to save her. But perhaps she has a plan to save herself.

I've been observing not only Anya and Ezra, but Kostya as well. The three of them have started spending more time together. I caught them once in an intense conversation where most of it was in Russian between Anya and Kostya, which in itself was odd because Ezra only speaks English.

It gave me an inkling that they may be planning something. I didn't know what and I didn't know when, but I knew it would be significant and soon. My obsessive observations over the last few weeks have allowed me to pick up on their subtleties.

Anya grew increasingly more agitated as Ezra's performance carried on, wavering between shifting uncomfortably in her seat and tense stillness. I wouldn't have thought much of it, given how pregnant she is and past her due date. It wasn't her obvious physical discomfort that caught my attention—it was the way she tried to hide it.

Even more telling was the way that Kostya popped from his seat the moment Ezra's performance ended. He rushed up the aisle to exit as a standing ovation was given for the talent. His face was tense and he was in a hurry, which seemed unnecessary. And the way Ezra's tension on stage ticked up after his performance was done—as he darted glances between Kostya's retreating form and Anya standing in the aisle—put me on edge.

I just know they're planning something.

But what?

An escape?

Murphy and I linger in the foyer just outside Nobility Hall as others filter through a narrow hallway which connects back through to Mikhailov Manor. It's blistering cold outside—winter in the Russian wilderness. No one is exiting through the doors that lead outside, all choosing to use the interior connecting hallway instead.

That's why I find it odd when I spy Kostya creeping around outside. I only spot him because I'm looking for him, wondering where he rushed off to right after Ezra's performance. I look away after I spot him, trying not to draw attention to him.

Instead, I turn to look at Murphy standing beside me, waiting to ensure that Anya and Ezra make it back to the reception.

Somehow, I know they don't mean to make it back to the reception.

Help them.

Cause a distraction.

I reach out my hand to hold his, squeezing his palm gently. His eyes drop to where our palms touch, his brow furrowed in confusion before looking up to meet my gaze.

Okay, I have his attention.

Now what do I do?

The number of people filtering through is waning and the theater is nearly cleared out. My heart pounds as the final groups of people exit the theater, and I don't know what the fuck to do.

What would distract him?

What would get his attention?

By luck or some miracle, one last person exits the theater alone, and it gives me an instant idea. It's a stupid, childish idea, but one that should work to distract Murphy, nonetheless.

Renata Vittori breezes by, giving both of us a once over as she moves past. Before she can exit through the connected hallway, I swallow my apprehension and pick a fight.

I put on an expression of pure rage, as if I've been slighted, and turn my head with disdain toward Renata. "What the fuck did you just say to me?"

She stops. "Excuse me?"

I don't want her to stop, I want to get them both into the hallway. I let go of Murphy's hand and circle her like a predator about to pounce on its prey, lining up to push her back where I need her to go.

"She just called me a bitch, Murphy," I lie smoothly.

"What?"

"Say it louder, Renata. I dare you."

She gives me a look of disgust, pulling her head away from me. She's got a good two inches of height on me, but I can take her. Adrenaline punches through my veins in preparation for a fight.

"Oh, sweet girl," she purrs condescendingly, giving me a real reason to want to kick her ass, "if I wanted to call you a bitch, I'd say it loud enough for your husband to hear."

Murphy's jaw ticks and he steps forward, trying to get between us—it's actually a little heart-warming, but I don't have the time to unpack that feeling. I need to get them out.

Before he can step between us, I lunge for her. I put my hands on her shoulders and shove her backward toward the open door leading into the connected hallway. Renata stumbles back on her heels but quickly rights herself.

Her eyes pop in surprise that I've laid hands on her, but honestly, it was probably just a matter of time before someone did. She has power, but it's unearned. She's a bitch and nobody likes her—except for Cordelia, but she's a bitch, too.

"I didn't call you a bitch," she argues, "but I will now, you filthy tramp."

"That's my *wife*," Murphy growls, but I don't allow him to intervene.

I shove her again and she moves back, closer to the hallway entry. This time, I don't stop moving; I keep marching toward her and she keeps backing away. For being such a big talker, she sure is afraid of a real fight.

I breathe a sigh of relief when she crosses the threshold and enters the hallway backward. Murphy quickly follows behind me, so I chase after Renata, leading him away from Nobility Hall.

I need to keep them both moving.

"Stella," Murphy warns as I keep pushing her back.

He's right where I need him to be, following right behind me, his attention on my behavior and the ensuing fight with Renata. I've got some pent-up rage to let out anyway, so maybe this worked out well for all of us.

"Are you going to hit me, Stella? Go on. I'll turn your entire family against you if you do—"

I ball my fist, rush her, and land a punch squarely against her perfect fucking cheekbone. Pain shoots through my knuckles, a sharp rush followed by a slow-aching bruise. Her body twists as the force of my hit turns her sideways and she stumbles, catching herself against the wall.

"Stella!" Murphy shouts, and I feel his fingers wrap around my elbow.

I yank free from his grip as I shake my hand. Renata touches her cheek, her mouth open in shock as her eyes start to water. I can't stop my smile, and I do nothing to hide it—I may as well let loose because I have both of their attention fully on me now.

Fury slips down her features, washing her face in anger, and I welcome it. I hold my arms out to my sides, welcoming her to come after me. She drops her hand from her face and lunges for me, shoving me sideways and slamming my back to the wall.

"Renata!" Murphy shouts.

But I don't need him to defend me with her.

I wrap my fist around her swinging black hair and pull her head down, forcing her neck to crane at an uncomfortable angle. She lets go of me when her hands come up to try to loosen my grip, and I use the leverage to swing her around and shove her to the wall instead.

"You disgusting *cunt!*" she spits.

My eyebrows shoot to my hairline at her insult. I draw back my fist and swing, hitting somewhere on her face. I don't get to see the result of my strike because Murphy's arms wrap around my waist and drag me backward. He spins me around and moves between me and

Renata, blocking us from each other.

He hovers over her as she slumps to the floor, wagging a stern finger in her face. "I'll hit you myself if you *ever* call her that again. She hates that word, and I think it's pretty disgusting coming from you, too."

My pulse thrums at the way he defends me. He turns to me, putting his hands on my cheeks as I pant to catch my breath. "Are you okay?"

I grin slowly. "Yeah, I'm fine. Don't worry about me."

He flashes me a quick wink, then turns his attention back to Renata. He grabs her by the elbow, hoists her pathetic ass from the floor, and marches her up the hallway toward the manor. "Let's get someone to look at your fucking face because that's gonna bruise."

Thank God that worked.

I run in the opposite direction as soon as they start moving. I cross the threshold into the foyer of Nobility Hall, grab hold of the door, and slam it shut behind me, pressing my back against it.

Anya and Ezra are both standing there, wide-eyed and fearful.

"Where's Kostya?" I ask quickly. "He's coming. Murphy's coming."

We all startle as Kostya whips open the exterior door from the outside. I see the exhaust from a car he's got running just beyond the door.

They're planning to run.

Yes, they have to run.

"Go," I tell them quickly. "I can stall him. But you have to hustle. Get the fuck going!"

I can finally breathe when they move. Anya and I share a glance, a look of concern in her eyes. I'm sure she's fearful for what they're about to do, so I try to grant her some encouragement with a small smile.

And in the next moment, they're gone, disappearing through the exterior doors. They're gone from the theater, but they aren't off the grounds yet. They still need more time. And the more I can give them, the better.

I have to stall Murphy.

"Stella?" I hear him through the door at my back as he jiggles the handle, trying to push it open. "Let me through."

I steel myself and turn to open the door, but I don't let him through. Instead, I rush him, tossing my arms around his neck and hugging him close.

"I'm sorry," I lie. "She just…I swear she called me a bitch under her breath, and I just lost it. I *hate* that woman."

He hugs my waist, holding me sweetly, and it makes me feel guilty. "It's fine; I don't like her, either. We'll have some explaining to do to our families, but it's nothing that hasn't happened before."

I pull back to look at him. "Someone's tried to break her jaw before?"

"I don't know that anyone's actually struck her before. Hell of a right hook, by the way, sweetheart. Are you okay?"

He strokes his hand down the side of my head and I allow myself to melt to his caring touch, just a little. "I'm fine. Better now. That felt good."

"I'll bet it did."

"You're not angry?"

"I probably should be, but I'm not. It might have turned me on a bit to watch, though."

My cheeks flush with heat, because maybe it turned me on a little, too. It really was a rush to slam my knuckles into her smart mouth. There's an opportunity in this, a way to distract him for a little bit longer.

I grab hold of his lapels and tug him with me as I walk backward toward the theater doors. "Let me fuck you in the back row."

His eyes flash with the desire he always has for me. He slams his body against mine, turns us, and pins my back to the wall. "What's gotten into you?"

He wants me, though his jaw is tense with his restraint, with his caution.

He knows.

"I want you," I tell him.

It's not even a lie.

I do want him, even though I'm not supposed to.

He slaps his palms to the wall on either side of my head, bending over me, trapping me. My breath catches and I struggle to steady it with the way he watches me. His eyelids fall to hood his narrowed eyes, his head falls to the side in consideration, and I feel the steady pulse of his suspicion.

"I can't recall a time since I brought you home that you asked me to fuck you, Stella."

I arch my back to curve my body against him. "Well, I'm asking you to fuck me now."

He dips his head, bringing his mouth a whisper of an inch in front of mine. His tongue slips out to wet his lips and he leans in, about to kiss me, but he stops short. He turns his head away with a snap. "Where are Anya and Ezra? They should be out by now."

I reach up and grab his face, turn it toward me, and kiss him hard and fast. He lets out a strained groan against my bruising kiss—a kiss I've given him willingly, a kiss he didn't have to steal. I feel something like shame ripple through me as I use my sexuality against him this way…shame I don't deserve to feel for doing what's morally right.

I wonder if he can feel it, like a rolling wave of guilt vibrating across my lips. I don't have to wonder long. Suddenly, he jerks back. He knocks my hands away from his cheeks so he can grab my face instead.

"What did you do?"

My lips part, but no words come out. I just shake my head against his hands.

"What did you do, Stella? What did you *do?*"

"I didn't do anything. I just—"

He doesn't let me finish. He releases me with a huff and storms over to jerk open one of the doors into the theater. He steps inside the empty house and bellows, "Anya? Kostya?"

I run after him as he storms down the aisle toward the stage. "They're probably just backstage."

"Anya!" His voice echoes eerily through the empty space.

He waits a beat, and when he gets no response, he whirls around to face me. He stomps back up the aisle, coming after me with fury painted across his features. I step back, but he catches me before I can retreat, his hand latching around my throat as he comes in close.

"Where are they? You know something. Tell me. Tell me right fucking now."

"I don't know where they are."

"Yes, you do!" he shouts, but his rage is masking his fear.

I can see it flicker behind his eyes and it changes something within me. It pulls out some long-dormant need to comfort and care—something I haven't had the urge to do for him until this very moment.

"Baby," I whisper. I lift one hand to lightly touch his wrist, and his grip around my neck loosens. "It's okay."

"Where are they?"

I hesitate, but I can't stand to see that fear behind his beautiful eyes. I know I shouldn't say a word; I shouldn't tell him anything. I try to stay strong and keep my mouth shut, but when he softens, when he drops his arm and comes in close, it takes everything I've got just to keep air moving through my lungs.

He wraps his arms around me and pulls me close. "Stella, please. Tell me."

What do I do?

He's going to find out one way or another, and I don't know how long I can delay him.

What if they don't get away? What if the four families realize they're gone first, and then go after them? I have to tell him...but how can I keep him from stopping them?

I hug his waist and hold tight, knowing I can't tell this lie effectively if I'm looking in his eyes. "I helped Kostya plan their escape." He starts to pull away from me, but I squeeze, refusing to let go of him as I lie. "I knew they were going to do it. I helped them plan it. I was involved with all of it, Murphy, and I'm…I'm scared. What will they do to me when they find out I was involved?"

He's rigid in my arms, but a brief, sudden tremor shudders through him. It scares me a little. His grip on me tightens and that scares me a little more. But this is what I need from him. I need him connected with me, emotional and fearful for me given what I've done.

Though I lied about planning it, I did help them escape—regardless, this will get me in trouble with the four families. It puts Murphy in a precarious situation, and I need to keep him on my side. I firmly press into his hold, letting my cheek rest against his strong chest.

"I helped them escape. What will the four families do to me?"

"Fuck," he mutters. "Fuck, Stella. What the fuck were you thinking?"

The tremor in his voice, the way he clutches me so tightly, scares me even more now as it really hits me. I *had* aided in their escape, and very real consequences might fall upon me for that.

"What do we do?" I ask.

He releases me, grabs my wrist, and starts up the aisle, dragging me after him. "We're going to fix this."

"What do you mean?"

"We're going after them."

I plant my feet and jerk back, trying to shake free from his grip, though he holds me firmly. "Let them go, Murphy."

"Absolutely fucking not." He tugs and manages to make me move, and I stumble after him in my high heels.

"Murphy!"

"Shut the fuck up! This isn't a negotiation! Your life is now at stake for what you've done, but there's still time to rectify this, and I *will* rectify this." He shoves the theater doors open and pulls me through.

"Let them punish me for it. I don't care. Anya and Ezra deserve to be free!"

His fury reaches a peak as he stops, spinning to face me, coming in close. "I don't give a shit about them. I give a shit about *you*. They've killed for lesser offenses than this. *I've* killed for lesser offenses than this. But I'll be damned if anyone tries to take you away from me."

The raw truth shining in his eyes halts me, stills me.

He pauses, swiping his palm over his beard. "Listen to me. You got us into this, and you're gonna help me get us out of it. I need you to be still and quiet. We're gonna go get keys to one of the vehicles, and you and I are going after them. If you keep fighting me, you will raise their suspicions and that will be problematic for everyone. I suggest you calm the fuck down and pretend you didn't just aid in an escape, or else the four families will go after them and deal with *all* of you in an equal manner. Is that what you want?"

I want them to be free.

I want to be free.

The only chance of that happening is to keep the four families out of this and let Murphy handle it. There's hope that they'll be gone before we reach them, and I choose to hold on to that.

I stop fighting him. "Okay," I agree. "Okay, let's fix this together."

His grip slips from my wrist to my hand and our palms clasp together. There's a lightning bolt that bursts through our palms, a thunderous flash of light that blinds me with the knowledge that we need each other—we both actually need each other right now.

I recall him slicing my palm and drawing blood before our consummation—from the very hand he holds now. He'd told me, "*Our blood is the same now. Yours and mine.*" I feel the meaning of that in our grip—his loyalty and devotion, the way he takes ownership *with* me, viewing my choice as his choice, a problem that we have to solve together.

"I won't let them take you away from me," he says gently.

I lock our fingers together and hold his hand tightly, for the first time feeling stronger with him at my side than I feel on my own.

CHAPTER 30

Stella

THE NARROW ROAD that cuts through the dense forest is slick with ice. Murphy drives cautiously, but quickly down the path. Snow drifts down through the trees, covering the ground, though the bare branches of aspen and pine trees slow the snowfall's descent. There's no light except for the moon and the beams of our black SUV.

It's eerily calm and quiet.

I glance over at Murphy, who's on high alert, his fists clenched around the steering wheel. We haven't said a word to each other since we got the keys and snuck out of the manor without drawing attention.

"I'm sorry." I don't know why those words come out of my mouth. Maybe because his tension is so unnerving—I feel his anxious energy pulsing and it overwhelms me.

"I'm part of every choice you make, every decision. I don't know what's so difficult for you to understand."

"I'm a person on my own—"

"You're my *wife*. It's my duty to stand by your side and if you fuck up, then I fuck up, too."

He releases one hand from the steering wheel to swipe it across his beard, his stress palpable.

"I only wanted to give them a chance. They're in love. Don't they deserve to be free and happy?"

He glances at me. "Don't *we* deserve to be free and happy? You could be killed for your involvement. I could be killed for failing to notify the board immediately. Would it have been worth it to help them then? To do what you did?"

Silence falls and remains for beats, the thickness of it making my pulse quicken.

"I'm trying, Stella," he says quietly. "I'm trying to be a better man for you. I'm trying to do what's right for you."

My eyes are glued to his face, though his features are shadowed in the darkness.

"I know I destroyed the life you had before. I understand that. I don't regret making you my wife because stubborn and bull-headed as you are, I can't stand to think of what kind of man I'd be without you."

My heart flutters and I stifle a gasp.

"I want to make this life good for you. I want to make you happy, and I have the power to do that. I have the power to be better than my father was. I have the power to influence change, but I can't do that when you pull shit like this that I have to fix."

"You weren't meant to fix it. They were meant to be free."

"And you were meant to be mine, but the facts don't require your acceptance to remain true."

"How can I believe something is true when there is no proof of it? How could I ever believe you want to be a better man when you haven't shown me?"

A sound from above interrupts our conversation—the whirring sound of helicopter blades chopping through the air far above the trees. We both lean forward to peek out the windshield, and I can spot the lights of the helicopter flying overhead.

"Fuck," Murphy mutters. He lifts his hands and beats them against the steering wheel. "Fuck!"

"They got away…"

We crest at the top of a hill. As we arc over the top, I see two lights in the distance at the bottom of the hill. We coast down the incline and a scene comes into view in a snow-covered clearing at the bottom of the hill.

"Murphy," I warn, pointing toward it.

But he's not looking toward the clearing, he's looking at the road ahead. "What the fuck?" he mutters, squinting. "Hold on."

He presses the brake smoothly, but I can feel the way the icy road makes the tires slip. The back end veers left and his arm snaps out, a protective instinct to hold me in place as the car swerves. My pulse quickens along with my breaths, nervous energy building within my gut. I let out a sigh of relief when he somehow manages to bring the car to a crooked stop, sideways on the road, just before the bottom of the hill. He doesn't say a word to me, but he parks, pops open his door, and climbs out.

I quickly follow suit, carefully walking in my heels on the icy road to move around the SUV. I meet him at the side of our vehicle to find him looking down at the ground, where our tires were meant to travel, and my eyes follow his gaze. There's a metal strip covered with thick spikes laid across the entire width of the road.

"What is that?" I ask.

He lifts his head to look at me. "A spike strip. Someone put it here to keep anyone from leaving."

"Did you—"

"No, I didn't know anything about this." His jaw tenses. "I should've been told about this."

Movement catches my attention from the corner of my eye, drawing me back to the lights I saw in the small clearing up ahead. Squinting, I stare in that direction, and realize I can see the shadow of a person moving nearby.

Headlights—that's what the lights are. Two headlights aiming at the trees in the distance, so close to the tree trunks that the lights are haloed and dull.

I step wide over the spike strip and walk as quickly as I can toward the glow.

It's easily below freezing and I'm already shivering. The icy roadway is particularly slippery in high heels, so I step off the side of the road and slowly trudge over the snowy dirt shoulder that lines it. After only a few steps, Murphy appears and falls in step beside me. He grabs hold of my elbow, but doesn't pull me back, doesn't try to stop me. He holds me so that I don't fall.

Moonlight casts a dull, eerie glow over the clearing as we approach, casting unwanted light on a scene that makes my veins hiss from a wave of adrenaline which floods me.

Snow painted crimson.

Anya's motionless body lies atop a pool of blood, her blush pink gown tattered, torn, and bloody.

Oh, God.

Oh, my God.

My hand clamps over my mouth.

Kostya rushes away from her side, coming toward us. "Murphy, I'm sorry. I did not—"

"Save it," Murphy replies. "I'm not the one who put that fucking spike strip across the road."

"Please, don't—"

"My wife told me everything, Kostya. I know every detail of your involvement in this attempted escape."

"Then kill us now," Kostya says. "Kill us before they come for us."

Us?

"She's alive?" I shake from Murphy's grip and run to Anya, unconcerned for the way the freezing snow bitterly bites at my toes. "Oh, my God." I drop to my knees beside her, landing in the blood-soaked snow. I glance over my shoulder at Murphy as he approaches. "Murphy. Please. We have to help her."

"You've already gotten me into enough fucking trouble with your involvement, Stella. And where the fuck is Ezra?"

"He's gone," Kostya replies. "With the baby. On the helicopter that left ten minutes ago."

"She's bleeding…" My voice quakes as I take in the sight of this strong woman, pale as the snow, blood pooling all around her. "Did she give birth? Out here? Oh, my God. Murphy…*Please*. You told me you could change. You told me you could be a better man for me. You told me you had enough power now to make changes and be a better father than your own. I'm fucking begging you. Don't let this poor girl die. Not like this."

He moves in close behind me. "You don't understand, Stella—"

I leap to my feet, anger and heartache rushing through my veins. I whirl around and jab my blood-covered index finger into his chest. "No, *you* don't understand, Murphy. You find a way to save her life, or I go to the board and tell them everything. I'll tell them how I helped Kostya plan her escape, and you know what will happen to me then. Are you willing to let me suffer those consequences? Or can you step the fuck up right fucking now?"

Silence falls, and though I feel frantic, I dig deep to hold steady, to stare him down, to stand firm, because I'm not going to let Anya die like this.

I can never love him if he lets her die like this—and my pulsing soul knows how much I want to love him.

"Well, fuck," he mutters, running his hand over his beard. "Let's get her outta here before the rest of the four families come looking."

"Where are we taking her? And what about Kostya?"

"I have a plan. Go get my phone from the car so I can call our pilot. I can stall the rest of them from coming out here for maybe a half hour. We need to move quickly. I can't afford any suspicion on my head. We'll tell them they all got away on the first chopper and you and I went after them in the second. Understood?"

My heart skips a beat and gratitude seeps from my pores. "Thank you." I throw my arms around him. "Really, thank you, Murphy."

Something strange wraps around our embrace, like a crackling forcefield of electricity that coils and sparks. It's a moment where the universe pauses and shows me that I'm right where I was always meant to be.

I was a lost soul before, just waiting to be found…and Murphy O'Shea was meant to find me. I was meant to save this woman from her death; I was meant to bring Murphy here to this place and time.

I was always meant to be his.

CHAPTER 31

Murphy

STELLA PACES A trail across the rug in my office, her arms folded tensely across her chest as we speak in hushed tones. A month has passed since we rescued Anya from the forest. By some miracle, she survived and recovered, and I've secretly given her shelter in our factory in Oslo.

"It's only a matter of time before they all find out. We should just let her leave."

"If we let Anya leave Oslo, the families will find her."

"Well, it's only a matter of time before your family realizes that you cleared out the entire factory. The girls you let go, the people who helped them leave… they'll talk. People always talk, Murphy."

"They won't talk. They've all been given monumental sums of hush money, enough for them to live out the rest of their lives comfortably."

She stops beside my desk and looks down at me. "Your family will realize how much money you've spent. They'll know."

"My family doesn't have the privilege to access those bank records. Only the other Heads of House do, and currently Leo Leblanc is the only one. I've thought this through clearly. I know what I'm doing. Have a little faith."

Her anxious features soften as she side-steps closer. She leans back against the desk in front of me, dropping her arms and curling her fingers around the edge of it at either side of her hips. "I'm trying," she says softly, her deep brown eyes catching hold of mine.

The look takes my breath away. I roll my chair toward her, spread my legs wide so I can move in closer. I put my hands on her hips and look up at her. "I know you are, and I'm grateful for it."

She smiles at me, though stress still holds her expression. "For what it's worth, I'm proud of you for doing this." She presses her eyes shut and takes in a deep breath. When she opens them again, I see nothing but raw sincerity. "If you continue down this path, I'll be proud to call myself your wife."

Proud.

She's proud of me.

The thought strikes my chest like a hot iron and fills me with instant warmth. To have her pride is as fulfilling as having her unconditional love.

It's greater than love.

It's acceptance.

It's gratitude.

It feeds my soul in a way that makes me realize for the first time that I was starving.

I push to my feet and eliminate the space between us. She slips up onto the edge of the desk and opens her legs for me, letting me settle between them so I can wrap my arms around her. She hugs me freely, closely, her cheek pressing against my beating heart.

"You know your soul was never lost," I say against her ear. "It was only searching for mine so you could heal me."

She lifts her head and looks up at me, her forehead creasing as she searches my face. I let go of her so I can take her cheeks in my hands.

"I would do anything for you." I kiss her sweetly, gently, tasting her appreciation for the changes I'm making on her tongue.

Fuck, she's everything.

I destroyed her world to bring her into mine, but she's so goddamn powerful that she's convinced me to burn it all down to ashes. She moans into my mouth, and I wonder if she can taste my love for her, my gratitude, my obsessive, undying passion for her.

She gradually pulls her head away, just enough to break the kiss. She pants as her hands slide back around the sides of my waist, and she pushes them up my chest, over my shoulders, and around the back of my neck. She digs her fingers into my hair and tugs me forward, bringing me down so our foreheads touch. Her skin is flushed pink from our kiss, and I lick my lips, hungry for more.

But she stops me with her words when I tilt my chin.

"I love you," she whispers, and it stops my heart. "I love the man you're becoming. I won't fight it anymore…I don't want to."

I take in a deep breath, inhaling the sweetness of her words. I open my mouth to tell her that I love her, too, but a fucking fist pounding on my office door disrupts our perfect moment. We both let out a sigh of annoyance. I kiss her lips once more, then step away from her, moving across the room to open the door.

Cordelia shoves her way through the door and stomps into the office, whirling around to face me as I push the door closed behind her—I have a feeling this is something I don't want anyone else hearing.

Bailey jumps to her feet, head down and tail wagging, a low growl rumbling through her chest. I wave my hand at her to hold and she tensely sits. Bailey's never taken much to Cordelia, but I've never seen her hop on guard this quickly before.

"Where's the money?" Cordelia demands.

"I don't know what you're talking about."

"The *money*. Millions have disappeared, and I want to know where it went."

I narrow my eyes at her.

She doesn't have access to the bank records.

How the fuck does she know?

I remain firm in the territory of playing dumb. "Nothing has disappeared. I don't know what you're talking about."

"Vigo gave me access to everything well before he died. I've seen it all. I know that money has disappeared, I just don't know where it went, and I demand to know right now."

I shouldn't be surprised to hear that Vigo Vittori was spilling secrets to Cordelia before he died. He knew she wanted my power, and the sick bastard enjoyed ruffling feathers.

"You have no right to that information, and I'll ensure your access is stripped within the hour."

She stomps toward me, coming in far too close, but I let her. I would never take a step back for her.

"Where is our *money?*" She spits her words with a fury I've never seen from her.

Stella quickly moves to my side and Bailey pops up, moving in front of her. "Back the fuck away from my husband."

I hold out my arm in front of Stella, preparing either to hold her back or protect her from my cousin, knowing the former is more likely than the latter.

Delia's gaze flickers to Stella, then back to me. "It has something to do with her, doesn't it? Did she swindle you out of our family's money?"

I step forward, forcing Cordelia to take a step back. "It's her money, too. Stella is as much of an O'Shea as you and I."

"She's not our blood, Murphy."

"Our blood became one when we consummated our marriage."

She scoffs, turning her attention to Stella. "What did you do with our money?"

Stella's face shows cold, impassive dignity. "I spent it on new shoes, of course. I felt it only fair that I should show the same level of entitled pretension on my feet as you do. I am above you in rank, after all."

In a swift motion far too quick for me to catch, Cordelia slaps my wife across the cheek. Bailey barks and snaps. Fire erupts in my gut and sets me ablaze. I snatch her bony wrist in my grip, twist her arm behind her back, and shove her forward into the bookcase.

"How dare you lay a finger on my wife? I should cut off your hand for touching her!"

"Murphy," Stella says softly, her hand landing on my shoulder.

I release Cordelia and step back with a snap. "Get the fuck out of my office. I want the whole goddamn family in the living room. Now!"

She whirls around to look at me with narrowed eyes. "You've just lost my good favor."

"And you've fucking lost mine!"

Her upper lip snarls. "Then I have nothing to lose." Her furious eyes glance toward my wife, looking her up and down with disdain.

I move into Cordelia's space and point my finger over her shoulder toward the door. "Get. Out."

I could fucking throttle her. She's lucky she has the good sense to leave. She whirls around, yanks open the door, and marches her pompous heels right out of my office.

I turn and pace away, grabbing my cell phone from my pocket and sending off a group text to the family to have their arses in the living room in five minutes. I shove my phone back into my pocket.

"What are you going to do?"

"I'm going to set an example."

"How?"

"Cordelia wants to question our authority and lay hands on my wife? Then I'll show them exactly what happens when they cross us." I grab her hand and pull her toward the door.

"Murphy, wait." She stops, tugging backward on my hand and forcing me to stop with her. I'm huffing with anger and fire blazes in my veins, but her eyes wash across my face like water dousing the flame.

A sly smirk curls the corner of her mouth. "You've never been hotter than you are right now."

Fuck.

I let go of her hand, lasso my arm around her waist, and drag her against me, bending to bruise her lips with a powerful kiss.

My eyes squeeze shut as I let myself taste her and feel the power of her love. I was meant to be a king on my own until I turned forty, but I wonder now if that rule was only ever meant to dampen my power. Alone, I could rule my kingdom in the four families' world, but with her, I can conquer the universe.

I open the door and hold it wide for her, letting my queen lead the way. As she steps across the threshold, Bailey rushes after her, turns as Stella exits the office, and starts barking like mad.

"What are you—" Stella begins, but then the universe implodes.

A flash of orange hair catches my attention first. Cordelia is standing right there, far too close to my wife, whose lips are parted in shock. Cordelia's face is twisted in rage but singed with satisfaction. My eyes draw down in disbelief to see Cordelia's fist against Stella's stomach. Cordelia grunts and draws her arm back in a swift motion, and that's when I see the blade pull free from Stella's flesh. Her lips part as pain and shock wash the color from her cheeks; instead, color floods from her middle, crimson seeping through her shirt.

The shock that registers in her dark brown eyes is what sets off the adrenaline in my veins. Her gaze drops to see the deep crimson stain spread across her stomach. Blood spills from her, and when she slumps, reality strikes me.

She's been stabbed.

I rush forward to catch her beneath her arms, falling to my knees with her as she drops to the floor. Bailey circles us madly, yipping and whimpering.

"Stella!" I hear Declan yell from somewhere down the hall. "Fuck! I'll call the physician."

"Call a fucking ambulance!" I shout at him. "She needs a surgeon!"

I frantically scan all around me, searching for Cordelia, searching for help, trying to figure out what the fuck I'm supposed to do here. That's when my eyes land on Cordelia, casually striding away down the hall, dangling the bloody dagger in her fingers, leaving a trail of crimson dripping down the hallway.

It all happened so quickly. She must have already had the dagger on her when she came into my office. She was prepared, ready to attack, and she did it with all the demonic grace of a monster.

She's a monster.

"*I have nothing to lose*," she'd said in my office.

I see Cormac round the corner with Tally, and I shout to him, "Stop her! Hold her! I'll cut off her fucking head!"

I don't wait to see if he follows my orders as my attention is drawn back to Stella, her arse on the floor between my knees, slumped back against me.

Stella looks up at me, her entire body tremors in shock. "I'm okay," she whispers. "I'm okay…right?"

"You're gonna be okay."

She nods, but I see the fear in her expression. Her eyes turn away from me to glance down and she sees the horror that I see—a pool of blood soaking through her clothes and spreading wildly.

"Shit," she mutters. "Oh, shit, that's a lot of blood. That's all from me?"

Declan appears at her side, slamming down to his knees. "Fuck. I called a private airlift. An ambulance would take too long. They'll be here in fifteen minutes."

"We might not have fifteen minutes!"

"What?" Stella's voice cracks. "It's not that bad, right?" Her eyes lock onto mine.

"You'll be all right," Declan tells her. "Just fifteen minutes and help will be here."

"Am I gonna die?" Her voice catches on the words and fear brings burning tears behind my eyes.

"No. You're too strong. No one can end you that easily. Just hang on."

Fiona appears, dropping to her knees opposite Declan. "We have to put pressure on the wound." She leans forward, lifting Stella's bloody shirt. "This might hurt," she warns before putting her hand over the spot where blood spills.

A scream bursts from my bleeding wife, ripping through my chest, echoing hauntingly through the hall. I hold her steady as she cries in pain, as Declan holds her hand, as Fiona keeps pressure against the injury.

"Oh, Stella…no!" I hear my mother's voice echo sorrowfully as rushed footsteps approach us.

As minutes pass, Stella's sobbing fades into silence and her trembling, rigid muscles suddenly go lax before she falls heavily in my arms.

"Stella."

She doesn't respond.

"Stella!"

A distant sound chops through the air, the blades of a helicopter swiftly approaching.

My air has been stolen from me. I can't breathe. Her blood pools around me and mine might as well drain with hers.

If I lose her, I have nothing.

The family, the wealth, the prestige, the power…it doesn't mean a goddamn thing to me anymore.

I want her.

I only want her, and I don't care about anything else.

"Stay with me," I whisper as I bend to kiss her hair. "You can't leave me now. My soul will be lost forever without yours."

CHAPTER 32

MURPHY

I'VE BEEN SITTING in this hospital waiting room for hours while Stella lies alone in surgery. I hate that she's alone and that I'm powerless to help her. She fell unconscious in my arms back home, and I haven't seen her gorgeous brown eyes since.

The doctors came out once to update me, told me that she was lucky—*lucky*—because a few millimeters difference might have cost her life. It's almost as if Cordelia knew where to stab her, where to cut her to cause the most damage, as if she'd planned to do it all along. She's always resented Stella for the way she came into her position, thinking her unworthy, jealous that Stella held rank above her. Yet it still took me by surprise.

"Murphy," Declan says gently.

I slowly lift my head from my hands, exhausted, stressed, and overwhelmed.

When I see Fiona peek out from behind him as they enter, it snaps me to attention and I jump to my feet. "Why did you bring her here?"

He doesn't need to answer my question because I can see on Fiona's face why she's here. Her pale cheeks are painted with the tracks of tears, her eyes red and swollen from crying. I let out a sigh and move toward them, thankful that we're the only people in this waiting room.

"Come here," I tell her, opening my arms, and she comes to me for comfort.

"Is she going to be okay, sir?" she asks me.

"I don't know." I hate that this has to be my answer. The not knowing makes my breath catch and my eyes burn with the welling of fresh tears.

"Are you okay, sir?"

"Don't call me that here."

I let her go and move back to my chair to sit. Fiona and Declan follow suit, sitting in the chairs on either side of me.

Declan sets a duffel bag on the floor in front of him. "I brought Stella's glasses and some clothes for her," he says. "There's clothes for you in there, too. I expect you're not planning to leave anytime soon."

I nod a little as I lean forward, placing my elbows on my knees, and dropping my face into my palms. "Thank you."

I'd ridden with Stella alone on the airlift that brought us here. My mother and father had met me here and sat with me a few hours ago, but I sent them home. There was nothing they could do for me. My father hasn't been well recently and truthfully, they were only adding to my stress. But Declan's presence is comforting, even Fiona's concern provides some warmth in this cold space.

I feel Fiona's soft touch on my shoulder. "Do you need anything?"

She sniffles, still trying to get her own emotions under control, but I've so effectively manipulated her into servitude that she puts my needs first.

I turn my head to glance over at her. "Why are you so upset, Fiona? Why are you here?"

"I'm worried about Stella. And I'm worried about you."

"You don't need to worry about me."

"I'm meant to take care of you, of the family, sir."

"I told you not to call me that here."

"I'm sorry. I just want to make sure you're okay."

"I'm not okay."

I drop my head, breathing slowly, trying to hold back the fucking tears that keep threatening to spill. But Fiona's hand on my back, rubbing in a slow, comforting circle makes it hard to control my emotions.

What kind of life is this for her? A life of service to our family, only to be killed to make space for the next talent slave one day? The slave that my future son will bring home?

"Fuck." I shove to my feet and pace across the room.

My life has been disrupted by chaos since the day I met Stella—chaos that's ripped through my world like a tornado. She's torn through my beliefs, my understanding of our traditions; she's broken my hardened exterior and left my remaining humanity exposed and vulnerable.

She's changed me.

She's changed *everything*.

I'm not angry, or confused, or disappointed by it. I'm *grateful* for it. And I'm terrified I'm going to lose her. I'm terrified I won't deserve her when she wakes up from this.

I spin back to face them. "I have to let you go, Fiona." I reach into my back pocket and pull out my wallet. I slip out one of my credit cards that's under a false name, one with a higher limit, and hold it out to her. "Take this. Get a flight, get a hotel, *leave*. I won't keep you anymore."

She rises slowly and steps toward me, but she doesn't take the credit card from my hand. "No, sir."

I grab her hand and place the card on her palm, forcing her to take it. "Don't tell me no. Get the fuck out of here. I'll track the card and find you and wire you some money in a few days. Then you can take it and run, and I won't be able to track you anymore. I'll pay you sufficiently for your silence about my family."

She tries to give the card back to me. "Please don't make me, sir."

"Just *go*."

"I'm not going. Stop asking me. Please, sir."

"Why won't you leave?"

"I have nowhere to go."

"You can go home."

"My home is with the family."

"Fiona, stop it," I hiss. I grab her by the wrist and drag her toward the door.

She plants her feet and manages to stop me. "I'm not going!"

I whirl around to face her. "Why?"

"Because my life with your family is better than it was with mine!"

I'm silent for a moment as I watch her, as I register the truth in her eyes. She holds up her hand with the credit card, waving it sharply for me to take, which I refuse. She turns on her heel, marches back to Declan, and hands him the card instead. Then, she sits.

"Stella made me a promise," she says quietly.

I don't respond.

"She promised that she'd make sure I was okay. And I'm going to do the same for her."

"I didn't know that you've spoken with each other."

"We haven't...not much. You've done a good job of keeping me away from her. But you know your wife, sir." She chuckles. "She does what she wants."

I rub my palm over my face. "Yes, she does."

"I want to be here for her."

I sigh, moving back to my seat.

"I want to be here for you, too," she continues. "I don't feel the need to run from people who make sure I'm taken care of. My family never did that. They only pushed me from one singing audition to the next. They exhausted me."

I was always aware of her family and how she was treated. They misused the money I gifted them to fund her talent as a meal ticket. Though her talent had developed, they'd pushed her to exhaustion—they'd abused her, too. I knew that for years, but I never cared, never thought of it, never did a damn thing about it. I was pleased by it when I selected her to be my talent slave because abused women are easier to break.

I'm as monstrous as the men we sell to, and I never could've seen that if it hadn't been for Stella drawing the curtains on my dormant empathy.

I drop my face into my palms and Fiona tries to comfort me. Her compassion is unsettling, but it's also humbling.

I lift my head and look at her squarely. "I'll make sure you're taken care of, Fiona. Stay or leave."

She nods, giving me a small smile. "I know, sir."

"Mr. O'Shea?"

My head snaps toward the door to see a woman in scrubs standing there. "Please come with me," she says without expression.

I rise and walk, the rest of the world quickly fading into a blur as I follow the woman alone down the sterile hallway.

CHAPTER 33

Stella

I AWAKEN FROM a deep, dreamless sleep to an insistent steady beat. I feel peaceful and sleepy as I'm unwillingly dragged from a perfect slumber. I blink a few times, but it takes me a few moments to become aware of my surroundings.

White, cold, and sterile.

I look down and see the plain blankets covering me, the railing on either side of the narrow bed where I lay propped up on pillows. My nostrils are irritated, and I lift my hand to rub my nose only to find rubber tubes there, pumping me with oxygen.

"There she is," a kind, female voice says, an unfamiliar hand touching my shoulder. "You're all right. We can take that off in a bit if you're feeling okay."

"Where…" My voice is scratchy. I swallow a dry lump in my throat and try again. "Where am I?"

There's a warm, familiar touch wrapping around my hand. I feel comforted by it, and I start drifting off to sleep again. My brain won't let me stay under though, dragging me away from the calming darkness into the harsh light of reality.

The familiar touch squeezes my hand and I know it's him right away. His rings kiss my flesh, and my fingers immediately curl to grip his hand.

"You're in hospital," he says. I open my eyes again and slowly roll my head to the side to see him leaning over me. "You were in surgery, but everything's fine, sweetheart."

I was stabbed.

Cordelia stabbed me.

The memory alerts me to the pain in my stomach, and I feel my face contort as the complete awareness ripples through me.

"It hurts."

"I'll let the doctor know you're awake and see if we can get your pain meds started. I'll be right back with juice for you." The kind woman slips out of the small space.

"I'm okay?" I ask Murphy.

"Yes. You will be. You'll need some recovery time, but I'll make sure you have everything you need at home to rest as much as you need to."

I was stabbed.

The fear I felt when I was bleeding on the floor in Murphy's lap comes rushing back to me, and I suck in a sharp, gasping breath, my heartbeat quickening.

I was stabbed and I could've died.

I could've died and Murphy would be alone.

His rough hands grab hold of my cheeks as he bends over the railing, lowering his face to mine. "Take a deep breath, sweetheart. You're safe now. I'm here. I'm so sorry I let this happen to you."

"It's not your fault."

"I should've known…I should've seen it coming. It should've been me."

"No. I wouldn't be able to…to breathe if you were in this bed instead of me. I wouldn't be able to…I couldn't…Murphy, I love you. I love you and—"

He cuts me off with a kiss to my dry chapped lips, and the passion behind the chaste touch tells me how much he cares, how much he needs me, how much he wants me, even at my worst.

"I feared I might lose you," he whispers against my lips. "I didn't know what would happen to you. My soul would be lost without yours. I don't think I could ever survive without you now that I know what it's like to be complete."

My fear drips from my eyes in the form of tears. Tears of connection, longing, and true love for this man.

He blinks and pulls his head back as his own tear slips down his cheek. He sniffs and wipes it away quickly with his knuckle.

Sleep tries to take hold of me again, but I want to stay awake. I want to keep talking so I'll stay awake.

"Lost souls collide and shatter lives." I don't really know what words I'm saying because I'm so groggy, but I feel what I mean in them. I just hope he feels it, too.

"Right." He chuckles a little at my incoherence. "You shattered my life," he whispers, kissing my cheek and petting my hair, "and I shattered yours. I want to pick up what's left of our two lost souls and make one together. You and me, king and queen. I'll do whatever you ask of me to make myself worthy of the love you've given me, Stella. I swear, I'll do whatever it takes to make you happy."

I drift away again, the anesthesia reluctant to release its grip on me, but I blink my eyes open a few moments later. "Would you destroy the four families for me? Would you find a way to end it all?"

It's quiet for a few beats and sleep threatens again.

But then he gathers my attention when he speaks. "Is that what you want?"

"It's the only way for me to know you've changed for good." I briefly wonder if I'm dreaming this whole exchange.

His voice is so crystal-clear that I know it's real. "Then I'll do it for you. We'll do it together."

I feel his sincerity cover me like a warm blanket and somehow, the promise alone gives me peace.

Peace with him.

Peace with myself.

Peace with the reality of our future and the knowledge that he and I are linked for life.

Greater than that, we're linked for eternity.

Lost souls collide and shatter lives.

My foggy mind knows better than I do when I'm fully cognizant.

He and I were both lost souls. Our lives collided the night we met and shattered the realities we both knew. The journey has been painful, toxic, aching, and desperate, but the mending of our shattered souls is making something better, something brighter, something that will last long after we're gone from this Earth.

He and I are going to become one, irrevocably and irreversibly one celestial soul.

I smile through my physical pain because the joy of my lost soul finally recognizing its mate is more powerful than any ache.

"We'll do it together," I repeat his words, "and I'll be yours forever."

With my palm in his, I carefully lower into the armchair normally reserved for Murphy. He stands beside me as we wait for the family to gather in the living room. Cordelia kneels before us, facing outward to receive her judgment, her hands tied behind her back and duct tape covering her lips.

I was only released from the hospital two days ago, and I can hardly walk without pain, though the doctors say that will get better in time. Cordelia had nicked a nerve in addition to all the other damage she caused with her dagger, but I'll take the pain today to ensure she is punished for what she did to me.

As soon as the rest of the family is settled in the sunken space, Murphy takes a step forward, standing just behind Cordelia, and he begins to speak.

"We all know why I've asked you to gather today. Cordelia has committed a treasonous crime against our family and for that, punishment must be forceful and swift. Stella's injuries were severe. She could be dead right now if the blade had slipped mere millimeters from where it sliced through her. Stella and I have discussed how this matter should be handled, and we've come to a common decision. Stella?"

He takes a step back to allow me full view of the family from where I sit. I start to lean forward, but a pinch of pain shocks me, shooting through muscle, and I'm forced to still myself. Murphy strokes his hand down the side of my head, granting me encouragement, letting his palm rub over my shoulder and rest between my shoulder blades.

I swallow a lump in my throat and take in a steeling breath. I know there was no other choice Murphy and I could have made regarding Cordelia's fate—she tried to kill me, and almost succeeded—but I still feel unsettled by it.

Unsettled isn't the right word.

I feel horrified by it.

But what she did to me is unforgivable. The changes that Murphy and I are trying to make together, the lives we're trying to save, the secrets we're trying to keep, it's all at risk with Cordelia in our presence.

"I think it's best that I just say it quickly. Cordelia has been sentenced to death for what she's done to me." The words feel cold slipping from between my lips, but they had to be said. The decision had to be made. I expected to hear murmurs of surprise from the family, but instead, I'm met with silence. "The sentence will be carried out immediately to rid our family of the threat that she has posed to us all."

Our family.

It's mine and Murphy's family now.

I have to own that to take control of it, to be the wife that Murphy needs. He has to continue growing to destroy the four families for good, and he will…because he was always meant to rise and destroy them. I was always meant to help him discover his purpose, to challenge his beliefs, to strengthen him with love despite our differences.

We both know that truth now.

He was never really the monster I thought he was. He's a product of his upbringing, of twisted traditions and ridiculous rituals.

Yet we still need to participate in one last appalling rite to ensure that our remaining family knows it's place…so we can move forward and effect real change. Cordelia has to be made an example of to ensure we're never questioned again, especially when factories start closing and money starts disappearing.

I feel sick to my stomach as Murphy removes his dagger from his calf holster and steps forward.

"Blood taken requires blood given," he says clearly, and my heart beats in an overwhelming flurry. He circles around in front of Cordelia and looks down at her. She tilts her chin up to look at him, though she can't speak because the duct tape covers her lips.

Murphy looks at me, pausing and asking silently for my permission one last time. I nod at him, grateful for the final ask, though we've talked this outcome to death.

It has to happen, I remind myself.

She stabbed me in cold-blood, with no motive other than her ridiculous idea that I had taken money from the family. In truth, I'd had nothing to do with Murphy's decision to pay off the entire Oslo operation to allow Anya and Kostya a safe place to hide. Yes, I had asked him to save Anya's life, but every decision he'd made from there, he'd made on his own—he'd grown in *empathy* on his own, and my love for him only grew stronger.

Though what he's about to do is horrid, I know that it has to happen or we'll never be safe. We'll never be able to do the work we need to do in order to save lives.

Murphy circles Cordelia, coming around behind her again. He steps wide and plants his feet on either side of her legs. I'd asked him to end her quickly, to minimize her suffering, though she deserves to suffer as much as I did when she stabbed me so cruelly.

I see him wrap his fist around her hair and jerk her head back. "The matter is settled with Cordelia's death. Let this set a precedent that anyone who crosses me or my wife will meet the same fate."

I feel sick.

In one swift motion, he slashes the blade across her throat. The squelching sound of metal slicing through sinew and vein makes my stomach lurch and my shoulders shrug with tension. Her parents and sister cry, their sobs breaking through the silence as blood spurts from Cordelia.

I feel like shit.

This is too much for me.

He nudges her sideways and she topples to the floor, her body limp and lax within a minute. Blood continues to spurt from her in bursts that slow with her beating heart.

"Murphy." His name tumbles from my lips and he steps back, taking heavy breaths while holding the bloody dagger in his hand. My eyes are drawn to it, and it triggers a reminder of the pain in my stomach, the pain triggering the fear I felt when I thought I was dying in his arms. My pulse quickens as I beg, "Put it down."

I slip my hand up to my throat, squeezing briefly and dragging my fingers back down to my chest—a previously agreed upon signal between us that I'm overwhelmed and that I need him. I need him to get me away from here so he can help calm me. I've been unusually anxious since the attack.

He nods at me in understanding. He quickly bends to return the coated blade to his calf holster—he's soaked in her blood, regardless, so it doesn't matter that it drips down his leg.

"I want it known that Stella is the reason your hands remain clean today. I wanted everyone's involvement in this, and I wanted her death to be slow and painful for what she did to my wife. But Stella didn't want that for Cordelia; she didn't want that for any of you. Her dignity and grace far exceed what any of you possess. She asked that you be spared participation in this death and for that, you owe her your gratitude."

"Thank you, Stella," Declan says graciously.

"Thank you, Stella," Bridget follows.

A chorus of thank you's—some reluctant—echo in the room and fill me with a sick sense of pride that twists in my gut. That pride only upsets me further.

Murphy wipes his bloody palms on his slacks, then moves in front of me, holding out his hands to help me to my feet.

"Cormac, I expect you to arrange for removal and clean-up," Murphy says quickly as I stand.

He wraps one arm around my waist and walks beside me as he leads me toward the hallway. My anxiety and pain work together in a way that makes it all worse. I grab hold of his belt, gripping tightly as my breaths quicken and make me light-headed.

"Are you okay?"

"I just need to be away from them…alone with you. I need to lie down."

"How's the pain?"

"It's fine."

"Don't lie. How bad is it?"

"Eight out of ten. But it will get better once I lay down."

"Almost there."

He takes me into a bedroom he's set up for me on the first floor, just down the hall. Stairs are off limits for a while, and really, I'm not supposed to be walking much at all, but I refused to be in a wheelchair. He opens the door for me, and we're greeted by Bailey—we'd shut her in to avoid the bloodshed. She's proven to be a fantastic emotional support dog.

Murphy helps me lower onto the bed and I twist to put my feet up. I lay back slowly on the pillow, wincing at the pain on my way down. "I'm good. Go get cleaned up."

He heads off to the connected bathroom, and I hear the faucet running for a minute before he returns. His hands are clean, though his clothes are still soaked in Cordelia's blood. The sight of it makes my stomach roll.

He hands me a glass of water and holds out his palm—a white pill rests there and I pluck it from his hand. I pop the prescription pain medication into my mouth without putting up a fight like I normally do. This whole thing has just been too much for me. I swallow it down with a gulp of water from the glass, and he sets it on the bedside table.

I settle back against the pillow and wave my hand. "Go. Go take a shower. Please. The blood is too much."

He disappears into the bathroom. Bailey jumps up on the bed and settles by my feet as I hear the shower turn on. I close my eyes and breathe slowly, working hard to force images of death from my mind.

It had to be done.

She had to die.

Murphy isn't in the shower long. After just a few minutes, I hear the door click and I open my eyes, rolling my head to the side to look at him. He exits the bathroom stark naked, soaking wet, his muscles glistening with water. My heart pounds as I watch him cross the room and open the wardrobe. He pulls out a towel from it and turns to face me.

"Forgot a towel."

"That's totally fine, baby. You don't really need one. Just stand there and drip dry while I enjoy the view."

He grins, and the shift in his energy is palpable—his joy gives me the calm I need to force away the horrors of the day. "While I love having you objectify me in that way, I'm pretty sure sex is off the table until you're healed, sweetheart."

"I didn't say anything about sex. I'd be thrilled to enjoy the view without the benefit of a happy ending."

He smiles at me, drying himself with the towel. He moves to sit beside me on the edge of the bed, reaching out to stroke his hand down the side of my head, his palm coming to rest on my cheek. "How are you?"

"I'm okay. That was really…overwhelming."

"I know. But it had to be done."

"I understand that, but that doesn't make it any easier to experience. I feel ashamed, like I should be sad that she's dead because she's a human being like the rest of us…but I'm not sad. I feel relieved. And that makes me feel guilty because I'm responsible for her death."

"She was responsible for her own death. She chose to hurt you, and she knew what the consequences would be for that. I'd made it very clear to my family before you arrived that no violence against you would be tolerated."

"I still feel responsible. I feel like I killed her myself."

"I don't want you to feel that weight."

"I think it's unavoidable at this point. To do what we want to do… to bring it all to an end."

"I need you to let me take the guilt of that, sweetheart. It's my responsibility to bear."

"I don't want you to bear it alone." I grab his hand and pull it from my cheek so I can lock our fingers together. "I'm in this with you. I'm here for you. I'm the one who asked you to make it all right, so I have to take responsibility for all the changes you're making."

He unlocks our fingers and his palm moves around mine, gripping my hand and lifting my knuckles to kiss each of them in turn. "I love you, Stella. I won't allow you to carry guilt on your shoulders. You've done nothing to earn it. I brought you into this world, and I'm going to make it right for you."

I sigh, smiling, knowing there's no point in arguing with him right now…I just don't have the stamina for it. I let my eyes fall shut. "When I have the strength again and I'm back to normal, I'm going to be stubbornly aggressive with you about sharing the weight of the world on our shoulders."

"I promise you, sweetheart, when you're back to normal, we're going to be aggressive with each other in a variety of ways. I've started a rather filthy list to keep track of my ideas."

I grin at the reminder that I've met my match in this man. It was so easy to see him as my true soulmate when we were stripped bare of the actions we were forced to take as products of a cruel world. His essence is pure and good, and I may be the only woman in the world who can see it, but that's all that he needs to become the man he was always meant to be.

"Promise?"

He bends and places a kiss to my forehead. "I promise."

CHAPTER 34

Murphy

TWO YEARS LATER

"THAT'S IT," I say to Declan, ending the call on my cell phone, "it's done."

He lets out a heavy breath. "When are you leaving?"

I scrub my hand across my beard, swallowing a painful lump in my throat. "After I tell Stella."

"Tell me what?" She appears in the doorway to my office, my stunning, perfect wife, sauntering joyfully into the room. "Never mind, it'll have to wait because I have something I need to tell you first." Her smile is broad and unyielding, and it makes my heart drop into my stomach. "Declan, will you give us a second?"

"Stella—" he starts.

"Your news will have to wait," I tell her, then look at my brother, tilting my head toward the door to indicate he should go.

He gives me a sad smile and nods, slowly exiting and closing the door behind him.

Fuck, this is gonna hurt.

Her head tilts to the side and her unyielding smile gradually gives way the longer she stares at me. I can't hide the ache of my soul for what I have to tell her. This is going to break her. It's going to break me. But this decision has been a long time coming and there's no going back now.

For two stressful years, we skillfully and intentionally misled the other families. It was easy enough to do in the chaos of Anya and Ezra's escape. I'd managed to convince them that Anya and her baby were dead—that they'd died at a hospital in Russia shortly after they escaped the forest on the helicopter. I'd led the charge to hunt Ezra down, producing and presenting fake leads for them to chase.

It was all in the name of keeping them occupied and distracted while Stella and I dismantled what we could. We both knew what would ultimately need to be done, but I'd promised her we had more time together. I didn't know we'd be here so soon…that I'd have to have this conversation with her now.

"Okay. So, tell me," she insists, crossing the room and circling my desk. I roll my chair back and let her move in front of me, leaning against the edge of the desk. "What is it?"

"Well, good news first. The Copenhagen factory is officially closed."

Her eyes widen and the smile returns to her face. "That's fantastic. That's five O'Shea factories now." She reaches out for my hand, and I let her take it. She bends to plant a few soft kisses across my knuckles before holding it in her palm, laying it in her lap. She studies my face carefully. "Why are you shaking?"

"There wasn't enough money to pay off all the girls we let go."

She shifts uncomfortably. "What did you do?"

"No one got hurt," I rush to assure her. "They were all let go."

"Oh," she breathes out in relief.

"Our family is bleeding money with all the factories we've been closing. I had to make a choice." I squeeze my fingers around her hand, holding on tightly. "I had to make sure there was enough to provide you with the long, happy life you deserve."

Her brow furrows. "What are you saying? You're making me nervous."

I pull my hand from her grip, push to my feet, and pace away from her. She stands, turning to face me. "You wanted me to destroy the four families, and we've made great strides in that direction. But it all comes at a price. Paying off the captives for their silence has been an expensive venture, and I've always known their silence was never guaranteed. I thought we'd be able to close a few more factories before everything went public, but…we've reached our financial limit. I thought we'd have a few more years, but there's no time left.

"I've prepared a written statement confirming that you were my captive, taken against your will, and forced into marriage. I've stated that you had no knowledge of and no control over business decisions made on behalf of the four families. You never attended a board meeting. You never saw our documents and sales reports. You attempted to escape on several occasions, and you sought to escape every chance you got."

"None of that is true…"

I turn to face her. "It's what I've written, and you will not deny it, do you understand me?"

She shakes her head. "No. No, I don't." She crosses to me, grabbing my cheeks with her hands. "Tell me what this is all about."

"I've sent twenty-two million into an untraceable offshore account. My accountant will be in touch with you in two weeks to let you know how to access it. You'll be comfortable for the rest of your life."

Her grip on my face tightens. "What are you *talking* about? Tell me right now."

"I'm turning myself in."

She gasps and sucks all the air from the room. Her hands drop from my cheeks and the look on her face makes my heart sink heavily.

She whispers, barely audible, "When?"

"Today."

Her hands lift to cover her mouth as her eyes scan my features. I stand before her, steady and feigning calm, as she watches me, as she takes in the news. Her brown eyes glisten as tears fill them, as the realization hits her that I'm going away for a long time, possibly forever.

Forever without her?

Her chest rises, and as the sob forces its way out of her, I step forward and throw my arms around her. I drag her against my chest, against my pounding heart which beats only for her.

She cries in my arms, and I cry with her because we both know that I might never return once I turn myself in. It's ironic, really. To become the best version of myself, to be the man she truly deserves, I have to do this. I have to turn myself in and hand over all the information I have about the four families to be worthy of her love. And it means I'll likely be imprisoned for life…it means I'll likely never be with her again.

"You can't…" she forces out the words through her tears. "You can't do this now. You said we had more time together."

"I thought we did. But I needed to ensure you and my family would be taken care of when I'm gone, and the money only stretches so far."

Her arms, which were pinned between us where she covered her face in shock, snap down and lasso around my waist. She hugs me tight, like she's afraid to let me go.

She *is* afraid to let me go—because when she does, I'll be gone.

I let her cry and hold me for as long as she needs to, minutes stretching on as her tears soak my shirt. I inhale her scent—sweet and strong—then press a kiss to the top of her head.

"I have to do this," I whisper to her, though I say the words for myself.

I have to do this.

There's no other way for me to redeem myself from the horror I've caused countless lives. If it weren't for Stella, none of this would have happened, nothing would've changed. I'd still be kidnapping women and selling them as slaves. I'd still be vile and vicious, a ruthless king of masters.

It's because of her that I saw the truth, the reality of our business.

She took the spark of humanity left buried deep within me and rekindled it, fed it, helped it grow into a flame that consumed me. From the ashes, we melded together and became one soul that could take on the world.

I don't know how I'll live out my days without her.

She lifts her head after several minutes to look up at me. "How am I going to do this without you?"

"You're strong, far more capable than I am. You're going to be just fine on your own. Declan will be around to help you, at least to get you back on your feet. You can move to New York if you want, spend more time with Cora and Josh—"

"That's not what I want. I want *you*."

I cradle her head in my palm and pull her against me again, holding her firmly to my chest. "You can come visit me." I try to keep my voice steady, but it falters.

"It's not enough!"

She cries until her body has exhausted itself, until she's drained of tears and emotionally spent. At some point, she relaxes her hold on me, leaning back so she can look at me. Her voice is quiet and sad. "I came in here to tell you something."

I stroke my hand down the side of her head and rub my thumb across her cheek.

"I know they said they weren't sure it would ever be possible, given all the scar tissue from when I was stabbed..."

No.

My heart stops.

She can't be. Not now.

Stella tilts her head to the side, her cheek leaning into my palm. "But it is possible because I'm pregnant, Murphy. And now you're leaving, and I don't know what to do. I can't do this without you."

I grab hold of her face with both my hands and kiss her hard. I kiss her with all the joy, madness, and anger that's coursing through my veins. I feel cursed and blessed all at once. Blessed that she's my wife, that she's giving me a child, a family. Cursed that I have to walk away and leave it all behind.

The pain of healing, of growing, of making myself a better man to be worthy of her climbs out from deep within my heart and claws its way up my throat, filling every sense, overwhelming me with pressure, and forcing its way out through burning, aching tears.

I drop to my knees in front of her, grabbing her hips and pulling her close so I can kiss her belly before wrapping my arms around her tightly. I hold her and cry for the future I'll never get to see…the future I've created for her and our child.

I did this for her.

It's the future she deserves.

"Am I worthy of your love?" I whisper through my pain, lifting my head to look up at her. "Have I done enough to earn your heart?"

She looks down at me and I see the softness in her eyes, the kindness, the empathy, the loyalty. "You've earned all of me. All of me, heart and soul."

She falls to her knees, grabs my face, and kisses me with enough passion to last a lifetime.

This kiss may very well be our last.

CHAPTER 35

Stella

THREE DAYS.

My love, my heart, my soul…he's been gone for three days, and it may as well be a lifetime. A quick glance at my phone screen tells me it's one o'clock in the morning, and though I'm exhausted, I haven't slept a minute.

I roll onto my side and slip my arm beneath his pillow, hugging it close and inhaling deeply. I can still smell the sweet peppermint of his aftershave and I'm grateful that the scent remains. I cling to it, but the longer I breathe in his scent, the stronger my emotions grow and the deeper the pain burrows into my soul, and it all fucking hurts.

He turned himself into the authorities just so he could spill the secrets of the four families and bring them down…all because I asked him to change for me.

A selfish part of me almost wishes he hadn't changed—that part wishes everything remained as it was when he first stole me away from my life and made me his unwilling bride. It still takes my breath away to think about how far we've come since then, all the factories he's closed and the work he's done to chip away at the power the families hold from within.

He's done nothing but amaze me for the last two years. He became my whole world, everything I wanted and needed.

And now he's gone.

He's gone and I don't know how I'm supposed to live without him.

The tears come again, for the millionth time in so many days, and I can't fight them no matter how hard I try. They spill onto his pillow as I sob, as my soul splinters and cracks, and it rips my heart in two.

I don't know how much time passes. I almost feel tired as the tears gradually let go of me. I let my eyes fall shut, hoping sleep will take me away from this pain, but I know it won't.

I hear a click at the door, the old familiar beep as the lock code is entered. Bailey barks once, popping her head up from where she lays behind me on the bed. Declan's been in to check on me every few hours since Murphy left and each time, he's found me a sobbing mess. I hate that he's left to deal with me, because I know he's hurting too, and I can't comfort him. I can't even comfort myself.

"I'm fine, Declan," I whisper into the darkness of the room as the door pushes open slowly, then clicks shut again. "Go to bed. You must be exhausted."

"I'm fucking knackered, but there's no way I'm sleeping tonight."

I jack-knife, shooting up from my prone position at the sound of his voice. "Murphy?" I scramble for my glasses on the bedside table and slip them on.

Bailey leaps over me, yelping and barreling across the room. The lights flick on, and I flinch at the sudden burst of light through the room. I blink as my eyes come into focus.

It's him.

He's here!

"What…*How?*"

I don't even care if he responds. I toss off the covers, leap from the bed, and run to him.

We collide with each other, just as our souls had.

He lifts me to meet him, and I lock my legs around his waist. I kiss him deeper than I had before he left, desperately, achingly. I paint kisses across his cheeks and over the wrinkles of his crow's feet as he smiles the most spectacular smile.

I wrap my arms around his neck and hug him tight. "How are you here?"

"A miracle."

I drag my head back to look at him, locking my fingers behind his neck to hold myself up. "A fucking miracle." I grin. "What miracle?" My face falls. "Are they going to take you back? Will they arrest you?"

He swallows the sadness behind his eyes as they lock onto mine, burrowing into my soul. "Maybe someday. But not now and not for a while."

"What do you mean?"

He lowers me to my feet, but I don't let go of him, my fingers coming around to grip the collar of his shirt which is unbuttoned at the top.

"The men that my family have paid off over the years were quite surprised at my arrival and confession. I spent hours locked with them in a small room trying to help them understand that the family will soon be out of money to buy them off. They were rather upset by this news, only because it puts them on the line if I'm prosecuted." He sighs. "It took us a full day to put together a plan, another to settle it, and the last to get back home to you."

I grin at him, shaking my head. "Well, what's the plan?"

"Immunity in exchange for information about the four families." He smiles. "Takes us all off the hook, because as far as anyone else knows, Detectives Walsh and Byrne had never met me before I turned myself in."

"It can't possibly be that easy."

"It's not. The process will be complicated, and we'll have to be diligent about how we move forward." He puts his hands on my shoulders, rubbing down my arms and back up again. "But I'm confident that it will all work out given what's at stake for Detectives Walsh and Byrne."

"I'm confused. Are you home to stay or not? Do we have to live in fear you'll be arrested?"

"No. No fear, sweetheart. If all goes according to plan, and I'm confident it will, I'll never be prosecuted. If I am, then we'll at least have some notice to prepare for it. Either way," he bends and lifts the cuff of his pants, revealing a little black box with a blinking red light attached to his ankle, "we will be homebound for quite some time."

He grins at me, happy and carefree. Though the potential for him to be arrested in the future weighs heavily on my heart, I trust the joy in his expression and let worry drip from me like melting icicles. "We can be homebound forever as long as I have you here."

His eyes glance down at my mouth as I smile, and he licks his lips with intention. "You'll have me, sweetheart. And I think I'll have you now, too."

He bends to kiss me, his lips sparking against mine, striking like a lightning bolt. Electricity prickles along my skin, lifting the hairs on the backs of my arms, lassoing around my heart, and shocking me back to life…back to passion.

I jerk back and swat his chest. "I thought I'd never see you again. I thought I'd never kiss you again." I tighten my grip on his collar and tug him to meet my lips again.

He moves as he kisses me, forcing me to walk backward toward the bathroom behind me. He walks me until we're both stepping onto cold tile that sends a creeping shiver up through my bare feet. He breaks away, but only long enough to reach inside the glass-enclosed shower to turn the water on.

"I thought I'd never be able to touch you again…" My voice sounds sadder than I meant it to be, but it's the raw truth that slips out from between my lips. "Why didn't you make love to me one last time before you turned yourself in?"

I feel anger toward him rising in my chest, because it hurt that he hadn't left any time for us once he'd made the decision. He told me and then he left.

He stops and stills in front of me, his transcendent gray-green eyes scanning my features. His forehead creases and he tilts his head. "If I had, I wouldn't have been able to leave you. I would've been selfish, and I would've stayed."

My breath catches in my throat as tears rise and burn behind my eyes. "You could've stayed."

He shakes his head slowly, cupping my cheek in his palm. "I had to finish what we started. We both know I had to do it." His other hand comes up and he holds my head steady as he bends closer, heat spreading between us. "The fact that I'm here with you right now is proof that it was the right thing to do. The universe knows we belong together, but I had to do this to deserve you. I did what was right and it brought me back to you. It's why I have faith that you and I will be together forever."

He kisses me softly, his pillowy lips pressing into mine, gently encouraging mine to part for him. His tongue seeks mine for a sensual dance, and I taste the essence of him as he feeds me his love. His heat flows inside me, spreading across my body and melting me to desire. I moan and my knees sink as the kiss deepens, as my back arches while he bends over me.

His hands fall away from my face to grip my hips, turning me sideways and pushing me backward. He takes me into the shower, where the water is already warm and steam swirls at our feet. I gasp as he pushes me past the flow of water and soaks us both in our clothes. Our kiss breaks, but our need grows.

My back slams against the wall and he pins me there with his body as his lips drop to my neck, frantically kissing along the curve. I quickly remove my fogged-up glasses and fumble to set them awkwardly on the built-in shelf beside me. He grips the hem of my tank top, lifting and tugging it off over my head.

He dips to lavish my breasts with his need, kissing, licking, dragging his teeth, as if he's starving for me.

We're both starving for each other.

I reach for the buttons on his shirt, my fingers working as quickly as they can to unbutton the fabric. He groans his impatience, grips the two sides of his shirt, and with a sharp yank, tears it open. A button bounces off the tile as he quickly pulls his wet shirt from his shoulders and tosses it away.

My lips part to let out a heated breath as my head falls back against the wall. I lift my hands to his chest and rub my palms over his pecs, caressing his skin and tracing the lines of his tattoos—lingering over the purple rose on his heart, recalling the day I drew it for him.

It seems so long ago now that he asked for this tattoo that matches the rose on my hip. We hardly knew each other then. He must have known from the beginning that we were meant for each other.

Our eyes lock as he removes the rest of his clothing, watching each other with heated, anticipatory breaths. He grabs hold of my gray sweatpants and slowly peels them down, his body lowering with them until they're around my ankles and he's on his knees in front of me.

"Murphy," I beg for him as I step out and he tosses the last barrier of clothing aside.

His large hands land on my thighs, fingers digging in painfully, passionately, as he pulls at them, encouraging them to part. My chest heaves as I watch him on his knees in front of me, like a sinner praying at the altar, preparing to worship.

I spread my legs for him and he dives between my thighs, his thick tongue sticking all the way out to lick me from the back of my pussy all the way to my aching clit.

"Oh, my God," I moan, my fingers digging into his hair and holding him against me.

He groans as he licks me, alternating between long, lavish strokes of his tongue and quick flicks over my clit. I'm sinking, slipping, falling into the pleasure he builds deep down in my core. His fingers curl, gripping my thighs tighter as he frantically tastes me.

"I thought I'd never taste you again," he says against my pussy. "I'd die without your perfect cunt."

My grip tightens in his hair and I yank his head away, forcing him to look up at me. He pants on his knees, my wetness glistening on his lips, streaking his beard.

"You know I hate that word," I tell him with a small smile.

He grins and it's positively devilish. "I know."

"But I love the way you say it." I lick my lips, craving his perfect filth—the kind of filth I could only love with him.

He lets go of my thighs and pushes to his feet, making me lose my grip on his hair. "Taste it," he says before kissing me so deeply that he steals my breath.

I fade away into his touch, my mind intoxicated by the way he makes my body feel. I'm only half-aware of what's happening as I'm lifted from the tile floor. My arms and legs wrap around him purely by instinct as he hoists me high and then lowers me slowly.

It's like pure fucking magic the way he can move us so precisely, so perfectly, angling me just right so he can slide inside me before settling me against his hips.

I'm pinned against the wall, trapped by his strong body, and I feel overwhelmed in the best way possible. My hips move, rocking into him slowly as he grips my ass.

He buries his face in my neck as he pushes me harder to the wall, his hips pushing forward and up, sinking deep enough to make me ache. He starts to pull out, but I stop him, my arms and legs tensing around him, locking him against me.

"No," I moan, "don't move. Hold me up and let me fuck you."

He groans, biting into my neck, then licking across it to soothe the sting. His lips brush the shell of my ear. "Make yourself come on my cock like a good girl. Welcome me home, sweetheart."

My hips move, rocking against his hardness, which is buried

painfully deep within me. Pleasure coils low in my belly, promising me a quick climax from this position. He holds me up so strongly that I can grind easily, rocking and thrusting my hips frantically to chase the high of coming undone in his hold.

My cheek touches his as I hug myself around him, tightening my grip and letting tension build. "I love you so much," I whisper. "Don't ever leave us again…"

Us.

I've been so lost to despair the last few days that the fact that I'm pregnant truthfully keeps slipping from my mind.

He pulls his head away to look at me, his expression an odd mixture of love, fear, and gratitude. He lets his head fall forward and our foreheads touch as I move, driving myself toward the release I so desperately need.

"I love you," he says. "Fuck, I'm so in love with you, Stella."

I whimper, his eyes and voice reaching inside me, tugging on the cord of my climax, tugging and tugging as I fuck him.

"Oh," I breathe out, my body curling around my center, my womb dragging tension from the rest of my body into a heavy ball that sinks, then drops through my core and bursts through my pussy. "Murphy!"

He groans with my climax and trembles with me, his jaw setting as his hardness leaves me, only to thrust inside me again. "That's my good girl, always my good girl," he says as he fucks me. "Hold still, sweetheart. Hold still and let me take from you."

I can't hold still as my body trembles from the powerful release. The relief of it is so pure, so carnal, so satisfying that it floods me with emotions that threaten to spill from my eyes.

Murphy pounds into my flesh, fucking me with lust and filling me with passion. I need his aggression, his violent desire, his obsessive possession.

"Take me," I whisper. "Take me as hard as you love me."

A rumbling groan vibrates through his chest, and he moves fast.

My feet hit the floor and he turns me toward the back wall, shoving me forward against it. He pushes into me, his cock hard at my back as he pins me in place. "Hands on the wall," he demands, and I obey.

He grabs my hips and pulls them back harshly, forcing me to arch my back as he pulls my ass away from the wall. I bend for him, pressing my palms to the tile. Though my knees shake, I fight through the post-orgasm weakness to hold my position for him because I need to feel him fuck me viciously.

His fingers curl around my hip bones, digging in harshly as he rubs his cock along my crack, teasing me and brushing over my wetness. I moan, my pussy pulsing to be filled again. He lines up and plunges deep, thrusting into me so brutally hard that I have to lock my elbows to keep myself from slamming into the tile.

He fucks me, thrust after thrust, but I need more.

"Harder," I beg. "Make it hurt."

He grabs my arms, swiftly yanking them from the wall. I gasp at the sensation of falling, but he keeps me upright, twisting my arms behind me and locking them with bent elbows behind my back. His hands snap around me to squeeze my breasts, and he bends us forward, holding me to his chest.

One of his brutal hands rises, quickly crawling up my chest. I sigh as he reaches my throat and pinches the sides. My eyes flutter shut, my body relaxing into his hold as he chokes me into a breathless high.

"You're so fucking beautiful like this," he says against my ear. "Breathless, wet, and at my mercy."

He thrusts, his cock driving deep, making me gasp. My lips part with a smile as my pussy clenches around his hardness, suddenly begging for another release. His fingers circle my nipple, rubbing across it, rolling, pinching, tugging. My insides melt to liquid, sending a mad rush of molten heat to my core.

Words pop into my mind as I suddenly remember something he once told me…

"There never was a choice for you. Not from the moment we met each other."

The truth of that fills me with more joy than I ever hoped I could have in this life.

"There was never a choice for me to be yours," I whisper as we pant together, as he finds a steady rhythm that quickly drives us both toward a perfect release. "Not from the moment we met each other."

He groans and fucks me faster, pounding into me as his hand on my breast drops lower, dips between my legs, and circles my sensitive clit.

My eyes pop wide as another sharp climax takes hold of me. He grunts and groans as he swells inside me, as my pussy clenches around his cock. We come together—a perfectly unplanned, synchronous orgasm that tears through our flesh and cuts into our soul.

Our soul—the mended product of our two lost souls coming together.

I'm unaware of the movement as I come down through the high, but suddenly, I'm facing him, limp and lax in his arms as he holds me against his naked chest. I breathe deeply, my eyes fluttering shut in ecstasy to focus on this perfect moment.

"We never stood a chance," he breathes, kissing the top of my head. "We were made to save each other."

I find peace in knowing that no matter what comes for us, we'll be saving each other for the rest of our perfectly unknown days.

EPILOGUE

Murphy

THREE YEARS LATER

"WHAT DO YOU think?" I hear Stella say from the kitchen as I round the corner.

"Pretty, Mama!"

I move past the kitchen island, crossing in front of the sunlight which bathes us from the long expanse of windows and sliding glass doors. We're finally settling into our new home in the Irish countryside, built to Stella's specifications perfectly.

Liquidating the O'Shea estate had been made part of the immunity deal I'd struck with the authorities, so we'd had to leave our castle home behind. Our family lost nearly everything—except for the money I'd secretly set aside prior to turning myself over to the authorities.

I'd put aside accounts for Stella, for Declan, my parents, and for Fiona. Cormac and Tally had dissociated themselves from us long before, and the last I knew, they were living off her family's fortune.

My mother bought a modest seaside home, and Boyd is with her, along with their in-home nurse. As a part of my own immunity deal, I'd insisted on Boyd's immunity from the crimes he committed in his tenure as the Head of House, as well. Given his old age and how his health has affected his mind, I doubt any judge or jury would see reason in prosecuting him now, anyway.

His health had started deteriorating a long time ago. Dementia had taken hold of him, which was only fortunate in the sense that it allowed me and Stella to close so many of our factories early on without interference. It was unfortunate in every other way and in every sense of the word.

I suppose he'd told my mother at one point that he'd wanted to be near the ocean, so that's where they are as his condition worsens. We visit them every so often, but the nurse in residence with them is paid well and cares enough for both of them that we don't have to worry too much.

Fiona has a small home a few kilometers from ours. She has enough money to go wherever she wants, but she's chosen to remain close to us. I promised her a long time ago that I would make sure she's taken care of, and I've held good on that promise. Stella had become a sort of big sister figure in her life, and they've grown closer over the years. She's living independently and enjoying her life, but we're happy to see her often.

And Stella and I are here, in this perfect home she's created for us. Her eye for aesthetics translated to more than just tattoo artistry. Our comfortable home is modern and bright, with sunlight peeking in wherever you turn. It makes sense to have a home with so many windows when you have a view like ours.

Our land is so much like the castle grounds, though still unique in its own right. The back of our home opens atop a large, grassy hill that gently slopes downward, opening to a field of blue and purple wildflowers. We often picnic in that field beneath the oak tree in the distance.

"What's pretty?" I ask as I grab Stella's neglected cup of coffee from the kitchen island and bring it over to her at the table.

"Thank you." She smiles at me, taking the mug. "Take a look, Daddy."

Fuck, it kills me when she calls me that. It makes my chest swell with pride and my heart pound with joy for the family Stella's made for us—and it makes my dick throb with the need to show Stella my undying gratitude for all of it.

My sweet little lass raises her hand to show me. On the back of it, Stella's drawn a purple rose. "Pretty flower," Molly tells me, pride glowing on her perfect pink cheeks.

Our daughter is just over two years old now and has enough attitude in her little toe to rival Stella. She's loud, ferocious, determined, every bit the definition of what you'd expect as a "terrible two," and I wouldn't have her any other way.

"Stunning, my love." I grab her tiny hand and bend to place a kiss on the rose that matches mine, that matches Stella's.

"Kiss, Daddy," Molly says, making a kissy face at me. I give her a quick peck on the lips, and she smiles proudly.

She could ask me for the moon and I tear it down from the sky for her. She humbles me. She makes me proud. She frightens me and makes me understand myself in ways I never thought I could.

From the moment she was born, I saw in her the face of every girl I'd ever trafficked, every girl I'd ordered to be stolen away and sold, every girl who lost their life at my hands.

That understanding had broken me for a while. I'd been depressed for much of Molly's first year, and it wasn't easy for me to heal. I still struggle with it from time to time, but the guilt is at least manageable now. I might've crumbled under its crushing weight if it hadn't been for Stella.

I look at my wife and see all the good in the world. This woman, this perfectly imperfect woman saw me through the worst of it and stuck by me through it.

She had every reason to run, yet she stayed. She could've taken Molly from my life and gone to live anywhere she wanted. She was the only one of us who could access the money I'd set aside for her, but she didn't take it and run. She stayed by my side, forgave me for the villain I was, and every day she celebrates the man I'm learning to be.

Her love is healing me, and I won't ever take that for granted.

"You ready to go? Josh and Cora's flight should be landing soon. I want to get to the airport early so I can hold up this embarrassing sign I made for her." She pushes back from her chair and stands, picking up a piece of poster board from the table, and holds it in front of her. "Do you like it?"

WE DON'T SERVE ASSHOLES, it reads.

I chuckle, shaking my head. "Don't you think that's a tad inappropriate?"

"Absolutely not." She grins. "Cora's opening up a second shop in two months, so she needs another sign."

Bailey walks by, on her way to the water bowl, and Molly slips from her seat at the table to waddle after her.

"Are you disappointed we couldn't go back to New York?" Part of my deal requires me to stay in the country—I'll never be able to travel outside of Ireland again.

She sets the sign down and reaches for me, dragging me into her arms. "No, not at all. Maybe there's some part of me that misses the city, but as happy as I was there, it was never home. It never could be. I have to be with you to be home."

I sigh, stroking my hand down the back of her hair. "You're too good for me."

"Oh, I know," she smiles, "but the sex makes up for it." She winks and lets me go, turning like she's just gonna walk away from me after that.

I grab her hips and pull her arse back against my cock, turning her and pressing her forward against the island counter. I brush her hair back over her shoulder and lean in close, kissing her cheek.

"I think I have some making up to do later, don't I, sweetheart?"

"With Cora and Josh staying with us? That would be quite the welcome for them to hear me screaming your name, wouldn't it?" She mimics me with her terrible rendition of my Irish accent, "Don't you think that's a tad inappropriate?"

I reach down to pinch her arse cheek and she yelps. "They won't hear a thing if I gag you properly."

Her back arches. "Shit."

Something soft hits my leg. "I save you, Mama!"

I look down to see Molly brandishing her toy foam sword, pulling it back and preparing to hit me with it again.

"I save you from dragon!"

"That's right, little princess, kick his ass," Stella encourages.

"Kick it!" Molly yells as she hits me again.

I turn with a snap and roar like a dragon. She screams and giggles, but she doesn't run away, not my little girl. She turns the foam sword, angles it upward, and stabs it into my stomach.

"You got me!" I yell, dramatically dying, slowly dropping to my knees before tumbling sideways on the floor.

"Double tap," Stella tells her. "You make sure that dragon is dead."

I try to hide my ridiculous grin, but it's pointless to try. As Molly drives a final, fatal blow to my stomach, an odd memory creeps inside my mind. It's a memory from my childhood, in one of our factories, though I can't tell which one. I remember giving a butterscotch candy to a girl, handing it to her through bars that locked her in…then there was a conversation with my dad.

"What do you know about sacrifices?"

"I heard that word in a movie. They were talking about taking a princess to a cave and leaving her there as a sacrifice for the dragon. They said it would keep him away from the village for another year and keep everyone safe."

"Right. It's like that. Our clients are like dragons, and we have to sacrifice a few princesses to keep them away from our villages. We sacrifice

others to save ourselves. We feed the monsters to provide for our family."

"I don't want anything to happen to my family."

"That's right."

"Thank you for saving us from the dragons, princess."

The memory makes me shudder. I was groomed to be a villain from the day I was born. Our clients were no more monstrous than we were. *We* were the monsters, lying to ourselves, pretending our family was more valuable than any other.

The so-called princesses we sacrificed didn't go willingly to their deaths; they didn't do it to serve some greater purpose. They did it because we forced them, because we accepted that it was their responsibility to satiate the beastly men of this world. We sentenced them to die, not knowing what they were truly made of or who they were truly meant to be.

Who could they have been if they'd had their lives, their freedom?

Having Molly has taught me what a princess truly is. She's not just the daughter of a king and queen, she's every little girl who was ever born into this cruel world.

A princess is a warrior, a fighter, a survivor.

A princess is a queen waiting to rule.

And my little girl is a princess who will someday set this world on fire with her mother whispering encouragement every step of the way.

The doorbell rings.

"You slayed the dragon!" Stella cheers.

I peek one of my dead dragon eyes open to watch them both raise their arms above their heads and jump up and down cheering. Then Stella reaches her hand over my body and Molly takes it.

"Now step over that dead dragon daddy, toss your hair, and sashay away."

I roll onto my back and open my eyes to watch both my girls walk away with their heads held high. Neither of them need a man in their life, yet they both choose to love me. And I'm fucking humbled.

I climb to my feet as Stella opens the door and greets Declan, here to watch Molly for a bit while we head off to the airport to pick up Cora and Josh.

"Who is this?" Stella asks with a high-pitched curiosity in her tone.

I come upon them to see Declan lift Molly from the floor to give her a hug, but there's someone behind him. I move quicker toward them, immediately protective to see a man I don't know at my home.

"Right, who is this?" I ask Declan.

"Good to see you too, mate." Declan smiles. "I take it your wife forgot to tell you I was bringing Kiernan along to meet you."

Kiernan. Declan's new boyfriend, who I know very little about. I did run a background check on him when they first started dating a few weeks ago, but otherwise, I know very little about him.

Stella opens the door wide to let them in and Kiernan smiles as he reaches out a hand in greeting. "Good to meet you."

I shake his hand. "Likewise."

"Uncle Declan, who's that?" Molly asks.

He shifts her to sit on his hip. "That's my boyfriend, Kiernan."

"You got a boyfriend?"

"I sure do."

"We won't be too long," Stella tells them. "Molly just ate lunch but will probably want a snack before we get back."

"Go on," Declan says. "I know where everything is."

"I just need to get my sign and my purse, and we can go."

I stare Declan down as Stella gathers her things. "I don't know him." I point at Kiernan. "You watch him with my daughter."

"He has three nieces, I'm sure he'll be fine."

"Declan, eyes like a hawk."

"Murphy, arse out the door." He grins. "You know I wouldn't let anything happen to her."

Stella breezes through, stopping to give Molly a quick snuggle and kiss. "They'll be fine," she says. "Come on, Daddy."

I bend to kiss Molly on the head. "You keep your eye on them," I tell her.

"Okay, Daddy." She giggles.

I smile at her because I see the mischief sparkling in her dark brown eyes—just like her mother's.

Eventually, I tear myself away from the little beauty and head to the car, climbing inside the driver's side, Stella already in the passenger seat.

"Did you forget to tell me he was bringing his new boyfriend?"

Stella scrolls on her phone, staring at the screen to avoid my eyes. "Um…did I forget to tell you? Or did you forget that I told you?"

"Don't play that game with me."

She grins. "I have no idea what you're talking about. Oh, look!" She turns her phone toward me, leaning closer to show me. "Anya posted a new video."

Stella thinks it makes me feel good to watch her videos on social media—clips of her and Ezra dancing, often with their children—but truthfully, it's a reminder of all the women who didn't get lucky like they did. It makes me think of all the women who didn't get a chance at life because of me…they didn't get a chance at love because of me.

I feel her eyes on me as my smile fades. Some days it's harder than others to ignore my guilt and keep the evidence of it off my face.

"Baby, look," she says as she lets the clip replay. "Look how happy they are. *You* did that. She'd be dead if it weren't for you."

"And she might've suffered a lot less if—"

"If what? It's not your fault what she went through. Yes, you did some terrible things, but that's not who you are anymore. It was never really you."

I turn my head to look at her, searching her deep, beautiful eyes.

She puts her phone down in the cup holder and turns to face me, climbing onto her knees on the seat and grabbing my cheeks.

"I love you. I love all of you. Your past, your present…our future. I need you to find a way to make peace with yourself. We'll keep working on it together, okay?" She smiles.

The same smile spreads across my cheeks, mirroring hers. It's impossible to be unhappy when she glows so radiantly with forgiveness and love.

"Show me the video again."

She shakes her head, but her smile doesn't fade. "I'll show you the next one she posts. I have a better idea to lift your spirits before we head to the airport."

"Oh?" I lift my eyebrows in curiosity.

"Let's drive to that little spot we found in the trees at the edge of our property. We can park there, and I can fuck you in the backseat."

"Only if you let me get filthy as fuck with you." I start the engine, put the car into gear, and turn it around in the driveway.

She quickly settles in her seat.

"I would expect nothing less from you, Daddy."

"Tease." I grin.

"Asshole," she plays.

"You'd better tear up that fucking sign because you're about to serve this one."

"How about you tear me up instead?"

"Oh, sweetheart, I promise you, I will."

I turn to look at her in time to watch a bright smile spread across her cheeks. "I love you so damn much, Murphy O'Shea."

I slam the brakes right there in the driveway, reach over to stroke my hand down the back of her head, and tug her close. With a sigh of gratitude, I rest my forehead against hers.

"I will never stop loving you," I tell her.

And I never did.

BRYNN'S BOOKS

The Four Families Trilogy
Counts of Eight
Dance with Death
Pas de Trois

The Four Families Spin-Off
King of Masters

Ember Glen
Spark of Madness
Blaze of Misery
Embers of Mercy

Standalones
Jagged Line Paradise
Sugar Wood

Lawless
Coming Soon!
The Darkness We Hide

CONNECT WITH BRYNN FORD

Website

Click "Newsletter"
to subscribe to my author newsletter!
www.brynnford.com

Goodreads

www.goodreads.com/brynnfordauthor

Bookbub

www.bookbub.com/profile/brynn-ford

Instagram

@brynnfordauthor
www.instagram.com/brynnfordauthor

Facebook Page

www.facebook.com/brynnfordauthor

Facebook Reader's Group

bit.ly/brynnsdarlings

ACKNOWLEDGMENTS

I'm so grateful that Murphy and Stella came to me and told me to write their story. To the readers who knew they had a story to tell, this book is for you!

Danielle, Mary, and Maria, THANK YOU. The way you girls enthusiastically obsessed over Murphy as much as I did really brought this book to life. If I could give you each a turn with him as a thank you for your support of this book, I would, but we all know he only has eyes for Stella.

Rachel, you crazy, beautiful, no-nonsense, floppy disk friend of mine. Without you, Rachel, I'd be dropping characters names eight times in a single sentence, Rachel. Thanks, Rachel. :)

Dear husband and children, thank you for letting me disappear and do my thing. I couldn't get these stories written without your support.

To my Facebook reader's group, Brynn's Daring Darlings, thank you for voting and choosing Bailey as the name of Murphy's dog!

To my street team and ARC team, you are amazing! I'm overwhelmed by your support and commitment to helping spread the word about my books and providing honest reviews to other readers. I'm so lucky to have you on my team!

To the incredible design team at Najla Qamber Designs, your work continues to blow me away! From the beautiful cover art to the stunning interior, you always impress me.

Silvia, my marvelous editor. You were among the first to push for Murphy and Stella's story, and I'm so grateful you did. As always, you made my words sparkle and shine!

My final thank you goes directly to you, reader. You picked up this book, you read the words I wrote, and for that alone, I am grateful. If you connected with the characters or the story and enjoyed this read, just know that you and I have met through these words, and I'm forever thankful you took the journey with me.

ABOUT THE AUTHOR

Brynn Ford is a USA Today Bestselling Author of dark romance for daring readers. She writes emotionally heavy love stories that will twist your soul and shatter your heart before pulling you back together with a hopeful happily-ever-after.

Brynn's books are dark, sometimes disturbing, and often overwhelming. But they're always brightened by an insistent, spicy romance that will live rent-free in your head long after you've turned the final page.

When Brynn isn't obsessively writing, you may find her binge-watching favorite shows while eating far too much junk food or fanatically reading, always seeking to lose herself in the emotional roller coaster of a damn good story. She's a firm believer that her characters continue to live outside the pages in the minds of her readers. Stories don't end just because there aren't any more pages to turn.